Beyond
the
Shadowed Earth

BEYOND
THE
SHADOWED
EARTH

JOANNA RUTH MEYER

PAGE STREET
PUBLISHING CO.

PAGE STREET
PUBLISHING CO.

Copyright © Joanna Ruth Meyer

First published in 2020 by
Page Street Publishing Co.
27 Congress Street, Suite 105
Salem, MA 01970
www.pagestreetpublishing.com

Distributed by Macmillan, sales in Canada by The Canadian Manda Group.

24   23   22   21   20   1   2   3   4   5

ISBN-13: 978-1-62414-820-0
ISBN-10: 1-62414-820-4

Library of Congress Control Number: 2019941878

Cover and book design by Ashley Tenn for Page Street Publishing Co.
Cover image: Mountain and eagle © Creative Market/Bakani, Crown © Creative Market/ FleurArt, Clouds © Creative Market/Feanne, Star map © Creative Market/Digital Curio

Printed and bound in the United States

For my dad—this book is pretty weird,
but I hope you like it anyway.

And to J. R. R. Tolkien and
Megan Whalen Turner: thank you for
your words and your worlds.

Prologue

HER FATHER USED TO TELL HER THE story on summer nights, the tall windows in their parlor flung wide, the tangy air blowing up from the sea:

Once there was a boy who made a deal with a god.

It was centuries ago, far away in Halda, and the boy's name was Erris. He lived in a hut on the edge of a wood with his twin brother, Cainnar, and their widowed mother. Erris was fiercely devoted to the gods and brought offerings to their altars every week; Cainnar scoffed at Erris's beliefs and did not bring any.

One day, an oracle came to the hut with the news that the gods had chosen Cainnar to be Halda's first king. The boys' mother was overjoyed, and Cainnar was quick to accept the declaration of the gods he did not believe in. He went to live in the glittering new palace on the top of a hill by a bright lake, and Erris stayed in the hut with their mother.

In the winter, their mother fell ill and died, and Erris packed his few belongings and went to the palace on the hill. He thought

Cainnar would welcome him gladly, but Cainnar had grown proud. He refused to acknowledge that Erris was his brother—he refused to acknowledge him at all. So Erris became a servant in the palace, because he had nowhere else to go, and he thought in time Cainnar would accept him.

Cainnar did not. Day after day Erris saw him, dressed in silk and dripping with jewels, the gods' chosen king. And day after day, Erris's envy grew, until he could no longer bear it.

And so he left the palace and climbed up Tuer's Mountain. Tuer was the first god to be formed on Endahr and was said to be more powerful than all the other gods combined. Erris built an altar to Tuer and waited beside it for nine scorching days and nine freezing nights.

On the tenth day, Tuer came, and he looked at Erris with deep sorrow. "What is it you wish of me, son of the dust?"

"I wish to be king in place of my brother," Erris told him.

"And what offering do you bring to me, that I might grant your request?"

"My devotion," said Erris.

"That is not enough," said the god.

"My life, then."

"What good is it to be king if you are dead?"

Erris thought. "My brother's life."

"He was chosen by the gods already—his life is not yours to give."

"What is mine to give?"

"Your soul," said the god. "Your time. Your heart."

"Take them freely," said Erris.

Eda always interrupted the story at this point: "Why would he give those things up so quickly?"

"Because he was a fool," her father said, "and because his hatred blinded him."

"Very well," said the god. "If you are certain." And he spoke a Word of power that burned into Erris's forehead.

Erris went down the mountain again.

When he returned to the palace, he was astonished to find the walls crumbled away, reduced to ancient weathered stones scattered in the grass. He wandered awhile among the ruins, until he came upon a child with a shepherd's crook.

"What happened here?" asked Erris.

"This was the palace of a mighty king, centuries ago," said the child. "But there is no king here anymore. Oh! I see you are king."

And Erris reached up to find a crown upon his head.

"Here," said the child, "I shall make you a throne." He piled up stones and laid leaves on them for a cushion.

Erris sat. He was bewildered, but felt neither loss, nor anger, nor sorrow, for he had given away his heart, and was incapable of feeling anything.

"Long may you rule," said the child. Then he bowed, and went away.

Erris sat on the makeshift throne as night fell and dawn came again. He sat as the seasons changed from fall, to winter, to spring. He sat as the centuries spun away and he did not age, and he did not die, for he had given away his soul and his time.

And there he sits still, the king of nothing, the ruler of emptiness.

"It doesn't seem very fair," Eda always said when her father finished the story. "He was only jealous of his brother."

"But he should not have made such a reckless deal with Tuer," her father told her gravely. "The gods are bound by the One who formed them to fulfill their oaths and honor their promises."

"Is there no way to free him?"

"Perhaps there is a way, and perhaps he found it, in the end."

"I hope so," said Eda. "I don't like to think of him sitting there even now."

"One must always take care when treating with gods," said her father. "It might not be worth the risk."

Which is why, when Eda was nine years old and made a deal of her own, she took very meticulous care. After all, her parents were dead and there was no one to look out for her but herself.

Part One

STONE AND CROWN

Long ago, when the world was young but not quite new, a man dared stand against a god, and the god struck him down.

Chapter One

E DA SWORE.

Rain pounded sharp outside the open window of the council chamber, a gust of wind whipping aside the gauzy curtain to display the sprawling city below the palace. Blue-tiled roofs, silver-spired towers, a maze of stone streets—all were as familiar to Eda as breathing, all gleaming wet in the rain. Bells clamored from the spires, warning of the storm that was already here.

She swore again, with heat.

"Is something wrong, Your Imperial Majesty?" The Baron of Tyst blinked at her from his place midway down the polished ironwood table. He'd been droning on and on for the last quarter hour, to the rapt attention of her other Barons and assorted nobility, but the sandalwood oil drenching his stubby beard was so distractingly potent she hardly knew what he was saying. The courtiers had barely listened to the young steamship engineer she'd brought in to address them earlier; he now sat on her right, looking for all the world like a scrawny, cornered rat.

Eda reminded herself of all the reasons she shouldn't strangle the Baron of Tyst and reined in her irritation. "I fear the rain might delay temple construction."

The Baron's eyes shifted away from hers, and Eda glanced down the length of the table to find most of her Barons unwilling to meet her gaze.

All except for Rescarin Haena-Ar, Baron of Evalla. He sat opposite the Baron of Tyst, his arms folded across his chest. Rescarin was somewhere in the neighborhood of thirty and more elaborately dressed than anyone else in the room. His jaw was smooth, his dark eyes filled simultaneously with laughter and disdain. "Construction is already delayed, Your Imperial Majesty."

Eda's whole body went cold. "Why?" Her voice was low, dangerous.

Rescarin raised his eyebrows, as if daring her to react further. "We've used all the stone. There can be no further progress until the next shipment arrives from Halda."

"That is absurd. The plans for the temple haven't changed— we ordered the correct amount of stone. There should have been enough."

Rescarin had the audacity to shrug. "We can't produce building materials out of thin air, Your Imperial Majesty. Halda wasn't able to send it all in one shipment, and the second one has been delayed."

It took all Eda's willpower to keep herself from lunging across the table, dagger in hand. Gods, how she hated him.

Enduena was made up of six provinces, five under the command of Barons, the sixth under direct Imperial control. Each province had its own army, ostensibly to protect itself but also to temper the power of the Emperor or Empress. Most of the Barons ruled their provinces as a kingdom unto themselves, and the two most powerful provinces—Evalla and Tyst—kept the firmest check on the Imperial seat, as well as keeping a check on each other.

Rescarin had been governing Evalla ever since he'd made himself regent when Eda's parents had died. He was respected by the other Barons, and any attempt to replace him would have caused an uproar she was not equipped to handle. She had the loyalty of the Imperial army, but it was not a large enough force to subdue all of her Barons and their armies at once. It was a delicate, maddening balance—she needed the Barons to support her in order to remain in control, and they begrudgingly gave her their support to avoid the all-out civil war that would ensue if they got rid of her altogether.

And so when Eda ascended the throne she'd made Rescarin a Baron, which was higher than her parents' former ranks of Count and Countess. She'd also officially given him the Governorship of Evalla, with the understanding that he would drastically reduce the size of Evalla's military. That was one thing the other Barons had wholeheartedly supported her in—they didn't like the threat of Evalla's army any more than she did. Rescarin had agreed to her terms and disbanded half of his army. But his power in the capital still held nearly as much sway as hers, so she was left with these endless council sessions, pretending she was wholly in charge when everyone in the room knew she was really not.

"How long until the next shipment arrives?" Eda asked through gritted teeth.

"Could be half a year."

"Gods *damn*."

Her Barons and other courtiers shifted uncomfortably, but Eda didn't care. She touched the elaborate gold filigree cuff that circled the length of her left forearm, trying to focus her anger. She'd had the cuff made shortly after her coronation, a replica of one thought to have been worn by Caida, goddess of fire, millennia ago. Eda wished she had an ounce of Caida's power— she could turn these fools to cinders with an eyeblink.

She glanced at the young woman with the oval-shaped face and large eyes seated near the back of the room: Niren Erris-Dahril, Marquess of Dyas, who had the esteemed honor of being the only person alive that Eda actually liked. Diamonds hung heavy in Niren's ears and at her throat, gleaming against her rich bronze skin. No one looking at her would have guessed she'd been a sheep farmer a year ago. Niren regarded Eda with a wry, quiet humor. She gave the slightest shake of her head, lips twitching, and Eda understood her meaning: *Why are you being so fanatical about your ridiculous temple?*

But Niren didn't know everything. Eda refocused on Rescarin. "The temple must be finished by the Festival of Uerc. Construction *will* move forward. Find the stone somewhere else."

Rescarin tapped his fingers against his etched-metal wine cup and didn't bother hiding his eye roll. "The royal treasury is depleted enough as it is. There's no money to obtain stone elsewhere, even if it could be found. Wait for the shipment."

Domin Odar-Duen, Baron of Idair, squirmed in his seat. He might one day prove to be handsome, but at present he was gangly as a cricket and couldn't grow a beard. At sixteen, he was the youngest courtier among them and rarely spoke up during council sessions. But he spoke now, very quietly. "No one wants a temple anyway, Your Imperial Majesty. If the gods ever existed at all, they've long since stopped caring for the people of Endahr. They don't need us, and we don't need them."

"You're wrong," said Eda coolly. "It is high time Enduenans resumed our devotion to the gods. Only a fool would deny their very existence."

Outside, the storm was getting worse. A gust of wind blew the rain in, and an attendant went to shut the window.

"The new temple has been a foolish endeavor from the start," Rescarin said. He took a swig of his wine and then frowned into the bottom of his now empty glass. The attendant who had shut the window hurried over and refilled it. "We have the old palace temple. That should be enough."

Eda curled her hands into fists, nails digging into her palms. The temple he referred to was in an ancient wing of the palace and hadn't been in use for nearly a century. She'd wandered there often as a child, drinking in the murals of the nine gods painted by some long-dead artist's brush, mourning the cracks in the plaster, the crumbling walls and sagging roof. There was an altar at the back of the room, the stone worn smooth from several millennia of royal offerings. Cobwebs and dust were its only supplicants now, joined by the odd sack or two of grain when extra storage was needed.

"I am not offering the gods an old, ruined temple to mark Enduena's return to devotion."

Rescarin sighed, like he was dealing with the nine-year-old child he clearly still saw her as. "Your Majesty, the late Emperor abolished religious practices for a reason. Trying to reinstate them is troublesome at best. Forget the temple."

She ground her jaw, ready to put Rescarin in his place despite the consequences. But then she looked at Niren, saw the crease of concern in her friend's forehead, and forced herself to appear outwardly calm. "As I have told you many times, Baron Rescarin, that is not for you to decide." She fixed her eyes on each of her Barons in turn. "The temple *will* be built before the year is out. The money for the stone will come out of *your* provinces' treasuries, and if there is none to be found, you will tear apart your own cities and use that."

Rescarin shook his head. "Your Majesty—"

"Your *Imperial* Majesty," she spat at him. "I am your Empress, and I will have your respect." It was a daring move, reprimanding him in front of the others.

For a moment, Rescarin didn't react or respond. Then he gave her a small, mocking smile and dipped his head in the semblance of a bow. Raiva's beating heart, Eda wished she could eviscerate him.

She took a breath and settled deeper into her chair. "As for the matter Baron Lohnin has been speaking about so eloquently"— she glanced at the Baron of Tyst and thought she could practically *see* his beard dripping oil—"we will not be pursuing a treaty with Denlahn. We will continue to arm ourselves against them and prepare to conquer them for the glory of the Empire."

Forty years ago, the late Emperor, bent on expanding his domain, had sent an army by ship to conquer Denlahn. He'd thought it would be easy, like conquering the island province Ryn had been. But Denlahn was filled with trained warriors, as Ryn was not, and the attack on Denlahn ended in slaughter. Enduena suffered heavy losses, and took decades to recover. There had been no further attacks after that first one, on either side, but the Emperor had spent the rest of his reign arming Enduena against Denlahn, and plotting ways to take over the enemy nation. Eda meant to finish what he'd started, all those years ago, but she was going to do it properly—she wasn't about to repeat the Emperor's mistake. When she'd conquered Denlahn, she'd build temples there, too, and bring their people back to the gods.

"That's exactly why I brought my steamship engineer to speak with you all this morning, or were you *not* listening to his detailed explanation, Your Grace?"

Eda nodded at the engineer, who nervously adjusted his spectacles and stood up to go over his plans again.

But Baron Lohnin frowned and waved him back into his seat before he could even open his mouth. "These new ships are untested. They—"

"They will *work*." Eda bristled at the dismissal of her engineer. "The steamers will be more than twice as fast as your outdated sailing ships. They will enable the Empire and our religion to spread quickly."

Baron Lohnin flicked his dark eyes to the other courtiers around the table as if to say *You see how unreasonable she is.*

Eda tried not to grind her teeth.

"If you would *consider* a treaty," said Rescarin, in that bored-sounding tone she hated so much.

"A treaty is not what we're here to discuss!" Eda jerked from her seat, barely reining herself in.

None of her courtiers stood out of respect for her, as etiquette dictated. They just sat there, staring carefully past her.

But Rescarin locked eyes with her. "I wonder why you hold these sessions at all, Your *Imperial* Majesty, if you have no intention of listening to your councilors' advice."

"And I wonder, *Your Grace*, why you bother coming to them, since you always do exactly as you please."

Outside, the rain fell harder, sharp as stones on the tile roof. Lightning flashed, and thunder answered with a resounding *craaaack* that shook the whole palace.

Eda's eyes were drawn to the foot of the table, where a figure stood suddenly beside Niren, its clothes or body made of rippling shadow. Eda stared, horror freezing her in place. For a moment, the figure raised its head, fixing Eda with those shining eyes she remembered so well from her childhood.

"Tuer." The god's name dropped from her lips in the barest whisper.

He didn't speak, just touched Niren's brow with one shadowy hand.

Niren's forehead creased in pain, and Eda cried out and leapt toward her.

But then she blinked and the shadow-god was gone. She stood trembling in the center of the council chamber, rain pounding on outside the shuttered window, lamps flaming orange from their wall sconces.

All the courtiers were staring at her.

Eda didn't care. She couldn't take her eyes off of Niren, off the faint shadowy marks that lingered on her friend's forehead where the god had touched her.

Dread pooled in Eda's stomach, a terror awakening that had never been real to her until this moment. "How long since the stone ran out?" she asked quietly, to no one in particular.

"Your Imperial Majesty?" said Domin, the youngest Baron, confused she would go back to harping on the temple at this moment.

"How *long?*" she shrieked.

"What's wrong, Your Imperial Majesty?" asked Niren. Sweat

was beading on her brow, though she didn't seem to notice.

"Construction stopped yesterday," offered the Baron of Tyst. "Does it matter?"

"Why didn't you tell me?" Eda demanded, trying and failing to conceal her panic. *"Why didn't you tell me?"* She couldn't look away from the marks on Niren's forehead, the spots of shadow, sinking into her.

Gods gods gods. Eda hadn't thought this would happen so soon—she hadn't thought it would happen at all.

She'd thought Tuer would give her more time.

They discussed her fate like she was a hound or a chair—to be put aside and forgotten. They didn't even wait until her parents' burial.

She stood outside her father's office the night after they died, listening like the shadow they thought she was. Lamplight flickered orange in the hall, shadows dancing. Her nightgown hung off her thin form, overlarge since the illness that had taken her parents but not her. She trembled, even though the air was warm, and put her ear to the door.

"She can't inherit, that much is obvious."

"A regent, then. But who?"

"I know you're itching for the job, Rescarin."

"I'm a cousin, of a sort. It makes sense."

"We'll take it to the Emperor."

"But you'll support me?"

"If you'll keep the size of my army from him."

"You know that's treasonous, Lohnin."

They both laughed, and she didn't understand how anyone could laugh when her parents lay as cold as marble two rooms away.

"But what to do with the girl?" asked Lohnin.

"It doesn't matter."

"We have to do something with her. We can't just throw her out in the desert and forget about her entirely."

More laughter.

"Take her back to Eddenahr with you," said Rescarin. "Find her a nursemaid."

"Now you're not coming back at all?"

"Someone has to put Evalla's affairs in order. If I'm to be regent—"

"That isn't decided yet."

"You know it is."

"Fine. I'll take the girl with me. What are we to tell her?"

That's when Eda shoved the door open and marched into the room, so horribly, horribly angry that tears were pouring down her face.

They didn't interpret her tears correctly.

Rescarin knelt down to make himself her height and took her small hand in both his large ones. "Poor child is distraught, Lohnin, you see?"

"I'm not a child!" she shouted, or at least she meant to shout. The words came out all strangled and damp.

Rescarin laughed a little and patted her head. "You have nothing to worry about, you know. It's off to Eddenahr tomorrow. Won't that be grand?"

"I don't want to go to Eddenahr. I want to stay here."

"You can't," said Lohnin, stacking papers neatly on her father's

desk then kneeling beside her and Rescarin. "Your parents are gone and there's no one to look after you."

"I can look after myself. I'm to inherit Evalla—my father told me."

"You're not inheriting anything. Best to get to bed, now. You've a long journey ahead of you in the morning."

"I want to stay here!" Eda kicked Rescarin in the shin, as hard as she could, and he howled and jumped backward, knocking his head against the desk. She saw the rage come into his face, but she wasn't expecting the blow, a sharp, stinging slap across her cheek.

She gaped at him, so angry she could barely breathe.

"Get her out of here," snapped Rescarin.

Lohnin grabbed her arm and yanked her from her father's office, dragging her all the way back to her bedroom.

Eda didn't sleep. She waited until Lohnin's footsteps faded, and then crept down the hall to the room where her parents' bodies lay. She sat between them all that night, praying to the gods that it was all a mistake, that both of them would stir, and open their eyes, and come back to her. Make everything right.

But they didn't. They just lay there, dead, dead, dead.

In the morning, Lohnin put her in a carriage bound for Eddenahr.

That was the day she decided she would become Empress. The last day someone other than herself would command her own fate.

Chapter Two

E DA CLIMBED THE HILL IN THE TORRENTIAL rain, the normally dusty road a swirl of sucking mud beneath her feet. Rain ran into her eyes and plastered her clothes to her body; she hadn't brought a canopy or a cloak—she wanted to feel the full weight of the gods' storm. Dread had seized hold of her in the council chamber and wouldn't let go. How much time did she have before the gods took what she had promised them?

A pair of guards trailed up the hill behind her. There were always guards. That was the price she paid for being Empress of half the known world: never any privacy, not even the illusion of it. She was grateful for the loyalty of the Imperial army, comforted by the fact that she had an entire garrison of soldiers at her command just outside the city. Still, the lack of privacy— even though it ensured her safety—grated on her.

The Place of Kings loomed ahead, Eddenahr's ancient royal burial ground built on top of an even more ancient temple. Millenia ago, it had been erected in honor of Tuer, Lord of the Mountain, first and most powerful of the nine gods. All that remained of the temple now were a few crumbling pillars circling the brow of the hill and, mostly obscured behind fallen gravestones, a low doorway spilling down into darkness. Eda had discovered it as a child when she'd first been brought to Eddenahr. *Too fond of death,* her nursemaids always said, *a lover of shadows.* But that wasn't it at all. She'd come here because few others did—to think, to plan, to prepare for the day she'd be crowned Empress.

Since then, she'd come to offer a daily oblation to the gods, as the ancient kings and queens of Enduena had done.

Today, she was here to ask for more time.

She couldn't shake the image of Tuer in the council room, of his shadowy fingers brushing Niren's brow. Eda had no illusions as to why he had come: to remind her of her oath price, of what it would cost her if she didn't hold up her end of the bargain.

Eda reached the top of the hill and ordered her guards to wait for her there. All Enduena knew about their Empress's religious habits, but she had no wish for her petition to be observed. The guards were clearly unhappy with the command, which meant them standing for an unspecified amount of time in the driving rain. But she fixed them with the knife-sharp gaze that had won her an Empire, and they obeyed, leaving her to wend her way between the gravestones, memorials, and raised marble tombs on her own.

She went straight to the old doorway, squeezing behind the slanted stone, out of the rain and down into darkness. She scrabbled in a niche in the stone for the matches and candle that she kept there. A tongue of orange flame flared bright, illuminating the interior. Dust lay thick on the floor, centuries upon centuries of dead flowers and ashes, disturbed only by the track of her own footprints. Other than that, the chamber was empty.

Eda walked to the center of the room, dripping rainwater on the floor, and knelt down, her candle wavering. She dipped her finger in the jar of ashes and oil she'd brought, smearing it across her forehead and pouring the rest onto the floor, an oblation to mix with the rest. Sometimes she brought bread or wine; sometimes gold. The evening before her coronation she'd sacrificed a goat, its blood hot and sticky on her hands. But more often than not she brought oil and ashes, which were ancient symbols of petition, of humility. They felt simultaneously slick and gritty against her skin.

"I'll get the stone," she said, her voice strong in the echoing chamber, "I'll finish the temple and serve you all my days, just as I promised. But you can't take Niren. I haven't failed you."

"It has been a year already," came a voice behind her, soft as a whisper, light as spring rain. "Still there is no temple. Still the people do not turn back to the gods."

Eda swallowed a curse and shook where she knelt, her fear nearly smothering her. Despite Tuer's appearance in the council chamber, the gods had not spoken to her since the day she made a deal with Tuer as a child. She stared at the floor, where dust consumed her offering, and the puddle of rainwater vanished like smoke. "What must I do?" she whispered.

"You must honor your promises."

"I'm *trying*."

"The gods will have their payment."

"I'll get the stone. I'll finish the temple."

"But how? When? Will it be soon enough to save me?"

Eda jerked her head up and gasped. Niren stood in the

doorway, staring back at her.

But she wasn't Niren as Eda knew her. Her form was blurred about the edges, her skin gray, her eyes blank and haunted. She looked like a shadow of Niren, or the memory of her, beginning to fray.

Eda's heart stuttered. "What are you?"

"A warning. The Circles are fracturing apart. Soon, the spirits trapped in the void will be free, and if you do not honor your vow, my death will be only the beginning."

"You're not going to die!" said Eda fiercely.

Niren's shadow vanished.

Eda jerked to her feet, cursing, and dropped her candle in the dust. The oil caught fire and flames leapt high. Smoke poured through the temple. Eda fled up the stairs and out into the rain, coughing and coughing. Her eyes and lungs burned.

For a long moment she stood there, tilting her face to the sky, letting the rain wash the ashes from her forehead, trying to quell her terror.

Behind her, the fire sputtered and died.

"Eda?"

She jerked up from her dressing table and wheeled toward the door, dropping the jar of perfume she was holding. It shattered on the marble tiles, filling the whole room with the overpowering scent of jasmine and lilies. "Niren?" Eda whispered.

"Of course it's me."

Outside, the rain went on and on, echoing off the domed

roof. The late monsoon would temper the summer fury of the sun and make the air breathable again, but it would also flood the city streets if it went on too much longer. It was already midafternoon, and it had been raining for hours now. Eda's attendants had persuaded her to close the heavy wooden shutters to prevent water flooding through her windows, so the cloying perfume had nowhere to escape. It clung to her, choking her breath away.

Niren closed the distance between them, a wry smile on her lips, and grabbed a rag off the dressing table. She knelt down to wipe up the mess. "You are jumpy as a jaguar today. I came to see if you were all right after the council session this morning. You were acting . . . strangely, to put it mildly."

Eda crouched beside Niren, the heel of her sandal grinding the shards of the perfume jar into powder, and touched her friend's arm. "Leave it. One of the attendants will sweep it up. And I wasn't acting *strangely*."

Niren raised an eyebrow and shook Eda off. She finished wiping up the biggest pieces of glass and then straightened up and threw the perfume-soaked rag into the dustbin beside the empty fireplace. Remnants of the perfume jar were still scattered over the marble. Niren stepped carefully over them and pulled out the stool of Eda's dressing table, waving her onto it.

Eda sat, unnerved by the memory of Shadow Niren in the Place of Kings, so wholly different from her warm, vibrant friend. She caught Niren's eyes in the mirror, trying and failing to tamp down her panic.

Niren picked up the carved ivory comb from the dressing table and began working it slowly through Eda's hair, which was wet from the bath she'd taken to wash away the smoke from the temple. "I don't think you should press the Barons so hard about the temple. It isn't the best way to win them to your side, especially when you start threatening them about the stone and then . . . act like you did."

Eda gritted her teeth. "The gods are relying on me to build the temple. How else am I supposed to reinstate a religious order in the Empire?"

"Perhaps reinstating religion isn't the best use of your time."

"You believe in the gods more intently than anyone else I've ever met. Why are you so resistant to the idea of organized worship?"

It was a conversation they'd had almost daily since Eda had brought Niren to live in the palace. Neither of them ever seemed to tire of their arguments.

Niren finished with the comb and began braiding Eda's hair. "Belief is a personal, individual thing. Worship shouldn't be forced on anyone."

"I'm not forcing it, I'm offering it."

"And you think an Empire-mandated temple will compel the people to serve the gods willingly?" Niren pinned the braid on top of Eda's head, and swiftly started on another one.

"I do."

"And if they don't?"

Eda shrugged, always uncomfortable when the conversation reached this point. "If they don't, the temple will be there for them anyway."

"And how do you intend to feed your priests and priestesses? Out of the royal treasury?"

Niren knew full well that the treasury was depleted, and Eda scowled at her in the mirror before glancing around the room. Lamps burned bright from their gold-plated wall sconces, designed to look like stars caught in the bare branches of trees. The flickering flames danced out of time with the rhythm of the rain, glinting off the mosaics that covered the walls from floor to ceiling. The tiny pieces of colored glass formed scenes from mythology, crafted by some long-ago artisan. They needed to be restored, but Eda had allocated the funds she could have spent beautifying the royal suite on the temple. The rest of the treasury funds had gone to paying her guard and all her various supporters who had helped pave her way to the throne. There wasn't any left.

Eda's eyes snagged on the archway that led into her bedchamber, where the old Emperor had died. She still had a hard time thinking of him as her father, even though that was the claim she had made when she seized the Empire: an illegitimate daughter, the Emperor's only heir. It was strange, occupying the rooms where so many royals had drawn their first—and last—breaths. According to the histories, a young king had even been stabbed in his sleep by his own sister here. There was no reason given, but if the king had been anything like Eda's Barons, she could think of several without trying too hard.

"Niren, what do you know about the spirits?" said Eda, watching her friend's nimble fingers continue to braid and pin her hair.

"The One made the spirits at the beginning of the world, to help the gods in their tasks. No stories tell how many there were—some say as many as the stars, some say more than the grains of all the sand on Endahr."

Eda was not surprised that Niren knew about the spirits—she was probably more well informed than the head palace librarian, since all she ever seemed to do was read. "What happened to them?"

Niren pinned another braid. "They were powerful and clever, and many began to imagine themselves as equal to the gods, even higher than them. There was one spirit who seduced the god of the sea and took his power for her own. There were some who taught the sacred Words of the gods to mankind. There were some who spun evil diseases into the world in order to erradicate mankind, whom they deemed unworthy. And there were some who sought to swallow the sun, the last unclaimed Star, and become gods in their own right. But when the spirits banded together to slay Raiva, goddess of the wood, the gods at last took notice. The gods bound the spirits with the Words of power and sent them into the void for eternity, all but a few who had proved themselves faithful. Some stories say one of a handful of remaining spirits is the servant of Tuer. Why do you ask?"

Eda played with the ring resting in a little ivory-latticed jar on the dressing table: a heavy gold band shaped like a tiger chasing its tail, with rubies for eyes. Just like these rooms, it had belonged to the Emperor. She should know—she'd taken it off his finger. "Something made me think of it this morning, but it doesn't matter." Eda chewed on her lip. "Are you angry that I brought you here?"

Niren shrugged. "You took me away from my mother and sisters last year without warning. I haven't even seen the city you made me Marquess *of*." Niren's tone softened her words.

"You're my only friend, Niren. The only person I can trust." For an instant, she blinked and saw Shadow Niren in the mirror, dead eyes watching her, dead hands binding up her hair.

But the next instant it was living Niren, pinning the last

braid into place. "And who's fault is that, Eda?" Niren stepped back to examine her handiwork. "How do you even know you can trust me? We were friends when we were young, when you were a child on your parents' estate and didn't understand the differences in our stations. I felt it even then."

Eda tried to shake the image away. "But we are friends?"

Niren shook her head in obvious exasperation. "Of course we are."

Eda made no apology; Niren didn't expect one.

Niren glanced toward the door and then back at Eda. "Now I'm afraid I have to tell you something you will not like."

Eda fidgeted with the clasp on her jewel case, flicking it open and shut, open and shut, watching the play of the light on the metal. "The Barons have sent you with unpleasant news," she guessed. It wouldn't be the first time.

Niren rubbed a hand over her eyes, mouthing a quick prayer. "The envoy from Denlahn has arrived."

Eda thought she'd heard incorrectly. "What?"

"The envoy from Denlahn is here." Niren shifted uncomfortably. "For the peace treaty talks. The Barons arranged it without you, months ago. There's to be a party tonight to celebrate their arrival."

Eda slammed the lid of the jewel case shut so hard the perfume bottles on the dressing table bounced and knocked together. So that's what the Barons had been getting at during the council session. They weren't petitioning for a treaty—the bastards were informing her it was already underway.

Chapter Three

A PAIR OF MALE ATTENDANTS HELD A CANOPY over Eda's head to keep the rain off. It was bright orange, a blur of color in the uncharacteristically dreary day. She'd selected the male attendants to accentuate her height—she stood eye to eye with one, and was taller than the other—just as she'd chosen the orange canopy to set off her appearance, which was meant to evoke the image of Caida, goddess of fire. Her skirt was a swirl of red and gold Itan silk, so thin it was nearly translucent, her sleeveless top studded with rubies, her bare midriff gleaming with gold-flecked oil. Her intricately braided hair was woven through with gold threads connected to a filigree crown that matched her arm cuff, and her lashes and brows and lips were dusted with gold powder.

But the dagger at her waist was the only thing that gave her any comfort. Unlike her Barons assumed, it was every bit as functional as it was decorative.

Just outside the palace's grand front entrance, a carriage flanked by six horsemen lurched to a stop, mud from the wheels spattering up across the door. Eda descended the wide palace steps like a blazing star, four guards at her back. She paused a few yards from the carriage, observing the new arrivals as if she had known all along they were coming and wasn't completely blindsided by their appearance, as the Barons had intended. She wanted the first show of power the Denlahns saw to be hers, and hers alone.

Two of the horsemen swung down from their mounts, futilely attempting to wipe the rain from their eyes, and one moved to open the carriage door and offer his arm to the young lady inside, while the other stepped toward Eda.

He was a tall man, at least a head taller than her, which irked her, and had the dark brown skin of his native country. He looked about sixty, his close-cropped, tightly curled hair silver, and she could see the outline of a sword underneath his dense rain cloak. He did not bow. "I am Oadem Jaer, Ambassador of His Majesty Desares Emohri of Denlahn. Who might I be addressing?" He spoke in accented but confident Enduenan.

Eda didn't deign to let her anger show. She looked Oadem squarely in the eye and said coldly, in smooth Denlahn, "I am Her Imperial Majesty Eda Mairin-Draive, gods-blessed Empress of Enduena, Queen of Ryn, and Ruler of Od."

Oadem's expression didn't change, but he dipped his chin with some measure of respect. "Your Imperial Majesty. Allow me to present to you Their Highnesses Prince Ileem Emohri and Princess Liahstorion Emohri." He gestured behind him, beckoning forward the other dismounted horseman and the young woman from the carriage. Both of them bowed to Eda.

She took great pleasure in watching them straighten up again and struggle not to ask why she hadn't yet invited them in out of the rain or offered them a canopy. The prince was

shorter than the ambassador, on eye level with Eda, and broad
shouldered. He was probably about her own age, maybe a little
older. He had a sharp jawline, piercing eyes, and tightly curled
black hair cropped short against his head like Oadem's. There
was a silver cuff on his left ear, molded to fit all along the rim of
it, and it was crimped and stamped with some design she couldn't
make out from where she stood.

The princess looked a little younger than her brother. She was
dressed in deep blue brocade robes, with a thin silk scarf pulled
up over her cloud of black hair that was doing a bad job keeping
the rain off. She had gleaming dark eyes and was scowling sharp
enough to wound.

Eda stood, radiant and dry under her canopy, and smiled
grandly. "Welcome to Eddenahr. I would apologize for the rain,
but it's always wanted in the desert, isn't it?"

"Indeed, Your Imperial Majesty," said the prince. "A gift
from the gods themselves." His voice was sonorous and rich and
had the cadence of a singer; he spoke her language easily, with
hardly any accent.

Eda focused her smile on him. She was about to invite them
inside at last, when Baron Rescarin strode up behind her. He
smiled broadly at the Denlahns, but she didn't miss the anger
burning in his eyes. He spoke in careful Denlahn, and Eda
wondered if he thought she couldn't understand it. Bastard. "Ah,
Your Highnesses! Welcome to Eddenahr! I see our little Empress
has come out to greet you."

As if she were some eager pet hound—Eda wanted to tear
him to pieces. Maybe she could, if she made it look like some
kind of unfortunate accident. She pondered throwing him into
the tiger pit and almost missed Rescarin's next comment.

"What do you think of her, now that you see her?" And then to Eda, in Enduenan, "I do hope you've been polite, Your Imperial Majesty. You've never had a suitor from quite so far away before."

"A—a *suitor*," Eda stammered before she could stop herself.

Rescarin pretended to ignore her, his smile widening as he took the prince's arm and led him past Eda and up toward the palace. The princess and ambassador followed.

Rain poured over the edge of Eda's canopy as she stared after them, dumbfounded. She did not like surprises, and she most certainly did not like this one.

She squared her shoulders and climbed the steps in the others' wake, her star a little dimmed.

By the evening, it had finally stopped raining. Beyond the open balcony at the back of the enormous ballroom, bright stars spangled the night sky, thick as spilled milk. Eda swept into the room emulating Raiva, goddess of trees and spinner of starlight, second in power only to Tuer of the mountain. For her coronation, Eda had copied the dress and crown depicted in Raiva's mural in the old palace temple. Tonight's gown was more fanciful, patterned after an illustration in one of Eda's childhood books: it was bright blue, with an airy light gold sash shimmering with flecks of diamonds. Her black hair tumbled loose behind her shoulders in carefully arranged waves, and instead of a crown she wore a sapphire on her forehead, heavy and cold against her skin.

Niren was standing near the balcony, in the middle of what looked like a heated discussion with one of the palace scribes.

It seemed to be a challenge among all the scholars and library apprentices to best Niren in a debate over the finer points of mythology. As far as Eda knew, in the year Niren had lived in the palace no one had ever done it.

Eda wished she could go and join Niren, but she had Barons to call to heel and Denlahns to banish from her shores.

As if reading her thoughts, Rescarin stepped up to her, wine goblet in hand, the diamonds in his ear flashing in the lamplight. "I hope our little surprise this afternoon didn't rattle you overly much, Your Imperial Highness," he said smugly, taking a sip of his wine.

Eda imagined shoving the goblet down his throat and making him swallow it, which allowed her to offer him a brilliant smile. "Not at all, Your Grace. I approve of a council that can sometimes take initiative. The key word, of course, being 'sometimes.'"

"I understand perfectly, Your Majesty. We will consult with you before we take any other such steps."

She couldn't help but admire, at least a little, how smoothly he lied.

"But now that Prince Ileem is here, I do hope you will consider the match—it would do more toward uniting our countries than war and be less costly."

She despised the good sense in his words, but called out his real motive: "You care more about transferring my power to someone you can more easily control than you do about what might be less costly for Enduena. I implore you not to forget, Your Grace, that I could give your title—and your lands—to someone more willing to obey my orders."

The threat was empty, and Rescarin knew it, but he gave her a little bow of acknowledgement anyway. "I endeavor, as always, to please you, Your Majesty." He turned away before she could dismiss him. Jackal.

As Eda strode farther into the ballroom, attendants trailing in her wake, every eye in the place fixed directly on her. Most of her courtiers were ambling around the room, eating glazed meat off skewers or nibbling sugared cakes and drinking wine. Some lingered by the food tables near the back, waiting for more substantial fare to be served.

Niren had finished her debate and hovered apart from the rest of the crowd, looking bored and out of place. She never seemed to have any interest in conversing with the other courtiers, no matter how many times Eda told her they all admired her, and she might have already garnered a number of marriage proposals if she'd paid any of the young men even an inkling of regard. Niren hadn't told her as much, but Eda suspected she'd left her heart behind her in Evalla. Eda didn't feel guilty about it. Far better for Niren to marry a rich courtier she liked a little, than a penniless farmer she fancied herself in love with.

"Your Imperial Majesty?" Lohnin, the Baron of Tyst, had approached without her noticing. He frowned behind his wretched beard. "You've not yet formally welcomed the Denlahn envoy."

And you've not yet formally perished in the void, Eda barely kept from replying. The Denlahns waited awkwardly near the wide dais opposite the food tables: the two royals and the ambassador, with a pair of guards standing stiff behind them.

Eda stepped past Baron Lohnin without acknowledging him and gave the Denlahns her sharpest smile. She snapped her fingers at one of the attendants, and a wine glass was pressed into her hands. She raised it high, addressing the whole room: "To our honored guests, Prince Ileem Emohri and Princess Liahstorion

Emohri of Denlahn. May the gods guide your steps and give you the grace to walk." It was an old platitude she was attempting to resurrect, to little success.

Most of her Barons grimaced at her, but all the courtiers raised their glasses and drank to the Denlahns' health. Niren caught her eye across the room, lips twitching—she recognized the platitude, even if no one else did.

The ambassador, Ileem, and Liahstorion approached, and Eda deposited her glass with another attendant in time for the ambassador to take her hand. He pressed it briefly and released her.

"You are all looking very well, and rather more dry than when we saw each other last," Eda greeted them.

The ambassador gave a forced laugh, while Prince Ileem smiled. Princess Liahstorion just glared at her.

"I'll leave you to get more acquainted, Your Highness, Your Majesty," said the ambassador in his accented Enduenan. "I have much to discuss with your Barons." He bowed and left them.

Eda thought that if she chopped up the ambassador and all her Barons and put them in a stew, they would have even more to talk about. How arrogant of him to assume she was to be left out of their discussions!

"You're scowling, Your Majesty. Do you find me so repulsive?"

She snapped her eyes to Prince Ileem, whose tone was dark and tense. He seemed almost to crackle with energy, like there was something wild in him he could barely contain. He wore a pair of loose trousers and a long fitted shirt embroidered in silver, with silver buttons marching down the front of it. The whole ensemble nicely set off the cuff on his ear.

"Do you?" His voice grew even tighter.

"Of course not, Your Highness. I was only imagining all my

Barons chopped up in a stew, and wondering what seasonings I might add to make them remotely palatable."

She didn't know what possessed her to tell him that, but he gave a short bark of surprised laughter and seemed instantly more at ease. "I take it you don't like them very much."

"They're far more trouble than they're worth."

He smiled and offered her his arm, which she took after only a slight hesitation. They walked together toward the balcony, and courtiers parted to make way for them.

Princess Liahstorion, who hadn't said a word throughout this exchange, followed.

Eda smoothly drew her arm out of Ileem's as they stepped up to the balcony's rail. The air smelled fresh and new, of damp stone washed clean of dust. She breathed it in. "I'm gathering your sister doesn't like *me* very much." She could feel Liahstorion's glare without turning around.

Ileem smiled again, but his eyes held danger. "Don't flatter yourself. She doesn't like many people." His ear cuff flashed in the starlight. "Although you Enduenans *are* responsible for our father's death, which would give her reason to harbor personal hostility toward you."

Wind stirred through Eda's skirt and a chill curled up her spine. "Your father?" she said carefully.

"The late King of Denlahn. He fought in the war your Emperor brought to our shores. His wounds maimed him, and slowly poisoned his blood until he couldn't even lift his head from his pillow. We watched him waste away our entire lives, and two springs ago—we watched him die."

Eda's hand went to her dagger. "You're here to kill me."

Ileem raised both eyebrows. "Kill you? Certainly not, Your

Majesty. We're here to make peace, so no one in either Denlahn or Enduena will ever have a childhood like ours."

"But you hate me, surely."

"Our father's death was not your doing." Ileem looked out over the balcony, down into the sprawling city. Lights appeared in the streets below, lanterns in windows to combat the dark. "That is precisely why we are here—to forge peace in this new generation, an alliance strong enough to atone, at least in part, for the shadows of our past."

Eda glanced behind them to Liahstorion, who had listened stone-faced to her brother's impassioned speech. "I appreciate your sentiments," Eda told the prince, "but I don't trust you."

"And nor should you, not yet. All I ask is that you don't judge me—judge *us*—too quickly."

His earnestness surprised her. "I'll endeavor not to."

Ileem bowed very low. "Thank you, Your Majesty."

Liahstorion shifted where she stood, drawing Eda's eye. Her deep violet skirt pooled like water around her ankles, her bare brown arms traced with swirls of silver that gleamed in the light spilling out of the ballroom. "I'm thirsty," she said. "I'm going in." And she left them.

Ileem looked after his sister. "She doesn't agree about the treaty. She wants war. Vengeance."

"Then why did she come?"

Ileem shrugged. "To look after me, I suppose. She doesn't trust me to keep out of trouble."

"I thought you were the older sibling."

"I am. Well, I'm the youngest of seven sons, and she's the youngest of us all, but she was born to be a queen."

"And you?"

He eyed her intently, his expression unreadable. "I was born to bind together the might of two great nations and make them stronger than anyone ever thought possible. I was born to fulfill the will of my god."

A chill shuddered through her. "Your god?"

His hand went unconsciously to his ear cuff. "My mother pledged me to the god Rudion when I was born. At twelve, I made her vow my own and took the god's mark. It is my sworn duty to serve him all my life."

Eda's thundering heart already knew the answer, but she asked him anyway. "Who is the god Rudion?"

"The Lord of the Mountain. The god you call Tuer."

She couldn't help but gape at him, her world shifting into a strange new pattern. Had Tuer sent Ileem to her? Was he her answer? "I too serve Tuer," she told him. "I'm building a temple in his honor."

Ileem smiled, swift and fierce. "A noble undertaking indeed, Your Imperial Majesty. I'm glad my vow has brought me here." His whole body seemed to relax, tension she hadn't realized was there melting out of him. "Do you dance at Enduenan parties?"

"I have only to give the musicians the word."

He held out his hand. "Then give it. Dance with me."

She thought for a moment while he waited, his hand still outstretched. Then she took it, his skin warm and rough beneath her fingers. "I will dance with you," she said. "But it remains to be seen whether or not you can keep up."

It was later than she wanted when she stepped into Baron Domin's private suite in the royal wing of the palace, an hour or two before dawn—she and Ileem had danced a long while, the knowledge that they served the same god pulsing warm between them. She'd come via the roof to avoid her guards, swinging down onto Domin's balcony and stepping in through his window.

He was, predictably, asleep, sprawled out on his silk sheets, his head lolled to one side, drool soaking his pillow. She stepped up to his bed, knelt, and shook his shoulder. She liked Domin a very, very little, but more importantly he liked *her*, and she wanted to keep it that way. He was hardly more than a boy, and she knew he fancied himself in love with her. She tried to encourage that as often as possible, while still making no promises of an amorous nature. "Domin, wake up."

He shifted, yawned, stretched, and opened one eye at a time, looking at her with some degree of confusion but no alarm. "Your Imperial Majesty?"

"I need to know how the Denlahns entered my country without my knowledge."

He blinked and yawned again.

"Get up, Domin. Ring for tea if you need it."

Domin gave a sigh of resignation and climbed out of bed. He flushed to realize how little his thin nightshirt conserved his modesty, but Eda didn't blink, just raised an eyebrow, impatient with him. There was a robe lying haphazardly on his dressing table, which he grabbed quickly and put on, then walked with her over to the armchairs arranged next to the balcony.

Eda sat, folded her hands in her lap, and eyed him expectantly. "Well?"

He sat too, jiggling one foot and avoiding her eyes. "It's been a plan for a while, Your Majesty, from before you were even crowned."

"And yet you neglected to inform me."

Domin shifted in his seat. "The others made me swear on my rank. It was the only way they would allow me to take the Governorship of Idair after my father died."

Even though he'd only been fourteen and not of age yet—they certainly hadn't afforded Eda the same courtesy on her parents' deaths. "Tell me now," she said, trying to keep the anger from her voice. "The whole plan."

"They were going to take the Empire for themselves, divide it among them—at least that's what they claimed, though I'd swear on the gods' graves that Rescarin and Lohnin at least had an eye on the crown."

"Don't make such reckless oaths!" said Eda sharply before she could stop herself.

He looked at her quizzically, but went on. "The Emperor was sickly. He had no heir. It was the ideal time for a transference of power. And they thought that a peace treaty with Enduena's greatest enemy would go far toward easing the people's minds about the change. So they set it in motion, before you announced yourself as the Emperor's heir last year."

"And the marriage alliance?"

"That was Rescarin's idea," Domin confessed.

Eda frowned, tapping her fingers on the arm of the chair. "He isn't even the heir."

"Your Majesty?"

"Prince Ileem. He's last in line for the throne, apart from his sister. They couldn't have sent a more complimentary suitor?" Vow to Tuer aside, such a low-ranking prince was a horrific insult.

Domin squirmed. "Prince Ileem and his sister spent the last year in Halda on a religious pilgrimage, but the whole truth is they were sent away from Denlahn for causing trouble for the rest of their siblings."

Well, that was unexpected. "What kind of trouble?"

"I don't know, Your Majesty. But a Denlahn ship collected them earlier this year and brought them here instead of taking them back home."

"So his own family is trying to get rid of him and sent him to try his hand at being Emperor?"

Domin shrugged. "Perhaps an oversimplification, Your Majesty, but . . . it seems so."

Or perhaps Tuer himself had had a hand in it, though Eda didn't particularly want to pursue that line of thought. She shook her head, trying to make sense of it all. "And when do treaty negotiations commence? Or was I to be included in them at all?"

Domin flicked his eyes briefly up to hers. "Tomorrow morning, Your Majesty."

She rose from her seat and he did too. He shrugged. "Forgive me, Your Majesty. They made me swear. And you should know . . ." He shifted his feet, wary and uncomfortable. "The Barons are questioning your legitimacy. If the marriage alliance isn't realized, they'll investigate. Turn the people against you. Take the throne, one way or another."

"My legitimacy? I have my father the late Emperor's documents, signed in his own hand. I have the ring he gave me."

Domin avoided her glance. "Documents can be forged, rings stolen. There are some who don't believe the Emperor died of a natural illness."

"Who doesn't believe that?" she demanded.

He didn't answer, but he didn't need to. "Rescarin," she said. "Damn him."

"He also finds it suspect that the attendants who supported the claim of your rival, Miss Dahl-Saida, have all vanished."

"She was a traitor and I sent them away."

"What proof do you have of her treachery?"

"She was conspiring with Denlahn—"

"Your Barons had dealings with Denlahn all along," said Domin carefully. "Don't you think they would have known if Miss Dahl-Saida did, too?"

Eda had no answer for that. She reined herself in, giving Domin a smile and lightly brushing her fingers across his wrist. "Thank you for the warning, Domin. You're my most faithful supporter, and I will continue to repay you handsomely."

Domin grinned, suddenly all boyish relief. "Thank you, Your Majesty."

She offered him another smile. "Until the morning."

She left his room via the balcony, and climbed back onto the roof the way she had come, quickly, before he saw how angry she was. She told herself none of the Barons, not even Rescarin, could prove the Emperor's death had been at her hand. Nor could they prove that she wasn't the Emperor's daughter. *She* didn't even know if she truly was or not, a fact that haunted her during many a sleepless night. She'd told herself, over and over, that he *was* her father, that all the evidence pointed to it, that he would have told her so himself the night he died.

That is, if he hadn't already been so weak when she administered the final dose of poison.

Chapter Four

EDA ARRIVED EARLY TO THE COUNCIL CHAMBER, wearing a light green skirt sewn with hundreds of tiny, flashing mirrors, and a sleeveless top embroidered with gold thread. Her crown sat once more upon her black hair, and she wore a gold cuff on her ear as a complement to Ileem. She hadn't slept for even an hour, but she wasn't tired in the least, refreshed by a cool bath and a bracing pot of cardamom tea.

Her Barons were clearly unhappy to see her, but not surprised. Eda had expected Domin to tell them about their meeting, so she hadn't been counting on her presence being a shock.

The lower-ranked courtiers were absent, including Niren. This would be a private session, only the governors of provinces having a say in negotiations.

Eda took her rightful seat at the head of the table, and beckoned to one of the attendants hovering outside the door. "Tea, at once," Eda instructed. "And wine and cakes. And breakfast, while you're at it."

The attendant bowed and went to carry out her commands.

The Denlahns arrived, Ambassador Oadem leading the way with Prince Ileem and Princess Liahstorion just behind. Two of their guards entered and stood at attention by the door.

Eda gave them her most brilliant smile and waved the prince and princess into the chairs on her right and left hand, displacing Rescarin and Lohnin. Ambassador Oadem insisted on sitting next to Prince Ileem, which forced Rescarin to move farther down still. Eda could barely contain her delight.

Opposite Rescarin and Lohnin were the Barons Tuell and Dyar of the provinces Duena and Irsa, respectively. Tuell was as ancient as the mountains and had been with the late Emperor from the beginning of his reign. He was already beginning to doze, his weathered chin tipping forward onto his chest. Dyar had been Baron only for a year; Eda had awarded him the province of her former rival Talia Dahl-Saida in exchange for his immense support leading up to and during her coronation.

With the arrival of breakfast, Ambassador Oadem opened negotiations, speaking Enduenan out of respect for his hosts. "Many thanks for receiving us, Your Imperial Majesty, Your Graces." He nodded to Eda and then to each of her Barons, in turn. "We've come here to discuss how Denlahn can serve Enduena and Enduena, Denlahn." He drew a packet of papers from beneath his robes and handed it to Rescarin.

Eda struggled to suppress her impatience. If she'd wanted to spend the morning *reading* she could have wandered into the palace's labyrinthine library and lost herself among centuries of paper and dust. She didn't suppose the Denlahns' treaty would be any less dull.

Rescarin glanced through the papers briefly and frowned.

"There is no mention of a marriage treaty."

Eda had to remind herself yet again why she couldn't execute him. "You forget yourself, Your Grace. If a marriage treaty is ever to be discussed, *I* will be the one to draw it up. Until that day comes, *if* it does, it is neither your business nor your concern. This morning we will discuss the possibility of a peace treaty, and that is all we will discuss." She held out her hand for the papers and Rescarin, after a moment, handed them over.

She took her time with them, making the others wait, making it clear exactly who was in charge. When she was finished, she passed them down to Domin, who nervously met her eyes and gave the papers a cursory glance before handing them on to Lohnin, whom he clearly thought was further up in the hierarchy of control than himself. Baron Tuell started audibly snoring, and Baron Dyar jiggled his knee, obviously annoyed the papers hadn't gone to him next.

"You want reparations," said Eda to the ambassador before anyone else could finish reading, "for a war fought forty years ago?"

Princess Liahstorion glared at her, tension all throughout her frame. "You brought battle and death to our shores, then sailed away as merrily as you please without suffering any consequences. You maimed our king, my father. You set our country back *decades.*"

"No consequences!" said Eda. "The soldiers who actually made it back to the ships barely escaped with their lives. The rest you slaughtered like swine and left to rot on your cursed beaches. Don't you dare demand reparations for *that.*"

Liahstorion jerked up from her chair, her dark eyes flashing. "You deserve to die for what your father did to mine! We should be demanding your crown, not just gold. You're not fit to be Empress, and if the rumors are to be believed, you're not even of royal blood."

Eda stared her down, not letting it show how close Liahstorion's words cut to her deepest insecurities. "I had understood, Your Highness, that these negotiations were to be civil. If they're to be otherwise, I suggest we end them immediately before I get very angry and decide taking you as my hostage would be a better way to proceed."

Ileem stood and reached across the table, taking his sister's hand, gently drawing her down into her seat again. He was wearing a deep green robe this morning, with an elaborate collar that looked like it was made of silver-plated brambles. He met Eda's eye. "Forgive us, Your Majesty. We *are* here in peace, no matter how hot my sister's temper runs."

"Indeed, Your Imperial Majesty, there is no need for such steps," said Ambassador Oadem all in a rush. "Her Highness spoke out of turn. Perhaps we can discuss reparations a little later on in our proceedings."

Three hours later, Eda called an end to the session, her head swimming with fatigue and irritation. She'd decided to add the ambassador and Princess Liahstorion to her Baron stew. She hadn't yet made her mind up about Ileem, vow or no vow— he was quiet, severe, only speaking up occasionally, but always spouting extreme good sense. She didn't trust him at all.

Her guard attached himself to her heels as she swept from the council chamber, and a few moments later, footsteps echoed behind them. She didn't pause or slow down, forcing whoever it was to nearly run to catch up.

"Your Imperial Majesty."

She glanced back—Ileem. She scowled, thoroughly tired of political conversation. "Negotiations are finished for the day, Your Highness. I've nothing more to say to you."

He grabbed her sleeve and she wheeled on him almost as quickly as her guard, who already had a saber at Ileem's throat. "You *dare* touch the Empress?" the guard demanded.

Ileem scrambled backwards, hands raised in the air, a spot of blood showing bright against his dark skin. "I mean Her Imperial Majesty no harm."

"Withdraw your saber," Eda ordered the guard. And to Ileem: "What do you want?"

"To have a word with you, Your Imperial Majesty. In private. It won't take long."

Eda massaged her temples. "Fine." She commanded her guards to follow at a distance and beckoned the prince through an archway that spilled out into an enclosed courtyard.

The sun burned white-hot overhead. Eda led Ileem to the only shade: a stone bench by the back wall underneath a trellis of honeysuckle. It was a little cooler there, the air dripping with the sweet scent of the bright orange blossoms. Eda sat, but Ileem did not. The warm wind rifled through his robes.

"First of all, I want to apologize for my sister's behavior, Your Imperial Majesty. Whatever her temper would suggest, we *have* come in peace. I will keep her from attending future council sessions." His words were passive, but an intensity lurked in his eyes that belied him.

Eda leaned against the wall, the still-cool stones pressing into her shoulder blades. A honeysuckle flower fell into her lap and she brushed it dismissively onto the ground. "I appreciate your sister's passion, Your Highness—and her honesty. Do you truly harbor no ill will against Enduena, or are you just playing a part to infiltrate my palace?"

Ileem smiled, quick and confident as a lion. "You don't trust me at all, do you, Your Majesty? I'm glad." He ducked under the trellis and sat down beside her, closer than was appropriate—his knee bumped hers, and she could feel his heat through the thin material of her skirt. "Only an immense simpleton would trust me, especially seeing as your Barons arranged our visit without your knowledge or consent."

Eda opened her mouth to object, but he held up a hand to forestall her. "Please, Your Majesty—extend me the courtesy of the truth, as I am doing to you." Ileem imitated her posture, lounging back against the stone wall and stretching his long legs out in front of him. He was near enough she could see the markings on his ear cuff: they were words in an ancient Denlahn dialect, engraved in a flowing script. She knew enough to recognize the language, but couldn't read it.

Eda glanced to her guards, who were watching from a few paces away, their hands on their saber hilts. "All right, then. What's the truth?"

He turned his face to hers, and she saw there were flecks of gold in his brown eyes. "The truth is, ever since I was a child, since before I pledged myself to Rudion, I was taught that Enduenans were monsters from the lowest Circle of the world, without souls or hearts. I wanted to grow into a man, so I could come here and slaughter you all, wielding the vengeance of the gods. When my father died—" Ileem swallowed, his eyes shifting away. He pulled an orange blossom from the vine and twirled it in his lap. He stared at it, his voice growing husky. "It broke me, Your Imperial Majesty.

My father was the best man to ever live. I wanted to board a ship and sail to Enduena. I wanted to burn you to ashes in your beds. I wanted all of you to suffer, as I had suffered."

"What changed?" Eda's eyes fixed on the orange flower. From over the wall, she heard the parrots calling from the aviary.

"Rudion came to me in Halda. He gave me a vision."

Eda grew very still. "What vision?"

"Of my city in ashes, the stones tumbled down into the dust, my mother and brothers and sister bloodied and dead, lying in a pit of bones. Of warships filled with Enduenan soldiers, death in their eyes. Of the whole world, consumed with war, weeping, dying. Of winged spirits from the void, devouring the sun. And then Rudion himself spoke to me."

She tried to appear calm, though her every nerve was on fire. "What did he say to you?"

Ileem tucked the honeysuckle blossom behind Eda's ear. "That if I followed the path of my vengeance, the vision would come true. That I would destroy the world with my anger, that there was a better way." He touched her cheek with his hand, his fingers calloused and warm. "Once more I swore myself to my god. Once more I made a vow to him: a vow to forsake my anger. To continue to serve him with the whole of my being. To forge peace, instead of war. I want a better world, Your Imperial Majesty. In the name of my god I want peace. With *you*." He let his hand fall. "I want to help you. Let me prove to you that you can trust me. That the vow I made to Rudion was in earnest."

Her ears buzzed, her skin burned where he'd touched her. She saw the truth of his words, but she trusted him less than before. He was volatile, a flame burning too close to a vat of oil. A needle of jealousy pricked through her that Tuer spoke to him so freely, when she was left grasping at shadows. "What are you proposing?"

Casting a swift glance at her guards, Ileem gingerly folded Eda's hand into his. "Let me help you solidify your power. Let me help you put your Barons in their place. And when I do it, when *we* do it . . ." She could feel his pulse, sharp and quick, in his wrist. "Marry me."

Eda jerked out of his grasp, gaping.

Ileem didn't move to take her hand again, he just watched her, the sunlight filtering through the honeysuckle vines and tracing lacy patterns on his skin. "We could be so strong, together. Stronger than your Barons—stronger than anyone. You would be under no one's rule."

"I am Empress of half the world," she spat at him. "I'm under no one's rule now."

"Aren't you?"

"I'm handling my Barons," she said huffily, though both of them knew very well that wasn't true.

She felt horribly exposed before him, like he could see all her darkest secrets. She rose from the bench, and he did, too. "I feel it only right to return honesty for honesty: I have no intention of adding a marriage clause to our treaty. I will work toward peace with Denlahn, in the name of the god we both serve, but that is all."

Ileem bowed low. "Perhaps you will allow me to change your mind, Your Imperial Majesty. In any case, I thank you for hearing me."

Eda strode quickly from the courtyard, trying to shake the knowledge that Tuer had indeed sent Ileem and that he might be her best chance at permanently subduing her Barons.

She refused to admit to herself that he might be her only chance.

Chapter Five

"SO WHAT *HAPPENED?*" SAID NIREN, WITHOUT LIFTING her head. She was bent over her drawing table in the center of her sitting room, an illuminated manuscript opened before her. Light flooded through the glass dome of the roof, pooling soft and golden all around her, like she was a goddess from the very book she was slowly copying out. She used swift, bold strokes, replicating the work of whatever unnamed scribe had first written and illuminated the book. Niren couldn't bear to be idle, and had inserted herself into the rotation of apprentice librarians and scribes who routinely copied manuscripts for the palace library. The head librarian had welcomed her gladly, because even though she'd had no formal training, Niren's skill was unmistakable.

Eda had watched Niren copy manuscripts many times—it was horribly boring until Niren put down her pen and picked up her paints to fill in the color. Right now she was still at the dull black-and-white phase, but a glance at the original made Eda's breath catch momentarily in her throat: between and around the neat square letters that made up the text, a petitioner knelt before the god Tuer, who had a mountain for his throne and a crown made of stars. Ileem's voice ran through her mind: *Once more I swore myself to my god.*

"Well?" Niren prodded, actually looking up from her work to catch Eda's eye. "What happened at the council? Did Rescarin steadily undermine you while Domin drooped with love and Lohnin frowned over his awful beard? Did Princess Dagger Eyes try to murder you? Did Prince Silver Ear propose?"

This was enough to shake her from her reverie. Eda laughed. "You're not far off. No proposal, but Prince Ileem did ask to speak with me, alone."

Niren gave Eda a wicked grin. "*Alone*, hmm? Must have been all that dancing last night. Tell me everything!"

Eda did, glossing over the prince's mention of his vision and his vow to Tuer. Niren listened with interest, the manuscript forgotten.

"Do you think you'll sign a treaty?" Niren asked. "Is there any possibility you'd consider marrying him?"

"Gods' hearts, no! I'll do just enough to appease them and then send the Denlahns home."

"Meeting them doesn't change your mind about war?"

Eda looked at the illuminated manuscript again, not able to tear her eyes away from that image of Tuer. *Had* it changed her mind? It was easier, certainly, to think of sending a ship filled with soldiers across the sea to conquer a land she'd never seen, a people she'd never encountered. She'd always considered it part of her vow—expanding the Empire, building temples in every province, compelling all the world to return to the gods. But as Ileem's own vow proved, Denlahn was not the backwards, godsless nation Eda had always thought. . . . Perhaps war wasn't the answer. Perhaps it never had been.

The light from the glass dome ceiling grew suddenly dim—a cloud must have passed over the sun. But when Eda glanced out the window, the sky was clear, sunlight refracting off the spired towers, heat shimmering in waves above the rooftops. She repressed a shudder. Why had it grown so dark?

She left Niren and went over to the window for a closer view. If she squinted just right she thought she could see a crack splintering through the air, a host of winged spirits flying toward the sun. But then she blinked, and there was nothing.

She turned and stifled a scream.

Shadow Niren hovered at real Niren's shoulder, limp hair brushing her living counterpart's smooth skin, the marks of Tuer's fingers glowing like live coals on her brow.

The sun was at its zenith by the time Eda rode out of the city, a single guard on horseback accompanying her. Sweat ran into her eyes and pricked at the back of her neck. Heat spiraled up from the ground in waves, yesterday's rain all but forgotten. Eda swiped a hand across her forehead and nudged her red mare, Naia, toward the mountains that marched across the desert like a scattering of jagged spearheads. She'd have to hurry if she wanted to get to the sacred pool and back before nightfall.

Good thing Naia was the fastest horse in the Empire— she'd won the races at the Festival of Uerc a few years back. Eda kicked the mare into a run, not sparing a backward glance for the mounted guard a few paces behind her. She leaned into the wind, letting it wrap around her, trying not to think about her vision, trying to squelch the horror of seeing Niren's ghost, of those telltale marks left by Tuer's fingerprints. The gods were taunting her. Showing her what would happen if she failed.

But she wasn't going to fail. She refused to fail.

Eda spat a curse into the wind and urged Naia even faster.

An hour later, Eda and her guard reached the foot of the mountain, where an ancient stone stair wound upward, out of sight. Eda swung off her mount and handed the guard her reins. "Wait here," she told him, five steps up before he could object to her going alone.

It was cooler in the shadow of the mountain, a little breeze fanning her face and bringing with it the scent of sagebrush and wild jasmine. The climb wasn't difficult, but it took another half hour before she reached the top of the stair, where a small courtyard led to an ancient shrine built into the side of the mountain. The stones were weathered and overgrown with vines, the images carved into the pillars so worn they were unrecognizable.

Long ago, the shrine had been dedicated to the river god Hahld, built as it was around an underground spring. Eda could hear it now, burbling from inside the mountain: the sacred pool. It was a common place for petitioners and pilgrims to come and seek the gods, even after the old Emperor had abolished religious practices. In centuries past, Enduenan royalty had bathed there the morning of their coronation—Eda had revived that tradition. The pool had been as freezing as the godless void, and when she'd stepped from the water, a weathered old priest had blessed her.

There weren't any young priests, not anymore. That was one of the things she was working on changing, one of the ways she was serving the gods and fulfilling her vow. She had started an informal school for future priests and priestesses, setting a handful of young men and women to study ancient library texts for hours every day so they'd be well versed in sacred duties and traditions.

The gods just had to give her the chance to finish the temple, and then she could put them to work in earnest.

Eda crossed the courtyard and stepped between two worn pillars, descending a few shallow steps to the edge of the pool. Dark water lapped over her sandals, washing the dust from her feet with icy, whispering fingers. She peered across the pool to the other side of the shrine. "I would speak with you." Her voice echoed strangely, bouncing off the walls and the surface of the water and wobbling back to her. She drew her dagger and slashed it across her palm, pain sharp and sudden, blood hot and wet. "I would speak with Tuer. Or Hahld, if Tuer cannot come." She trembled at the names of the gods—did that brief glimpse of Tuer yesterday and Ileem's recounting his vision make her think he would just appear at her command?

She squeezed her hand together, blood dripping into the water, and waited. Her toes grew numb; the stale, damp air seemed to choke her breath away.

A light flared in the dark, and the priest who had presided over her coronation peered at her across the pool, his face lined and spotted with age, his hair limp and ragged. He wore robes in the ancient style, wound about his torso and hanging loose to the ground, girded with a length of leather cord. He lived up here all alone, a hermit and caretaker of the sacred pool. She couldn't begin to guess his age, and he had no name that she had ever heard of.

"Tuer is not here, child." In stark contrast to his frail appearance, the priest's voice was strong as the mountain. "Nor Hahld either. They are both of them bound, far away: one in stone, and one in water. What do you want with them?"

Eda wiped her palm on the thigh of her loose riding trousers and waded into the water. It lapped up to her shins, then her knees and her waist, soaking her trousers, washing over her bare midriff and the bottom edge of her beaded silk top. She stopped in the center of the pool, ignoring the cold and the pain in her hand, her feet sinking ankle-deep in shifting sand and mounds of long-forgotten petitioners' coins. "I want Tuer to tell me that a few missing stones won't cost my friend's life. I want him to tell me that the vision I saw today will not come to pass."

The priest studied her in the wavering light of his candle. "What does Tuer care for a little girl who plays at being Empress?"

Rage coursed through her, but she hadn't come to let this wretched priest make her into a fool. "Tuer made a deal with me."

"Impossible. Tuer has not been seen in this Circle of the world for millennia."

Her anger burned. "*I* saw him." As had Ileem.

"You saw his Shadow, perhaps, a sliver of himself. But the god is gone, child, chained in his mountain far away. If you wish to speak with him, you will have to find him."

"If you won't help me, old man, I'm not going to waste any more time." Eda turned in disgust and started sloshing back through the pool. Her palm pulsed with pain.

"Something burns inside you that was never meant to be there," said the priest quietly. "You can feel it, can't you?"

She jerked around again, heart unaccountably pounding. "What are you talking about?"

The priest's face creased suddenly, as if he was in pain, and his eyes rolled back into his head. The candle fell from his hand and landed, sputtering, on the stone. Somehow it seemed to flare brighter than before. "The world is broken," the priest whispered. "The Circles are closed and they cannot get through. They're trapped in the dark. The sun will be swallowed. Time will end. All will turn to shadows and dust."

In one swift movement, the priest stepped into the pool and grabbed her arm, hauling her toward him, his strength startling and fierce. Now his eyes met hers, and they blazed with light. "Seek the god. Fulfill your vow. Unlock the doors."

"Get *off* me!" Eda wrenched herself from his grasp. Her skin burned where he'd touched her. "What do you think I'm doing right now? I *am* seeking him. I *am* fulfilling my vow. What about *Niren*? What about my temple and the Empire?"

The priest shrank into himself again, his eyes dull and blank. He studied her impassively. "You came seeking answers. That is your answer."

"Will Niren die?" She hated how her voice shook, how the words choked out of her. "Will the gods take her from me? Will she—will she turn into her shadow self?"

"Seek the god," the priest repeated. "Fulfill your vow." For one brief moment he brushed his fingers across her forehead and she felt a flare of heat. But then he withdrew his hand and stepped out of the pool, vanishing into the darkness.

Eda slapped the water and it splashed up into her face. It touched her lips and tasted bitter.

Chapter Six

E DA ARRIVED BACK AT THE PALACE JUST as the sun disappeared over the western horizon. She was dirty and tired and angry, and her hand gods-damned *hurt*, blood still slowly seeping from the wound; she hadn't had time to bandage it properly. She could taste the grit of her long and fruitless ride, feel it caked on her skin. She longed for a bath. Huen take the doddering priest and his cursed riddles to the depths of the earth—she'd wasted nearly an entire day.

A young female attendant met her at the door, obviously flustered. She couldn't seem to look directly at Eda, twisting her fingers in the loose material of her silk trousers.

"What is it?" Eda snapped, coming up the steps and sweeping past the young attendant. It was cooler inside, the arched halls and marble floors helping to circulate the air and keep the heat at bay. Down the corridor and around a corner, Eda saw a flare of orange—another attendant, lighting a lamp.

The attendant's eyes found the floor, and her knees started

shaking. She mumbled something incoherent.

"Speak clearly to your Empress, girl!"

"Your Barons have been in the council room with the Denlahns all afternoon. They've——" Her whole body started shaking. "They've signed the treaty," she whispered.

Eda went cold and, for an instant, shock outweighed her fury. Then she straightened her spine, staring at the quivering attendant and felt her rage *burn.* "Where is he?"

"Who, Your Imperial Majesty?"

"Baron Rescarin. *Where is he?*"

"In the dining hall, Majesty. The court has—the court has just sat down to dinner."

Eda's fingers coiled tight around the hilt of her dagger, and the girl gasped and scrambled backwards, pressing up against the wall of the corridor. Eda looked at her in disgust. "I've not yet stooped to slitting the throats of servant girls, you sniveling creature. You've delivered your message. Now get out of my sight."

The attendent bowed and was gone in the space of a heartbeat.

Eda strode into the dining hall ready to murder Rescarin.

He was sitting on the right hand of her empty seat at the head of the table, the Denlahn ambassador beside him, the prince and princess opposite. An uncorked bottle of what Eda recognized as the late Emperor's centuries-old vintage lay half empty at Rescarin's elbow, which shocked her unduly—the Emperor himself had reportedly touched it only once a decade.

Eda swept up to the table and grabbed the bottle, corking it firmly. "What do you think you're doing?" she demanded, past caring to present an aloof exterior to her Barons.

Rescarin eyed her mildly, lifting his glass in her direction. "Toasting the signing of our treaty with Denlahn, of course, Your Majesty."

Eda could practically taste her anger. "You have no right to sign a treaty in my name."

"Oh, not to worry, Your Majesty—we have left the marriage clause up to you, to sign or not, as you wish." He smiled, smug as the viper he was, and patted her arm like she was still the child whose province he'd snatched up before her parents' bodies were even cold.

She drew a sharp breath, the rage eating her up from the inside. "No treaty can stand unless it is affixed with the Imperial seal."

Rescarin swirled the wine around in his glass. She stared at the priceless liquid and imagined it was his blood. "You can affix it in the morning, my dear. But tonight is for celebrating the long overdue cessation of hostilities between our two nations. Have a seat, won't you? Join us."

His dark eyes glittered in the candlelight, and Eda was suddenly aware of the other courtiers seated around the table, watching her, waiting to see what she would do.

She glanced at Prince Ileem, who raised one eyebrow, the expression on his smooth face unreadable.

Rescarin smiled, saluting her with his wine glass as if to say, *Your move.*

She didn't deign to answer, just strode from the hall without another word.

Exhaustion was making Eda's ears buzz by the time she shimmied down the roof of the guest wing and arrived at Ileem's window. She'd bathed, changed, and eaten in her chambers, then stopped to briefly check on Niren before clambering up on the roof. She rubbed at the grit in her eyes—if she didn't sleep at least a little tonight, she would be absolutely useless tomorrow. Eda rapped on the window frame and crouched on her heels to wait, cursing the limitations of mortality.

Ileem appeared after a moment, a silver dressing gown tied about his slim frame. He raised his eyebrows at her sudden appearance, but gave no other indication of his surprise. "Come in, Your Majesty." He sounded amused.

Eda stepped lightly through the window, ignoring Ileem's proffered arm. She settled herself on a blue velvet couch with carved ivory legs that sat facing an empty fireplace, running her fingers through the waxy leaves of a potted orange tree that stood to her left. Ileem took the matching armchair adjoining the couch, then crossed his legs and folded his hands over his knees. He regarded her with mild interest, clearly waiting for her to speak first.

"I have one condition," said Eda, without preamble.

"Just one?"

"My Barons have halted construction on the new temple. I need you to help me finish it by the Festival of Uerc."

"That's mere weeks from now. Why must it be completed so soon?"

Eda plucked an orange—it was small to suit the size of the potted tree, and fit easily in the palm of her wounded hand, which she had properly bandaged after her bath. She took the dagger from her waist and began to peel the orange, slowly. "Enduena forsook the gods during my late father's reign—I mean to reinstate them. The temple—" She paused, deliberating how much to tell him. "The temple is part of a vow *I* made at my coronation."

"A vow to the people?"

The orange peel fell from the fruit and coiled into her lap like a tiny bright snake. "A vow to the gods. To Tuer—to your Rudion."

Ileem stiffened and leaned forward in his chair. "Then we have both treated with him."

She brushed the peel onto the floor and tore the orange in half. She handed one half to Ileem and kept the other for herself. "Tell me about your vow. What did you offer him? What did he promise you in return?"

He fiddled with his orange while she tore off slices and ate them until they were gone.

"I was twelve when I made my first vow, as I told you yesterday. My mother had always hoped her youngest son would serve the gods, not be consumed with vengeance and war like my father and my brothers. But her vow alone could not bind me. I chose it for myself.

"I went to our temple, and I shaved my head, and I knelt on the stone floor for nine nights and nine days, neither eating nor drinking. The gods' wills alone sustained me. Every morning I sliced open my palm, spilling my blood into the dust, begging Rudion to come, to take me for his own, to mark me. And at last, he did."

She could hardly breathe. "What did he look like?"

"A tall, shadowy figure with bright eyes that pierced me down to my core. He accepted me as his servant. He touched my ear with fiery fingers, burning the gods' own mark into me." Ileem eased the silver cuff off his ear so Eda could see the scorched, mangled flesh concealed underneath. "I collapsed after he touched me, and when I revived, I commissioned the metalsmith to craft cuffs for my ear, so I might always remember my vow." Ileem fitted the cuff back on. "Each one is engraved with Rudion's name in the old language and prophesizes my death by the blade if I ever deny him what he asks. I am his servant indeed—his arm, his mouth, his oracle to the mortal world. I am bound to do his will as long as there is breath in my body."

Juice from the orange clung to Eda's chin and fingers and stained the stark white of her bandage. "You've told me he wills peace with Enduena. Will you help me?"

He tossed his own half orange up into the air and let it dance over the back of his knuckles, all the while his eyes never leaving hers. "What did you bargain?" he asked quietly.

She forced herself not to look away. His words burned through her. "My life in service." It was the truth, or part of it.

"For?"

"For a peaceful reign." A lie, but flavored with enough truth that she could tell it convincingly. She didn't know why she was compelled to hide the whole truth after his revelation. Perhaps she was intimidated by the strength of his connection to her god. Perhaps she was envious. Perhaps both.

Ileem frowned, and dropped the orange. "It is dangerous to treat with the gods for something so trivial."

Eda lifted her chin. "It wasn't trivial, and I do not fear the gods." Another lie.

He shook his head and toed the fallen fruit with one bare foot. A silver tattoo curled up his ankle and disappeared under the cuff of his pants.

She watched him decide something, a hardness coming into his face. He stood from the chair and came to kneel before her, crushing the orange underneath one knee; its scent burst tangy in the air, enveloping both of them. "My god compels me to help you. It's why he sent me here in the first place. But I am wary of your vow, wary that it will be at odds with my own."

"It is my vow, not yours. I will not hold you to it, and neither will our god."

Ileem nodded.

She was suddenly, acutely aware of him, his tall frame folded before her, the heat emanating from his body, the strength in his arms underneath his silk robe. He could overpower her so easily, and fear bit at her, causing her to clench her dagger hilt. But he'd asked her to trust him. She let out a breath, and took her hand off her dagger. "Are we in agreement?"

He smiled, something sparking in his dark eyes. "We are, Your Imperial Majesty."

She smiled too, relieved. "Good. Now get up and tell me what you propose to do about my Barons."

He did, sinking down beside her on the couch so close their knees touched, his knee still damp from the crushed orange.

They talked for an hour, the tang of citrus fading from the air until all that was left was Ileem's scent, heady cedar and sharp iron, and the sensation of power, buzzing just beneath his skin. Eda thought she might get drunk on it.

But at last her lack of sleep got the better of her, her head drooping, eyes closing of their own accord. Ileem touched her shoulder and she started awake.

"Perhaps it's best we reconvene tomorrow, Your Imperial Majesty."

She nodded, rising and returning to the window. She fumbled for the latch.

"Are you sure you shouldn't take the conventional route?" Ileem gestured at the door.

"My attendants think I'm sound asleep—it isn't worth upsetting them."

"Attendants are awfully excitable," he agreed. "But let me come with you—to make sure you don't fall?"

She was offended. "I would never *fall!*"

Ileem raised an eyebrow as she climbed up onto the windowsill and nearly tumbled off. "Do you think our god would catch you? You look drunk as a cat. Please let me come."

She scowled. Even through her haze of exhaustion, she knew it was reckless to bring him with her over the rooftops. Alliance or not, vow or no vow, she still didn't quite trust him, and there was really nothing to keep him from shoving her to her death and returning to his bed with no one the wiser.

But she was in a reckless mood. "Oh very well, though I didn't think so refined a man as yourself would ever be caught clambering about on a roof."

He grinned, joining her at the window. "Whoever told you I was refined was woefully misinformed."

It was strange, having company as she scrambled over the maze of blue tiles back to her bedchamber. Ileem was quiet, and steady on his feet, his eyes gleaming in the soft starlight. They reached her window before she was quite ready; the night air had revived her a bit, and she no longer wanted to go to bed. For a few moments they both crouched there, considering each other in the dark, the air awash with night-blooming jasmine and the buzz of cicadas.

Ileem smiled at her, soft and slow, and briefly took and pressed her hand in his. "Until tomorrow, Your Imperial Majesty."

She envied the way he wore his subjection to Tuer, as easily as a loose shirt. It suited him, made him seem shiny and strong. She didn't know what possessed her, but she reached out and touched his cheek. His stubble was rough under her fingertips; he was human after all.

He didn't react beyond his deepening smile. She drew her hand back, fighting her flush. "Until tomorrow, Your Highness."

She grabbed the top edge of her window frame and swung down into her room, where she went, at long last, to bed.

Chapter Seven

E DA STOOD ON THE DAIS IN THE BALLROOM, hugely refreshed after her half night's sleep—she felt ready to conquer the world. She'd risen early to bathe and dress before the treaty ceremony, and her formal crown weighed heavy on her brow. Green and sapphire skirts pooled around her ankles while her bare arms were painted with silver designs imitating Ileem's tattoo.

Ileem, Liahstorion, and the Denlahn ambassador Oadem stood beside her on the dais while the gathering crowd of courtiers glanced about with obvious confusion, wondering where Rescarin and the other Barons were.

This was deliberate. On Ileem's advice, Eda had moved the ceremony an hour earlier and had her personal attendants inform the courtiers but not the Barons. It was a subtle but effective start at undermining their power while emphasizing hers.

The room grew stifling as everyone waited, the courtiers fidgety. Eda sank back onto her ivory throne and instructed her attendants to bring up an elaborately carved chair for Ileem.

He sat beside her, and they chatted amicably as they nibbled at a platter of candied mangoes and pretended not to notice the courtiers' deepening confusion. Oadem stood frowning on the edge of the dais, clearly at a loss without Rescarin.

Liahstorion didn't speak to Eda or Ileem, just held her scowling post beside the ambassador. She was dressed beautifully this morning in a gauzy rose-pink dress, with a gold headdress to rival Eda's crown sweeping back her cloud of black hair.

Niren, from her place among the waiting courtiers, looked a mess, her hair unkempt and her trousers wrinkled, her fingers streaked with paint. Eda didn't doubt Niren had been up most the night working on copying her manuscript.

Eda waited until just a few minutes before the Barons were to arrive then stood from her throne and beckoned Ileem to do the same. "We may as well begin. Count Tarin, may we have the documents?"

Count Tarin, the Imperial Record Keeper, was a wizened little man with long white hair that he tied at the nape of his neck in the old style. He came forward and spread a large scroll of parchment out onto the waiting pedestal table, keeping it in place with a pair of beautiful glass map weights. He drew out a peacock-feather pen and uncorked an ink bottle.

Eda gestured to Ileem to sign first. He accepted the pen and wrote his name in cerulean ink at the bottom of the parchment. Oadem signed next.

Eda flicked her eyes to the ballroom entrance, taking the pen from Oadem and signing her name with a flourish just as the Barons swept in like a flustered brood of hens, the edges of their long embroidered coats flapping ridiculously behind them.

"Baron Rescarin," said Eda with a lazy smile as he and the

others ascended the dais, "so nice of you to join us."

He glowered at her and reached for the pen. "Your Majesty."

Eda gave a calculated, playful laugh and batted his hand away. "My signature is the only Enduenan one needed, Baron—the treaty is between the Empire and Denlahn. And you see I've already signed. Count Tarin, my seal?"

The count gave it to her, and she melted the wax herself, dripping it onto the bottom of the parchment before pressing the seal into it firmly: three stars, stamped in blue.

"And now," said Eda, straightening up again and smiling at Ileem as if Rescarin and the other Barons weren't even in the room, "in honor of the treaty, let us exchange gifts between our two mighty nations."

Ileem gave her a little nod—*job well done.* "Denlahn brings to Your Imperial Majesty this humble but priceless offering, in the name of Rudion our most mighty god." He snapped his fingers, and a pair of Denlahn guards came through the courtiers, carrying a sapling with white bark and trembling silver leaves. They set it before Eda and bowed, taking up posts on either side of the dais.

Eda brushed her fingertips across the leaves, understanding the gift for what it was—a true gesture of goodwill and trust.

Ileem smiled at her. "This tree was grown from a seed in my father the king's court, a precious spark of life from our desiccated land. May it grow here as a symbol of our flourishing peace and our joint devotion to the gods our countries share."

Eda bowed to Ileem. "All Enduena thanks you and offers this gift in return." She nodded at the guards waiting at the back of the room, and they opened a door to usher in another guard leading a tiger cub on a length of braided leather cord.

The courtiers gasped and drew back as the guard brought the

cub up to the dais. Eda accepted the cub's lead and handed it to Ileem, who was doing a good job concealing his surprise.

Liahstorion immediately knelt down by the little tiger. It nuzzled up against her knee and she broke into a radiant smile.

"Like this cub," said Eda, "may the peace between our nations grow fierce and strong and never be broken."

Rescarin frowned—he had not known about the gift, and he clearly disapproved of it. "Your Majesty—"

"And now I think we should all have breakfast," said Eda brightly. "I believe it's been set out for us in the dining hall. Shall we?"

The Denlahn and Enduenan guards collected the tree and tiger respectively, with Liahstorion trailing in their wake, while Eda and Ileem descended the dais together. If he seemed at all slighted by the gift of the tiger—a hint that she didn't trust the peace treaty, that the cub very well might grow up to turn on either one of them—he gave no sign.

They were halfway out of the ballroom before Rescarin caught up. He grabbed Eda's shoulder and wheeled her around, his anger palpable. She was annoyed that her guards didn't keep him from touching her, but not surprised. Ileem stood beside her, quiet and wary.

"What do you want, Rescarin?" she demanded. "You got your treaty."

"*My* treaty," he said curtly. "Not yours. If you think you can cut me out after all my years of loyal service to the Empire—"

"The only thing you've been loyal to is yourself. I'm done letting you manipulate me. Done letting you use me for your own gain."

"Proud words from a little girl who wouldn't be *anywhere* without me."

Rage burned through her. "Your days as Baron are numbered, Rescarin. I would beware if I were you."

He smirked, folding his arms across his chest. "Curious. I was going to say the same to you. It's only by *my* generosity that you are still in power at all. The instant I wish to, I can prove your illegitimacy—and your treason—and have you deposed. You'll be dead and forgotten in the space of an eyeblink."

Her hand twitched to her dagger. "If that were true, you would have deposed me already. The god I serve would never let you touch me."

"The god you serve is a fraud."

"You *dare* impugn Tuer?"

"He's a story," Rescarin snapped. "Just a useless children's story you should have outgrown years ago. Perhaps that is what makes you still a child."

Eda stared him down. "When you die, when you are sent to burn alone in the freezing, gods-less void, you'll wish you'd put more stake in children's stories."

She left him abruptly, shaking with fury. Ileem caught her arm just outside the ballroom, and she could barely force the words past her tight throat. "He mocks our god."

Ileem's eyes flashed with a fury equal to her own. "He will be sorry. No one mocks Rudion and lives long to boast about it."

His anger scared her, and she took a step away from him.

His face softened, saddened. "I've come for peace, Your Imperial Majesty. No matter how hot my blood runs, I swear to you I've come for peace."

Gods help her. She believed him. She took a breath. "Come see the temple with me tonight. See what you've promised to help me build."

He smiled, and the last of the anger melted from his face. "I would like nothing better."

In the evening, the pulsing heat of the day fading bit by bit with the westering sun, Eda and Ileem rode out of the city, each accompanied by a pair of guards.

A wide expanse of barren desert unfolded before them, the Place of Kings silhouetted against the sky to their right. Dust swirled up all around, shimmering in the last remnants of the sun. It wasn't a long ride, just two miles outside of Eddenahr.

They reached the temple site with enough light yet to see by, the half-completed building Eda had been so proud of a week ago looking dismal and forgotten to her now. What would Ileem think of her, now he saw her poor offering to the god they both served? She swung off her horse and handed her reins to one of the guards, who lit torches for her and Ileem. She glanced aside at the Denlahn prince, nervous for his reaction.

But he only nodded. "Show me everything."

The temple was being constructed in the ancient Enduenan style, the main building meant to resemble a mountain peak, with the central spire soaring straight up into the sky. But construction hadn't progressed nearly that far. Eda led Ileem up a hundred wide, shallow steps and through a yawning archway into what would be the temple proper, holding her torch high. The walls of the inner sanctum were only knee height, the rest of the building open to the yawning sky and the hesitant, newly wakening stars. When the structure was complete, floor tiles would be laid in an elaborate pattern of intertwined blue and gold. A stack of the tiles waited in one corner and Eda knelt and touched one, reverently.

Ileem knelt with her. "It's beautiful."

She met his eyes and knew then that he saw what she saw: the temple in its completed state, a thing of true magnificence. Her heart eased. He took her hand and pulled her back to her feet.

They wandered all through the interior of the temple, Ileem not letting go of her hand. She didn't mind, and so didn't shake him off, his fingers warm and strong around hers. She had felt for so long like she was on the brink of collapse, and here was someone who could perhaps steady her feet again. But she wasn't ready to relinquish her autonomy, not yet.

The night grew cooler around them, and as they paced toward the back of the temple, where small living quarters would be erected for the priests or priestess on duty, a sudden, icy wind tore past them, ripping Eda's hair from its careful braids, extinguishing her torch with a drawn-out *hiss*. The sudden smell of incense and dried flowers rose strong in the air, and she turned and clapped her hands over her mouth in an attempt to stifle her scream.

"Your Majesty? Your Majesty, what's wrong?"

Horror twisted through her like venomous snakes. Two figures stood in an unfinished alcove, staring back at her: Shadow Niren, her silver skirt flapping violently in the wind, and an old man in a stained dressing gown—the garment he'd died in. Eda could still feel the hard vial of poison in her hands as she'd administered the last dose, the dry papery awfulness of the Emperor's trembling lips. His last breaths. His sudden, shocking stillness.

"Your Majesty? Eda?"

But Ileem's words didn't reach her. She stepped toward the two figures, trying and failing to keep herself from shaking.

"What do you want from me?"

Silent tears slipped down Shadow Niren's face, and the Emperor's ghost looked at Eda with immense sorrow. "The Circles are closed," he whispered. "I cannot get through. No one can."

"The god of the mountain is waiting," said Shadow Niren. "You are the only one who can help him."

"That was not part of my agreement!" Eda hissed. She was vaguely aware of Ileem coming up behind her, placing one warm hand on her shoulder.

Shadow Niren shook her head. "Seek the god. Fulfill your vow. Only then will you be free."

The words unsettled her, echoes of the ones uttered by the priest of the sacred pool. "I'm not a prisoner. And what about *Niren*? How can you wear her face when she still lives and breathes?"

"Oh Eda. Do you truly not know me?" Niren's shadow slipped closer, brushed her fingers across Eda's brow; they were soft and cool as rain. "How I've missed you."

"Niren—"

But Eda blinked and both Shadow Niren and the Emperor were gone. Wind blew dust over the stone, taking with it the scent of incense and dried flowers. Ileem watched her in the flaring orange light of his torch, but didn't ask her what she had seen.

"This was a mistake," she said. "We shouldn't have come here."

She swept back across the length of the temple and through the archway, Ileem hard on her heels. She practically tumbled down the steps, then swung up onto Naia and kicked the mare into a run.

But even the fastest horse in the Empire couldn't outpace Eda's terror.

The heat was oppressive in the Emperor's bedchamber, the fire stoked hot, though it wasn't needed in the warm spring evening. The attendants had kept the fires burning all day, desperate to chase away the Emperor's chills and keep death from coming.

They had no way of knowing it wasn't a fever attacking his already frail body.

They had no way of knowing that Eda had poisoned him. She had made herself invaluable to him over the past year—a courtier he could trust. Rely on. She'd used the rumor that she was his illegitimate daughter as an excuse to get close to him. Close enough to put the poison she mixed herself into his food and drink, drop by drop, day by day. Tonight, she'd given him the final, lethal dose.

She sat by his bed, holding his tremulous hand as he took his last rattling breaths. The firelight cast eerie shadows on his sunken face.

She stared at him, watched him die.

And she felt nothing.

She rose from her place at his bedside and rang for the attendant. This was her moment—she would seize it before it was taken from her, like so many things in her life.

"My lady?" The attendant at the door was young—no older than Eda's own seventeen years. She looked frightened, her eyes big and round.

"The Emperor, my father, has passed," Eda told her. "I will be announced as his heir in the ballroom in a quarter hour."

Somehow, the attendant's eyes grew even rounder than before. "But my lady, Miss Dahl-Saida is announcing herself as heir."

The name rankled her, even though she'd made preparations. Eda straightened her spine. "I know. That is why I'm bringing the Imperial Guard. Send for soldiers from the barracks to stand vigil around my father. And it's Your Imperial Highness, at least until I am crowned tomorrow."

The attendant drew in a sharp breath and bowed very low. "It is an honor to serve you, Your Imperial Highness." She left to do Eda's bidding.

Eda smiled. She felt the power of the gods, filling her up.

She swept from the room and went to claim the Empire Tuer had promised her.

Chapter Eight

THIS TIME, IT WAS ILEEM WHO APPEARED at Eda's window, his form melting out of the shadows on the rooftops.

She'd been sitting on the sill, knees pulled up to her chin, staring blankly out into the night and trying desperately to get a hold of herself. She hadn't spoken a word to Ileem on the short ride back to the palace, had barely even glanced at him in her haste to return to her rooms. And he hadn't pressed her.

Now he was here, crouched expectantly outside of her window with only the jasmine-soaked night air between them. "May I come in?" he asked.

"No."

"Then will you come out?" He raised a bottle of wine into her view.

She blinked and saw the image of the Emperor's ghost pressed behind her eyelids. She realized how much she didn't want to be alone. "All right. But only because of the wine."

She clambered through the window and out onto the roof,

letting Ileem choose their path. They climbed up a ways, onto the main dome of the library, and stretched out on the sun-warmed tiles. The moon was at its zenith, and it seemed all the world was flooded in silvery light. It would be beautiful if Eda could shake the image of the Emperor's ghost from her head, if she could forget her mounting terror for Niren.

Ileem took several healthy swigs of wine before passing the bottle to Eda. If it was anyone but Ileem, she would have said something scathing about Empresses not drinking from bottles, and *certainly* not directly after someone else. But it *was* Ileem, and she found she didn't mind her lips touching the same thing his lips had touched. She took a long drink—the wine was strong, and burned in her throat on the way down. Excellent. She took another drink.

"I've always had a thirst for vengeance," said Ileem, stretching out his long legs and leaning back onto the roof. "Even after I swore myself to Rudion."

His dark skin gleamed in the moonlight. He looked otherworldly, gods-touched. Eda shuddered. How awful it must be to truly bear the gods' mark.

"I wanted to right all the wrongs of the world," Ileem was saying. "Make my father well again, protect my sister, demand my brothers serve the gods with proper reverence. I was always getting into fights, letting myself be provoked. I liked to think I was carrying out the gods' judgment, but it was really my own. Not even bearing Rudion's mark could cool my temper— if anything, it fed the flames. When my father died, I couldn't control myself anymore. I broke a man's nose for mocking my devotion to Rudion. I broke another man's leg when he questioned my choice of song in our darkwinter Feast of Stars, a song Rudion himself had given me to sing. And then . . . then I killed someone by accident."

Eda scraped her fingernails against the wine bottle. The Emperor's death had not been by accident. It had been a calculated choice, a necessary step. She'd thought she was resigned to it: the gift from the gods that allowed her to seize what they owed her. She'd never felt guilty about it before. She never thought she'd needed to.

But now she couldn't stop seeing the Emperor's haunted eyes.

"It was supposed to be a boxing match," Ileem was saying. "A harmless bit of fun. But he made me angry. He mocked me and my family and my god. He said I was a whipped cur, slinking back to the temple again and again to the god who kept me on a leash. I couldn't stop beating him. I couldn't *stop*, like it was someone else controlling my hands, someone else's screaming that made my throat raw and my hands ache. By the time a guard pulled me off of him, it was too late. He was gone."

Ileem's jaw tensed; he stared out over the rooftop, every line in him evincing his regret. "That's when I decided I had to leave Denlahn for a time, make a pilgrimage to the monastery in Halda and atone for my sin. I also hoped to meet Rudion there, in the mountains, where they say his presence lingers strongest of all. I hoped to see more than just a shadow. I hoped to gain new purpose in my life. Liah came with me to keep me from getting into any more trouble. I don't think she minded. I think she was bored at home. As the youngest of us all, she hadn't a lot of opportunity for adventure. And she's always been fond of me, for reasons I can't fathom."

Eda took yet another drink. The wine tasted sweeter now than it had at first. She closed her eyes, losing herself in Ileem's story.

"My brother was pleased when we went away. I really don't know that he meant to ever have us back in Denlahn again. The monastery, Tal-Arohnd, was different than I expected. Filled with power and peace. It broke my world apart and slowly pieced it back together again. I repented. I healed. I grew used to the thin mountain air and the cold and the remoteness. I grew used to the Haldans' way of life and how religion touches every part of it."

"That's what I want for Enduena," said Eda. "That's how it should be."

"The Haldans' weeks are divided into nine days, one for each god, and the monks relegate their duties accordingly: on Huen's Day, they dig hollows in the earth, sit in them, and pray; on Uerc's Day, they sit with their animals and sing to them. On Raiva's Day, they tend their gardens, and so on. It was such a contrast to the frenetic pace of court life, but I learned to love the rhythm of it. Liah would paint the views from the mountain and I saw how at peace she was—that made me content."

"What did the monks do for Tuer's Day?" asked Eda quietly. "What did they think of the mark from your god?" She washed her questions down with more wine.

"They were wary of the mark at first. Wary of me. But the third month I was there they at last let me take part in Tuer's Day. They climb partway up their cliff, and sit with their backs against the mountain, looking west toward Tuer's Rise. That's where they say Tuer's Mountain is hidden."

Eda nearly choked. "Tuer's Mountain?"

Ileem peered up at her. "The monks believe Tuer himself is there, somewhere. Trapped in his own mountain. They claim they can hear him sometimes, his weeping tangled up with the wind."

She tried to force herself to breathe evenly. The wine was making her head spin. She took another swig because she might as well, now.

"I heard it, too. I always hear my god, which is how I know the monks were telling the truth, even though I also know Rudion isn't trapped. He can't be—I've seen him."

"We've both seen him." Eda clenched the wine bottle tighter and lay back on the roof tiles beside Ileem, her head mere breaths away from his.

His dark eyes pierced her, and something more than the wine seared through her veins.

"I climbed up the cliff alone one morning at dawn. Liah had told me there was nothing like watching the sun rise over the peaks. She was right: the mountains turned to molten gold. That's when Rudion came to me."

"When he gave you your vision."

"Yes. And when he'd finished admonishing me about my thirst for vengeance and the blood I'd spilled in his name, he looked straight through me and said 'Find her. Free me.' And then the sun was wholly above the peaks and Rudion was gone. That's when I vowed to come here to forge peace. With you." Ileem turned his left palm so Eda could see the crisscrossed map of scars that shimmered there, some old and white, from the time Rudion had marked him, some fresher, as if they had only recently healed. "I told Liah that Rudion had come to me. I told the monks, too. But they said it was impossible, that the god was lost to this Circle of the world long ago."

The words of the Emperor's ghost shuddered through her: *The Circles are closed. I cannot get through.* Shadow Niren had said something about the Circles too, in the Place of Kings.

"What did they mean by 'the Circle'?"

Ileem raised his eyebrows. "You've never heard of the Circles of the world?"

Eda shrugged. "It's an expression. Something we say when someone dies—that the One who was before everything gathers their soul to paradise, beyond the Circles of the world."

"It's more than an expression in Denlahn. Halda, too."

"Tell me," said Eda.

"There are four Circles. The first is the Circle of the Living." Ileem gestured to the rooftop that spread out before them, the sky, the stars. "It's the world itself, where we walk and breathe and *are*. The second is the Circle of the Dead, where souls wait to be gathered to paradise. The third is the Circle of Time, and the fourth and final the Circle of Sorrow."

"How can the Circle of Sorrow be outside of Time?"

Ileem caught her eye. "Because sorrow can be greater than anything. Even time."

Unbidden, Eda saw her parents, dead and cold as marble, wrapped in white sheets. She understood.

Ileem lapsed into silence and Eda focused on her surroundings: the press of the roof tiles into her shoulder blades and her spine, the kiss of the night air, the steady sound of Ileem's breathing. But it couldn't keep her panic at bay, couldn't keep the words of the Emperor's ghost and the ancient priest from the sacred pool from repeating themselves endlessly in her mind:

Seek the god.

Fulfill your vow.

Ileem turned toward her, his sleeves scraping against the tiles and sending a shower of tiny pebbles skittering. "All that to say, Your Imperial Majesty—whatever happened at the temple site this evening, whatever it is you saw——you can tell me. I'll believe you. Or if you don't want to tell me, I'll understand. But I'm sure it's nothing to be afraid of. And if it has to do with *your* vow, I understand that, too. It is not an easy thing, to be fixed in the eye of a god."

Eda blinked at him, lost in his gaze, in the sound of his voice. He intoxicated her, even more than his ridiculously strong wine. She wanted to forget everything else. She wanted to drown in him.

"Your Imperial Majesty," he said softly, brushing her cheek with one finger. "You seem very far away."

She just needed to breathe. "Then perhaps you should come closer."

And then he was kissing her, his mouth wet and warm on hers. He tasted like the wine they'd been drinking. He tasted like the star-streaked sky. Every inch of her was aware of every inch of him, and she pulled him closer, until his heart beat beside her own, a matched set, pulse for pulse. Her foot knocked against the wine bottle and it went clattering across the roof tiles and smashed noisily somewhere far below.

Eda flung her head back, breaking the kiss. Someone would have heard that. Her fingers were still tangled in Ileem's shirt.

"Your Imperial Majesty?"

She touched his lips. "'Eda' will do just fine."

He smiled. "Eda."

She heard that musical cadence in his voice again, and she wanted suddenly, desperately, for him to sing for her. "I have to return to my chambers. Someone will come looking."

"What if that someone were me?"

Heat poured through her at his implication. "You are not Emperor yet, Your Highness."

Another smile, a little slyer than the first. "I suppose I am not."

They climbed down the way they'd come, Eda swaying and stumbling and more than a little drunk. For now, Ileem and the wine had driven thoughts of shadows and ghosts from her head.

She'd only just slipped in through her window and brushed the dust from her knees when an attendant rushed in, dark eyes wide with fear.

"What is it?" Eda asked her.

"It's the Marquess, Your Imperial Majesty. She's collapsed, and the physician cannot revive her."

She beat against the stone with her fists until the skin split, and blood burst bright. She screamed into the dim interior of the half-tumbled-down temple, screamed at the altar and the image of a god whose features had been worn away by wind and time. Her blood dripped down into the dust, and the sun slipped through cracks in the stone, making sweat pool at the nape of her neck.

"Show yourself to me!" she screamed, her small voice cracking. "I call upon the most mighty god of all! I call your name: Tuer! Show yourself to me!"

But there was no answer.

She collapsed on the ground in front of the altar, sobbing. It was all for nothing: her escape from the palace, her long journey home on horseback, the climb up to the old family temple. There was nothing here. She was alone, and she always would be.

"Child of the dust," said a voice behind her.

She yelped and turned.

A figure stood there, clothed in shadow so dark she could barely make it out. There was a pair of shining eyes somewhere in its depths, and shadow rippled and moved around it like water.

"What god are you?" she whispered.

"I am Tuer's Shadow—the only piece that is left of him in this Circle of the world." His voice sounded like rain on stone, like wind swirling through dust. "This was my temple, long, long ago. What is your request?"

She squared her shoulders and stared straight into Tuer's eyes. "I want to be Empress of Enduena."

The Shadow laughed. "But you're so small."

Eda felt the fierceness take her, same as it had when her parents died, same as it had when she'd snuck from her palace rooms, stolen a horse from the stables, and ridden all the way here. "I will be Empress."

"Very well," said Tuer's Shadow. "What do you offer the gods in return?"

She thought of the story her father used to tell. Tuer always kept his word, but not always in the way his petitioners wished. She must be careful. "Make me Empress in my lifetime, and I will serve the gods. My life in service, in exchange for ruling the Empire."

"Stand up," said Tuer's Shadow. "Let me look at you."

Eda stood, dust and blood clinging to the knees of her linen trousers.

The shadow-god circled round her, and she felt a strong, cold wind breathing through her hair, across her skin.

"It is not enough," said the god. "I need to be sure of you. I will honor any promise I make, but there is no surety that you will honor yours. I require something more."

She felt a tightness in her chest, disappointment crushing her. "I have nothing else to offer."

"There must be something," said Tuer. "There always is. Something precious to you."

Laughter rang suddenly outside the temple, and Eda peered through a crack in the stones to see her friend Niren playing with her two younger sisters at the base of the hill. Eda realized what the god wanted: Niren, with her laughing dark eyes and serious face, her mischief and good sense.

The dark cold of Tuer's Shadow blazed beside her, and Eda turned to look at him. "I won't forsake my promise. I will serve the gods all my life."

Tuer's eyes bored into hers. "And yet I still require an earnest."

One last glance through the crack in the stone, as Niren and her sisters passed out of sight. Eda knew what her answer would be. She screwed her eyes shut, saw her parents, lying dead in their bedrooms: her mother's dark hair splayed across the pillow; her father's ashen face and vacant eyes. The Barons dragging her from the house, shoving her into a carriage that hurtled her away from her childhood home. The regent, Rescarin, taking her father's place as Count of Evalla, forever to command her fate.

She opened her eyes again. Tuer's Shadow stood before her, dark and cold and strong, and Eda was suddenly afraid. "The Empire for my life in service," she whispered. She dug her nails into her palms. "With Niren's life as earnest. But it won't come to that."

She felt rather than saw Tuer's smile. His Shadow seemed to grow darker, gathering more substance. He stretched out one dark hand and touched Eda's forehead. Light burned through her, searing white-hot, and she gasped and sank to her knees. Stars wheeled before her eyes. She saw a god weeping in a dark room, bound with chains. She felt iron close around her heart, sealing her promise. Her forehead pulsed with faint heat.

"Take care, child of the dust," said Tuer. "The gods will have their payment."

A sudden wind tore through the temple—it smelled of honey and roses and fire.

When Eda opened her eyes, Tuer's Shadow was gone.

Chapter Nine

EDA SWEPT INTO NIREN'S SUITE, TERROR MAKING her head spin. The palace physician was waiting for her, a middle-aged woman with silvering hair and a healer's sigil pinned to her emerald-green sash. She hovered in front of the doorway to Niren's bedroom, blocking her from view.

The illuminated manuscript Niren had been copying still lay on Niren's drawing table, open to the page of Tuer's petitioner, hands outstretched to the god of the mountain. The illustration seemed to bob and dance in the lantern light.

Eda stood still, bracing herself for the worst.

"The Marquess is dying, Your Imperial Majesty," said the physician. "I'm afraid she hasn't much time left."

"Surely you can do something for her." Eda stared at Niren's manuscript, that cold, tight knot of fear in her chest making it hard to breathe.

"The Marquess isn't responding to any treatment. I'm doing everything I can for her, but—I fear it won't be long."

Eda stared at the doorway to the bedroom, wondering how awful Niren must look if the physician felt the need to forestall her in this way. "How long?" The words choked her.

The physician shook her head. "Two days. Perhaps three, if the gods are kind."

That was the wrong thing to say. Anger flooded Eda like an ocean tide. "Get out."

"Your Imperial Majesty?"

"The gods are never kind." Eda clenched her fists, digging her nails into her palms, the fingers on her left hand pressing into the wound she'd made at the sacred pool, hardly scabbed. She felt the skin break anew, the blood drip warm. It hurt, and the pain grounded her. "GET OUT!"

The physician bowed low, and quit the room.

Eda burst into Niren's bedchamber, unprepared for the stark horror of the form laying in the bed.

Gray. Niren looked so gray. Everything about her was drained of life, her body still between cream sheets, her dark hair a stain on the pillow. Her face was shrunken, and veins showed blue and spidery on her hands. The marks on her forehead where Tuer's Shadow had touched her were purple-black bruises. There was little difference, now, between Shadow Niren and the real one.

Eda collapsed to her knees beside the bed, folding Niren's hand in her own. All at once she was crying like she hadn't in nearly a decade. Tears poured down her face, soaking through the thin sheets.

She had learned long ago that crying gained her nothing but pity and scorn, so she'd stopped crying, even behind closed doors. Now she'd given in and she felt horribly weak. That made her angry.

She took a long, long breath, and bent to kiss Niren's cheek, waxy and cold beneath her lips. Her resolve sharpened. "I'm

going to save you, Niren. Gods and ghosts and vows be damned—
I'm going to save you."

She came into Domin's rooms without waiting for the guard
to announce her. Domin was sitting cross-legged at a low table,
halfway through a glass of wine and dressed only in a pair of
loose silk trousers. He started at her arrival, blushing horribly.

Eda didn't care. She grabbed his ear and hauled him upwards,
forcing him to look at her. There were crumbs on his lips. His
breath smelled of alcohol and honeyed mangoes.

"Y–Y–Your Imperial Majesty?"

"Where is the *stone*, Domin? Why does my temple still
languish half-built in the desert when you *promised* me you
would find the stone?"

Sweat popped out on his brow. "Your Majesty, there *is* no
stone—"

"LIAR!" She flung him bodily against the wall and he hit it
with a satisfying *crack*, his head jerking sideways, blood bursting
from his temple.

But she wasn't finished. She came toward him, drawing the
dagger from her waist.

He shrank back. His scrawny, coddled frame was no match
for her menacing height or her strength or her weapons practice
in the dead of night with the retired captain of the guard whom
she bribed heavily to keep up the illusion of her helplessness.

She pressed Domin into the wall, palm splayed across his
chest, her other hand holding the dagger to his throat.

"Please, Your Imperial Majesty," he whimpered, actual gods-damned *tears* rolling down his miserable cheeks. "It isn't my fault. I can't control what the others do."

She ground her jaw. "Tell me something useful. Now. Or I swear on my parents' graves I'll slit your throat and leave you to wallow in a pool of your own blood."

"Rescarin means to depose you."

That wasn't really a surprise. She adjusted her grip on the dagger. "When?"

"Soon. Before the Feast of Uerc. He has documents. Witnesses."

"What documents?"

Domin shuddered, his eyes wild. "I haven't seen them, Your Imperial Majesty. But he says they disprove your claim to the throne."

"Could you get them? Bring them to me?"

He took a breath. Two. "I think so."

"Can you do it or not?"

"I can, Your Imperial Majesty."

"Good. I need them by tomorrow."

"Tomorrow? But—"

She applied the tiniest amount of pressure to the dagger. "Tomorrow. Swear on your life, Domin Odar-Duen, if you value it."

"I swear on my life, Your Imperial Majesty. I won't fail you."

Eda withdrew her dagger and rewarded Domin with her most dazzling smile. "No, Domin. I don't expect you will."

Eda was just swinging up onto Naia, her guard already mounted, when Ileem appeared in the stable courtyard, a light blue head scarf wound about his cropped hair.

Dawn glowed red on the horizon, and terror made her heart seize.

Ileem grasped her bridle. "I only just heard about your friend. Wherever you're going, send me instead. I'm sure you'd rather stay here, be with her. Please, Eda."

Eda shook her head as Naia danced beneath her, sensing her anxiety. "It has to be me. There isn't time."

"Then let me come with you." Ileem jerked his chin at a stable boy, who bowed and disappeared back into the rambling whitewashed building to fetch him a horse.

"I can't wait," she said.

Light flooded the courtyard, shimmering in the folds of Ileem's blue and gold robes. Eda caught the sudden scent of citrus oil and sun-warmed figs. His eyes bored into hers. "I'll stay if you tell me to."

Her body screamed at her to go, go. Niren's life depended on it. But her traitorous heart whispered that it would be nice to not go alone.

Eda pulled Naia away from the stable, nudging her toward the gate. "Come, then," she called back to him.

Their horses ran, hooves pounding the hard ground, long legs eating up the miles of desert that stretched endlessly ahead. The only thing that marred the dirt were rocks and scrubby bushes and the occasional ironwood, jagged and black against the colorless sky. The rush of air made the heat easier to stand, though Eda could feel every inch of exposed skin slowly burning. She tried to let her mind go blank, tried to just focus on the wind and her horse and the mad pace of her heart, but she couldn't stop thinking about Niren. Eda whispered a prayer to Ahdairon, the wind goddess, to lend them speed.

But their mounts couldn't keep running indefinitely, and Eda and Ileem were soon forced to pull them back to a walk. Glancing behind her, Eda realized that she and Ileem had vastly outpaced her guard. She wasn't sorry, but she knew they'd better let him catch up.

"How much farther?" said Ileem, loosing a water skin from his saddle and taking a long, long draught.

Eda undid her own water skin and followed suit. The water was warm, but it tasted sweet. She wiped the sweat from her forehead. "A good six or seven hours, due south. I think."

"You've never been there before?"

Eda shrugged. "It's an ancient holy site. Raiva's Well. Although anyone who knows anything about the gods knows that Raiva—"

"—is supposed to be on Od somewhere," Ileem supplied.

"Perhaps it dates back to the time before the continents were formed."

Ileem patted his stallion's neck, and Eda noted his long arms glistening with sweat. Her thoughts turned to soft lips in softer moonlight, and she rubbed her own arm to distract herself from the heat spreading up her neck.

"Why are you seeking Raiva?" Ileem asked.

"Because Tuer will not hear me."

"When we get to the well, I'll invoke him for you."

"Does he come every time you call?" Anger and jealousy rankled her. She had promised Tuer everything, even more than

Ileem had offered. Why did Tuer snub her?

"No," said Ileem tightly. "Not every time."

"But he does speak to you? Tells you what he wishes you to do for him?"

"He speaks to me in visions and dreams. In stories and songs. In the words of others and the fire of a sacrifice. He speaks to me in many ways, but not always when or how I wish him to. And you, Your Imperial Majesty? Does he speak to you?"

"Only once, long ago when I was a child." She tried to keep the bitterness from her voice.

"And you want him now to save your friend's life."

Her chest hurt. "Yes. Raiva is second only to Tuer in power. Maybe she can do something for Niren."

"The gods are at work there, aren't they?"

Eda nodded, wholly miserable.

"Somehow, Niren's life is bound to the temple. That's why you want it built so quickly. That's why you're so angry with your Barons for halting construction. And that's what had you so frightened last night."

He saw so much, when no one else saw anything at all. "Yes." The word was hard and tight inside her throat.

"Why is Niren's life bound to the temple?"

This time she told him the truth. "I offered it to the gods as earnest, in case I didn't fulfill my end of the bargain."

He waited, correctly assuming there was more.

"I pledged my life in service to the gods in exchange for being made Empress. They required an earnest."

"Building the temple is your way of serving the gods."

"Yes."

He adjusted his headscarf, the cuff on his ear blindingly

reflecting the sun. "Did you ever consider that a temple isn't what the gods want from you?"

"The temple is just the beginning. I'm going to reintegrate religion into the Empire, restore the priesthood and the holy days. All of it."

"But what does that mean, personally, for *you?*"

The question bit deep. Eda tried to consider it from all angles, but it only made her frantic, frustrated. "I'm serving the gods in the only way I know how. I'm not going to give up the Empire and become a priestess or join the monastery in Halda and dig holes in the dirt every nine days."

"Even if that's what the gods want from you?"

Eda peered across at Ileem. His face was unreadable. "If it was, then why would they make me Empress?"

Ileem shrugged. "To see if you really meant the words of your vow."

"I really meant them," Eda snapped. "Why else would I be out riding in the desert in the heat of the day?"

His eyes pierced down to bone. "Because you're afraid there's really nothing you can do for Niren. Because you don't know what else to do with your guilt."

A hot wind tore across the scorched earth, making the hairs stand up on the back of her neck. She ground her jaw, and in that moment thought she hated him.

"I'm not blaming you, Eda. I understand. It's how I felt when I killed that man in Denlahn. Restless. Angry. Guilty. It's why I made my pilgrimage. I found healing in seeking the gods. That's what I would wish for you. Anger doesn't solve anything. I just—I just wanted you to know I understand."

She let out a breath, and he was forgiven again.

"I'm going to keep my promise. I'm going to help you finish the temple and save Niren. I know that's why Rudion sent me here."

"But will it be soon enough?"

His face grew hard, his eyes drifted away from hers.

She didn't blame him. She didn't know the answer, either.

"Tell me about the circumstances of your taking the crown," he said.

Eda's hands tightened around her reins. "My father named me his heir before he died. I ousted the traitor who dared claim my birthright and ascended the throne."

Ileem didn't answer right away. He rubbed his mount's neck. "What's the truth?"

It spilled out of her, without her really meaning it to. "The truth is I don't know who my father is. I saw my opportunity— I *made* my opportunity. And then I seized it."

"And the Emperor?"

She couldn't quite bring herself to tell him everything. "He was poisoned."

"So we blame it on Rescarin. We prove he murdered the Emperor and have him executed. Simple."

Simple. But even so, a sense of danger twisted through her. "Ileem—"

He raised one hand to forestall her. "We have an alliance, Eda. I would never betray your secrets. I help you take down Rescarin, and you consider marriage. Then together, we serve our god. That was our bargain, wasn't it?"

She thought once more of the taste of his lips in the moonlight. Her whole body warmed. "It was, Your Highness."

He smiled.

Chapter Ten

T HEY REACHED RAIVA'S WELL JUST AS THE sun was beginning to sink in the west, sending long blue shadows
across the desert. Eda's guard had caught up to them by
then, and she dismounted and handed him her reins without a
word. Ileem followed suit and went to stand beside her.

Raiva's Well was deceptively simple on the surface: an octag-
onal dome with a metal spire on top shaped like a tree. Somehow
the metal was untarnished by age; it flashed and danced in the
slanting rays of the sun. The dome itself was supported by eight
marble columns, the designs once carved into the stone worn
away now by sand and time. As Eda and Ileem drew near, a set of
narrow steps came into view. They spiraled down to the next level:
a stone floor and another eight pillars. More steps led down to the
next level, and the next. Eda couldn't see how many levels there
were—the bottom of the well was swallowed up in darkness.

She'd come prepared with lanterns and oil, and she filled and
lit two, handing one to Ileem and keeping the other for herself.

They descended into the well as the last of the sunlight slipped beyond the horizon.

Eda felt very much like she was being swallowed, climbing down and down into the earth as the sky grew ever farther away. The air became increasingly cooler as they went on; the sweat dried on her face and arms, and she began to shiver. The stairs were not wide enough for two, so Ileem came just behind her. His lantern light mingled with hers, sending shadows spinning wildly, making her feel as though a thousand dead souls were dancing round them as they continued their descent.

And then suddenly they were at the bottom of the well, a simple bare room, twenty feet square, with a shallow pool of water in the very center. Wax drippings lay mounded all about the pool, and the water itself was thick with coins. It was more than a little disappointing, less impressive than the sacred pool just outside the city.

Still, she'd come all this way. Perhaps appearances were deceiving.

Eda paced around the room, lifting her lantern high, while Ileem came quietly behind her. She studied the carvings in this last set of eight pillars: birds and beasts marched round them in endless loops, with trees between rows. There were three empty sockets in the center of each pillar where jewels might once have been set to represent the original three Stars.

Other than that, there was nothing down here but dust.

Eda knelt beside the fountain with a frustrated huff, and Ileem knelt beside her. It was strange and almost unsettling to have him there, to not be alone in her supplication to the gods. She drew out her pouch of ashes and oil and smeared part on her forehead and part against the edge of the pool, then handed the pouch to Ileem, who did the same. She cut her palm with her dagger, a new wound to join the one that was barely scabbed, and let her blood drip into the water. Dimly she was aware of Ileem slicing into the map of scars on his own palm, of his blood spilling out to mix with hers. She stared at her reflection, her dark eyes and shadowed hair, mingled strangely in the lantern light with the coins mounded under the surface. She wondered how many supplicants had come here, how many had left empty-handed. Beside her, Ileem closed his eyes, his lips moving in silent prayer.

"Raiva," said Eda quietly to the water, "hear my supplication." She shut her eyes, too, and crouched back on her heels, waiting, the cut in her palm pulsing like a second heartbeat.

She didn't expect anything to happen.

But a light touch on her shoulder made her start and turn. A tall, tall woman stood there, her hair mingled strands of beech-tree white and ash-tree brown, bits of shimmering jewels flashing on her forehead. Her skin was dappled, like sunlight through forest leaves. She was dressed simply, in a white robe girded with a violet cord, and her eyes were very dark.

Eda stared, so startled she nearly tumbled backward into the water.

But the woman came forward, took her hand, drew her to her feet. Up close she was several heads taller than Eda. Eda gaped up at her, unconsciously pulling her hand away.

"What is it you would ask of me, daughter of the dust?"

Distantly, Eda wondered if Ileem saw her too, or if he was still kneeling in prayer at the side of the pool, unaware that Eda's had been answered.

"You have a request," the goddess said gently. "Speak. I will hear it."

Eda scrambled to find her tongue. "I—my friend is sick. I think she's dying, and—it's not a natural illness."

"You seek a cure."

Eda nodded.

The goddess—Raiva—touched Eda's forehead, and Eda felt a sudden intense heat boring into her skull. It burned and burned; she thought it would split her apart. Raiva drew her hand back again, and the pain was gone.

Eda took a sharp breath.

The goddess frowned. "We have met before."

"We have not, my lady."

"But I know you. You are gods-touched." Raiva circled her, her white robe leaving a trail in the dust. "You bear my mark." Raiva turned to Ileem, who was indeed still kneeling by the pool, oblivious to her presence. "As your friend bears his."

For a moment, Eda stared at Ileem's shoulders and had the feeling that she had strayed somehow into the realm of the gods, that he would not see Raiva even if he lifted his head. "He made a vow to Tuer. I made a deal with Tuer."

"A deal you do not honor."

"I'm trying," said Eda desperately. "I just need more time to build the temple, time Niren doesn't have, and I never thought it would really mean her life. It can't. I won't let it."

"And if the gods have need of your friend?"

"What use do the gods have for a mortal?"

The goddess lifted her shoulders. "They treated with you."

Eda bit back a curse. She felt it would be deeply, deeply wrong to swear in front of a deity. "Can you cure her?"

Raiva's eyes softened, deep sorrow radiating from her face. "Little Empress. Your friend is on her own path now. Just as you are on yours. I understand now, what he did, why he did it, even though I do not agree with how it was done."

"What who did? My lady?"

Raiva put her hands on Eda's shoulders, her grip light and strong at once. "You met Tuer's Shadow when you were a child. Now you are grown, and you must seek Tuer himself. He's calling you, little one. There is no one else who can save him."

"I don't understand."

Raiva smiled, though grief lingered in her eyes. "Seek the god, dear one. Fulfill your oath."

"But—"

"That is your answer. I am sorry it is not the one you wished to hear."

And then Eda blinked and she was kneeling beside the pool, her hand still slick with oil and ashes, the blood drying rusty-brown on her palm.

Ileem turned to look at her, his blood running red down his arm. He looked shaken, as if he had stared into the mouth of a shadow creature and been eaten. "What did you see?" His voice shook. His whole body shook.

Eda realized she was shaking, too. "Raiva keeps her own council. She won't help me."

He nodded, briefly touching his ear cuff then letting his free hand trace the stream of blood on his arm.

"What did you see?" she asked him softly.

"Rudion came to me. He showed me everything. Eda, he showed me how to save Niren." Ileem's eyes focused on hers, and he grew steady again. Calmer. "Rescarin is lying about the stone for the temple. It's already here, in Enduena, in a herder's village east of the city."

Her heart skipped a beat. She forgot how to breathe.

Ileem grasped her bloodied hand with his. "Let's go find it. Let's go save Niren."

They rode hard across the desert and into the starry night, dust swirling up from their mounts' hooves to cling to their skin and choke their breath away. Eda could barely think beyond the words Ileem had spoken to her down in the well. They pulsed through her, hope tangled up with her anger at Raiva's riddles, at her terror for Niren and the fear they were already too late.

Ileem had told her the rest as they climbed the endless steps back into the night. Rudion had given him a vision of the stone held hostage by part of the army Rescarin had sworn to Eda he'd cut in half, of mercenaries swelling the ranks of that army, of them drilling on their practice grounds down in Evalla's capital city of Eron. Of Rescarin's trap, carefully, painstakingly laid, to take her crown and subdue the other Barons. To make himself Emperor. To destroy the temple she'd tried so hard to build.

On and on they rode, the night spooling out behind them like threads of darkest blue. She wanted to go faster, faster, to outpace her fears, but the horses needed rest, and Eda herself was aching with weariness. Her guard called an apologetic halt about three in the morning, spreading his cloak out for her over the hard ground. She collapsed onto it, and Ileem sat beside her, gleaming like a god in the moonlight. Eda had never felt so frantic, so vulnerable, and he exuded safety, steadiness. She stared at him, wondering how she'd ever thought someone so beautiful could be her enemy, wondering how beauty suddenly held meaning to her when it never had before. She wanted to sink into him, to kiss him until she could no longer breathe, to forget that such things as gods and vows and empires existed. To run away from this life she'd fought and clawed and killed for. To not look back.

And yet she also wanted to run on alone into the desert, find the stone, save Niren. She couldn't stop. There wasn't time to stop.

"Get some rest," Ileem said, giving her hand a quick, reassuring squeeze. "The gods will keep her safe. Rudion promised me."

She took a breath, and her eyes shut of their own accord.

She woke to the rosy glow of dawn to find Ileem curled up a few feet from her, snoring softly. He looked younger when he was sleeping, an innocence about him she hadn't realized was absent when he was awake. The shadows lengthened in the advent of the sun, golden light spilling over the planes of his face, sharpening their edges. And then he opened his eyes, and the innocence was gone.

Moments later they were back in their saddles, thundering on across the desert, the sun beating down relentlessly to make up for its all-night absence. Sweat soaked her clothing, grit clung to her skin and her teeth. Her heart roared inside of her, begging the gods for more speed.

It was maddening to have to stop and rest more and more often as the heat grew increasingly intense. They took a midday rest, sheltering in the insufficient shade of an overgrown bush, its leaves scraggly and sharp.

Ileem seemed as tense as Eda felt. They shared a water skin, passing it back and forth between them, and she liked to imagine she could feel the ghost of his lips on hers when she drank after he did.

"Did Rudion say anything else?" she asked softly.

He sat with his knees pulled up to his chin, sweat trickling down his forehead and into his eyes. He wiped his brow with the back of his hand. "Only that I have done well, that everything I've longed for will soon come to pass." He met her eyes, and once more she sensed in him that power, lurking just below his skin.

"Peace," she said and flushed, thinking of the bargain they'd made.

He smiled. "Peace."

Chapter Eleven

T HEY RODE ON IN THE LATE AFTERNOON, when the heat of
the day began to fade, little by little, and their horses were
rested enough for another run. They passed Eddenahr
as the sun sank in a fury of red and violet. It hurt to leave the
city behind, not knowing if Niren still clung to life or if she had
faded wholly into the shadow version of herself.

They took one last halt in the early evening, stars glimmering
to life, the last of the day's heat pulsing up from the ground. Eda
paced while her guard and Ileem shared a meager meal of meat,
dates, and cheese. She wasn't hungry. She didn't think she could
have stomached food even if she was.

It was deep night when at long, long last they set out on
the final leg of their journey. Her mare ate up the miles, hooves
pounding into the hard earth. Eda couldn't help but think that
the gods were watching her from their unreachable realms,
waiting to see what she would do.

Waiting to relinquish their hold on Niren's life.

She pushed away the horrible niggling feeling that it wouldn't be enough, that she would find the stone and finish the temple, and Niren would die anyway.

Ileem's words chased themselves around in her head: *The gods will keep her safe. Rudion promised me.* She clung to them, even though she didn't know if she really believed them.

Just when she thought they would be riding forever, they were thundering up to their destination. The village was so small it didn't merit a name. It was only occupied part of the year, when herders brought their horses through to eat the new growth of scrubby desert bushes and train for the annual races. Right now, the village was empty.

Or it would have been, if not for the mounds and mounds of stone blocks stacked by the central well.

A fire burned orange in the shadow of the stone, and half a dozen armed soldiers crouched around it, playing dice in the flaring light. The soldiers looked up as Eda, Ileem, and her guard approached, pulling their mounts to a stop. The soldiers jerked to their feet and drew their sabers in one swift, scraping motion.

For several heartbeats, Eda assessed the situation, calculating the odds of three against six, when she herself had only a dagger. Firelight danced along naked blades, and Eda glanced at Ileem. He nodded almost imperceptibly. It gave her courage.

She took a breath and swung off Naia, striding up to the six soldiers with her hands palm up in front of her, showing they were empty. The soldiers did not lower their sabers.

"I believe there has been some mistake about the shipment," said Eda coolly, stopping a pace away. "This stone was supposed to be delivered to Eddenahr for the new temple."

"I'm afraid, Your Imperial Majesty, that we are under orders to keep the stone here," said the silver-haired soldier on the end. "It's not to be moved."

"Whose orders?"

The soldier shifted uneasily, the point of his saber trembling. "Baron Rescarin, Your Imperial Majesty."

"And does Baron Rescarin command the Empire?"

"He commands us."

Eda put out one hand, touching his saber, pushing it gently down to his side. The edge sliced her fingers, and blood dripped into the dust. She didn't even flinch. "The stone goes to Eddenahr. Tonight."

The soldier's face hardened, and he raised the saber again, putting it to her throat. "I'm sorry, Your Imperial Majesty. But the stone stays here."

"Did you not *hear* her?"

Eda didn't take her eyes from the soldier's as Ileem paced up beside her. She sensed that energy in him, that volatile flame.

The soldier's glance flicked from Eda to Ileem and back again. "Baron Rescarin has ordered us to arrest anyone who attempts to take the stone. That includes you, Your Imperial Majesty."

From the corner of her eye, Eda saw a tall, shadowy form waver into existence beside Ileem. A tremor went through her, while Ileem drew a sharp breath and dropped to his knees. "My lord Rudion."

The Shadow stepped passed Ileem, glancing at Eda for the barest instant before stretching out one shadowy arm to touch the soldier's heart.

The soldier gasped, his eyes flaring wide, and dropped dead into the dust, his saber clattering at Eda's feet. The Shadow vanished.

Eda swallowed a scream while Ileem rose from his knees and

folded his arm in hers. Together, they turned to the remaining five soldiers. Eda forced her voice not to shake: "The stone goes to Eddenahr, tonight, and if you will not help us, our god does not have need of you, either." She gestured at the dead man on the ground.

The soldiers sheathed their sabers and bowed, very low.

The night seemed to spin on with a silvery strangeness, like a half-remembered dream. The wagons used to transport the stone from the seaport were gathering dust just outside the tiny village, the horses that pulled them safe in the herders' stable. It seemed Rescarin was ready to move the stone with a word, or he would have left neither.

It took hours to load the stone, the five soldiers and Eda's guard sweating and straining in the moonlight. Eda and Ileem paced between the wagons, overseeing the work. She tried not to see the body that lay where it had fallen; she gave no orders for its removal. But its presence gnawed at her, shook her to her core.

"Why did Rudion kill him?" she asked Ileem quietly as the last of the blocks were being hauled onto the wagons.

Ileem set his jaw, every inch of him burning with power and certainty. "Because Rudion takes care of his own."

Eda swallowed. "Did you call him?"

Ileem lifted his left palm into her view, and the fresh red mark slashed across his web of scars was her answer.

They started back to Eddenahr just before dawn, Eda and Ileem at the head of the stone-laden wagons. Every mile was agony,

Niren's uncertain fate eating Eda up from the inside. Over and over she sent a prayer to the gods, to Tuer: *Let us be in time. Let us be in time.* She tried not to think of the soldier, toppling dead to the ground at the barest brush of Tuer's shadowy hand.

It was nearly noon before Eddenahr came into view, its white walls and silver-spired towers hard to look at in the glaring light of the relentless sun. Sweat crawled along the back of Eda's shoulders, dust and grime ground into every ounce of skin.

As they drew nearer the city, Eda sent the wagons to the temple site, a fierce hope going through her at the thought of her temple being completed. Of Niren growing well and whole again.

She and Ileem and her guard thundered on to Eddenahr, pulling up at the gates in a cloud of choking dust.

To her surprise, they had a welcome party.

Rescarin was waiting there, the other Barons behind him, all dressed in their formal robes, heavy chains of office weighing around their necks. The envoy from Denlahn was present, too: Liahstorion, in a cloud-pink gown that hugged her slim form and accentuated the muscles in her arms and legs; Ambassador Oadem wearing his ever-present frown; a dozen Denlahn guards.

The entire space between the open gates was filled with Rescarin's soldiers, the Evallan crest emblazoned on their crimson sashes: a rising blue wave, a silver star.

Rescarin strode toward her, his stance assured, his expression beyond smug. "Eda Mairin-Draive, you are under arrest for the murder of our late Emperor and the unlawful seizing of his crown."

Rescarin's soldiers swept forward and surrounded her.

One of the soldiers dragged her from her horse and put his saber to her throat, forcing her onto her knees before Rescarin.

Chapter Twelve

E DA'S FAITHFUL GUARD DREW HIS OWN SABER, and Ileem dismounted, his form solid and still an arm's length away. Her eyes sought his and he gave her an assuring nod, which helped to quell the panic roiling inside of her. She stared up at Rescarin with as much indifference as she could affect and held her body rigid as a spear shaft.

"Baron Rescarin," she said coolly, around the point of the saber, "you understand that threatening the Empress of Enduena is treason."

He laughed. "You're the Empress of nothing. You're just a bastard who thought she could fool us into letting her parade about in pretty dresses and a crown. But you've been found out. Your ruse is at an end."

A hot wind stirred through the company at the gate, drying the sweat on Eda's neck, rustling through the dirty silk of her loose riding trousers. Ileem stood silent, his fingers twitching to the dagger on his belt.

Eda swallowed, carefully, the saber scratching her throat.
Would Ileem call Rudion again? Did she want him to?

Rescarin crouched in front of Eda in the dust. He grasped
her chin with one smooth, ring-covered hand, his nails digging
in, pulling her face toward the saber.

She fought him, straining hard, but he forced her throat into
the blade. Panic crawled behind her eyes. Pain bit hot.

"Baron Rescarin!"

He released her, and she stumbled backward in the sudden
absence of his pressuring hand.

She stared up at Ileem, who had drawn his dagger and raised
his left hand, showing the cut that was just beginning to scab.
Sunlight gilded him in gold, and it almost hurt to look at him.
"Do not make me call my god, unless you wish to be struck down
like your soldier in the desert, to be a feast for jackals, for worms."

Eda picked herself up, wiping the smear of blood from her neck.

Danger blazed in Rescarin's eyes. He snapped his fingers at
the soldiers who had relieved Eda of her horse. "Take her away
and throw her in the dungeon. We'll figure out what to do with
her later."

They seized her arms, jerked her toward the gates, but she
dug in her heels, resisting. Her eyes found Ileem's. She gave
him a swift nod, hoping he understood her meaning: *Call him.
Call Rudion.*

"Your graces, *wait!*"

Domin ran through the gate, kicking up a cloud of dust. He
clutched a sheaf of papers that made Eda's heart stutter. They
were affixed with the Imperial seal. "I have proof that Her
Imperial Majesty is who she says she is," Domin panted. "I have
proof that Rescarin is lying."

The soldiers relaxed their grip on her arms, and Eda shrugged them off. She approached the Barons, trying to remember to breathe, just breathe, forcing her face into an impenetrable mask. "Baron Domin," she said. "Show your proof."

Domin flicked his eyes to her, anxious as a rabbit, and nodded. He handed the sheaf of papers to Baron Dyar and Baron Lohnin, who immediately began to look them over.

Rescarin tried to snatch the papers away, but Lohnin held up one hand. "Is there something you'd rather we not see, Rescarin?"

That silenced him.

Eda waited, the hot wind curling round her ankles, while Dyar and Lohnin read. She knew what they were reading: she'd commissioned the forgeries herself, months ago.

After an agonizing few moments, Lohnin looked up with a frown. "What are you playing at, Rescarin? These are official documents: they chronicle the Empress's birth, with a statement signed by the late Emperor himself asserting his paternity. According to this, the Emperor planned on announcing her as his daughter the moment she was brought to Eddenahr as a child. Rescarin, *you* forestalled him, claiming it was better for her if she didn't know. Safer, to have a hidden heir, in case anything were to happen to his son. Which, as we all know, it did. Perhaps that was no accident?"

Every line of Rescarin's body evinced his rage. "Surely you can see those documents are fakes."

Domin turned on him, dark eyes flashing. "Then why did you steal them from the Empress? Why were they in *your* chambers? What were you going to do—burn them? Erase all proof of the Empress's claims?"

Rescarin faced him square on. "I was going to prove they

were forgeries, as more than a cursory glance would show."

"Except that isn't all that was found in your chambers."

Eda looked at Ileem with surprise. He swept past her, his face a study of controlled, righteous anger. "You were also hiding this." He drew something from an inner pocket in his robe, and held it up for all to see: a small glass vial that flashed in the sun.

Eda's heart seized. She knew that vial: knew its shape and its emptiness, knew what it had once contained. She should have smashed it and buried the shards. She should have gotten rid of it long ago, but she hadn't. She had kept it, in a little jewel case under her bed, a constant reminder of what she had done. How had Ileem found it? She hadn't even told him about the poison until their ride to the well. She hadn't even really admitted to using it herself.

And yet there it was, small and dark in his hand.

Ileem paced toward Rescarin. "The late Emperor was slowly poisoned for the duration of the last year of his life. You administered that poison, drop by drop, in his food, his wine. Didn't you, Rescarin? And when an unexpected usurper surfaced, imposter heir Talia Dahl-Saida, you gave the Emperor the final, lethal dose, planning to put yourself forward as a replacement. But because the gods are just, Her Imperial Majesty was there before you. Your every action over the last year has been purposefully designed to undermine her: making a peace treaty with my people without her knowledge or consent; halting construction on the temple to make her look weak and foolish; sowing mistrust among your fellow Barons. But you made one vital mistake." Ileem stopped so close to Rescarin their noses nearly touched. "You didn't realize the god-marked servant of Rudion was coming." Ileem jabbed the empty poison vial into

Rescarin's chest and let it fall to the dust. He ground it under his heel.

For a moment, Eda's eyes were drawn to the city gates, where the shadow-god stood, his piercing gaze meeting hers. Words echoed suddenly in her ears, and she knew that, at long last, the god was speaking to her: *Fulfill your vow. Honor your oath.*

She opened her mouth to reply, but Tuer's Shadow melted into dust motes swirling in the sunlight, and she was left to wonder if he'd been there at all.

"Your Imperial Majesty?"

She jumped, realizing Ileem was looking at her expectantly, realizing there was more to do. How long had she been staring after the god?

She drew a sharp breath, and turned to her Barons. "Perhaps Rescarin's biggest sin is that he did *not* reduce Evalla's army, as he swore to all of us he did. He's swelled its ranks with mercenaries instead, planning not only to depose me, but to get rid of all of you as well. He planned to march on the city next week. He planned to execute you, one by one." Eda had no idea if that last bit was true, but it had the desired effect.

Baron Lohnin drew his dagger and rushed at Rescarin, pinning him up against the wall beside the gate. "You traitorous *bastard!*"

"Lohnin, please," said Eda calmly. "Justice will be meted out in due time. For now——" She met Rescarin's eyes. "For now, take him away and throw him into the dungeon. We'll figure out what to do with him later."

Rescarin swore, batting Lohnin's dagger aside and lunging at her.

But the very guard who had taken Eda off her horse seized

him by either arm and dragged him away.

Eda crossed to where Domin stood, a little apart from the others. She gave him her most brilliant smile. "You are to be commended, Baron Domin, for bringing proof just when it was needed. My loyal subject. My most faithful servant."

She wasn't a fool. She knew Domin had been the one to steal those documents from *her* and take them to Rescarin—which is why he knew how and where to find them again. She knew he had been playing at double-crossing her this whole time, and that he knew that *she* knew it. But that just gave her one more hold over him. "To reward you for your loyalty, I'm giving you the Governorship of Evalla in Rescarin's stead. You command two provinces now, Domin."

Fear sparked in Domin's eyes. He understood she was telling him she owned him, that one more misstep and she wouldn't hesitate to get rid of him.

Domin bowed, very low. "What is your first task for me as Baron of Evalla, Your Imperial Majesty?"

"Take five hundred guards and see to it that the mercenaries Rescarin hired are sent away and Evalla's army is truly reduced. If he owes them money, you have my permission to take it from Evalla's treasury. See they are compensated immediately." She worked the ring off the littlest finger on her right hand, and offered it to Domin. "This is as good as my presence. Show it to Evalla's steward, and he will follow your every order."

Domin took the ring, and bowed again. "Thank you, Your Imperial Majesty." He strode from the courtyard with new confidence.

"As for the rest of you." Eda turned her full attention to the remaining two Barons, who stood eyeing her with new respect.

Ambassador Oadem looked bewildered, and Eda thought she saw a spark of admiration in Liahstorion's eyes. "There will be no more undermining my rule, my words, my decisions. You are to govern your provinces, bring me accurate and timely reports, and offer council if and when I request it. That is the sum and total of your duties in Eddenahr. Do I make myself clear?"

"Yes, Your Imperial Majesty," they said in unison, none of them quite daring to meet her gaze.

She issued a few more sharp commands, dismissing the army and sending everyone else away. For a moment she staggered where she stood, and Ileem caught her arm. "Go and see her," he said gently. "Go and see your friend."

Eda shut the door to the little bedchamber so she and Niren could be alone. There was no change. Niren was gray and still, more shadow than not. Eda smoothed the hair back from Niren's brow. She drew out a jar of ashes and oil and, opening it, smeared part across her friend's forehead and part across her own, as if Niren were a memorial stone Eda had come to petition beside.

"I'm not letting you go," Eda whispered. "I'm going to save you. I swear it." She kissed the mixture on Niren's forehead; flakes of ashes stuck to her lips, and the oil was bitter.

She left Niren and went to the stables, surprising the attendants there by saddling a horse herself—not Naia, who needed to rest from the last two days. Eda didn't wait for her guard to finish readying his own mount—she rode away alone, urging her horse as fast as it could run.

Hot wind rushed past Eda's ears; the desert blurred before her. Still she craved more speed, every pulse of her heart crying out *Please be in time, please be in time.*

She pulled up to the temple site in a blur of heat and dust. The masons and builders were back at work, unloading the stone from the wagons, stirring vats of mortar, hauling the stone up the temple steps with ropes and pulleys. The walls were already a little taller than when Eda and Ileem had been there last.

Eda swung down off her horse, and climbed the steps, weaving her way through the workers. Her body felt on the cusp of unraveling; she wondered what bound her together, if it was hope or fear or something else entirely.

She paced through the unfinished temple until she came to the place where the altar to Tuer would be, in the inner chamber. There was nothing there now besides a shard of broken glass, a mirror that reflected the blinding heat of the sun. Eda frowned and brushed the glass away. She knelt on the stone floor. She hadn't wiped off the ashes and oil from her oblation in Niren's chamber, and the oil, warm from her ride, dripped down her face like tears.

Eda stripped her sleeve and drew her dagger, staring for a moment at her left hand. Marks of previous petitions marred her, the worst one being the recent cut in her palm. She unlatched her gold arm cuff, and without further deliberation, sliced her blade across the middle of her forearm. The pain was sharp and swift, and the blood welled.

She let the blood drip on the stone until red obscured the dust before the absent altar. "Send her back to me," said Eda. "Send her back. The temple will be finished, just like I promised. The people will turn to you. You have no cause to take her, now.

I'm fulfilling my oath. I'm honoring my vow. Honor yours. Send her back. Please."

There came no answer, no ghosts, no gods, but it seemed like the world held its breath, a great hush resounding through the temple. And then a gust of wind ripped past her, tearing at her hair and drying the oil on her face. It smelled like roses, like fire. She blinked, and the blood on the stone was gone.

Eda stood, sheathing her dagger, cinching her arm cuff back on over her wound. She had done her part. Tuer had heard her.

Now it was time for him to relinquish his hold on Niren. To return to Eda the price of her vow.

Chapter Thirteen

E DA POINTED HER HORSE BACK TOWARD THE PALACE. The heat of the day was overwhelming, and she longed to be back inside, to have a languorous soak in her marble bath, to be *clean* for the first time in what felt like a very long time. But most of all she wanted to be back at Niren's side. She wanted to be there when her friend awoke, and if she didn't wake, if the gods took her despite everything—

Well, then Eda would make them pay.

A rider came toward her across the plain, and her heart seized up when she recognized Ileem. He had changed, since the gate, into a bright yellow robe that flowed around him like liquid light, with a matching headscarf sewn with diamonds that flashed and danced. He was bright as the sun, and she realized how much she wanted him always shining in her sky.

A strange hopeful eagerness welled up inside her as he reined in his mount next to hers. But his dark eyes were serious, almost angry. "You went to the temple alone, didn't you? You called the gods *alone*. Why didn't you wait for me? I would have invoked Rudion for you."

Something went tight and hard in her chest. "I was invoking the gods long before you came, Ileem Emohri. It's my vow in question. My friend's life hanging in the balance. It had to be me, and it had to be alone. You couldn't do it for me. Not this time."

His expression softened, and he looked suddenly stricken. He reached out to tuck a loose strand of Eda's hair behind her ear, caressing her cheek as he drew his hand away again. "Forgive me. I understand that my bond with Rudion is different from yours. That it must be. Did he come to you? Did he speak to you?"

The scorching wind dragged dry fingers across Eda's face. "He accepted my offering. I hope it will be enough."

"The gods have favored us since Raiva's Well. They will not forsake your friend, not now."

She studied him, and asked the question that was gnawing at her. "Where did you get the vial?"

"Rudion gave it to me, the night of my arrival. He said to keep it close, that I would have need of it. I didn't know what it was until . . . until our ride to Raiva's Well."

"And you don't despise me, even though—"

He smiled at her, soft and sad. "I don't despise you, even though. I know it was Rudion guiding your hand. It's how he allowed you to take the crown. It's how he punished the Emperor for his crimes."

The knot inside her eased, and she found she didn't feel the heat as much as she had a moment ago.

Once more Ileem's hand found her face. He stroked her cheek and she shut her eyes, leaning into him. "You kept your promise," she told him. "Helped me destroy Rescarin. Enabled temple construction to resume."

"So I did, with the aid of my god."

"Our god," she corrected gently.

"Our god."

She opened her eyes to find Ileem's face a breath away from hers, his dark gaze piercing through her. "Might I ask for an amendment to the peace treaty between our two nations, Your Imperial Majesty?"

A thrill went through her. She brushed her fingers along the line of his jaw. "You may."

He cupped both his hands around her face, drawing her close as their mounts shifted underneath them.

The gold specs in his irises seemed to dance; his breath was laced with the scent of cardamom tea.

"Will you be my wife, Eda of Enduena?" he asked.

She closed the remaining distance between them with a kiss, and let that be his answer.

Later, much later, she sat at the window in her bedchamber, staring out at the white stars. She tried to examine her joy about Ileem but she couldn't quite make sense of it. How could she be happy when Niren lay still as death in her bed?

There had been no change in her when Eda arrived back at the palace—none at all.

"What were you expecting?" the palace physician had asked Eda with a quizzical frown. "A miraculous recovery?"

Beneath her arm cuff, her wound itched and ached. Yes.

That's exactly what she expected.

The night stared back at her, empty, blank. She swore at the stars.

She rose and put on her favorite dressing gown, the deep green one with the white embroidery. If she couldn't sleep, there was no reason Rescarin should.

She left her rooms by the respectable route, collecting her guard from the corridor. She made her way confidently through the palace, across the courtyard, and down a set of narrow, dirty stairs to the lower level. To the prison.

She hadn't been down here in over a year, not since she'd paid a similar visit to her erstwhile rival. Even thinking about Talia made Eda's lip curl in disgust, though she was far away in Ryn and wasn't Eda's problem anymore.

Eda came to the first locked gate and barked at the guard who kept it to let her through. He did, bowing hastily, and ordered the guard beyond to escort her to Baron Rescarin's cell.

Eda was pleased to find that Rescarin had been installed in the darkest, dingiest cell possible at the very back of the prison. She grabbed a torch from the wall and brought it near the cell door, illuminating the interior. She was pretty sure there was a dead rat in one corner. The whole place smelled awful, like human waste and mold and fear.

Rescarin had been curled up on the narrow stone shelf that served as a bed on the back wall, but he scrambled to his feet at her arrival, tripping over himself and landing in a heap on the grimy floor.

Eda sneered down at him, in the safety of her torch and the bars between them. "Oh Rescarin, look at you. You're not bearing up at *all* as well as I thought you would."

He didn't seem affected by her jibe, a kind of wan humor in his eyes. "I underestimated you, Eda. I hadn't thought you'd ensnare that Denlahn jackal to do your dirty work for you."

"I rather like my Denlahn jackal. We're to be married, you know."

Rescarin gave a bark of laughter. "*Are* you?"

"At the Festival of Uerc."

His grin stretched to his ears. "I never thought our little Bastard Empress would lose her heart to anyone, let alone a foreigner. An enemy."

"*You're* the one who wanted peace with them. And he suits me."

Rescarin shook his head like she was some kind of witless child. "You have known him, what, a week? And you fancy yourself in love? You don't know anything about him."

"I know enough. And what's it to you, anyway? You'll be dead soon."

"That's rather tiresome. I'd hoped you had some sort of ridiculously elaborate banishment planned for me, like you had for that other courtier—what was her name? I don't remember. She was forgettable."

"Shut *up*. I didn't come down here to listen to you prattling."

His eyes met hers with a sudden, deadly seriousness. "Then why did you come? To make yourself feel powerful? Empires rise and fall, Eda. I would take care for yours."

"I'm disbanding your mercenaries. There's no other threat to me."

He laughed again, his eyebrows tilting upward. "You'll regret that, I think."

"I've won, Rescarin. I would think you would show a little more respect to the person who holds your very life in her hands."

"I'm not afraid of you, Eda. I know you put on a good show, but the truth is, you're still that scared little girl who would rather sit in a room with her parents' dead bodies than do anything to fight for the province she claimed to love so much."

"I was *nine!*" she screamed. "You took everything from me, and I swore to myself that one day I would take everything back. One day, I would repay you for everything you did that night. Everything you stole. Now I can."

Rescarin shrugged. "Then kill me, if you like. Afterward you'll have nothing left to hate, and no one to blame for your failures but yourself."

His words were calculated, and hit their mark. They bit deep. Eda hated that he knew it. She would never stop hating him.

"Perhaps I won't kill you," she said quietly. "But I can certainly make you regret being alive."

She wheeled on the prison guard. "Cut his fingers off. All of them. Send word when it's done."

"What's wrong, Your Imperial Majesty?" called Rescarin. "You don't have the stomach to see it done?"

She turned for one last look at the man she had hated since childhood. "You mistake me, Rescarin. I'm afraid if I stay any longer, I'll kill you myself."

She dreamed of climbing down into Raiva's Well, down and down, but no matter how far she went, she could never seem to reach the bottom. Then she was in the sacred pool in the mountain, the water lapping up over her waist. But she looked down and saw it wasn't water at all—it was blood. Rescarin laughed at her, reaching for her with scarlet hands, and the goddess Raiva turned her face away.

Far away, someone was weeping. A great darkness came into view, a god in chains. His head was bowed, his shoulders shaking, and she knew it was the god who wept. She stepped up to him. "What is wrong, my lord?"

But he didn't answer.

The room filled up with blood, and Eda woke, gasping, to a sharp rap on her door.

She jerked upright in bed, heart pounding wildly. A glance at the window told her she'd slept late—well past midmorning.

The palace physician stood there, her eyes wide with shock. "She's awake. Your Imperial Majesty, the Marquess is *awake*."

Chapter Fourteen

E DA DIDN'T STOP FOR ANY OF HER usual morning rituals. She stepped from her bed, grabbed a fresh silk dressing gown and shrugged into it as she brushed past the physician.

Out in the corridor, she ran. For the first time in her life she didn't care who saw her or what impression she made. Nothing mattered but reaching Niren's side as quickly as possible, to see for herself that her friend had truly rejoined the land of the living.

She burst into Niren's chambers, pushing past the gaggle of attendants and a few exceptionally nosy courtiers who had come to gape. She spared a backwards glance at her guard. "Get them out of here."

"Your Imperial Majesty?"

"Get them all out!"

And then she flung open the bedroom door to find Niren sitting up in bed, warm color in her cheeks.

Eda's heart wrenched. Tears pressed against her eyes. She stared at Niren, disbelieving.

She shut the door, and settled into the chair by Niren's bedside.

Her friend regarded her with a quiet smile, but something haunted lingered in her eyes.

Eda grabbed her hand. "I thought I'd lost you." Her voice was raw. Cracked.

Tears dripped down Niren's cheeks, and she turned her face away.

"Niren?"

"You didn't lose me, Eda," Niren's voice was hoarse with disuse. She shuddered and wept.

Eda sat with her awhile in silence, waiting until Niren was ready to speak.

"I saw the Circles of the world," said Niren, still not turning back to Eda. "I saw the spheres and the spaces between, the great void and the spirits trapped there. I saw the realm of the One and the gods and men alike who dwell on those shores. I saw death and time and sorrow. I heard the gods calling my name. And I knew they had a purpose for me. I knew I was destined to serve them there, as I could not do here. As I cannot do now." At last she met Eda's eyes; her face was wracked with sorrow. "You ripped me away from all that. I didn't *want* to come back. But then it seems to be *your* purpose in life to take everything that matters to me."

Eda blinked, throat constricting. "Niren—"

"Go away, Eda. I don't feel like talking to you anymore."

"I couldn't let you die, Niren. It would have been my fault. When I was little, when my parents died, I—"

"Eda." A strange gentleness came into Niren's tone. "Not everything is about you, you know."

"But I made a vow, and the gods—"

"The gods work according to their own designs, and the design of the One who created them. Do you really think a vow made by you or me or any human born on Endahr could alter the gods' plans? They released me for now, Eda. But they might call me back again. And when they do—when they do, you have to let me go. Do you understand?"

"I saved you once. I can do it again."

Niren sighed and shook her head, but a little smile touched her lips. "You're not listening. You've never listened. Not even when we were children."

"I found the stone, Niren. Construction on the temple has started up again and I sealed it with my blood. That's what saved you."

"Oh, Eda. I don't think my life or death is wrapped up in blood and stone. Perhaps the gods had pity on you. Perhaps they saw you couldn't do without me just yet."

Eda thought of Raiva's words to her down in the well, and a hard knot of anger pulled tight inside of her. "The gods have never had pity on me."

Eda had asked Ileem to sing for the company, to celebrate their formal engagement as he'd told her was tradition in Denlahn. The engagement had happened that morning, up in the Place of Kings during an arduous, drawn-out ceremony. They'd spent the rest of the day listening to outraged petitioners explain in loud, passionate detail why the marriage was a horrible idea. Some objected to Denlahn in general, others to Ileem in particular, and it had taken every ounce of Eda's willpower not to order them all dragged off to prison.

Even after that, Ileem had agreed to perform. Seeing him now, standing alone on the dais in the ballroom, took her breath away. He wore midnight-blue robes embroidered in silver, with a matching silver headdress, Enduenan-style sash, and his ever-present ear cuff obscuring the mark of Tuer. He held an ivory-bone lute, which looked small against his tall frame, like a child's instrument in the hand of a god.

Stars were just glimmering into being outside the balcony, and a breeze stirred through the ballroom that smelled, faintly, of autumn, of the coming relief from the summer that had lasted more than half the year.

Eda sat in a carved ebony chair, cushioned with velvet, that faced the dais. Her Barons and other courtiers waited behind her, some standing, some seated on the pillows strewn about the floor. Niren was among them, ruby skirts making a perfect circle around her, a red jewel flashing on her brow. Niren had been strangely quiet when Eda had told her about the engagement. She'd been strangely quiet all week, in fact, like she'd left a part of herself in the realm of the gods and would never again be truly whole.

But Eda pushed those thoughts from her head and locked eyes with Ileem as his fingers twitched over the lute strings. He gave her a swift fierce smile.

And then he opened his mouth and began to sing.

His voice was soft at first, barely audible over the twangy hum of the lute, but it grew fuller and richer with every note, and its beauty overwhelmed her. Bewitched her. He sang in the ancient Denlahn tongue, and though the words were unfamiliar to her, she still felt their power. She almost imagined she could *see* them, glinting gold on his lips.

The song ended abruptly, and Ileem took a breath and started another before anyone had a chance to applaud. This was a rhyme Eda had known from earliest childhood, sung in her own language. She hadn't thought about it in years, and listening to it now made her grow very cold.

Seek the god, fulfill your vow
He's calling, calling you
Shut in his mountain far away
Where chains of sorrow heavy weigh
He's calling, calling you
What need has he for temples?
What need has he for stone?
What need has he for gold or jewels
Trapped in the dark alone?
The sea will bear you hither
On wings you'll travel high
And past the mountain's doorway
The killing knife will lie
Seek the god, fulfill your vow
He's calling, calling you
Shut in his mountain far away
Where chains of sorrow heavy weigh
He's calling, calling you.

The song ended with an intricate and haunting countermelody on the lute, and then Ileem shifted into a third piece.

Eda stared at him. It was just a children's nonsense song.

But she didn't think those words were nonsense to the mountain priest or Raiva in her well. Shadow Niren wavered into view beside Ileem on the dais, her head in her hands, her shoulders shaking with sobs only Eda could hear.

Real Niren froze where she sat, her eyes locked hard on her shadowy self.

Horror plunged like a knife deep into Eda's belly and twisted.

Eda drew Niren into a corner of the room when Ileem's performance was over; she wasn't imagining that Niren's hand trembled in her own. "Niren, can you see her?" Eda asked bluntly.

Niren was so cold, a distant, unreachable star. "You haven't altered the future, you know. Just delayed it a little."

"Can you see her?"

"The shadow who bears my face?" Niren's jaw tightened. "Eda, I've always seen her."

Chapter Fifteen

"**Y**OU SEEM VERY FAR AWAY THIS EVENING, Your Imperial Majesty."

Eda glanced over at Ileem, her legs dangling from her perch on the rooftop overlooking the garden and the menagerie. It was near midnight—they'd danced for hours after Ileem's performance. Eda had at last retired for the evening and escaped up onto the roof to find her fiancé waiting for her. She'd come seeking solitude, but it was his company she actually craved, away from the eyes of the court.

"What made you choose that song? The one about seeking the god and fulfilling a vow?"

Ileem grimaced. "Did you find fault with my performance? Rudion brought it to mind, whispered it in my ear."

Her heart raced. "I didn't find fault with your performance in the least. Your tongue seems blessed by Raiva herself." She flushed at the memory of his mouth on hers.

He took her hands, lacing their fingers together as he

leaned close enough that she could feel his breath on her cheek.

And then he was kissing her and she was kissing him back, and he was salty and warm, the sea and the sun. She breathed Ileem, and Ileem breathed her, and for a while, nothing else seemed to matter.

But at last they drew back to breathe air again, and Ileem sprawled out on the roof tiles. Eda tucked her head into the hollow of his neck, drinking in the scent of him, drinking in this moment. "Do you know," she mused, running her finger along his ear cuff, "I think I'm in love with you."

He smiled, his own fingers tracing the line of her jaw. "I thank my god every day that he brought me to you. That we're to be married and our vows forged together into one." He caressed her neck, and lightning shot down her spine.

For so long, Eda had told herself she didn't need anyone, and she'd proved it to herself, over and over. But now that everything was set to rights again—Niren well and whole, her Barons subdued, Rescarin's threat eliminated—she found she no longer wished to be alone. She didn't want to have to sleep with a knife under her pillow, waiting for everything she'd fought so hard for to be ripped away from her.

She realized, all at once, what that meant. "I want to crown you as my Emperor," she told Ileem, "not just my consort. I want to share power with you. Equally, for everything that's mine to be yours." Her fingers curled tight around the material of his silk robe, the heat of his body emanating behind it. She swallowed, trying to quell the raging of her heart.

He brushed his fingertips across her cheek, her eyelids, her lips. She could hardly breathe.

"I would be honored to rule the Empire beside you, Eda."

Peace unfolded in her belly. She wrapped her hands around his jaw, and pulled his mouth once more to hers.

It was only later, when she slipped back in through her window in the dark hours before dawn, that she allowed herself to think about Niren's troubling revelation, and the shadow that wouldn't stop haunting her—the shadow Niren could see.

But Eda had won, hadn't she? Niren was alive, the temple was nearing completion, and Eda's throne was secure. *No thanks to the gods*, Eda thought, and then immediately chastised herself. After all, where would she be without them?

Here, Eda told herself. *What did the gods even do for me, really? I made myself Empress. I brought Niren back from the brink of death. What have they done?*

There was an attendant waiting by her door, half asleep. She jerked awake at Eda's arrival, and dropped a wobbly curtsy. "Apologies for the intrusion, Your Imperial Majesty, but there's a prison guard in the antechamber, waiting to speak with you."

Eda smoothed her hair and made an attempt at brushing the dirt from her trousers, then followed the attendant from the room.

Eda recognized the guard with a jolt as the one she'd ordered to cut off all Rescarin's fingers. Her stomach flopped over and she wondered that she'd pushed her encounter with Rescarin so far out of her head. "What is it?" she snapped.

"Your Imperial Majesty, I've come to inform you that Rescarin Haena-Ar, former Baron of Evalla, was found dead in his cell this evening."

She tried not to let her shock show. "Dead? Of what?"

"Complications from his wounds, Your Imperial Majesty. They became infected."

Eda had hated Rescarin for almost her entire life—now she hated that the news of his death made her feel sick. She waved one hand dismissively. "Send his body back to his family, and don't bother me with anything like this again."

The guard bowed. "My apologies, Your Imperial Majesty."

Eda went back to her bedchamber, but she didn't undress for bed. She sat by her window and stared out into the remnants of the night. She wondered how it had been so beautiful up on the rooftop with Ileem and was so wretched down here.

She drifted off just before dawn, cramped in the window frame, and dreamed of Niren, the Emperor, and Rescarin, walking together through a shadowy landscape, their ankles heavy with chains. "You did this to us," said Niren. "You trapped us here."

"But you're not dead," Eda objected. "I saved you."

Niren reached out her shadowy fingers to touch Eda's forehead. Heat pierced through her, as it had when Raiva touched her down in the well. "Oh Eda," said Niren sadly. "You haven't saved anyone."

The whole palace—the whole *city*—had turned into an anthill kicked by a boot. The preparations for Eda's seizure of the throne and subsequent coronation had taken place slowly and in secret. Wedding preparations, however, were being conducted very much in the open. And with the wedding date fixed for the main feast at the end of the nine-day Festival of Uerc, there were mere weeks left to get everything done.

Eda's approval was required on everything from the final selection of musicians to the color of the napkins for the table settings. It was driving her mad. And to make everything even more disagreeable, Ileem had similar demands on his time. She saw him briefly every morning, when they brought their joint oblations to the Place of Kings, but there was hardly a chance for more than a few words before their oblations were ended and their attendants pulled them off in separate directions. Eda began to despise the sight of the Imperial Steward, who seemed to desperately need her five hundred times per day.

Any time she wasn't with the Imperial Steward she was riding back and forth to the temple site, overseeing the finer details of construction, telling the artisans where their carvings and curtains and candles should go, instructing three brand new priestesses in their coming duties. It seemed her hands were always covered in dust.

She saw Niren even less than she saw Ileem. Niren rarely attended council sessions and seemed to prefer taking dinner alone in her room.

The morning before the first day of the festival—ten days before the wedding—the Imperial hairdresser came to Eda's chambers to discuss Eda's wishes for the ceremony. Eda sat down in front of her dressing table while Niren leaned against the wall, playing with the clasp of a sapphire necklace Eda had given her for her birthday. Eda had commanded Niren's presence like she was a wayward attendant, and to her surprise, Niren had actually come. She looked thin, tired. Her eyes wandered often to the corner of the room, where her shadow self watched them in ghostly silence.

"What do you think, Your Imperial Majesty?" said the hairdresser, laying down a comb and stepping back from the dressing table.

Eda inspected herself in the mirror. For her wedding, she planned to emulate the wind goddess, Ahdairon, in a nod to the ancient belief that Ahdairon blessed marriages because she was so content with her own marriage to the wind god Mahl. Part of Eda's hair was done up in elaborate braids woven with blue and gold silk ribbons. On the actual day, there would be sapphires and diamonds sewn in, as well as tiny wings crafted out of real gold. The ensemble would be completed with a gauzy gold veil. Eda turned to her friend, who had barely looked up during the entire process. "Niren, what is your opinion?"

Niren flicked her eyes to Eda's hair.

"Whatever Your Imperial Majesty wishes." Her voice sounded as washed out as she looked.

Eda jerked up from the stool and went over to Niren, grabbing her arm and hauling her into Eda's private sitting room. Tea was waiting on a low table, steam curling up from glass and metal cups accompanied by pots of honey and a heaping plate of candied dates. Eda pushed Niren into one chair and sat down across from her in the other.

"I'm tired of this," Eda snapped. "I refuse to apologize for not letting you die. Talk to me. Please, Niren."

Niren looked at her, really *looked* at her, and Eda was taken aback by her pity. "I know you mean well, Eda. But when the gods call me again, don't pull me back. I will be perfectly fine."

Something clawed its way up Eda's throat, and she found herself fighting tears. "But what about me? *I* won't be all right."

Niren smiled. "You've never needed me, not really. You have your Empire, and soon your husband. I'm just a crutch, Eda. A remnant of your childhood that you wanted to dress up to atone for some imagined sin."

"But—"

"Eda." Niren grasped Eda's arm. "Thank you for everything you've done for me. But you have to let me go. You have an Empire to run. I have the gods to serve."

"So serve in the temple. Be a priestess for the Empire."

"The gods don't want temples. They never did. They want truth. They want sincerity."

Eda's whole body sagged. "I don't know how to give that to them."

Niren pulled her into a brief, tight hug. "Then perhaps that's what you should be searching for."

And then Niren slipped from the room, leaving Eda alone with tea that was no longer steaming. She felt hollow and broken and cold. She knew Niren was right, and she didn't want her to be.

She canceled the rest of her appointments for the day and rode out to the temple site. It really was nearly finished now, the last roof tiles being fitted into place, the interior carvings and furnishings being brought in.

The temple was beautiful, but it didn't fill Eda's emptiness. She shut her eyes in the scorching wind, and sent a plea up to the gods. *Is this really not what you wanted?*

The wind spat dust into her face. She wondered if that was their answer.

Chapter Sixteen

"E DA?"

She looked up from her writing desk to find Niren standing in the doorway, her blue-green silk trousers pooling around her ankles, her dark hair for once combed neat and straight. She was hugging a cloth-wrapped, rectangular object against her chest. Lantern light cast haunted shadows on Niren's thin face.

It was late, past midnight—Eda had been caught up in her work, reviewing tax reports from her Barons. She laid down her pen, ink dripping black on her paper. "Niren, are you well?"

Her friend paced toward her, and without a word laid the rectangular object in Eda's lap.

Eda unfolded the cloth to reveal a heavy book. It had gold-edged pages and a red leather cover stamped with the three Stars and the one Tree.

"A wedding present," said Niren. "I was going to save it for your wedding day, but I wanted you to have it now."

Eda opened the book, and a page she recognized stared out at her: a petitioner, kneeling before the god Tuer, his throne a mountain, his crown made of stars. She looked at Niren with a troubled frown. "The manuscript you were copying?"

Niren knelt beside Eda's chair, her fingers brushing lightly over the book. "It's the original. The library has my copy. It's filled with the old stories we both love so much. I thought you should have it."

Eda swallowed past the lump in her throat. "Niren, you can't give me this."

Niren smiled. "Not even an Empress should turn away the heartfelt offering of her closest friend."

Eda bowed her head, humbled. "Then we are still friends?"

"Though death and time should drive a wedge between us, we will always be friends."

For a moment, they stared at each other, Niren's words bitter with foreboding. But then Eda smiled. "Thank you, Niren. I will treasure it."

Niren smiled, too, swift and bright. She pressed Eda's hand and, rising, left the room.

Eda sat staring at the illustration of Tuer's petitioner for a long, long while.

She tried to tell herself that the marks on Niren's brow were just shadows. They had to be. Because Tuer had sent her back— his fingerprints ought to have faded.

She touched the image of the god on the page and wondered what his petitioner had offered him and how high a price Tuer had demanded in return.

Eda shut the book and went to bed.

But she couldn't sleep, the weight of Niren's gift heavy on her mind. At last she got out of bed and brought the book over to the window, where moonlight flooded in, making the pages shine. Eda opened it at random, and began to read. The words leapt out at her. Devoured her. She couldn't look away.

Long ago, when the world was young but not quite new, a man dared stand against a god, and the god struck him down. The man's name was Tahn, and he wished to take a seed from the great Tree that had stood from the beginning and travel west with his brothers and sisters to plant a new Tree, and so help mankind to flourish and grow.

But the god, Tuer, did not want him to go, and so he slew him.

Death entered the world, darkening its edges, staining its joy.

And the god was haunted by what he had done. He had poisoned the world he was supposed to make beautiful and broken the people he was supposed to guide.

To atone for his sin, Tuer decided to seek the soul of Tahn, to bring him back to life and by so doing help to heal the world.

He prepared for a long journey, arming himself with Starlight and a sword made of Tree bark, forged in fire. He bound himself with Words of protection, and then he came out of his mountain and opened a door in the world.

He stepped through into darkness and strode a long way, shadows slithering over his feet. He had entered the void, the space beyond Endahr. But there was nothing to hold Tahn there, nothing for his soul to fix on. And so Tuer knew he was not there.

Long Tuer walked in the void, gathering it and binding it into a sphere that compassed the earth, so that it would catch any other souls that happened to perish before he could put an end to dying. And he named that sphere the Circle of Death. When he was finished, he made a door and stepped from the Circle of Death to what lay beyond.

And it was there that he forgot.

He forgot his name and his purpose. He forgot mankind and the Tree. He forgot about death and life and all other things.

Stars wheeled round him, swirling shapes and colors he did not understand. There were rivers of light and shining pools of a substance he had never seen. He wandered an eternity before he thought to look in one of the pools, and found what filled it up: it was memory. Memory of what had happened, memory of what was yet to be. Every pool teemed with it, and the memories reached up and pulled him under.

He saw all the ages of the world pass before his eyes. He saw its making and unmaking, saw his own death, saw all the lives of all mankind spinning out before him.

And he saw the soul of Tahn, shining like a star, dwelling in the realm of the One who made the world and existed outside of it.

And then he remembered his name and his purpose, and he stood and freed himself from the pool of memories.

With his sword and the light that blazed inside of him, he drew the memories from the pool and bound them all together. And he made a second sphere, and built a door out of it, and that he called the Circle of Time.

But he still had not reached Tahn or the realm of the One who was before all things. He had come to a nothing, a nowhere place that had less substance than the void.

He couldn't see or hear. He had no form. He didn't properly exist at all. He needed something to forge a pathway between the Circle of Time and the One's dwelling place.

But what is greater than time? What can contain it?

He didn't think of love, which would have led him straight to the realm of the One and then home again, for he had not experienced love in the same way as mankind.

But he had known sorrow.

And so he wove around himself a sphere of sorrow, large enough to encompass the Circle of Time, large enough to fill up all the space left in the universe.

But as he wove, the sorrow weighed on him, binding itself into heavy shackles around his ankles and his wrists. He built a door, but he could not bear to go through it. How could he go to fetch the soul of Tahn, drag him back through all the Circles to live again, when he was content in the realm of the One?

And so Tuer bowed his head and let the chains grow up around him like brambles.

And there he sits still, in the midst of the Circle of Sorrow that he made for himself.

Centuries ago, the Festival of Uerc had been a solemn occasion, a single feast of remembrance for the fallen god. Now it was a raucous celebration spread out over nine full days that mostly consisted of parties and feasting and betting on horses. Every morning there was a horse race. Every evening there was a ball.

The ball held on the sixth night of the festival had always been Eda's favorite—it was the most traditional and actually paid homage to the god of animals. This year, it marked only three more days before she made Ileem her husband—and her

Emperor. It was also the last time Eda would see Ileem before their wedding, as she was going to adhere to the traditional Denlahn custom of isolating herself for the two days leading up to the ceremony. The custom seemed particularly important to Ileem and she wanted to make him feel as at home in Enduena as possible since it was very unlikely he would ever return to his homeland after they were married.

She planned to enjoy the evening to the absolute fullest, which would be easier if the story from Niren's book would stop gnawing at her mind. *And there he sits still, in the midst of the Circle of Sorrow that he made for himself.*

Is that what Shadow Niren and Raiva had meant? That to fulfill her vow she was supposed to go and find Tuer in the Circle of Sorrow?

She dismissed the thought, as she had over and over since reading the myth. How could Tuer be trapped, when a piece of him walked the earth so freely, imbued with power? Who was to say the shadowy god she'd struck a deal with as a child *wasn't* Tuer himself?

But she couldn't stop thinking about it.

She swept into the ballroom anxious and distracted, but the instant she saw Ileem she relaxed. He was waiting for her in the center of the room, dressed in black and gold, his jaw freshly shaved and his ear cuff glinting in the light from the chandeliers. He came to join her, and she slipped her hand in his.

Music flooded the ballroom, a quintet of Odan singers dressed in yellow robes; their haunting voices filled the silence, and Ileem drew Eda close.

They danced, slowly, his breath in her ear, his chest next to hers. For a while, she forgot about myths and gods and vows, allowed herself to soak up his presence.

"I love you," she whispered.

He kissed her hair. "My god has blessed me greatly, bringing me to you."

She kissed his cheek and cursed the rules of propriety that kept them from kissing any more intimately than that.

"Are Rescarin's mercenaries disbanded?" Ileem murmured, playing with a stray curl of her hair.

"Scattered like so many ashes, so say the latest reports." The reports had also informed her that Rescarin had been buried, but that was another thing Eda didn't want to think about.

As the moon rose outside the ballroom, Eda and Ileem settled onto the dais to watch a mingled host of Odans and Itans perform a pantomime about the gods Uerc and Huen. Eda had seen it a dozen times before, but this year it struck a chord. Uerc, lord of the beasts, and Huen, god of the earth, were great friends until jealousy drove them apart. For centuries they wrestled together in Huen's halls deep below the ground, until Uerc was blinded in the light of Huen's great Star. Stricken with grief because he could no longer see the beasts he loved, Uerc climbed the great cliffs where his eagles lived and cast himself from their heights. Huen was consumed with guilt, because it was his actions that led to his friend's death. He retreated into his underground halls, and was never seen again.

When the pantomime was over, the courtiers gathered for one final dance. Eda tucked herself under Ileem's arm, and noted with satisfaction that Niren was paired up with a handsome count. The Odan singers picked up an ancient, haunting melody, and the Itans joined in, ringing scores of tiny pitched bells in an intricate counterpoint.

Eda laid her head on Ileem's shoulder and shut her eyes, letting the music and the movement wash over her. She had never felt more at peace.

And then someone screamed, and she opened her eyes to see Niren dropping like a stone from the count's arms.

Chapter Seventeen

NIREN COLLAPSED TO THE FLOOR, her head knocking against the marble, blood soaking her hair with red.

Eda was instantly at her side, screaming for a guard, a doctor, *anyone*.

It was Ileem who scooped Niren up in his arms, carried her through the ballroom and down the corridor all the way to Niren's bedchamber. He settled her into the bed, his face stricken.

"GET THE PHYSICIAN!" Eda screeched.

Ileem nodded once and disappeared.

Eda sank onto the bed, gathering Niren into her arms, wiping the blood from her temple. Niren was breathing, but only just—dry, awful rattles in her chest.

"Niren. Niren, stay with me. Niren."

Niren's body began to shake. Eda held her tight, unconsciously sobbing. The world blurred before her. She wound her fingers through her friend's.

Niren's breaths became fewer, with too much space between.

The pulse in her wrist faltered.

"Stay with me," Eda whispered. "Stay with me. I'm not letting you go. I saved you. I *saved* you!"

But Niren was suddenly, horribly still. Her breathing stopped. Her pulse was gone.

"Where is the physician?" Eda demanded. "WHERE IS THE PHYSICIAN?"

"Here, Your Imperial Majesty."

The physician rushed into the room, Ileem hard on her heels.

Eda clung to her friend. "Bring her back. Do you hear me? BRING HER BACK!"

The physician stepped over to the bed, felt for Niren's pulse, shook her head. "I'm sorry, Your Imperial Majesty. She's gone."

"She can't be gone."

"Eda." Ileem came up beside her. He loosened her hand from Niren's, drew her to her feet. "She's gone, Eda. She's gone."

Mutely, Eda allowed herself to be led from the room, ears ringing, eyes unseeing.

It didn't make any sense.

Gods above, it didn't make any sense.

She couldn't be gone.

She *couldn't*.

And yet somehow, she was.

They laid Niren to rest in the Place of Kings the night before Eda and Ileem were to be married. Ileem stood beside her, both of them breaking the Denlahn custom of isolation. She was glad he was there, glad he deemed her more important than his traditions. His presence made the world a little less sharp, a little more stable. Even so she could hardly bear to stand there, watching the guards lower Niren's coffin into the ground, while Niren's ghost stared at her from among the other tombs.

Besides Ileem and Eda's guards, the only other person in attendance was one of the new priestesses. There hadn't been time to send for Niren's family, and Eda was ignoring all kinds of rules by burying her friend in the Place of Kings. But Niren deserved to be laid to rest with honor. She deserved to be among kings. It was all Eda could do for her.

Tuer's voice, forgotten almost in the weight of the years, echoed in her mind: *The gods will have their payment.*

Ileem folded Eda's hand in his own, steady and solemn beside her.

The priestess, a girl of perhaps fifteen, uttered the formal words of burial in her wispy voice: "May your spirit be gathered beyond the Circles of the world and your body rest quiet until the end of time, when the world is unmade."

"Until the end of time," Eda, Ileem, and the guards chorused together. "When the world is unmade."

Eda turned away as the guards shoveled earth into the grave and erected the memorial stone. She couldn't watch. She let go of Ileem's hand and wound through the other memorials and tombs to the old temple's doorway, following the steps down into the darkness. He didn't follow, sensing her need for solitude. She lit a candle and placed it on the ancient altar. A smear of ashes and oil still stained the floor from her last visit. The air was close and dank in here; she couldn't breathe, couldn't think.

She paced the tiny chamber, footsteps raising clouds of dust.

Every part of her blazed with anger. Every part of her pulsed with pain. She beat her fists against the stone, like she'd done as a child. She screamed her wordless rage into the echoing room, and dropped at last to her knees.

"You tricked me," she spat at the dust. "I kept my promise, and you took Niren anyway. *You tricked me.*"

The words from the story in Niren's book filled her mind:

But what is greater than time? What can contain it?

He didn't think of love, which would have led him straight to the realm of the One and then home again, for he had not experienced love in the same way as mankind.

But he had known sorrow.

She climbed the stairs back out into the night, where Ileem was waiting for her—the priestess had gone, and the guards hung back at a respectful distance.

And there he sits still, in the midst of the Circle of Sorrow that he made for himself.

Eda and Ileem wandered together to the edge of the hill, where Eda put her hand on one of the ancient pillars that had stood through centuries of time and war and peered out into the desert. Stars glittered in the black sky. Somewhere, an owl called to its mate.

"My god came to me, in the night," said Ileem softly beside her.

Eda pressed her fingernails against the stone so hard a few broke off, leaving her with rough, jagged edges. "He did not come to me."

"He told me that Niren is safe. That she is honored. That her death was not in vain."

From the corner of her eye, Eda saw Shadow Niren flicker into view beyond another pillar. Anger hardened into stone. "Did he take her? Did Tuer take her?"

"Eda—"

"Did he?" She wheeled on him, not heeding the tears running down her cheeks.

Ileem glanced away. "Yes."

She could barely choke out her next question: "Because of me?"

He put one hand on her arm. "The temple isn't what he wanted. It didn't fulfill your vow."

Eda shook him off. "That doesn't make any *sense*," she said viciously. "I built the temple for *him*. What does he want? Why won't he speak with me himself?"

Ileem looked at her intently. "Have you sought him, Eda? Truly sought him? Ask him to come to you. Ask him to give you his mark. He'll come."

"And if he doesn't?"

Ileem brushed his fingers across her brow, and she longed to lean against him, to shut her eyes against the horror that was eating her up from the inside, to wake to a safer, better world.

"Honor the gods. Honor your friend. And keep asking until he does. But I've lingered too long. It's unlucky to speak with my bride the night before our wedding."

"Please stay," Eda whispered. "Please don't leave me alone."

He kissed her gently on the cheek. "After tomorrow, we will never be parted."

And then he walked away, leaving Eda on the hilltop, alone with her sorrow and her ghosts and a thousand wheeling stars.

Chapter Eighteen

S HE PASSED THE REMAINDER OF THE NIGHT in the new temple, kneeling before Tuer's altar. She sacrificed a goat, as she had the night before her coronation. She smeared her forehead with blood and ashes and oil. She pleaded with Tuer to come to her, to tell her what he wanted from her, to tell her why he took Niren. She slammed her fists against the stone. She screamed. She wept.

But Tuer did not come.

Two hours before dawn, a guard came to bring her back to her chambers, where an army of attendants were waiting to prepare her for the ceremony. Eda allowed herself to be bathed and dressed, sat quietly while her eyes were painted with kohl and her hair swept up in the previously discussed arrangement. Sapphires were hung about her neck and threaded through her ears. A gold cuff engraved with the ancient Denlahn phrase "loved of the gods" was fitted onto her ear, a wedding present from Ileem. Her skin was painted with gold-flecked oil to make her gleam. Jasmine essence was dabbed at her throat and behind her ears.

One of the attendants pressed a mug of cardamom tea into her hands and made her drink it, then proceeded to feed her orange slices and strips of honeyed flatbread like she was a parrot. She wouldn't have thought to eat, otherwise.

Last of all came the veil, a shimmering, gossamer gold that was draped over her hair and her face, hanging to her knees in front and her heels in the back.

The attendants ushered her from her chambers and outside the palace, where a quartet of guards handed her into a palanquin and hoisted it onto their shoulders. They carried her up the long, steep path to the Place of Kings just as dawn showed over the horizon and with it a dark mass of boiling clouds.

A wind whipped up, smelling strongly of rain, and the air seemed to crackle with power. The guards grunted, bending their heads into the wind and tightening their grips on the palanquin.

At the top, a second army of attendants waited. Eda tried not to let her eyes wander to Niren's grave as they folded back her veil, touched up her cosmetics, smoothed her dress, and rubbed out invisible specs of dust. One of them fed Eda strawberries while another cursed in frustration that no one had brought rain canopies.

Thunder growled in the distance as Eda stood there, lonely in the sea of people. The sun rose behind the clouds, a riot of color against the dark. The elephant arrived, lumbering over the brow of the hill. Its hide was painted with blue and gold whorls, and it wore a headdress of tinkling bells. The elephant keeper spoke a word to the beast and it dropped to its knees in a cloud of dust. Attendants slid a set of steps up to it, and what seemed like a hundred different arms helped Eda climb them. She settled herself in the high saddle, one final attendant climbing up with her and folding the veil back over her head before scampering down again.

And then it was time.

Bells sounded from down in the city, and bright silver trumpets pierced through the roar of the rising wind.

The elephant keeper spoke a word in the beast's ear and it lumbered forward, winding the long way back down the hill.

Eda had ridden an elephant once before, the day of her coronation. It had been hot and dusty, and the motion of the creature had made her sick to her stomach. That day had been filled with triumph. This one was tainted with regret.

She held tight to the front of the saddle and focused on looking like a goddess of old, untouchable, unshakeable.

When Ileem was her husband and bound to her as he was to their god, would Tuer come to her at last? Or was her deal at an end, now that Tuer had taken what she'd promised him? She would gladly trade away her Empire for Niren to be returned to her, hale and whole.

The procession wound down the hill and past the gates of the city, where all of Eddenahr was waiting. They rang little bells and waved scarves and threw flowers in the elephant's path.

As they approached the newly completed temple, the clouds blotted out the sun and the rain broke, driving and heavy. It shredded Eda's veil, plastered her priceless gown against her body, ruined her elaborate hair.

But something tight inside of her eased, because Ileem was waiting for her on the temple steps. He was dressed all in silver, and shone like the moon.

He is sun and moon both, she thought. A thrill went through her. If she had never made her deal with Tuer, would she even have met Ileem? Certainly she wouldn't be marrying him this morning. Was her friend's life worth this? Worth him?

Everything moved far too slowly for her after that. The Odans sang a hymn as attendants brought out another set of steps and helped Eda down from the elephant, holding rain canopies over her head that were rather too late to do any good. One of the new priestesses hung a garland of flowers around her neck and brushed a line of oil and ashes across her forehead.

The ancient priest from the mountain took Eda's arm and walked with her up the steps. It took an eternity to reach Ileem at the top, but finally, finally they did.

Eda took Ileem's hands in both of her own and tried to remember to breathe. It was almost cold, up there in the wind and the rain, but Ileem's presence warmed every part of her.

The ceremony was long, melding together Denlahn and Enduenan marriage traditions. The speeches and pledges filled up half the morning, and her legs began to ache from standing there for such an extended period.

At last the priest came to the formal words of binding. "As the Stars shone with one light, may you be one. As the Tree flourished upon the earth, may you flourish. Until the last Star falls from heaven, may your love endure. Until death parts you, may you be true. Until time itself is ended, may you be of one mind and one heart and one soul."

A shiver passed through her, her hands trembling in Ileem's, and she knew in her heart of hearts that this, at least, Niren would not blame her for.

"Do you bind yourself to this man?" the priest asked Eda. "To guard him and keep him for all of time?"

"I bind myself," she said, her voice swallowed up in the echoing rain. "For all of time."

"Do you bind yourself to this woman?" the priest asked Ileem. "To guard her and keep her for all of time?"

Ileem smiled, smoothing his thumb across Eda's skin. "I bind myself, for all of time."

"Then by the will of the gods and the One who created them, let it be so."

And then, then—Ileem was *hers*.

He wrapped his hands around her chin and drew her to him, kissing her long and deeply in the sight of everyone watching below.

Eda stepped back from him, joy pushing past her anger and her grief, filling her up. There was only one thing left.

She turned to the crowd, and called her Barons to join her at the top of the temple steps. Domin was still in Evalla, managing Rescarin's affairs, but Lohnin, Dyar, and Tuell were there, Lohnin holding a cedar box stamped with the emblem of the Empire.

None of the Barons were smiling. They looked as cross as wet hens. They looked *like* cross wet hens.

Eda accepted the box from Lohnin, and gazed out into the crowd. "Today I, Imperial Majesty Eda Mairin-Draive, Empress of Enduena and Ryn and Od, hereby crown as my equal in power His Highness Ileem Emohri, Prince of Denlahn."

She opened the box and took out the crown.

Ileem knelt before her, and she lowered it onto his head.

"Rise, Imperial Majesty Ileem Emohri, Emperor of Enduena and Ryn and Od. Long may you reign beside me."

Ileem grinned. Ileem *laughed*, and Eda hauled him to his feet. They turned together to the crowd and raised their joined hands.

They descended the temple steps side by side, and climbed up onto the elephant, Eda first, Ileem after her.

The rain slacked off as the beast lumbered back toward the city. Ileem wrapped his arms around Eda's middle and pulled her tight against him. He kissed her ear, her neck, her jaw, and heat shivered through her.

"You're mine, my darling," she whispered.

He laughed into her hair. "As you are mine."

The feasting lasted until evening, when the sun sank away westward and stars awoke once more in the dark. Ileem escorted Eda to the ballroom, hand locked tight in hers, and she marveled anew that he was her *husband*, that she never again had to face the world or her Barons or her Empire alone.

She'd changed after the ceremony, her attendants repairing as much of the damage done by the rain as they could, but her attempt to emulate the goddess Ahdairon was ruined. Eda didn't care. She had other things to think about.

She trailed her fingers up Ileem's arm to his neck, pulling his face to hers for a kiss. "How long must we dance, my darling? You are Emperor, now. I don't intend to return to my chamber alone tonight."

Ileem gave her a slow smile, but his eyes flitted around the ballroom, to the balcony and the door and then back to her. He seemed distracted. Nervous. There was tension in his shoulders.

A sense of uneasiness awoke in the pit of her stomach. "Ileem, are you all right?"

"Fine, Eda." He kissed her forehead, then drew her to the center of the room. "It's not every day we are married. Dance with me."

They wheeled about in time to the music, Enduenan instrumentalists having taken the place of the Odan singers. A harp and a flute twined together in an intricate counterpoint, chased by a pulsing drumbeat that echoed through the chamber.

Ileem's hand was tight against the small of her back. He gripped her other hand so hard it hurt.

"Ileem."

He kept looking toward the balcony, his usually steady feet stumbling over the simplest steps.

The uneasiness took root. "Tell me what's wrong. Please, Ileem."

And then suddenly bells began to ring down in the lower city, a clamoring chaos of noise.

Alarm bells.

Eda was thrown back all at once to the night over a year ago when she'd burst into the ballroom with an army at her back to stop her rival from taking the Empire. For an instant she thought she saw Tuer, his tall, shadowy form striding through the dancers. But then she blinked and he was gone.

Eda looked sharply at her husband. "What's going on?"

Ileem smiled, the tension melting out of him. "My god is here. He blesses me once again."

The bells rang louder, wilder.

The dancing and the music stopped.

Eda stared at Ileem, stared and stared. Her mind understood what was happening, but her heart refused to believe it.

And she didn't believe it.

Not until she felt the sudden prick of pain beneath her jaw and found Ileem's dagger at her throat.

"There are three ways to appease a god, once you've made a deal with them," said Eda's father. They had climbed together to the top of the limestone tower, where a rooftop garden awaited them below a fierce spray of stars. The air smelled like the garden's herbs, mingled with the sharp spice of tea steaming on a low table, and the ever-present salty tang of the sea.

Eda sat down at the table, tucking her legs underneath her, and took a sip of tea: it was very strong and very sweet, just as she liked it.

Her father sat across from her, his smooth face shining. "The first way is to fulfill your end of the bargain and accept whatever unexpected consequences come your way."

"Why would there be unexpected consequences?"

He smiled. "Because normally only fools make deals with gods. And they don't think through every detail before offering their vows. The gods can see much more than we can—they have a fuller picture of the world. They can twist our words, so that we think we have vowed something very different than we actually did."

"Then why make a deal at all?" Eda asked.

"Because mankind wants power. We always have, and we always will. The gods have that power. They are that power, and sometimes we're willing to make the sacrifice necessary to attain a piece of it."

Eda gulped more tea. She wished her mother had come up here with them, but she'd gone to bed early with a headache.

Her father coughed, suddenly and violently, and it was a moment before he stopped. Sweat beaded on his brow.

"Are you all right, Father?"

"Just tired, I fear. Perhaps we should end early tonight, little one."

"Not before you finish your story! What is the second way?"

He coughed again, but smiled at her reassuringly. "The second way is a little grim: take your own life."

Eda shuddered. A wisp of cloud seemed to come out of nowhere, dimming the light of the stars. She didn't want to admit it to herself, but she was beginning to feel unwell, too. "And the third way?"

"The third way," her father said, "is to kill the god."

Part Two

SHADOW AND BLADE

They forged the blade of iron, imbued it with Starlight, and crafted the handle from the Tree shard.

Chapter Nineteen

T HE DAGGER BIT HARDER. BLOOD TRICKLED WARM and wet down her neck. She couldn't stop staring at Ileem.

There was cruelty in his eyes and the curve of his lip. Cruelty that he'd hidden from her.

"What are you doing?" she whispered. She hated that tears pressed behind her eyes. She hated how weak she felt, when she'd fought so hard to be strong.

"I'm meting out my god's judgment, accepting the gift he gave to me," he said. "I'm taking the Empire. I'm avenging my father. And I'm making every last Enduenan dog bow at my feet and beg for Rudion's mercy. That includes you, my traitorous, blasphemous *wife.*"

The ballroom doors burst open and Denlahn soldiers flooded in. Blades flashed in the light of the chandeliers. People screamed and fell to the gold and white marble floor, throats cut, blood gushing scarlet.

Eda stared with a kind of distant numbness, not fully

comprehending what was happening. Ileem's fingernails dug into her wrist and her own blood continued to seep slowly into the neckline of her gown.

She didn't understand. Gods gods gods she didn't *understand*.

"You've asked me more than once why Rudion speaks to me and not to you," Ileem spat. "It's because I'm his faithful servant—his voice, his hand. You are nothing but a blasphemous dog who dared to raise herself to the position of a goddess. And that, above every other thing you've done, is why you will die, here, tonight: a blood sacrifice to *my* god, who laughs at your temples and scorns your offerings as he squashes you like the pathetic worm we both know you to be."

She blinked and saw Tuer's Shadow in the midst of the Denlahn soldiers, a blade in his outstretched hand that was wet with blood.

"Rudion is here," she breathed.

"Of course he is. Who do you think guides my hand? Who do you think clothed my soldiers in protection and silence as they crept through the city unseen? Who do you think put the crown on my head?"

"I did that," said Eda furiously.

"No. It is and always was my god. And now you will die, as he decrees, your miserable soul perishing forever in the black emptiness of the void."

"But . . . but the treaty." The words were more than foolish, and she knew it.

Ileem looked at her with obvious scorn. "The treaty was a ruse, Your *Majesty*," he hissed. "Now come with me. It's time our marriage was formally terminated." He dragged Eda toward the dais where a Denlahn soldier waited, a naked blade in his outstretched hand—she didn't have to imagine its purpose.

Her haze of shock broke, and she was suddenly glad she'd never demonstrated her weapons skills to Ileem.

She twisted out from under his arm, kneed him in the groin, and drove her own dagger into his leg, slipping and sliding across the bloody floor.

"STOP HER!" Ileem roared.

But no one heard him over the chaos of the ballroom, courtiers screaming and fighting back against the Denlahns as best as they could.

Eda tore her crown off and ducked into the writhing crowd, grabbing a fallen sword and fighting her way to the door.

Somehow, no one seemed to take much notice of her.

Somehow, she made it out to the corridor.

She ran until she was about to collapse, and ducked behind a pillar to catch her breath. Her mind was working furiously, trying to calculate her options, figure out her escape route. Her garrison of Imperial soldiers was stationed just outside the city. She would go to them, and they would break upon the palace like an ocean wave and have it back under her control before dawn.

That's what she would do. She forced breath into her shuddering body.

Someone seized her arm and hauled her into a hidden alcove.

Eda looked straight into Liahstorion's face. The Denlahn Princess was holding a sword of her own, grim determination pressed into her forehead. She stood in the archway, blocking Eda's path.

"Let me by," said Eda, forcing her voice not to shake. "Let me pass."

But Liahstorion didn't move. "You can't go to the garrison."

"What?"

"The garrison. That's where I would go if I were in your

place, but you can't. My brother poisoned every soldier during the wedding ceremony and even now is burning the whole place to the ground. There are men waiting for you there. You'll be dragged back to the palace and executed—Ileem doesn't mean for you to make it through the night alive. Now that he's been crowned Emperor, he doesn't need you anymore."

Eda stared, trying to comprehend what Liahstorion was saying.

The other girl grabbed her by the shoulders, shook her hard. "Are you *listening*, Eda? Your garrison is gone. My brother means to kill you. You have to leave, and you have to leave *now*. Do you understand?"

There was a roaring in Eda's ears, and around her the world seemed to shake.

Something in Liah's face softened. "Do you have somewhere to go?"

It wasn't the world that was shaking. It was Eda. "You're not taking me back to him. You're not handing me over to . . . to your brother."

"Not to my brother, and not to his god. I never wanted to come here, I never wanted to betray you. But Ileem wouldn't be dissuaded. He couldn't let go of his anger over our father, but more than that he—he thrives on chaos and confusion. He thrives on hurting people, and his god drives him to it, more and more."

A headache pressed between Eda's eyes. "But he—but he married me. He loved me. He swore on Tuer we were one."

Liah shook her head. "Eda. Listen to me. If you're going to survive you have to be steady. You have to use your head, and you can't let any of my brother's lies distract you. His one and only goal in coming here was to destroy you. You have to remember that. Can you?"

Eda forced herself to nod. She pressed her fingers against the wound in her throat and found it was still bleeding. Liahstorion ripped off a piece of her Enduenan-style sash and gave it to Eda to press against the cut.

"All right?" said Liahstorion, a storm of emotion in her dark eyes.

"All right," said Eda.

"Good. I'll distract Ileem as long as I can."

Eda took a deep breath. "Why are you helping me?"

A shadow of a smile touched Liahstorion's lips. "Because no matter what you've done or haven't done, no one deserves to die in the dark. And because I made a vow of peace—a true one. Now go."

Eda pressed Liahstorion's hand and ducked out of the antechamber, darting from shadow to shadow down the corridors, then through a servant's entrance and out into the night. The courtyard was still damp from the day's long rain. She stumbled over a stone and landed face-first in a puddle slick with mud, then picked herself up and barreled into the stable.

She had a moment's hesitation over whether or not to take an inconspicuous horse, but in the end she saddled Naia. Right now, Eda needed speed, and Naia could give that to her. She let a couple other horses loose for good measure, thinking maybe Naia wouldn't be noticed in the confusion. There was a pile of rags in the tack room; she grabbed one of the larger ones and pulled it over her hair, tying it at the nape of her neck. It smelled like hay and saddle oil and damp earth. There was nothing to be done for her blue beaded gown or her calfskin sandals; probably the mud would disguise them better than anything. She didn't even consider parting with her arm cuff—it meant too much to her, and she couldn't bear the thought of abandoning it in the muck.

She led Naia from the stable, out through a gate in the wall and into the desert. The dust had been washed clean from the air and she breathed in, deeply. But the tang of smoke made her jerk her head to the northeast, where her garrison had been. Dark plumes billowed high, and her stomach twisted. All those men, dead, because she'd trusted Ileem.

Because she'd *loved* Ileem.

Because she'd made him the gods-damned *Emperor*.

Part of her still didn't believe he'd betrayed her.

Part of her still yearned for his touch, his kiss.

Damn him, damn him, damn him.

She saw again those glimpses of Tuer in the ballroom, his sword dripping blood. Heard Ileem's voice. *"Who do you think guides my hand?"*

She forced herself to swing up onto Naia, to ride away from her city and her palace and her home. She urged the mare into a gallop. The world blurred before her, the night wheeled above, and the wind rushed past and stole away her tears.

Behind her, the garrison burned, and her courtiers lay slaughtered in the ballroom.

Her father's story burst in her mind, as if the gods themselves had reached into her memory and drew it out: *The third way is to kill the god.*

She burned with rage and a sudden, furious purpose. Tuer had betrayed her twice over, and never honored the terms of their agreement. She would make him pay for that. She would free herself from her useless vow. Somehow, she was going to find Tuer.

And when she did, she was going to kill him.

But first, she would win back her Empire, and she would do it the same way she had the first time: by herself.

Chapter Twenty

THE MARE RAN, HOOVES EATING UP THE miles, sweat flying off of her like sea foam. Eda pointed her northwest, toward Evalla, the only place in all of Endahr she could go. It was hard to force her mind to plan as she rode. She couldn't stop thinking about the way Ileem's skin shone in the moonlight, up on the rooftop with a bottle of wine in his hand.

She was a fool. She'd given her heart to the first man who'd smiled at her, the first man who kissed her and made her feel needed and told her lies about the gods she so desperately wanted to believe. She wished she could outrun the heat of her fury, the deep wells of her shame. But there wasn't a horse in the world who could run that fast—not even Naia.

And even Naia began to flag after a while; Eda pulled her to a walk. Moonlight bathed the desert in liquid silver, the scrubby undergrowth and spiny plants that grew between the cracks in the rock-hard earth casting long shadows across the dirt. To the north, the mountains marched stark against the brightness of the moon, and she felt utterly, awfully alone, like the thread of a song spun halfway out and then forgotten.

Just after dawn, she stopped briefly at the herder's village where Rescarin had held her stone hostage. A quick search garnered her a forgotten packet of dried meat and an empty water skin, which she filled in the central fountain before urging her reluctant mare on.

Naia dragged her feet as the sun rose higher, and Eda's entire body was coated with a thin sheen of sweat. Dust clung to her, irritating her eyes and making her breaths ragged and gritty. The cut in her neck had scabbed over, but it ached. She wanted so badly for this to be a nightmare, to wake in her bed with Ileem beside her.

But that was the lie, not this. Each of his actions had been calculated, his betrayal built with the stone of promises and moonlight, and mortared with every kiss.

She hated him.

And yet she still wanted him.

A few hours past sunset on the fourth day since she'd fled the palace, the ground began to rise, scrubby desert bushes turning greener and actual trees popping up here and there. The wind blew damp up from the sea. Eda breathed deep.

She hadn't been back to her childhood home since collecting Niren last year, and that had only been a brief visit. Part of her longed to pick up the threads of her old life: her mother's gardens and her father's workshop, the telescope on the balcony all three of them loved looking through. The sheep farm, just down the hill from the house, where Niren and her sisters ran barefoot through the mud and a warm plate of honeyed flatbread was always ready in the tiny kitchen.

But that life had been lost to her long ago.

Her chest tightened when the house came into view, high on the cliffside, Imperial banners snapping bright above its warm sandstone walls and arched towers. The sea crashed below.

There was no sign of the army—not that there would have been; the barracks were situated down in Eron, Evalla's capital city.

Eda kicked Naia into a run. They clattered up the flagstone path, through the high carved gate and into the courtyard. She reviewed her plans: regather the remnants of Rescarin's mercenaries and merge them with Evalla's standing army, then march back to Eddenahr with them at her back and Baron Domin at her side. She would probably have to marry Domin. Her people would mistrust her after Ileem, and a consolidation of power would do much to help win them back.

Eda gritted her teeth as she dismounted. Whatever happened, she was home now. Soon she would have Ileem at her mercy. She would make him kneel. She would make him *beg*.

And then she would find Tuer, and make him answer for everything he'd done to her.

A stableboy appeared from around the corner, and Eda handed over Naia's reins, then strode up to the front doors alone. She ran one hand over the carved ebony. She'd loved the doors when she was little: there were stories cut into the wood, gods and monsters parading endlessly before her, doomed to repeat their tales until time wore them away. She had little love for the carvings now. She rapped loudly on the wood and waited for someone to come and let her in, doing her best to brush the dirt from her ruined gown. There was no time for a bath and a change of clothes, which was a pity. She hated having to look less than her best when she was about to intimidate someone.

The door creaked open to reveal a young serving girl. She stared at Eda, belatedly dropping into an awkward curtsy. "Your—Your Imperial Majesty?"

"I need to speak with Baron Domin, at once."

The girl nodded. "He's in the drawing room. This way."

Eda didn't need to be shown through her own house, but she followed the serving girl anyway, eyes wandering to the mosaics in the floor, the domed ceiling set with colored glass, the tapestries on the walls. One of the tapestries—which depicted the wind gods Ahdairon and Mahl riding winged steeds—covered a significant crack in the plaster, where Eda had crashed headlong into it at the age of seven. She and Niren had been chasing a lamb they'd foolishly let loose in the house, and Eda wasn't looking where she was going. She still had the scar where the stitches had been, just behind her hairline.

The drawing room was not far down the main corridor, but it seemed to take an age to get there.

The serving girl opened the door and stepped in front of Eda. "Her Imperial Majesty is here to see you, Your Grace."

And then Eda came into the room and saw Domin lounging on a low-backed couch in front of the fire flickering unnecessarily on the hearth. His thin hand was curled around a wine glass, and rings weighed heavy on each of his brown fingers. He seemed somehow older than the last time she'd seen him, and something that she didn't like lurked in his eyes.

He didn't get up from the couch, just took a long draft of wine and watched as she crossed the room to him.

"Domin," she said, trying to keep the irritation out of her voice. Her head was beginning to spin with exhaustion and thirst, and she wanted to harangue him for not tripping over himself to accommodate her, as he usually would. She forced her voice to remain steady. "Ileem has flooded Eddenahr with Denlahn soldiers. He betrayed me."

Domin's eyes flicked up to Eda's, then down to his wine glass. He traced the rim with one finger, and suddenly she saw the tension in his shoulders.

She decided to ignore it. "What happened to Evalla's army and Rescarin's mercenaries?"

"Mercenaries take time to get rid of, Your Imperial Majesty. Some have gone, some are still camped outside of Eron." He waved his hand in the vague direction of the city.

"Good. We'll need them to retake Eddenahr."

Domin laid the wine glass on an end table. He lounged back against the arm of the couch, folding his hands behind his head. "They're my army now, Your Majesty. You made me Baron of Evalla, if you recall."

"So I did." She smiled at him, tried to be warm. Flirtatious. "And I mean to make you something more than that, once my current husband is drawn and quartered."

Sweat beaded on Domin's upper lip, but he smiled back. "He married you and *then* took the city? Bastard." This last bit was said with some degree of admiration.

Eda wasn't about to admit to Domin that she'd crowned Ileem Emperor, too. "How soon can we have the army mobilized? I'd like to start back to Eddenahr tomorrow, or the day after at the latest. Ileem can't have too much time to fortify the city. Domin, are you listening?"

He'd shut his eyes, and stretched the whole length of his lanky body out onto the couch, sandaled feet dangling over the end of it. He was dressed in silk, she noticed. Diamonds gleamed from his ears and his skin was dusted with gold-flecked oil.

Since when had Domin cared about finery?

"Domin. We have to act *now*."

He sighed, and jerked suddenly to his feet, pacing around her to the elaborately carved sideboard on one wall and taking out a bottle of her father's wine. Jealousy sparked through her—no one should touch her father's wine but her. He poured a glass, handed it to her.

She accepted it but didn't drink, watching Domin over the deep red liquid.

"Don't you trust me, Your Imperial Majesty? Or are you afraid it might be poisoned?"

Eda's heart jerked. She frantically reviewed everything she'd ever made Domin do, right up to stealing the papers from Rescarin—the papers that, if they were found to be forgeries, incriminated *her*.

"Eda—I can call you Eda, can't I?" He snatched the glass back from her, and took a healthy swig before dashing it against the wall. It shattered in a rain of red and crystal.

She stood very still, a dawning horror taking root.

"I know everything about you, everything you yourself choose to forget—or refuse to believe. You murdered our Emperor, poisoning him slowly so it seemed he was succumbing to illness. You banished the rightful heir to the throne and made yourself Empress in her stead, claiming the Emperor's paternity. But I know that is a lot of nonsense. You aren't royalty, Eda. You aren't even of noble blood."

He circled her, dragging one finger along her cheek.

She reached for the dagger that wasn't there and he laughed and grabbed her wrist, hauling her back over to the couch. He shoved her down onto it and stood over her, anger hardening every plane of his face.

She'd never known Domin could be angry. Gods help her, she'd never known Domin even had a spine.

"Do you know who you are, Eda? You're nobody. You're not the daughter of an Emperor. You're not the daughter of a Baron. You're the daughter of a gods-damned *sheep* farmer, your mother's childhood sweetheart. She married the Count of Evalla to cover it up, to give you some chance at respectability."

Eda's head was spinning. She couldn't breathe. She bunched the material of her filthy skirt tight in one hand. "What are you saying? What sheep farmer?"

"Oh, he's dead too," Domin spat. "Died years ago. But you would have known him when you were a child. He was the father of your friend, that wretched sickly thing you made into a Marquess."

Chapter Twenty-One

"DOMIN." SHE FORCED HERSELF TO BREATHE, FORCED herself to focus on his face amidst the black spots crawling at the edges of her vision. "Domin, how do you know that?"

"From Rescarin. He got it out of your friend's mother last year after the Emperor's death."

There was a roaring in her ears, every part of her screaming. Because if what Domin said was true, it meant Niren was her sister. Her *sister*.

And Eda had killed her.

She leapt off the couch, grabbed Domin by the collar, and pinned him up against the wall. "You're lying."

"I'm not." He shoved her off him, no knife at his throat this time to keep him from overpowering her. "You're finished, Eda. The Empire is done with you, and so am I."

"Domin, wait. We can retake the city, you and I. Together. I'll make you Emperor. You'll rule beside me. We'll—"

His face hardened with rage. "When have you ever done *anything* for *me*, Your *Majesty*? Ever since you were crowned you've manipulated me and controlled me. Bent me to your whims and your wishes, thinking I wouldn't notice you using my feelings for you to get you what you wanted."

"Domin—"

"That's all over, now." He turned his face to the door. "Guards!"

Four Enduenan soldiers stepped into the room, helms gleaming in the firelight. "My lord?" inquired one of them, a young man with a scar on his cheek.

"Arrest this woman," said Domin. "She's a traitor and a murderer."

"Domin—"

Domin slapped her, hard, across the face.

Her skin was still smarting as two of the guards grabbed her shoulders and hauled her from the drawing room while the other two followed, the points of their sabers biting into her back.

They locked her in a holding cell next to the stables.

It was dingy and dark, hardly ever used, and it stank of horse and moldy straw.

She crouched on the dirt floor and rocked back and forth on her heels. She was empty. She was blank.

She was nothing, nothing, nothing.

There were no tears, there was no anger.

She didn't know how to feel anything in the face of Domin's revelations.

Gradually, as the night deepened and cold air seeped into the cell, her utter shock dimmed, and Eda came back to herself.

She paced the confines of the tiny chamber, barely six feet square, and tried to make sense of her current situation, tried to see a way out of it.

All those years ago, Eda had bargained away her own blood. The life of her sister. And she'd never known.

But hadn't she, really? She'd felt that connection, since they were children. She felt it now. It ate at her, gnawed her down to muscle, to bone, to the delicate organs beneath that measured out the beats of her life.

Her only friend in all the world. Her *sister*.

Dead. Gone.

Because she'd bargained Niren's life away to Tuer.

And he'd betrayed her.

She couldn't stop seeing Tuer's Shadow in the ballroom, blood dripping from his blade. She couldn't stop hearing Ileem's words, racing endlessly through her mind: *Who do you think guides my hand? Who do you think? Who do you think?*

Tuer had promised to give her everything she had ever wanted.

And then, just like in the story her father who wasn't her father had told her as a child, Tuer had destroyed her.

Sometime during the night, hooves crunched over gravel outside her cell, leather creaking as a rider swung down. Eda jolted from her reverie, every nerve on fire with the need to *run*.

"The other Barons escaped the slaughter, my lord," came a male voice. "They're mobilizing their armies and preparing to march on the city in a fortnight."

"How old is your news?" Domin's voice, a hard edge to it.

"Four days. I rode day and night to get here."

"Then we have a week, no more. Thank gods the army is ready. We depart at sunrise."

"Did the girl come here?"

Eda bit back a snarl at hearing herself referred to that way. Domin laughed. "She's here."

"What do you mean to do with her?" The messenger's words were hesitant.

"Drag her along, of course. We'll make a spectacle of her execution, once we retake the city. Right after I'm crowned."

Eda smacked the wall of the holding cell, biting the inside of her cheek so hard she tasted blood. How dare he. How dare he plot to take *her* crown, which she'd fought and lied and killed for? Which she'd sacrificed her *soul* for?

Niren, dead on pale sheets.

Tuer's Shadow in the ballroom, his sword dripping blood.

Ileem's knife at her throat.

She should have recognized the anger in Domin, the yearning for power. No one had seen it in her. Why hadn't she seen it in him?

"And if we fail to retake the city?"

"We won't fail," said Domin. "But if we do, I'll slit her throat myself and leave her carcass to rot in the desert." He laughed again, and footsteps drifted away from the stable, leaving Eda once more alone in the dark.

She fell asleep without meaning to, and dreamed of a garden, flowers nodding in slanting sunbeams, bees dancing under a bright sky. In the center of the garden was a stone temple, half tumbled down and overgrown with moss and ivy. She stepped under a low doorway and found herself in a small square room, lit with a white light that seemed to come from both nowhere and everywhere. The room was empty save for a young man who sat at a table, writing in a book.

For a while Eda watched the movement of his pen, traveling rhythmically across the page. It never seemed to run out of ink.

And then he looked up at her. His arms and face were scored with scars. His eyes were dark; they burned with wisdom and age.

She felt compelled to kneel but she resisted the urge. She was Empress, still—she knelt to no one.

"Who are you?" Eda demanded. "Why am I here?"

"I want to help you, if you'll let me." His voice was rich and thick as honey.

"Do you have an army?" She scoffed. "I need an army."

"Is that what you need?"

His manner was so quiet, so unassuming that it took her aback. "Tuer betrayed me. He took my Empire. He took my friend, my—my sister. And now he means for me to die. An army is the only thing that can save me."

"Is it," said the man. "I see." He bent back over the book again, and continued writing.

"What are you writing?"

"The stories of the worlds. Endahr's story is here, and your piece of it."

"Then you know how it ends."

"It has ended, and yet it is still being written. There are many paths that it could take. Many paths that you could take."

Eda scrutinized him. "What god are you?"

He smiled. "I am not a god, child of the dust. Now. What path will you take? There is a task set for you. There is a story here, for you to follow. Will you follow it?"

"I follow the path I make for myself."

The man lifted his shoulders and turned back to his book. "Think on it, Eda of Endahr."

Eda woke alone in the holding cell, the incongruous scent of wildflowers lingering sweet on the air, to find the door ever so slightly ajar.

She didn't know how it was possible, whether man or god had unlocked the door, but she also didn't care. She slowly swung it open, peeking her head out to make sure she was alone before slipping through. The sea air wrapped around her, the burgeoning stars filled her up. She crept around the back of the stables, yanking a damp shirt and pair of trousers off a clothesline, and bolted up the hill.

She didn't mean to go to the old family temple, but some instinct pulled her there.

It wasn't much of a temple: a narrow doorway looking into a mound of grassy earth. There were symbols carved into the stone doorposts, but she didn't stop to examine them as she darted inside, panting for breath. She hadn't been back here since she was nine years old, when she'd met Tuer's Shadow and bargained Niren's life away.

A lantern and matches waited in a wall niche; she lit the lamp and raised it high.

Shadows slanted through the low-roofed chamber. She knelt in the dust beside the weathered stone figure at the back of the room.

What was she going to *do?* Gods gods gods.

Domin must not find her here, and she didn't have anywhere else to go.

Eda tilted her forehead against the stone figure. She screwed her eyes shut and saw Niren, lying dead on her pillow; the Emperor, taking his last rattling breaths; Rescarin, raising his bloody hands; an entire garrison of soldiers poisoned in their beds, burning and burning and burning. She saw herself, dragged onto a high wooden platform erected before the city gates, her head forced onto a block, the executioner's blade raised high.

"Stop it!" she screamed at the statue. "STOP IT!"

But there was no answer.

She pounded her fists against the stone until blood burst from her knuckles. She screamed herself hoarse.

But when all the fight had gone out of her she was still alone in a temple that felt like a tomb.

An Empress who'd lost her Empire.

An outcast with nowhere to go.

Eda jerked up and away from the statue. She paced, as she'd done in the holding cell.

There was an ancient wooden chest stuffed into a hollow in the stone near the back of the temple. Eda hauled it out, opened it, lifted her lantern. The chest was filled with scrolls and books, crackly, crumbling pages bound in faded leather. She pulled one of the scrolls out, uncapped the end of its casing, and unrolled the yellowed parchment. At the top of the page, in shaky handwriting, were the words *Of Tuer and Raiva and the Mountain of Sorrows*.

Eda cursed, and let the parchment roll back up again. She had the sudden impulse to touch her lantern flame to the books and scrolls and burn them all to ashes, but something stayed her hand. She sat back on her heels, running her fingers over the edge of the chest; the wood was worn and smooth.

Ileem's face rose unbidden in Eda's mind, his eyes shining in the moonlight as he sat with her on the rooftop and told her about his time in the monastery on Halda. How the Haldans believed that Tuer was hidden somewhere in the mountains.

Eda felt shaken and raw, seized by a strange frantic certainty. She would go to Halda. She would find Tuer. And she would make him answer for everything he'd done to her.

She changed quickly into the trousers and shirt she'd pulled from the clothesline and went out into the night, leaving her discarded gown to gather dust with the ruined statue of the god.

"But how are you supposed to kill a god?" Eda asked. She'd crawled up into her parents' bed to be with them, because they were all sick with the same crippling fever and she could no longer bear to stay in her room alone.

Her mother was asleep, her brow drenched with sweat. Her father was awake, his dark eyes glassy.

"What's that, my love?" His voice sounded horribly far away.

"The third way to appease a god you've made a deal with," Eda *explained. "How are you supposed to do it? The gods are immortal." She'd been puzzling over this question the last few nights; she needed the answer.*

A cough wracked her father's whole body, and flecks of blood clung to the stubble on his chin. He stroked Eda's hair with trembling fingers. "A god can be killed with the right weapon." He broke off into another fit of coughing. "Something as old as he is. Something just as powerful."

Eda clutched at the buttons on her father's brocade dressing gown. "But the only things as old as the gods are the Stars and the

Immortal Tree, and they're lost and gone forever."

"I don't know what to tell you, little one." He caressed her cheek. *"The stories say there used to be weapons like that, but I don't know what became of them. You should look in the scrolls in the temple. Perhaps there are answers in there."*

"I'll do that tomorrow," said Eda, *suddenly feeling very tired.*

But she didn't, because the next day she was so ill she couldn't move, and the day after that, and the day after that. And then she recovered, but her parents did not, and she was dragged off to the capital.

She forgot all about the scrolls in the temple, even when she made her deal with Tuer.

She forgot all about ancient weapons forged to kill the gods.

She didn't think she'd ever need one.

Chapter Twenty-Two

EDA REACHED THE SEAPORT JUST BEFORE DAWN, the sky brightening from black to gray to silver, for one fleeting moment the same color as the sea.

A steamer waited at the dock, its huge smokestacks and dark iron hull dwarfing the more traditional sailing ships. Eda was shocked at how ugly it was. She couldn't help but think of that day, not so long ago, when she'd tried to persuade her Barons that the steamers were the future.

She'd never meant *her* future.

But it would be the fastest way to get to Halda.

Eda shouldered her way through the chaos on the docks. Seagulls shrieked and sailors swore at each other, struggling to haul cargo on and off ships. At the end of the quay stood a squat stone building with a sign over the door that read STEWARD'S OFFICE. Eda ducked inside, a bell chiming overhead. The interior was lit by a single lantern, the ceiling low. Sea charts were plastered all over the dingy walls, with a fanciful depiction of the sea god Aigir framed in the center. He was surrounded by his daughters, the Billow Maidens, and an ancient Star blazed brightly from his finger.

The whole place stank of fish.

An Enduenan man wearing a blue sash and matching sailor's cap looked out at her over a worn wooden counter at the back of the chamber. "Can I help you?"

"I'd like to buy passage on the steamer to Halda. When does it sail?"

The sailor eyed Eda doubtfully. "This morning, but it'll cost a pretty penny."

Eda tore the gold wrist cuff from her arm and slapped it on the counter. "I'll need my own room, with meals."

"Gods' eyeballs, who do you think you are? The Empress?"

Eda's fingers twitched for the dagger at her waist that wasn't there. "Is it enough or not?" It had to be—Eda had the Emperor's ring as well, but it was far too distinctive to use for currency here—any Enduenan would recognize it. She'd braided it into her hair in the holding cell, saving it to exchange for money in Halda.

The sailor considered, running his fingers over the cuff. He took it, securing it somewhere behind the counter, then drew out a pen and ink and a blank paper ticket from a drawer. He printed the number 302 on the ticket, and glanced up again. "Name?"

For half a moment, Eda didn't know what to say. She swallowed back a demand for him to use her title, hating the sinking feeling that accompanied the recollection that she was now nobody. "Niren," she said quietly. "Niren Erris-Dahril."

The instant the name left her lips Eda wished she would have said something, *anything* else.

But the sailor printed Niren's name in bold black letters and handed the ticket to Eda across the counter. "Board quick,

Miss Erris-Dahril. The ship won't wait for you."

Back outside, Eda squinted in the sunlight, clutching the ticket so tightly the sweat from her hand made the ink smear. She walked out to the steamer and quickly climbed the gangplank.

A handsome steward in a smart cap looked at her ticket and escorted her across the main deck of the ship, down a set of stairs and through a narrow doorway into an even narrower corridor. It was carpeted in bright red, and the doors that marched in an orderly fashion on either side of the corridor were painted with gaudy gold embellishments. The steward led her to the door with the number 302 emblazoned on the front of it, and waved her in.

"Meals are served in the galley twice per day. You're responsible for washing your own clothes and linens—one of the girls will show you where. Daily water rations are brought to your room every morning, and lamp oil is available if yours runs out, just ask. Is there anything else you need?"

Eda gaped at him, her mind still snagging on the fact he expected her to wash her own clothes.

The steward tipped his cap. "I hope you have a pleasant voyage, Miss Erris-Dahril. Welcome aboard the *Empress of Enduena.*"

And then he was off down the corridor again, leaving Eda to gape after him, belatedly realizing he was talking about the name of the ship and not her.

She snapped her mouth shut, tight with the knowledge that the gods were mocking her, even here.

She stepped into her cabin. It was shockingly small: to her right was a narrow bunk with a single thin sheet; to her left, the tiniest closet she had ever seen in her life. A porthole looked out of the back wall, a washbasin on a stand just beneath, with a chamber pot tucked discreetly in the corner.

There was nowhere for her to sit unless she wanted to clamber up onto the bunk, so she collapsed onto the floor.

Somewhere overhead a bell clanged, and the vessel rumbled beneath her. The horizon through the porthole tilted left and right and left again, and Eda was suddenly aware that the steamer was moving, her body helpless to its subtle rocking. She took another look through the porthole, which turned out to be a mistake.

She barely made it to the chamber pot before she was suddenly, violently sick.

She didn't notice that the ship had pulled out from the dock, that Enduena was shrinking fast and far away from her.

Everything was awful, inescapable motion.

The rock of the steamer beneath her hollowed-out body, the sway of the overhead lantern.

The air smelled of sickness, and the sheets balled up in both hands were slick with her own sweat.

She didn't know how long she had been lying there—she didn't even remember crawling up into the bunk like a half-dead slug.

She was sick again, and then lay back on her pillow, shuddering. Her lips moved in a soundless prayer to Aigir, the sea god, to have mercy on her.

She slipped into dark dreams; she saw bodies twisted on the ballroom floor, Niren dead between pale sheets, Ileem's cruel smile, Tuer's bloody sword. Even in her nightmares she couldn't escape the motion of the wretched sea.

She woke in the dead of night to the face of the steward glowering at her in the lantern light, the silhouette of another man hovering just behind him. "I'm afraid there's been some mistake," said the steward.

Her body felt too heavy, her head like it was filled with sand. Still the ship rocked and rocked and rocked. She writhed with the agony of the nausea that wouldn't go away. "What's . . . wrong?" she managed.

"This cabin belongs to this gentleman." The steward waved at the man behind him. "You were shown here by mistake."

"I have a *ticket*," Eda hissed through gritted teeth. She tumbled headlong from the bunk and scrabbled in her pocket, pulling out the crumpled piece of paper. She held it out to him. Another wave of nausea hit her and she clutched her stomach, trying desperately not to be sick again.

He gave an exasperated sigh, as if she were being very tiresome. "You were a last-minute passenger, and the dock steward should never have promised you a cabin. I'm here to move you down to steerage where you belong."

"I *paid* for this ticket! Please. *Please.*" She was sobbing. She was begging. The Empress of half the world, and she was *begging on the floor like a dog.*

The steward wasn't moved. He grabbed her under the armpit and hauled her upright. Her knees buckled beneath her; she couldn't walk unassisted.

She could barely keep her eyes open as she attempted to walk with the steward. He half dragged her from the cabin and through the narrow hallway, then across the upper deck, swathed in moonlit silver. It made her feel as if she were caught in a dream, the kind that makes your body heavy, your legs sluggish. She blinked and was on the rooftops, staring into Ileem's gleaming eyes.

The steward nudged her ahead of him, down a set of cramped iron stairs. She tripped on the last few, landing in a heap on the lower deck, lit by a lantern affixed to the wall between a row of metal rivets. The motion of the ship was worse down here; her stomach cramped, and she was sick in the corner.

The steward cinched open a heavy metal door and brought her into the dark space beyond. It smelled of vomit in here, of sweat and sour milk. She had the dim impression of rows of pallet beds, of the hundred-odd people lying on them. Some were sleeping. More were moaning and hunched over buckets.

Toward the back of this awful place was an empty pallet. Eda collapsed onto it, the nausea and exhaustion blurring the edges of her vision.

"Nothing personal," said the steward.

And then he was gone.

She slipped into a place between dreams and waking, aware always of the sea's jarring, stomach-wrenching motion but seeing things she shouldn't if she were truly awake:

A door in a mountain.

A god in the dark.

Shadowy spirits, devouring the sun.

Beneath her, the rush of wide wings.

Inside her, nothing but sorrow.

She moaned and wept in her sleep, and eventually, someone was beside her. Soft hands touched her brow. The rim of a porcelain bowl met her lips. She tasted salty broth and swallowed, once, twice, before she pushed the bowl away.

She slept a little easier, after that.

Later, much later, she opened her eyes to find lanterns glowing softly from the walls all around the wide room. People talked in groups around their pallets or played at dice on the floor. The door to the lower deck was open, letting in a breath of salty air.

She felt woozy and weak, and had no wish to move from the pallet. She trembled where she lay, tears oozing from her eyes and soaking into her pillow.

A shadow passed before the open door—she recognized the silhouette of her god. For an instant he paused and turned toward her. His eyes pierced her through.

And then she blinked, and he was gone. This, too, was Tuer's doing. He showed how much he despised her even in the middle of the sea.

I'm coming to find you, she thought, *I'm going to make you answer for everything you've done to me. Everything you've taken from me.*

Niren. Ileem. Her parents. Her Empire.

I'm going to drive a knife into your heart, and see what color a god bleeds.

Once more she let the blackness claim her.

Chapter Twenty-Three

W HEN EDA WOKE AGAIN, SHE FELT A little steadier, and made the mistake of trying to sit up. Instantly, her stomach wrenched sideways and she collapsed back onto the pallet, desperately fighting the nausea.

"Slowly," came a woman's wispy voice beside her. "You have to take it slowly, at first."

Eda gingerly turned her head, and the woman came into focus: she was dressed in the Enduenan style, her hair cloud-white, her brown skin wrinkled and spotted with age. But the way she carried herself, even while seated, displayed her nobility, and her strength. Her eyes were watery, unfocused—as if she were mostly blind. "Don't worry, little one. The motion won't bother you after a while. In a week or two, you won't even feel it."

Eda groaned and ground the heels of her hands into her eyes.

The old woman laughed, which turned into a wheeze. She coughed into a handkerchief.

"Are you all right?" Eda croaked out, bewildered that the

person it seemed had been caring for her was in perhaps worse shape than she was.

"Just old, my dear. An ailment that comes to all, in time. I came to sit with you because I can't bear to see a creature in such torment. And because you remind me of home. I'm Lady Rinar. From the province of Duena."

Southwestern Enduena—Eda had never been there. She felt a keen sense of loss as she wondered if she'd ever have the chance to.

Carefully, Eda eased herself to a sitting position and glanced around the packed room. "Who *are* all these people?"

"Immigrants, many of them. Seeking their fortune apart from the Empire, or going to work in Halda's stone quarries and send money home to their families."

"Why would they want to leave the Empire?"

Lady Rinar shrugged her thin shoulders. "There's very little opportunity for common Enduenans to improve themselves or their stations. Land and power are squabbled over by the nobility, like my late husband, and there's nothing left for anyone else. If you're born poor, you are very likely to die poor."

Eda thought about Niren, who would have lived and died a sheep farmer's daughter if not for her. Didn't that mean Eda had improved her lot? And what about the temple? Eda had constructed it specifically *for* the common people. A traitorous thought wormed through her mind: *Temples do a poor job of filling anyone's belly*. She pushed it angrily away, forcing her thoughts back to the present. "Are you an immigrant, too?"

"I'm a pilgrim," said Lady Rinar softly. "Journeying to Tal-Arohnd. My son Torane made a pilgrimage there two decades ago and stayed to become a monk. I want to see him one last time before I die."

Eda didn't ask if Lady Rinar was ill—clearly her age would not allow her to make another such trip, if she even survived this one. "Tal-Arohnd," Eda mused. "The monastery in Halda."

The old woman nodded. "Then you've heard of it?"

Eda felt woozy again, her heart beating overly fast. She laid her head back against the wall and shut her eyes, fighting against the memory of Ileem lounging on the roof tiles, the moonlight kissing the curve of his cheek. *The monks believe Tuer himself is there, somewhere,* he'd said. *Trapped in his own mountain. They claimed they could hear him sometimes, his weeping tangled up with the wind.*

"Yes, I've heard of Tal-Arohnd. That's where I'm headed, too."

By the afternoon, Eda felt strong enough to drag herself out of bed. The ship still tilted alarmingly, but she remained upright, and the little bits of food she'd managed to get down stayed where they were supposed to.

She had no wish to stay cramped inside with strangers and sickness, so she stumbled out onto the lower deck.

Sea air hit her square in the face, cold and damp and salty, and beyond the ship's metal railing there was nothing but the endless waves. She clapped her hand over her mouth and turned away from the dizzying view—she was helpless out here, at the mercy of the merciless gods, impossibly far from land in every direction. She shuddered, and wondered what in all of Endahr would ever possess someone to become a sailor.

She wasn't alone on the deck. A mother sat nursing a baby

on a rough wooden bench that butted up against the outside wall of the horrid steerage cabin. The mother looked sickly and thin but the baby seemed content, one tiny fist curled tight around a length of the mother's dark hair.

For a moment, Eda stared at the child, seeing her own future with Ileem, a false future, one that had never truly existed.

And yet her traitorous heart still longed for it. What would her and Ileem's child have looked like? Smooth skin, black hair, dark eyes, surely. But what else? Ileem's singing voice, perhaps. Eda's dimples. Treachery, engraved into the child's very soul.

They weren't very different, her and Ileem. Like, calling to like.

Eda jerked her gaze away from the mother and baby, her insides roiling with more than nausea.

An Enduenan man and his teenage daughter emerged from steerage and went to stand by the rail. The daughter stared longingly out over the water, a faraway look in her eyes, and for some reason, she reminded Eda of Talia.

Caida's bleeding heart. Eda didn't want to ponder her old rival's fate, or contemplate with slightly guilty pangs the elaborate lengths she'd gone to to make doubly and triply sure Talia would be miserable for the rest of her life. Eda didn't want to think, even for an instant, that perhaps she had wronged Talia. Talia had been all the things Eda wanted to be, and was not: the true heir to the Emperor, a daughter of royal blood. *Somebody*.

But Eda was nobody, now.

She always had been.

The steerage passengers ate in a cramped mess hall adjoining their sleeping quarters. Portholes looked out to sea, where the setting sun sank fiery into the waves, and an Odan chef in a dirty apron spooned what looked like pig slop into tin bowls.

Eda took her slop, plus a mug of beer, and sat at a rough wooden table near Lady Rinar. Eda tried a bite from her bowl. It was some kind of stew, and thankfully tasted rather better than it looked.

"I was hoping you would join me," said the old woman with a smile in Eda's direction, though Eda had no idea how she knew it was her. "What did you say your name was?"

Eda opened her mouth to give Lady Rinar Niren's name, but found she couldn't do it. Her grief and guilt choked her. So she gave her own name. "Eda."

"Like the Empress," said Lady Rinar.

Eda looked at her sharply, but there was no suspicion in the old woman's face. "Like the Empress."

Lady Rinar sipped what appeared to be overly watery tea from a chipped mug. It smelled like dishwater. "What sends you to Tal-Arohnd? It is rare that the very young have any interest in religion, although you have the air of one who has seen the gods. Even treated with them."

Unbidden, the green meadow from her dream in the holding cell came into Eda's mind. She saw the stone temple where the scarred man sat writing in his book. All around the temple shadows slipped through cracks in the sky—shadows with teeth.

"I'm going to find Tuer," said Eda without meaning to. "He wronged me, and I mean to make him answer for it." She couldn't quite speak her true purpose out loud.

Lady Rinar's blind eyes fixed on her face. "That is a

dangerous quest, little one. But I fear you won't find him. The stories say he's trapped in the Circle of Sorrow, though no one but the Bearer of Souls could know that for sure."

The boat swayed, and Eda's stomach dropped. "What is the Bearer of Souls?"

"Who is," Lady Rinar corrected gently. "The souls of the dead cannot reach paradise—that land which dwells beyond the Circles of the world—on their own. Every century or so, the gods choose a mortal to be the Bearer of Souls—they are the one who gathers the dead and brings them through the other Circles to their final rest."

"I am a devotee of the gods. I have never heard that before."

"It is a Haldan tradition—my son wrote of it to me in his letters."

"How does the Bearer of Souls pass through the Circles?" Eda asked, a horrible suspicion unfolding inside of her.

Lady Rinar reached out one quavery hand and brushed her fingers gently across Eda's forehead. "I believe the gods mark the Bearer somehow, but it's been a long time since my son wrote of it to me." She dropped her hand. "I'm afraid I don't quite remember."

Eda crawled onto her pallet that night, the awful suspicion growing. Had the gods chosen her to be the Bearer of Souls? Was that the reason for the ghosts she'd seen back in Eddenahr, for the visions she kept having even now? Was that what Tuer wanted from her, not the temple she'd struggled so long and hard to build?

Is that why he'd taken Niren and driven Ileem to betray her?

She dreamed she was standing on a green hill pressed up against an iron sky. A shadow passed over the sun, slowly devouring its light. The world seemed to stretch out from her, out and out, so that she could see beyond the shadowed earth to the Circles of Death and Time. A host of dead souls, clothed in gray, marched between the Circles, and Niren stood before them all. She looked straight into Eda's eyes. "Help us," she said. "You're the only one who can."

Chapter Twenty-Four

E DA HAD NEVER REALIZED BEFORE HOW MUCH she thrived on activity. There was nothing to *do* onboard the steamer but sit on her pallet or stand at the rail or eat slop stew and stale biscuits in the mess hall and pine for her luxurious cabin on the upper deck.

She spoke with Lady Rinar sometimes, but the old woman grew weaker and weaker as the voyage wore on. Soon she couldn't stand at the rail or even sit on the bench. Before a month had passed Lady Rinar couldn't leave her pallet bed anymore. Tears leaked continually from her eyes, her lips moving always in prayer to the gods pleading that her body would sustain her for one last glimpse of her son.

Eda sat with her as often as she could bear it, but she hated the old woman's unshakeable faith in gods who didn't hear her. She hated the sound of Lady Rinar's breath, rattling in broken lungs, the way her skin shrank against her bones, the way her nails yellowed and her hair fell off in matted white clumps. But most of all, Eda hated the way Lady Rinar's dying reminded her of the Emperor's, of how his suffering, the unraveling of his spirit from his body, was her doing. An empty vial of poison for a crown on her head.

Two months into the voyage, Eda sat with Lady Rinar in the hush before dawn, half dozing over the old woman's paper-thin body. All at once Lady Rinar's eyes flew open and she seized Eda's hands with a sudden, desperate urgency.

"Hold me back!" Lady Rinar rasped. "Don't send me into the dark. The Bearer is trapped and cannot get through. I don't want to go to the shadows. Don't let me go! Hold me back!" Her body convulsed and she gave one last sharp cry before growing wholly, irrevocably still.

The ship rocked beneath Eda's feet, and she stared with horror at the husk of Lady Rinar. The gods were cruel. She had died far from her home, far from her son.

Eda jerked upright, stumbling through the steerage cabin to call for the steward.

Out on the deck, the wind was whipping, icy and wild. Eda leaned against the railing, and the freezing metal seared through her clothes down to her skin. The steward had sent two sailors down to steerage. They had unceremoniously wrapped Lady Rinar in sailcloth, then hauled her outside and hefted her over the rail, surrendering her to the sea. The waves had swallowed her whole, erasing her from existence as if she'd never lived at all. The sailors had uttered no benediction, just gone back to their duties on the upper deck as if they'd completed a routine chore. They didn't seem to care that they'd sent Lady Rinar's body to the fathomless depths, to be devoured by monsters, by time.

Eda hadn't moved since they'd gone. She just stood staring out into the fathomless sea, wrestling with her rage, her grief for this woman she barely knew. Was this how Eda would end? Alone and forgotten, with no one to mourn her?

She shuddered with more than cold and rubbed her arms to try and get some heat in them.

A wave broke against the side of the ship, drenching her arms and face; it tasted of salt and bitterness.

Would that she had the power of a goddess—she would break the world in half. She would bend it to her will, make it take the shape that she wished.

Clouds knotted tight and dark over the sun. Beneath the ship, the waves grew wild, *angry*, lashing the steamer, seeking to tear it to pieces.

And then the sea began to boil.

Eda gasped. A high, piercing wail echoed on the wind, an inhuman screeching that caused her to let go of the rail and clap her hands over her ears.

The world shook.

There came a resounding *crack* like some enormous piece of wood splitting in two.

The sea stopped boiling, but the waves rose high, and music seared the air: voices tangled up in an ethereal melody that made her want to weep and shout and leap into the sea all at once.

But then the music calmed, became a lament instead of a lure.

Something flashed out among the waves, a bright light that was immediately extinguished.

And then, impossibly, a chariot rose from the depths, filled with shadows and pulled by nine luminous horses. The chariot shot through the sky and disappeared in the clouds. Eda hardly had time to wonder about it before something else rose from the waves: a huge white bird with shining wings, carrying something in its talons. She had a glimpse of dark hair, a silver tail, and then the bird too was lost in the clouds.

For a moment, Eda thought that whatever had happened was finished, that all was well and calm again. But something angry muttered in the iron sky. Cracks splintered through the air, like lightning made of shadow. Darkness seeped through the cracks, a formless nothing that resolved itself into hundreds of . . . she could only call them spirits. They had dark wings and jagged teeth and wicked swords. Looking at them made her feel like a thousand fire ants had burrowed beneath her skin and were eating her, eating her through muscle, down to bone.

Eda scrambled back from the rail, shrieking and falling, covering her head with her arms.

And then—

The whisper of a touch on her shoulder. A glimpse of movement, passing around the curve of the ship. Eda got to her feet and followed.

The sky still crawled with those winged spirits, but she kept her eyes straight ahead, stopping as she saw who waited for her beneath the shelter of the upper deck.

He was less solid than he'd been in the ballroom; she could see through him to the waves that lapped silver beyond the ship.

But she knew the form of the god who had betrayed her. For an instant he turned, and his shining eyes met hers. "Come," he said. And then he stepped through the railing and out onto the sea, vanishing into the spray.

Eda followed the god.

She expected to hit the railing or plummet sickeningly into the icy waves, but instead she found herself stepping through a doorway into an ancient stone temple, open to a star-swept sky. Leaves rattled brittle over the flagstones, and in the midst of the temple, a white flame burned on a marble plinth, though there was no wood or oil to feed it.

It took her a moment to see the four gods.

Raiva Eda knew; she stood tall and solemn in a stone archway, her hand on the pillar. Another deity came toward Raiva, a rippling form of feathers and wind, rain and lightning tangled together in yellow hair: the wind goddess, Ahdairon.

Mahl, the wind god, stood in the center of the temple. His skin was dark as obsidian, his hair white as cloud. He was crowned with lightning, and his cloak was made of eagle feathers woven together with rain.

The fourth figure was more monster than god: he had the head of a lion and the twisted spine of a sea dragon. Tendrils of ragged weeds hung from his shoulders, and his mane was knotted with broken pieces of coral. At first Eda thought he must be the sea god, Aigir, but looking closer she saw he wore no Star on his finger—he was Hahld then, the river god. He stood apart from the other three, at the far end of the ruined temple, as if he was ashamed.

There was no sign of Tuer's Shadow.

"What are we to do?" said Raiva.

Eda didn't know where the rest of the nine gods were, or even if they still lived, but she understood that in their absence Raiva was their leader. Perhaps even their queen.

The goddess of the trees turned from the archway, and Ahdairon, Mahl, and Hahld looked toward her. "The Immortal Tree is no more. The Billow Maidens will bear the Dead of the sea as far as they can, but in the end they will be like all the rest: left to wander in the darkness, eaten slowly by death itself."

"We cannot help them," said Mahl. "The world is broken. The Circles sealed. The spirits we trapped in the void long ago begin to break free. Soon the Words we bound them with will not hold them; soon all will be lost."

"Then we bind them again," said Ahdairon, "and we find a way to unlock the Circles."

Hahld shook his lion's head. "It cannot be done. I was trapped for centuries by just one of those spirits—none can withstand all of them."

Lightning crackled from Mahl's crown. "Then it is to be war."

Raiva strode to the center of the temple, her gown dragging over the stone. "A war we cannot win. We four are not enough against the fathomless spirits, honed for centuries in darkness."

"If we could free Tuer," suggested Ahdairon.

Darkness clouded Raiva's face. "There is no help to be found in the god of the mountain. He made his choice long ago. He chose to leave us and loose his Shadow, and in so doing, break the world."

Ahdairon bowed her head.

"There is nothing we can do," Raiva went on, her voice the barest thread in the dark, "but watch, and wait, and hope that when the world unravels we are able to gather as many souls as we can and bear them through the shattered remains of the Circles to the One."

"That is not our purpose," said Mahl.

Raiva shimmered with sudden light, her sorrow so strong Eda could almost taste it. "And yet it is the only purpose remaining to us."

Eda shook herself as if from a daze and walked farther into the temple, meaning to catch Raiva's sleeve, to demand more answers. But in the darkness, where the starlight did not touch, loomed the Shadow she had followed here.

He turned toward her, becoming more solid than she had ever seen him. Dark wings grew from his shoulders, folded now against his back. There was a white sword at his side and a fiery crown glimmering on his head that burned but did not consume him.

An icy fear curled round her heart, tangling with her rage. "You haven't spoken to me since I was a child. I called for you. I screamed for you. I *bled* for you, and you didn't answer. Why didn't you answer?"

"Because you didn't need me, then." His voice grated in her ears, like stone scraping stone. "And because I was bound to another." The shadow-god slipped through the wall and out onto the hill.

Eda followed, stone parting around her like so much mist. "Do you mean Ileem?"

He stood silhouetted against the stars, the wind ruffling through his wings, his crown blazing brighter. "You still care for your enemy, little Empress?"

"*You* are my enemy."

"You think he would have been different were he not bound to me? He would not have. He would have put a knife in your heart the instant he saw you. All his lies were mine."

She hardened before him. "Have you abandoned him, now that you don't need him anymore?"

"The princeling didn't matter." Tuer's Shadow flexed his dark wings. "He never did. He was merely my way to you. And now you are on the path I brought you to, the path I made you for."

"I made myself. I come of my own accord."

"And yet." He smiled, his teeth flashing in the darkness.

"I'm coming to kill you," she spat. "To drive a knife into your heart and make you pay for betraying me, for taking Niren and my Empire. For leaving me with *nothing*."

"I upheld my end of the bargain, little Empress. You did not uphold yours. The Circles are locked—how do you think you will find me?"

She lunged at him, intending to push him off the hill into the valley below.

But her hands passed through him, and a terrible chill seeped under her skin.

He brushed one finger against her forehead, and her brow flared with heat. "You cannot kill a shadow," he said.

And then Eda blinked and she was standing at the ship's rail again, the sea calm before her, sun streaming through wooly clouds to pool like water on the deck.

Chapter Twenty-Five

T HE DAY WAS COOL AND STREAKED WITH clouds when Halda
came into sight on the horizon. The land was green and
white and gray: green trees, white cliffs, gray mountains.
As the ship crept closer, tiny brown specks came into view circling
the cliffs: the famed Haldan eagles said to be descendants of the
ones who spoke with the god Uerc long ago.

The steamer took an age to reach Pehlain, the port city, and
by the time it did, it was well into the afternoon, shadows slanting
long across the dock. All at once the ship's steward was shouting
instructions down at the steerage passengers to collect their
belongings—there wouldn't be another chance to retrieve them.

Eda didn't have much to collect, just a worn satchel she'd adopted
from Lady Rinar, but she got stuck at the back of the crowd, and was
nearly the last steerage passenger to squeeze out onto the narrow deck.

The first-class passengers were allowed to disembark first,
and then finally the steerage passengers were ushered up the
narrow metal stairs and out onto the dock, one by one.

As the people ahead of her left the ship, Eda was finally awarded a view of Pehlain: cobbled streets wound up from the quay toward squat stone buildings, banners snapping brightly from nearly every rooftop in blue and red and gold. Snatches of music leaked out from one of the nearest buildings, which was situated a little up the hill from the dock and was three times as tall as the rest of them. Eda realized it must be an inn. She still had the Emperor's ring, but she needed it for supplies for her journey—she couldn't afford to spend anything on accommodations, as much as she longed for *sheets* on a *bed*.

It was her turn to climb the stairs.

Eda's feet hit the dock, and the cobbled street after, her body swaying to offset the movement of the ship that was no longer there. Wind tangled in her hair, smelling of sea and salt and stone. She peered at the maze of streets winding up from the shoreline and, taking a deep breath, started walking.

She stopped to ask a Haldan boy for directions, thankful she spoke his language well enough for him to understand her. The city of Pehlain seemed, at first, to be a mess of disorganization: wandering, haphazard streets, buildings piled precariously on top of one another, a myriad of treacherous-looking trails leading up into the mountains.

But as Eda followed the boy's directions, she found a chaotic kind of order to everything. The streets were labeled with freshly painted signs on every corner. Similar businesses seemed to be grouped together, the flower shops down one row and the fish markets down another. The cobbles lay smooth and worn beneath her feet, and the banners snapping from nearly every rooftop were splashes of bright color against the gray sky.

She shivered as she walked, her thin trousers and filthy blouse unsuitable for the Haldan climate. She wondered how cold it must be up in the mountains, when it was already so frigid down here.

She came to a storefront in a row of buildings halfway up a steep hill. Charms hung from the eave of the roof, carved wooden figures strung on lengths of bright blue and yellow yarn. Eda recognized the figures as depictions of the nine gods, all skillfully carved. If the boy's directions were correct, this was a cartographer's shop, and clothes and other supplies waited for her the next street down.

She pulled the door open and stepped in. The shop was narrow but deep, lit by a half dozen blue globe lanterns fixed to the wall at regular intervals. Between the lanterns, the left wall was plastered with so many maps it made the whole building seem inches narrower than it ought to have been. The right wall was lined with wooden racks specially designed to hold hundreds more maps, rolled up and protected in cream-colored cylinders. The whole place smelled like dust and paint and ink. More wood and yarn charms dangled from the ceiling.

Eda walked to the back of the shop, wooden floorboards creaking under her feet, to where a boy of eighteen or so sat on a stool with his bare feet propped up on a worn counter, reading a newspaper. He had the red-brown skin of most native Haldans and straight black hair cropped short behind his ears. He glanced at her over the top of his newspaper. "May I help you, Miss?"

The young man spoke in fluent Enduenan, and Eda was relieved to hear her own language.

"I need a map of Tuer's Rise."

This clearly surprised him; he laid down the paper at once and took his feet off the counter. "Why in gods' green Endahr would you want to go up Tuer's Rise?"

Eda sighed. "Because I'm looking for Tuer's Mountain. Have

you got a map or not?"

He scratched his chin. "We have maps for everything. My mother is the greatest cartographer in the world, you know. But even she hasn't been *all* along Tuer's Rise. That requires an expedition, weeks of planning, tons of equipment and supplies."

"I just want a map," said Eda crossly.

"Tuer's Mountain is hidden from mortals. Most people who go up into the Rise don't come back again."

"I'm not most people. Are you going to help me?"

The boy shook his head, like he couldn't believe Eda still wanted the map after all his generous warnings. "Just a second."

He hopped over the counter and trotted partway down the room, his fingers running across the map cylinders as he peered at the brass-plated labels beside each one. He selected a cylinder and uncapped it, pulling the map out and uncoiling it. Eda peered over his shoulder, annoyed at having to stand so close to him.

The map was beautifully drawn and painted, paths winding up through the mountains, streams and valleys and caves all neatly labeled.

She pointed to the top of the map, where everything disappeared into a haze of gray. "Why does it stop?"

"I told you. Not even my mother has traveled the entirety of the Rise. The map stops there because that's as far as she went. But I swear to you, Miss—don't go up there alone. You'd die your first night." He looked her up and down. "Especially in those clothes."

What she wouldn't give for her dagger or a solid amount of guards at her back. "How much?"

He rattled off a sum that shocked her. She shook her head. "This is all I have."

She laid the Emperor's ring in his open palm, the metal

shaped like a tiger chasing its tail, with rubies for eyes.

The boy's eyes grew round. "That's pure gold. Where did you get it?"

She scowled at him. "It's mine. Do you treat all your customers like thieves?" She blinked and saw the Emperor lying against his pillow, his breath rattling in his chest as she slipped the ring from his finger.

The boy folded the ring back into her hand. "Take it to the money changer's the next street over. He won't cheat you." He gave her a searching glance. "Why do you want to find Tuer's Mountain?"

"Because Tuer wronged me, and I'm going to make him pay, locked Circles and evil spirits be damned."

His face blanched with shock. "How do you know the Circles are locked?"

Her bewilderment waged war with her annoyance. "Tuer's Shadow told me himself," she blurted before she could think better of it. "I see visions and ghosts. The gods send me dreams."

The boy sucked in a sharp breath. He leapt over the counter and put his hands on Eda's shoulders. "You can see them? You can see the Dead?"

Something about this boy made her want to divulge her darkest secrets to him. She settled for the truth. "Some of them. Sometimes. Why—do you believe me?"

He grabbed Eda's hand and pulled her around the counter, through a narrow door and into a dim back room. Shelves stretched to the ceiling, stuffed to overflowing with piles and piles of maps. A table stood in the center of the room, or at least what Eda assumed was a table—it was stacked with maps as well.

The boy waved Eda onto a stool and crouched near her on

another, shoving a stack of the maps onto the floor. "It's here somewhere. I'll find it, just a tick."

And then he was rummaging through the shelves, parchment flying everywhere. The mess was enough to make Eda's head spin. "What are you doing? Who *are* you?"

"Clet Morin," he said absently, still digging through the shelves. "This place is my uncle's, but it's true my mother is the greatest cartographer who ever lived. I manage the shop during the winter months while my uncle journeys south to collect all the latest maps from the southern part of Halda—and so he can escape the majority of the snow, I'd wager. The rest of the year he's here, and I'm up in the village with my family. But last year we lost our father to fever and my mother swore up and down she saw his ghost everywhere. She said that *he* said he was trapped. Couldn't move on. No Bearer of Souls to help him through the gates. That's when she decided to go up Tuer's Rise for the second time—she swore she wasn't coming back until she found Tuer's Mountain and saved my father. *Here.*" He snatched a map from the shelf and slapped it down on the table, weighting the edges with colorful glass globes. "This is the last map she made of Tuer's Rise."

Eda glared at him. "What about the one you were going to sell me earlier, Clet Morin?"

He had the good sense to look sheepish. "That's one of the ones we always sell to tourists. Sorry about that. And it's just Morin. Haldans give our surnames first when we introduce ourselves. Now look." He jabbed his finger at the base of the map. "This is the path she took last time. She said with more preparation, she wouldn't have to turn back. She was confident of success."

Eda shivered. "She really thinks she can find Tuer's Mountain?"

Morin nodded.

"She's sure of it. But I think—I think some part of her believes she can actually save my father, not just send his soul to rest, but bring him back to life." Morin's forehead creased, and he sagged back onto his stool. "I'm worried about her. My father was the love of her life, and I'm not at all sure she was in any state to go searching for a mountain no one's supposed to be able to find."

"How long has she been gone?"

"Since the middle of the summer. I'm hoping there will be news of her when I get home. I'm hoping *she'll* be home, too." Morin rubbed his eyes and took the glass globes from the corners of the map, allowing it to roll up. He found one of the map cases and stuffed the parchment into it, then handed it to Eda. "Please take it. No charge—I hope you'll forgive me, for before. Your best bet for heading up Tuer's Rise is to attach yourself to a caravan. They come through here every spring, a mixture of merchants and pilgrims going to Tal-Arohnd."

"The monastery," said Eda. She blinked away the image of Lady Rinar's body sliding into the sea.

"From there, you should be able to cobble together an expedition and gear in the village just beyond. And after that—" Morin shrugged. "After that, gods keep you."

No, Eda thought, *gods beware of me.*

Chapter Twenty-Six

E DA STEPPED FROM THE CARTOGRAPHER'S INTO A freezing rain. She followed Morin's directions to the money changer, who gave her a heavy pouch of coins for the Emperor's ring. After that she purchased sturdy traveling clothes from a tailor's shop, hired a mule, and bought a knife from a swordsmith just before he closed his doors for the evening.

By the time she left the swordsmith it was fully night, the icy rain hardly touching her beneath her new poncho. Her coins had diminished by half, and she needed every one to buy more supplies once she got up to the village beyond the monastery, but her feet still led her to the inn. For a moment, she stared through the window, watching the lodgers eat together at a broad wooden table, a roaring fire at their backs.

Regretfully, she slipped into the inn's stable and shook the rain from her poncho. She curled up in the straw in an empty stall.

She fell asleep, still feeling the motion of the waves underneath her. Dreams folded over her like water over a sunken ship.

She dreamed of winged spirits leaking through the void. Of agony and terror and darkness.

She dreamed she drove a knife into Tuer's heart. His blood was silver. His tears were red.

The world was healed, but it didn't matter. Tuer's Shadow seized her, and hurtled her into the void.

Agony, terror, darkness. There was nothing more.

There never would be.

Mules were stupid creatures. Eda learned that in her first five minutes riding one. The man she'd hired hers from had also advised her to attach herself to a caravan, which was due any day. But she hadn't wanted to wait.

Maybe she should have. Maybe in a line of mules, hers would behave himself instead of stopping to nibble at every blade of grass growing alongside the rocky trail, or planting his feet and refusing to move because a rabbit darted across the path three yards ahead. Before half an hour was gone, she was sweating and swearing with all her efforts to drive the horrid thing forward, and bewailed ever hiring him at all.

But as the trail grew steeper, the mule seemed to decide to get down to business; he proved sure-footed over the loose rocks and climbed steadily, his huge fuzzy ears pointed forward. Eda was begrudgingly grateful for him after all.

The map Morin had given her was marked with the most direct route up into the mountains proper, where the endless stretch of peaks known as Tuer's Rise began. It hadn't sounded so hard to her before, climbing a mountain and finding the god, but she hadn't realized she would have to climb *many* mountains, and that each one would take a ridiculously long time. At least once she reached the monastery and the village beyond she could replenish her supplies and hire a guide, then let *him* consult the map a hundred times a day to make sure they were on the right path.

She spent two miserable days on the first leg of her journey, huddling against the mule for warmth both nights because she didn't know how to build a fire. The third morning she found herself on a trail so treacherously steep she was forced to get off the mule and lead him behind her. She felt as if she were clawing her way up into the sky, that the earth was doing its best to keep her from it.

Several hours' hard climb brought Eda and the mule to a wooden platform built into the side of the mountain that looked very much like a dock for a ship. Strong wooden poles on the end of the platform stretched up into the sky, their tops lost in fog, with thick cables stretching out from them. A young Haldan girl was sitting in a booth on the platform, her nose stuck in a book and the hood of her poncho pulled tight over her ears. She looked up as Eda approached.

"They told me the caravan was due today," she said, yawning, as she came out of the booth and tucked the book under her armpit. "But there's only one of you." She had two short braids tied off with green yarn, and a spattering of freckles all across her nose and cheeks. She was skinny and slight, her knees and elbows poking out. Something about the girl's honey-brown eyes looked familiar.

"I'm trying to get up to Tal-Arohnd," said Eda.

The girl jabbed her finger at the wooden poles and the cables.

"Only way up to the monastery is in the aerial lift. I hope you're not afraid of heights. I'm Clet Tainir, by the way."

The surname sharpened the sense of familiarity, but Eda was foggy and exhausted from the long climb and couldn't quite place it.

"You can put the mule in there," Tainir added, jerking her chin at the small pen tucked around the side of the mountain that Eda hadn't noticed before. "I'll help you with your packs."

With Tainir's assistance, Eda had the mule unharnessed and all her belongings piled on the platform in the space of a few minutes. She was rather afraid to ask the question, but she did anyway. "What's an aerial lift?"

Tainir laughed. "You'll see." She ducked into the booth, and pulled the lever attached to one wall with a horrific *screech*.

Something came rumbling down the cables out of the fog: a narrow, gondola-like carriage that swayed in the empty air and bumped up against the platform with a jarring *thud*. The walls of the carriage came up as high as Eda's waist, with posts arching up over her head to the roof, which hung from the cables by a thick brass ring.

"Gods' bleeding *heart*," Eda swore. "I'm not getting in that."

Tainir just laughed again. "You are if you want to go to the monastery! Barring wings, it's the only way up."

Eda ground her jaw.

"It's not that bad," Tainir promised. "I ride it all the time. The view is beautiful, and it always makes me think deep thoughts."

Eda peered up into the nothingness of the fog, her heart tugging her onward. Somewhere up there, Tuer was chained in the Circle of Sorrow. Waiting for her. "Take me up," she said.

Tainir opened a door in the side of the gondola and waved Eda in, piling her packs in a heap on the floor. It was larger inside than it looked; there was probably room for a half dozen people to ride at a time, which would be useful for the caravan. A narrow bench was built into the walls of the awful vehicle, and Eda sat down.

"Don't worry," said Tainir cheerily, "it's never crashed, and I've operated it at least twice before."

Eda sprang out of her seat, but Tainir had already shut and latched the door and returned to the booth, where she yanked on another lever.

The gondola rocked alarmingly and then began to move.

Eda sucked in her breath, grabbing tight to the sides of the carriage, peering out into empty air. The lift didn't move very fast, just steadily, and after a few minutes she relaxed. The fog swallowed her, and she had the strange sensation of being lost in a place between heaven and earth, belonging neither to gods nor to mankind, wholly and utterly alone.

She didn't like it at all.

Now and then, a piece of mountain poked through the mist, and she saw rocks and trees and far, far below, the thin silver ribbon of a winding river. The air clung to her, damp and cold, traced with the sharp tang of winter.

For an instant she thought she saw a crack in the sky, a winged shadow slipping through, crowned with fire. But when she blinked again, there was only the mist.

All at once the gondola bumped up against another wooden platform, and the door was pulled open and she was pulled out. She looked into the bronze face and dark eyes of an Enduenan man who was not old, but no longer young. He wore rough-woven robes of deep green, and a white scarf wound tight about his head. There was a silver mark in his left ear; his right hand was tattooed with the image of the Tree.

Eda knew instantly who he was. He had his mother's eyes, the same regal way of carrying himself. "You're Torane. Lady Rinar's son."

He nodded, his face tight with grief. "She's gone, isn't she?" His unaccented Enduenan reminded her fiercely of home.

Eda blinked and saw the old woman's body, devoured by the waves. Something wrenched inside of her. "I'm sorry."

He smiled, quiet, solemn, and pressed his hands around hers. "Come, Eda of Enduena. We've been expecting you."

Chapter Twenty-Seven

ORANE HEFTED THE MAJORITY OF EDA'S PACKS onto his shoulders, leaving her with only her satchel. He led her down a well-trodden dirt path that hugged the side of the mountain, a steep cliff plummeting away into the fog on her right, and before they'd gone a few yards, the mist cleared and the monastery came into view.

Her heart stuttered. Tal-Arohnd was impossible and terrifying, a series of whitewashed stone structures built into the side of the mountain or—in some cases—built *out of* the mountain. They looked unnatural, as if the slightest wind or rain would make them tumble off into the valley far below. "They've been there for centuries," said Torane over his shoulder, reading her thoughts, "and they'll be there for centuries yet to come. The stories say that the gods wove Tal-Arohnd with Words of protection, so neither storm nor blade could ever harm it."

Eda didn't doubt the truth of those stories; she almost imagined she could see the ancient Words, glimmering gold where they bound the monastery to the mountain. It made her uneasy, and with an effort, she pushed away the thoughts of gods and their earth-shattering power. "How did you know I was coming?"

"She said you were."

"She?"

"The Denlahn Princess."

Eda's insides turned to sand. "Liahstorion."

"She was here with her brother, the vengeful prince. He claimed he served Tuer, but there was such darkness in him I cannot believe it. I think he must have pledged himself to an evil spirit instead."

Eda couldn't stop the flashes of memory: Ileem and Liahstorion, standing in the rain as Eda first welcomed them to the palace. Liahstorion's outburst during that first council session. Ileem sitting with Eda under a trellis of honeysuckle, the blossoms falling bright on his knee. Moonlight, gilding the rooftops with silver. Ileem's warm mouth pressed against hers.

Eda sagged against the cliffside. She'd wondered often during her long climb if Ileem had left any trace of himself at the monastery. Now she had her answer. He was caught like oil on her skin; she could not wash him off.

Torane turned back. "The princess said she had a vision of you, coming here. Climbing Tuer's Mountain. Healing the cracks in the world."

Eda gnawed the inside of her cheek so hard she tasted blood.

"But come." Torane put gentle hands on her arms. "You've had a long journey. Food will help set you to rights, and then I will give you what assistance I can."

Numbly, Eda started walking again. They drew nearer to the cliffs, and she saw that the buildings were arranged in levels, with narrow paths ascending and descending the mountain that connected them. The widest level—the very heart of Tal-Arohnd—was situated on a shelf of land jutting out from the cliff. It had space for rambling gardens and chicken pens, along with the great hall, which was the only structure not touching the mountain.

The temple was on this level as well, carved out of the cliffside. Eda looked quickly past it. Down a stretch of path beyond the temple lay a sprawling mountain village, which must be the one Morin had told her about. A scattering of people were walking up the path, some pulling goods on carts, some holding bundles of cloth and clay jars. One young man had a pair of goats trotting along behind him.

"They're bringing supplies up from the village for the feast," Torane explained, "and to welcome the caravan."

"What feast?"

Torane glanced back at her. "The Feast of Tuer. Do you not observe it in Enduena?"

Unease squirmed through her. "The old Emperor abolished the feasts. I—the Empress was trying to reinstate them."

Torane raised an eyebrow, not missing her slip. "And it didn't work?"

"The gods did not will it," she said bitterly.

And then they were passing through a wide empty field that stood before the great hall and on into the hall itself.

The interior was a single huge, rectangular room, vast carved pillars stretching up to the peaked wooden roof. On the long sides of the room, tall windows set with intricate stained glass let in the afternoon light, patches of stained violet, cerulean, and gold pooling on the floor. The whole place was a flurry of activity, more monks in the same rough-woven green robes and white headscarfs as Torane, carrying in heavy wooden tables or stocking the enormous fireplace at the back of the hall with logs. Others brought in garlands of flowers, which they strewed about the floor, while still others fit fat beeswax candles into intricately carved stone lamp stands. One monk didn't leave his station at the back of the room, where he knelt in prayer before a square altar that was stained with blood and wine from centuries of offerings.

Almost before Eda could make sense of the whirling scene, the villagers began to flood in, bringing jugs of goat's milk and wheels of cheese, colorful woven blankets, wine. A young monk in a green robe who was not wearing a white headscarf instructed the villagers where to lay their goods.

One of the villagers she recognized with a shock as Morin, who came in with the pair of goats. He looked very different than he had at the cartographer's shop, bundled in a heavy woolen poncho dyed bright blue and red, his dark hair tousled from the wind. She didn't understand how he could have possibly gotten here before her, but it was definitely him. She started toward him, but the young monk had apparently instructed him to take the goats somewhere outside, because he turned and left the hall again. Before she could follow, twelve Itan women swept in one after the other, the mist clinging to their long black hair like tiny glimmering diamonds.

"Priestesses from Ita," said Torane. "They must have come with the caravan. Will you excuse me a moment?"

He stepped away and Eda found herself suddenly surrounded by the priestesses. They bowed to her. The youngest priestess—a girl who couldn't have been more than fourteen—brushed her fingers across Eda's forehead. "You are gods-touched," she whispered in broken Enduenan.

Heat pulsed from Eda's brow and she jerked away, skin crawling.

The girl looked at her intently. "Our goddess Ahdairon called my priestess-sisters and I here to meet you—the girl who will heal the world. It is an honor, my lady."

"I'm not going to heal the world."

But the priestesses didn't seem to hear. They circled around her, tugging at her sleeves. "Come, come," said the youngest one. "We'll help you dress. We'll make you ready for the festivities. For the *qirta*."

Eda tried to shake them off but they held her tight in their midst, and would not let her go.

"*Qirta, qirta,*" they whispered all together.

"I'm not going to the feast. Get off of me. Get *off*."

And then Torane was at her elbow again, and the priestesses drew back, their white skirts dragging on the stone floor. They watched her with their dark eyes, silent and solemn.

"Come," said Torane, "I'll show you to a room for the night. You can rest before dinner and return here for the festivities, if you wish."

Eda followed him back outside, gulping deep breaths of the sharp mountain air, her nerves shattered to pieces. They walked along a path that cut through the gardens and chicken yards, then climbed a rickety stair up the cliff to one of the little white buildings that clung there so impossibly.

"I hope you will attend the feast and honor us," said Torane, then turned to leave her.

"What does *qirta* mean?"

For a moment, he looked back. His brows drew together. "It's an ancient Itan word. It means 'sacrifice.'"

Chapter Twenty-Eight

EDA DIDN'T GO INTO THE LITTLE HUT. She let her feet follow the path back up toward the main hall, and without really meaning to, took the turn that led to the temple. Somewhere beyond the mountains the sun was setting, and darkness settled thick and fast over Tal-Arohnd.

Eda put her hands on the carved stone doorposts. She could feel the power that teemed in the very bones of this place. It scared her, but it also called to her.

She stepped in.

It was more like a cave than any temple she had ever been in before, due to its having been dug out of the mountain. The ceiling reached far above her head, bleeding into darkness, and pillars sectioned the temple into private alcoves, some containing weathered altars, others shelves crammed with ancient books and scrolls. Lamps burned white in every alcove, so she felt like she was peering into a field of stars.

She paced past the alcoves, her footsteps echoing over the

stone. There was no one else here, the monks and any petitioners evidently all in the main hall for the feast.

A few of the alcoves were painted with beautiful, detailed murals, and she studied them as she went past. One showed a similar image to the one in the illuminated manuscript Niren had given her: a petitioner kneeling before Tuer, who was enthroned on a mountain and crowned with stars. But there was one difference. A shining spirit stood beside Tuer's throne, glimmering wings folded against his shoulders. On his brow was a crown of fire. Words sparked unbidden in her mind: *You cannot kill a shadow.*

Another mural showed a host of winged spirits rebelling against the gods. Another, the gods binding them and sending them into the void. Only that one spirit remained behind, steadfast at Tuer's side.

She stopped before one of the altars, thinking of the last time she'd made her daily oblation and streaked her forehead with ashes and oil: the morning of her wedding, months ago. There was a jar of ashes on a shelf beside the altar, a vial of oil. She could have knelt and prayed. She could have asked the gods to bless her journey.

But she turned away. She didn't need the gods. She didn't want them.

Still, something tugged her on through the temple, led her to an alcove where a book lay open on a reading stand, its pages cracked and yellowed. The words leapt out at her, making her breath catch hard in her throat, flinging her back to that day, long ago, when her father had told her about Erris, and the foolish deal he had made with Tuer.

Here was another story. One he had not told her.

There came a time when Cainnar, who was the first and mightiest king of Halda, found that he was lonely. He had everything his soul had ever desired, and more besides, but he remembered his old life with his mother and brother in the woods, and he missed them fiercely. His mother was dead and gone beyond the Circles of the world, but his brother Erris was a servant in the palace. Cainnar determined to make Erris a prince and raise him to a place of honor.

But when Cainnar called for Erris, Erris did not come. Cainnar's servants searched the palace high and low, but they could not find the king's brother, and no one knew where he had gone.

At last, a serving woman called Lumen came and bowed before the king. She was no longer young, but the light of the Stars shone in her eyes, and she was yet beautiful. She had loved Erris, and wished to wed him, but his jealousy had blinded him to her affection. "My lord king," said Lumen to Cainnar, "Erris went up the mountain to seek Tuer, to petition the god to make him king in your stead. But that was ten years ago. He never came back."

Cainnar was stricken, because he knew this was his fault. "I will go up the mountain myself and bring my brother home. And when I do, I will crown him king also, and he shall rule beside me."

Lumen didn't believe him—who among the race of mankind had ever truly wished to share their power? But she packed supplies for the king's journey and loaded them onto a sure-footed mule. She was sure-footed herself and went along with him, she too longing to know Erris's fate.

They climbed for days that seemed to never end and huddled at night around a fire that did little to banish the bitter cold.

At last they reached the doorway to Tuer's Mountain, but a spirit with a burning sword and flaming hair barred their way. "Tuer is not here," she said, "nor Erris either. The god is in Sorrow and the man is in Time, and you cannot reach either one."

"But I am king," said Cainnar. "Anything I demand is given to me."

"Not this," said the spirit.

"Can you tell us, at least, what has happened to Erris?" said Lumen.

"I cannot tell you." The spirit held up a shard of black glass, which glistered in the light of the setting sun. "But I am permitted to show you."

And the king and the serving woman looked into the glass and saw Erris sitting on a crumbling throne as time spun around him and he grew old but did not stir and did not die, a crown moldering on his head.

"He asked Tuer to make him king," said the spirit. "And there he sits for all eternity, the ruler of emptiness."

"Is there no way to free him?" Cainnar cried.

The spirit shook her head. "He made a deal with the god, and so is bound by it."

The king and the serving woman turned away from the mountain, weighed with anger and sorrow.

"There is a way to free him," said Lumen. "If we kill Tuer, that will sunder any bond he has with man—it will allow Erris to come home to us."

And because Cainnar was proud, and did not like to be denied things—even by a god—he agreed.

So together, Lumen and Cainnar forged a weapon to kill the god. From their temple, they took hallowed objects: a jar of Starlight, a sliver of the Immortal Tree. They forged the blade of iron, imbued *it with the Starlight, and crafted the handle from the Tree shard. For nine years and a day, Lumen wove the knife with the Words of the gods, Words of death and power, power and death.*

And then one day, finally, the knife was ready.

Once more Lumen and Cainnar climbed the mountain. Cainnar was growing old, and could not walk as well as he used to. He stumbled on the path, and before Lumen could catch him, he fell over the edge, struck his head on a rock, and died.

It was an ill omen, the death of a king, but Lumen gripped the knife tighter and continued on her way. She would free Erris, and be reunited with him at last.

She went into the mountain and trod the long, long path, through the Circles of Death and Time, and came at last into Sorrow.

There she found Tuer, kneeling in darkness, chained and weeping. The knife felt very heavy in her hand. Now she saw him, she knew she could not kill him. She pitied him too much for that.

So she bowed her head and went back the way she'd come, straying once more into the Circle of Time. There she found Erris on his throne, a crown on his head, his eyes staring into nothing. She laid the knife in his hand, to use or not as he saw fit, and she sat down beside him, determined to dwell with him for the rest of eternity, or until Tuer had pity on him, as she had had pity on Tuer, and set him free at last from his vow.

But there was no vow laid on her.

And so Time stole her away bit by bit until there was nothing left of her but dust and the knife she'd made in anger and sheathed in mercy, resting unused on Erris's knee.

Eda lifted her eyes from the book, head wheeling. She couldn't breathe. The knife she needed to kill Tuer not only *existed*, but it was waiting for her on the very path she had already determined to take, provided no one else had found it since Lumen's time.

A cold wind blew through the temple, rustling through the pages of the book, touching her neck with icy fingers.

Perhaps this was the sacrifice the priestesses meant. The sacrifice of a god, to heal the cracks in the world.

Eda would do it. Find the knife. Drive it into Tuer's heart. And then, then—

Then she would return to Enduena and take her Empire back, because a woman with the power to kill a god could do anything at all.

"Little Empress."

She wheeled to find the twelve Itan priestesses standing in the midst of the temple, their black hair bleeding into the shadows, their white gowns rippling about their feet. The youngest priestess stepped toward Eda, another white gown draped over her arms. "For you. To wear to the feast."

Dread curled down Eda's spine. "I'm not going to the feast, and I'm certainly not wearing *that*."

"It is an honor to be offered the garment of a wind priestess. It is a great offense against the gods themselves to deny such a gift."

"I already have my quarrels with the gods," said Eda carefully. "White is the color of mourning in Enduena. The color of shrouds and dead things. I *can't* wear it. I won't be your *qirta*." Her voice shook.

"You misunderstand," said the priestess, softer now. "You are not to be the *qirta*. You are to fight with us against the coming darkness. Honor us. Honor our goddess." Once more she held out the dress.

Eda swallowed, hard. "Very well."

The priestesses helped her into the gown, tugging the finely spun Itan silk over her head, fastening the three hundred buttons that ran from the high neckline all the way to the hem. The sleeves were long and came to a point over her wrists; the cuffs were embroidered in silver.

When she was dressed, the youngest priestess gave her a dagger in a supple white leather sheath and matching belt.

"What is this for?" Eda asked, uneasy.

"To serve you until you find Lumen's knife." The priestess buckled it tight around Eda's hips.

Chapter Twenty-Nine

T HE PRIESTESSES ESCORTED EDA FROM THE TEMPLE, their skirts and hers an ocean of whispering white silk, making her feel as if they were an army of ghosts passing through the Circle of the Dead. Her uneasiness sharpened as they stepped into the great hall, which shimmered with light and warmth and music. A fire roared at the back of the room, and platters of food were laid out on the long oak tables. Monks and villagers and people who must be from the caravan sat and ate together. The priestesses drew Eda to a seat near the end of one of the long benches, and all but the youngest priestess left her there and went to sit by the fireplace. To Eda's surprise, the youngest priestess waited on her as if she were an attendant back in the palace, serving Eda food and keeping her cup full.

For a while, Eda's hunger forced her attention wholly to her plate. There was hot, gamy meat with rice and herbs, fresh corn tortillas drizzled in dark honey, creamy yogurt, and clear cold water that tasted as if it had been blessed by the gods themselves.

It was the first good meal she'd had since her wedding feast, and she ate until she was actually full.

"Why aren't you eating?" she asked the priestess when her hunger had finally subsided.

"We do not eat on holy nights, so that we can listen to our goddess."

"And does your goddess speak?"

"Perhaps she will, and perhaps she will not. Either way we will listen."

Eda's fingers twitched to the knife at her hip. "How did you know about Lumen's blade? I had only just finished reading about it in the temple."

"Our goddess appeared to me in Ita, told me to forge that knife and sew the sheath and belt, that you would have need of it. It's the only reason I was allowed to take my vows and make the journey to Tal-Arohnd, even though I have not yet reached my twentieth year."

"You're a bladesmith?"

The priestess smiled. "We have many skills on Ita. We do not just make silk."

Eda's face warmed. "What's your name?"

"Ahdairon. We are all Ahdairon—we give up our names when we take our vows, and assume instead the name of our goddess."

"Doesn't that bother you?"

"I serve the gods, and they speak to me. That is worth more than a name, don't you think?"

Eda was about to retort that no, she didn't think that, when the younger monks rose to clear the tables while the rest of the company settled onto the floor facing the fireplace where the priestesses waited. The youngest priestess bowed to Eda and went to join them. With one voice, the priestesses began to sing in their ancient tongue, an eerie, awful melody that made Eda's skin crawl. Firelight shone orange in their black hair and danced in the fine weaves of their silk gowns. Eda wanted to run, far, far away. The music sank into her. Ate her.

Torane was suddenly at Eda's elbow, his face drawn and sad. "They sing of the felling of the Tree, of the day when Tuer slew a man and brought death and time into the world."

Eda's chest tightened. "The day when all mankind wept for the folly of a god."

Torane looked at her sharply. "Death would have come, with or without Tuer's anger."

"Would it? Don't you think the world would look wholly different now, without Tuer in it?"

"Dear one." Torane's voice was gentle, but held a note of deepest sorrow. "Do not blaspheme the gods. Do not offend them."

"They've offended *me*," she said fiercely. She clenched the hilt of the priestess's blade, itching to wrap her fingers around Lumen's knife. "Haven't they offended you as well? You've served them all these years, and yet they had no thought to keep your mother alive long enough to see you one last time."

Torane's face closed. "Take care, little one. The gods will require much of you in the end, I think." He left her, and Eda hated herself. Torane did not deserve her anger. Lady Rinar did not deserve her scorn.

The priestesses sang on, their voices reaching a high, keening pitch that echoed shrilly in the stone hall. Eda resisted the urge to clap her hands over her ears. The youngest priestess locked eyes with her, and the words she had spoken to Eda in the temple echoed in her mind: *You are not to be the* qirta. *You are to fight with us against the coming darkness.*

A sudden chill permeated the room, and the air in front of Eda grew crackly, bright, sparks of silver splintering out from her like threads of gossamer web. The world seemed to pull, to stretch, and the splinters joined together to form a massive crack. Behind it teemed shadow, power, rage.

And then the spirits burst through in a rush of dark wings, a dozen, no more. Eda caught a glimpse of empty white eyes, of noseless faces and gaping mouths filled with jagged, broken teeth, of bleached bone swords set with black jewels.

The spirits hurtled toward the crowd, swords swinging, teeth gnashing. Heads and arms tumbled to the floor; Eda's vision was a spray of red. She stared at a Haldan woman whose headless body stayed upright for one heartbeat, two, before falling in an awful, mangled heap beside several others.

The monks drew swords from beneath their robes and launched themselves at the winged spirits.

The villagers and people from the caravan stampeded to the door, screaming and shoving each other.

The priestesses lifted their hands, their song morphing into a single, monotone note. Wind rushed into the hall, harsh and cold and stinging like scorpions.

Eda just stood there, staring at the dead bodies littering the floor, at the widening pool of blood that crept toward her feet.

And then she blinked and one of the spirits stood before her, a spirit she knew.

He was even clearer now than he'd been on the ship: his wings rippled with dark feathers, his sword was made of bone and was set with a flashing white jewel. Flames licked round his brow, his fiery crown unable to consume him.

In one swift movement, he pulled her tight against his body and wrapped his wings around her. Clawed fingers cut through the white gown and into her skin. His breath was scorching hot in her ear: "Do not fear, little Empress. I will not let them harm you. You are to be queen, when the spirits are free. It's why I made you. Why I called you."

She writhed in his grasp, scrabbling desperately for the dagger at her hip. She tore it free from its sheath and drove it upward, as hard as she could, but it merely passed through him.

"I told you, little Empress. You cannot kill a shadow."

She twisted around so she could look into his eyes—their fathomless depths seemed to swallow her, and her hatred of him evaporated her fear. "When I find you in your Mountain, you will not be a shadow. I will kill you then."

He laughed. "Then run. Run to the Mountain. See what awaits you there."

He released her so suddenly she fell in a jumble, her right hand sliding in a pool of blood. For an instant all she could do was stare, horror clawing at the edges of her vision: the youngest priestess lay dead on the floor, a jagged red line slashed across her throat, her eyes staring vacantly at the ceiling.

And then a hand closed around Eda's, and someone pulled her to her feet, tugging her insistently to the door. She had a glimpse of a blue and red poncho and a boy's dark hair, before they burst out into the night, the spray of breathtaking stars savagely incongruous with the slaughter they had left behind.

She planted her feet and looked back at the great hall, her head wheeling.

"We have to go," said the boy. "We have to go *now*."

She allowed him to pull her down the path, stumbling over

loose rocks as she ran. She felt numb and strange, the shadow-god's words echoing in her ears: *You are to be queen, when the spirits are free. It's why I made you. Why I called you.*

A distant part of her realized the boy running with her down the mountain was Morin.

Chapter Thirty

E DA YANKED HER HAND OUT OF MORIN'S and stopped dead on
the trail, gasping for air.

He stopped too, though the tension evident in every
line of his body screamed his desire to keep running.

"What are you doing here? Where are you taking me?" She
couldn't stop shaking, couldn't shut out the images of the dead
priestess's eyes or the Haldan woman's headless body crumpling
to the floor.

"Up the Rise."

"What?"

He grabbed her hand again, his eyes intent on hers. "I'm
taking you to find Tuer's Mountain."

And then they were hurtling down the path again, the stars
a blur of silver above them.

They slowed a little as they reached the village, a haphazard
collection of stone cottages sprinkled about the sprawling valley. A
river curled away to the west, hugging the shoulder of the mountain.

Eda couldn't run anymore, pain stabbing up through her ribs, but she walked as quickly as she could, gulping mouthfuls of icy air. Beyond the outskirts of the village, Morin led her up a worn track to another stone cottage. Flags flapped on a line that stretched from the peak of the roof to the top of a stone well. A pen of sleepy goats butted up next to the house.

The door creaked open and a girl looked out—Tainir, the same girl who had operated the aerial lift. She looked older somehow than she had earlier, her hair tangled about her shoulders, her face smudged with dirt. Eda realized why her eyes had looked so familiar, why she'd recognized Tainir's surname—she must be Morin's sister.

"Is everything ready?" said Morin.

Tainir nodded. "We can leave as soon as she changes."

Morin waved Eda toward the door and she stepped inside. The cottage was impossibly cramped, a worn canvas couch facing the fireplace, an iron stove in the corner, a table under one small window, and a doorway hung with a leather covering that Eda assumed led back to sleeping quarters. Three huge packs were piled by the front door with coils of rope and a battered kettle.

A lantern burned from the center of the table, which was covered in half-drawn maps, ink bottles, and paint jars. An intricate collection of pen nibs and brushes marched neatly beside the inks and paints, organized by size. Eda was reminded with a pang of Niren and her illuminated manuscripts.

Tainir pressed a mug into Eda's hands, steam curling up. "Drink it quick—we've a long way to go before morning. You can change back there." She waved toward the leather-covered doorway.

Numbly, Eda slipped behind the covering, which concealed

a short hallway and two tiny bedrooms. In one, a set of clothes was laid out for her. With shaking fingers, she clawed at the priestesses' dress, having to rip the buttons off because she couldn't undo them by herself. The white silk puddled on the floor, spattered with red. She drew on the trousers, shirt, and thick poncho quickly, then gulped down the contents of the mug: gods-blessed Enduenan tea.

Morin and Tainir were waiting for her in the front room, each wearing a pack. Tainir helped Eda into the remaining pack, adjusting it on her shoulders and tightening the strap across her chest.

"Let's go," said Morin grimly.

All three of them stepped out into the night, Morin pausing to lock the door. He led the way up the path that wound behind the house, and Eda followed in a daze. She was dimly aware of a pair of graves a little ways off the trail, spread with wildflowers and illuminated by a single lantern. Tainir went to blow it out.

"My mother didn't make it up the Rise," said Morin in a choked voice. "I've only known since yesterday. I told Tainir this afternoon."

Eda's own dead paraded through her mind: her parents, the Emperor, *Niren*, all jumbled up with the slaughter in the great hall. "I'm sorry."

He just shook his head, waiting for Tainir to join them before starting to move again. The track wound ever upward, clouds scudding across the stars.

"Why are you helping me?" Eda asked. "How did you know to pull me from the great hall? How did you even get to the monastery before me?"

Morin glanced back. "Tuer sent me a vision, up on the cliffs. I've been preparing for our climb all day."

Unbidden, Ileem's words slid into her mind. *Rudion came to me in Halda. He gave me a vision.* Unease twisted through her. "What did he show you?"

"The girl I gave the map to stolen by a creature with dark wings. The whole world being swallowed up by darkness, unless I found her, and brought her up the Mountain. But he didn't show me why. Why are you here, map girl? Why are you searching for Tuer?"

"Because he destroyed me. And because I cannot kill a shadow."

"Tell us," said Tainir behind her. "Tell us everything."

And so she did: the story her father had told her as a child, the deal she'd made with Tuer's Shadow, her ascension to the throne, her squabbling Barons. The temple. Niren's death. Ileem's betrayal.

Morin and Tainir listened in silence.

The words poured out of her, and when she was done, she felt entirely empty.

"Are you sure the gods have wronged you?" said Morin then, almost apologetically. His boots crunched through the gravel. "Tuer kept his promise. He made you Empress."

"And then he ripped my Empire and Niren away from me."

"But maybe it was never about you. Maybe becoming Empress was just a distraction. Maybe Niren's life was never yours to give, and the gods were always going to take her, without any regard to you."

Guilt pierced her, and so she was cruel. "Did the gods have need of your parents, too?"

His jaw tightened. He didn't answer.

The silence was awful, after that.

They went on, and despite the icy wind, sweat trickled down

Eda's shoulder blades. She had nearly worked herself up to an apology when the trail came to a dead end against a sheer cliff wall.

"It's called Tuer's Face," said Tainir, waving up at the rock. "Catch your breath for a few minutes—it's a hard climb."

Eda tilted her head back as far as it would go, but the top of Tuer's Face was lost somewhere in the night. "We're climbing *that* in the *dark?*"

"No way around." Tainir shrugged out of her pack and started digging through it. "This is the shortest way up."

Morin glanced up at the sky, the clouds clearing away, the moon starting to rise. For a moment, he seemed to stare intently at something behind them, but then turned back to Eda with a forced smile. "There should be enough light to see by. How are you at climbing, Your Majesty?"

She didn't understand why, but it irked her to hear her title from his lips. "I've never done it before."

"I'll show you." Morin unpacked climbing gear, which looked to Eda like nothing more than a mess of ropes and buckles. To her surprise, he carefully explained the harness, and helped her put it on and tighten it around her. Next went her pack, with pouches at her waist for climbing spikes and a mallet to drive them into the rock. He demonstrated how to use them, and had her practice on level ground until he was satisfied she'd be all right on the cliff. He avoided her eyes the whole time.

Tainir flashed Eda a tight smile. "Gods keep you—see you at the top." And then she leapt onto the cliff like a mountain goat, quick with her hammer and spikes, a dozen feet up before Eda could even blink.

Morin waved Eda up next, and he came behind her.

At first, it wasn't so bad. She fell into the rhythm of the rock and the hammer and the spikes, the cord of the rope and the strain of hauling herself slowly upward. Sweat danced on her forehead, her shoulders and arms aching.

And then she made the mistake of glancing down at Morin, and saw how high she'd climbed already.

She yelped and pressed herself against the rock, heart slamming, head wheeling with terror.

But Morin put a gentle hand on her ankle. "It's all right, Eda. You're safe. The ropes will hold. Just keep on like you've been. I passed out on my first climb, and that wasn't on the sheerest cliffside in Halda. You're doing well."

She took a long breath, then another. She waited until her pulse grew steady again. "I'm sorry for what I said about your parents."

"The gods have taken from us all, Your Majesty. I don't blame you. Now climb, or we'll never catch Tainir." There was an urgency in his voice that hadn't been there before.

His forgiveness was an unexpected comfort, but the anxiety she sensed from him scared her. She turned back to the cliff.

On and on they climbed, Tainir so far above them that her form blended into the rock. Eda wondered if Tainir was actually part goat.

Beyond the mountains the sky began to lighten bit by bit, the world going silver at the edges. Eda glanced behind her, and thought she saw a glimmer of darkness on the distant horizon. She squinted, but couldn't tell if there was really something there or if exhaustion was making her see things. All at once, the sun lipped over the peaks, flooding the cliff with light and warmth, and whatever lurked behind them was swallowed by the dawn.

Another hour later, when Eda thought her arms were going

to break from the continual upward strain, Tainir came into view, leaning backward, black braids swinging. "We're almost there— just a little farther!"

That was enough to keep Eda climbing another hundred feet. Tainir pulled her onto a ledge in the rock, and Morin scrambled up after her.

For a moment, all Eda could do was stare. The ledge was much wider than she'd initially realized, at least the size of the palace menagerie, and was scattered with what looked like a dozen enormous birds' nests. A wooden hut was built against the mountain, brightly colored in whorls of cerulean and magenta and gold.

"They must be out hunting," said Morin, stretching his arms. "I'll call them back." He shrugged out of his harness and went inside the hut, emerging with a curved instrument made out of some huge animal horn. He blew three short notes that echoed off the cliffside with the harsh voice of some ancient beast.

Tainir tugged Eda toward Morin. "Keep away from the edge."

Morin lowered the horn and peered out over the valley. Eda's whole body tensed, uncertain what they were waiting for.

But she didn't have to wait long. Dark shapes appeared in the eastern sky, growing larger and larger against the rising sun as they came rapidly toward the cliff.

Fear crashed through her, her head wheeling with images of the winged spirits in Tal-Arohnd, of bone swords and splattering blood. But then the shapes resolved into massive birds, golden wings catching the sunlight.

Morin sagged with relief, his face splitting into a wide grin as he glanced over at Eda. "You asked me how I got to the monastery ahead of you." He strode toward the cliff, kneeling down and bowing as the enormous birds landed all around him in a roar of wings and talons. "I flew," he said above the noise.

Chapter Thirty-One

"WHAT DOES HE MEAN, HE *FLEW*?" Eda hissed to Tainir.

Morin was feeding the huge birds scraps of meat from his palm, which was terrifying—their hooked beaks were larger than his forearm.

"They're the ayrrah," Tainir said, "the giant eagles, descended from the ones who used to serve the god Uerc. And Morin literally means he *flew*. The ayrrah have been our family's secret for generations. My mother could speak to them, and Morin inherited her abilities."

Eda blinked and saw the maps plastering the walls of the cartographer's shop—incredibly detailed maps, like the person who'd drawn them had had an actual bird's eye view. "You can't mean—you can't mean he *rides* them."

"That's exactly what I mean. And you'd better hope the ayrrah like you, because we're flying, too. It's our best chance at making it all the way up Tuer's Rise. It's our only chance at finding Tuer's Mountain, which was something even our mother couldn't do." Tainir's voice caught.

Morin stood next to an eagle with dark wings, pressing his hand against its enormous head, leaning close to the creature's fierce eyes. All but three of the ayrrah gathered their wings and leapt off the cliff, and Morin turned to Eda and Tainir, his grin even wider than before.

"They'll take us," he said, trotting past them and back into the hut. "Get Eda ready, won't you, Tainir?"

Tainir helped Eda out of her harness, then shoved it and the climbing spikes deep into the bottom of her pack.

Eda dubiously accepted a hat, which was made of a bright blue knitted wool, with braided leather cords to tie under her chin.

Tainir laughed at Eda's obvious dislike. "Flying is *cold*. Trust me. You'll want it."

And then Morin came back, lugging a trio of odd avian saddles, which the eagles allowed him to strap on to their backs. The birds waited patiently for him to finish, and when he did, he waved Tainir and Eda over.

Eda went, reluctantly.

Morin took her hand and brought her to one of the eagles, who peered at her with sharp eyes and pressed its beak into her palm. Eda suppressed the urge to screech and leap away. The ayrrah's feathers were a rich chestnut brown, but their edges glimmered gold.

"This is Filah," Morin told her. "She was—she was my mother's favorite." The words choked him. "She'll bear you well. You have nothing to fear."

And then before Eda was ready, Morin boosted her up onto Filah's back. The saddle was small and light, made of supple, tooled leather, with a raised part in front for Eda to hold on to, and braided leather stirrups for her feet. Morin adjusted Eda's pack, making sure it was secure on her shoulders, and then stepped away to climb onto his own eagle, who had darker, almost black wings. Tainir's was gold and white and seemed to be younger than the other two; it stamped its taloned feet and bobbed its head about impatiently.

Morin hung a smaller version of the horn he'd used to summon the ayrrah around his neck on a blue cord. He lifted it to his lips and blew one piercing note. Beneath Eda, Filah gathered her wide wings and launched into the air so suddenly that for a moment, Eda left her stomach on the cliff ledge.

Wind rushed past her body, stinging her hands and her cheeks. At first, she could hardly open her eyes; when she did, it was to a dizzying blur of rock and trees and empty air. She thought she'd be terrified, like she had been climbing the cliff, but somehow, she wasn't. Filah flapped her wings once, twice, then soared for a while on a current of air.

Eda slowly made sense of what she was seeing: the mountains, marching beneath them, a river so far below it was a mere glint of silver. Clouds close enough to touch, treetops small as spiders. The thrilling sensation of *freedom*, untethered to the earth.

They flew almost due west, Morin's ayrrah taking the lead with Eda in the middle and Tainir just behind. It was freezing, which made Eda grateful for the awful hat. The wind numbed her hands, and she slipped them beneath the feathers on Filah's neck. Warmth crept tingling back into her fingers.

Morin looked back at her, an expression of pure joy on his face. "All right?" he called.

Eda couldn't stop the grin tugging at her own lips. "All right!"

They flew on, and every once in a while she caught Morin looking behind them, tension coming into his frame again. She got into the habit of glancing back, too. Sometimes, she swore she could see that wavering darkness on the horizon, but mostly there was nothing.

They'd been flying several hours when, to Eda's surprise, all three of the giant eagles spiraled closer to the peaks again and landed on a jut of rock in a rush of wings. Morin and Tainir clambered off, and Eda followed suit, confused when the ayrrah launched themselves back into the air.

"They may be descendants of Uerc's eagles, but they're still mortal, and we're heavy," Morin explained. "They've gone to hunt—they'll be back before long." He flopped down onto the rock, feet dangling out over empty air, and took flatbread and nuts out of his pack. He handed some around to Eda and Tainir. Eda didn't miss the worry in his eyes as he glanced frequently back the way they had come.

The three of them ate in silence, Eda still trying to catch her breath. She had no idea where they were, or how far they'd flown, but Morin found their jut of rock on the map, and circled it with a charcoal pencil. Eda studied the map. "It's not as simple as riding the ayrrah for a day up the mountain, is it?"

Morin shook his head. "It's faster than climbing, of course, but we'll have to take frequent breaks during the day for them to rest and hunt, and they don't see well enough in the dark to fly at night. And we'll have to do some climbing eventually—the ayrrah never want to go past the Singing Mountain."

"What's the Singing Mountain?"

Now Tainir was looking anxiously into the empty air behind them. "The stories say Tuer made it for Raiva, in the days before the Stars were plucked down from heaven. They say it really sings."

"Have you heard it?"

"We've never been that far." Morin let the map roll back up again and stuffed it into its protective cylinder. "But our mother said it was the strangest and most beautiful thing she ever encountered."

Both his and Tainir's faces closed at the mention of their mother, the grief still so raw.

"It was Filah who found her body," said Morin. "Carried her back to me. I don't know how far my mother made it or where she died. But she was long gone by the time Filah laid her at my feet." He shut his eyes and rubbed his hand against his temple.

Tainir wrapped her arms around him, her eyes swimming with tears. For a moment, brother and sister clung to each other like they were the only two souls left in the world.

Eda shifted with discomfort, not wanting to fall back into her own grief. "What do you both keep looking for?" she asked, after a while, desperate to break the silence.

Tainir lifted her head, her cheeks damp. She glanced at her brother.

His jaw tightened. "The spirits that attacked Tal-Arohnd. I think they're following us."

When the ayrrah returned a few minutes later and Eda and the others resumed their flight, she couldn't recapture the joy she'd felt before. Fear gnawed at her, and she looked back more often than she looked ahead.

Clouds knotted across the sun as the day spun on, and an icy rain began to fall. Morin blew several notes from the horn he wore around his neck, and the giant birds turned slightly to the north and landed high on the side of a mountain. Eda, Morin, and Tainir huddled under an outcropping of rock, as much out of the rain as possible.

Trees grew in a tangle from the mountain's edge, on far too much of a slant to provide any realistic shelter, but Morin was able to gather enough wood to make a fire. The ayrrah nested deep within the branches, tucking their wings over their heads and seeming to fall instantly asleep.

Tainir drew jars of goat cheese and hummus out of her pack. "We have to travel light," she told Eda by way of apology for the sparse fare. "But Morin did bring a kettle—we're not monsters."

Eda smiled, the knot inside her easing a little. "It looks a feast to me."

"Tomorrow, we'll have to hunt when the birds do," said Tainir, with distaste.

"Food might be a little scarce from here on," Morin agreed, eyes flicking in Eda's direction.

She shook her head. "I lost my appetite for an Empress's table a long time ago. You needn't be sorry on my account."

When they'd eaten, Morin made tea, and the three of them sat drinking it around the fire. The rain dwindled down to nothing.

"What will we do if the spirits catch us?" said Eda.

Morin put another log on the fire. "Tuer is calling you to the Mountain—we have to trust he'll protect us long enough to get you there."

The flames cracked and popped, glowing hot embers sparking red into the night, smoke swirling up to join the emerging stars.

"How can you trust Tuer after what happened to your parents?"

"Their deaths were not his doing."

Something twisted inside her. "How can you know that?"

He shrugged. "I guess I don't. But it's not something he would do—Tuer has always watched over us."

"You still think that after everything he did to me?"

Morin and Tainir exchanged glances.

"I don't think Tuer is quite who you think he is," said Morin.

"Then who is he?"

Tainir rubbed her thumb along the rim of her tea mug. "Who he is not is more to the point. What do you know about the spirits?"

"There were countless of them, formed by the One at the beginning to help the gods shape Endahr."

"So there were," Tainir agreed. "Some helped Raiva guard the trees and make them grow. Some helped Mahl and Ahdairon, the wind gods, harness the lightning and wield the rain. Some helped Uerc tame the beasts and teach them to speak. And there was one spirit who became the servant of Tuer, helped him raise mountains from the earth, and cast them down again."

Eda saw a flash of the murals in the monastery temple: a shining spirit, always at Tuer's side.

"This spirit was almost as powerful as Tuer himself," Tainir went on. "While most of the spirits were not faithful to just one god, but passed freely between tasks until they grew bored and roamed about Endahr on their own, this spirit stayed beside Tuer always, and so he was called, in the old days, Tuer's Shadow."

Eda drew a sharp breath, unease twisting through her. "I thought—I thought Tuer's Shadow was a *piece* of Tuer."

"No god can divide themselves," said Morin quietly. His eyes snagged on Eda's, but she only held them for a moment before looking away.

Tainir's story continued to spin out into the night. "When

the spirits rose against the gods and were sealed into the void, Tuer's Shadow remained. He went with Tuer into exile in the Circle of Sorrow, and it's thought that Tuer sends him out to do his bidding in the world. Some stories do not think Tuer's Shadow is benevolent. They say he's an evil spirit who manipulates Tuer, using the god's likeness to fool mankind into making hapless deals. In those stories, Tuer's Shadow goes by another name."

Eda forced herself to breathe as a horrible understanding unraveled her, thread by thread. "What name?"

Tainir's voice was small in the vastness of the dark: "Rudion."

Chapter Thirty-Two

E DA LAY AWAKE LONG AFTER THE THREE of them had crawled into their bedrolls and Morin and Tainir had drifted to sleep. Uneasiness bit at her.

How long had Tuer been trapped in the Circle of Sorrow? How long had he sent his Shadow—sent *Rudion*—to do his bidding?

She couldn't shake away Torane's words to her back in Tal-Arohnd: *He claimed he served Tuer, but there was such darkness in him I cannot believe it. I think he must have pledged himself to an evil spirit instead.*

Deep in the night, Eda left her bedroll and paced to the edge of the cliff. She stared out into the vast reaches of Tuer's Rise, a speck of dust amongst the stars. The wind curled round her, icily cruel. And then a shadow separated itself from the mountain, and she was no longer alone.

His wings stirred beside her. She could feel the heat of his fiery crown.

"What do you want with me?"

"What I have always wanted," he answered. "What my lord Tuer bid me."

Anger hardened her. "And what has the god bid you?"

"To draw you to his Mountain."

The wind tore past her, sending a cascade of pebbles skittering down the cliff. "He orchestrated all of this, didn't he. The deal I made. Niren's death. Ileem—Ileem's betrayal."

She felt, rather than saw, Rudion's smile. "Do you want to know what became of your prince?"

She bit her lip so hard she tasted blood and didn't answer.

"He's dead. Does that please you?"

Her traitorous heart wrenched and she wheeled on the spirit. "Why are you here? I'm doing what you want. I'm going to the Mountain. Leave me—I have no use for shadows."

Rudion lifted his hand and traced her cheek with one taloned finger. It bit into her skin. "I can take you to the god. I can bear you to the Mountain. Tonight. You need wait no longer to avenge yourself on him." His wings rustled in the wind. His sword gleamed white.

"I'm not going *anywhere* with you," she spat.

He hissed, showing his teeth, jagged and broken. "You will be sorry. You are the only one Tuer needs. I will not ask so politely again."

She took a breath and he was gone, nothing but the wind and the stars and her two sleeping companions with her on the mountain.

She woke to blinding sunlight pouring over the peaks, uncertain if her encounter with Rudion had been a dream. Morin and Tainir were already up, busy breaking camp, and Eda crawled hurriedly from her bedroll. Despite the sun, it was freezing.

On the edge of the cliff, where she had stood last night, rested a single black feather. She shuddered. "We should go," she told Morin. "As quick as we can."

He caught her apprehension and nodded, calling the ayrrah down from their trees. He showed Eda how to saddle Filah, which was not very different from saddling a horse, and she was surprised when he told her he'd made the saddle himself.

"Is there anything you don't know how to do?"

"Rule an Empire—but I suppose that makes two of us."

She scowled and punched his arm, belatedly realizing he was teasing her. Her cheeks warmed.

He rubbed his arm and laughed. "I suppose I had that coming."

Minutes later, the other ayrrah saddled, they all launched into the air.

They flew into the wind that tasted like lightning, like freedom, but fear bit at Eda in a way it hadn't yesterday. She couldn't stop looking over her shoulder.

Behind them, the horizon glinted dark, and sometimes Eda thought she saw black wings and a fiery crown. But it must have been a trick of the light—every time she blinked, it was gone.

Tainir sang as they flew, her fingers busy hand-knitting something from a skein of bright blue yarn. Morin pulled parchment and charcoal from his pack, and somehow had the coordination to sketch the landscape below, unconcerned with the plummeting drop.

The ayrrah set them down in a high meadow a little before noon and flew off to hunt. Tainir left to do some hunting of her own, which surprised Eda, considering the face she'd made last night at the mention of it.

But Morin just smiled, shaking his head. "She's prouder of her hunting ability than you would think."

The two of them built a fire, or rather Morin did after Eda awkwardly told him she didn't know how. He didn't tease her about this, just explained everything as he was doing it, and assured her she'd be an expert in no time.

With the fire lit, there was nothing else to do besides wait for Tainir. Morin sprawled on his back in the grass and stared up at the sky. Eda watched him, unsure why she felt so uncomfortable being alone with him. Her glance flitted often to the patch of darkness on the horizon, her skin crawling at the memory of Rudion's words.

"What is it like, to talk with the ayrrah?"

"It's like talking to the wind and having it listen."

"What do they say to you?"

Morin rolled onto his side and propped himself up on one elbow so he could look at her. "Nothing in words. It's more like . . . images. Emotions. Sometimes flashes of color."

"But you understand them?"

"Often, but not always. My mother spoke their language best."

Eda saw her own mother, dead between white sheets, and shuddered.

Morin's brow creased. "What's wrong?"

"The gods take. They take and take, and give nothing in return."

He studied her, his dark eyes seeing deep. "Nothing at all?"

His question hung in the air between them as Tainir appeared with a brace of rabbits hanging from her belt. She greeted Eda and Morin, then skinned the rabbits with neat efficiency. Morin turned his head away, looking more than a little green, but he was the one to dump the meat into their little cooking pot.

Eda was relieved when the ayrrah returned, anxious to get back into the air, to reach Tuer's Mountain before Rudion found her again. She brushed one hand against the side of Filah's head. "Let's chase the wind, swift one. I think we could catch it."

She flushed when she realized Morin was standing close enough to hear her.

They flew on, west and a little north, on the heels of the falling sun. Eda found herself glancing over at Morin, and tried to parcel out the reasons why. He confounded her, this boy who drew maps and talked to eagles, whose grief was as large as her own and yet had not made him turn away from the gods.

She was glad when the ayrrah set them down for the night on a flat rock ledge bare of trees or brush, then took to the sky again to find nests for themselves. Tainir scrambled down the cliff, like the mountain goat Eda began to suspect she actually was, in search of dinner, leaving Eda and Morin alone once more.

The last rays of the sun vanished and the stars came out, gleaming and bold in the vast inky sky. Morin let Eda build the fire, and she was pleased to have absorbed his instructions from earlier well enough to get a good blaze going. She helped him lay out the trio of bedrolls, and then crouched on her heels to watch him finish the map he'd been working on in the mingled light of the flames and the stars.

"Not nothing," she said after a while.

He looked up from the map, a question on his face.

"What you said before," she explained. "You were right. The gods don't always give nothing in return."

His eyes were dark pools of memory, of grief. They seared through her, down to her soul. "It is our choices that make us, Eda. What we choose to do with the things the gods give us."

A gaping discomfort opened inside of her. "What have you chosen?"

He answered without hesitation. "To take you on this journey. What have you chosen?"

She couldn't answer that. She looked away.

"Eda."

She glanced back. He put down his brush, paint staining his hands. He leaned toward her, grazed hesitant fingers across her chin. Wet spots of paint clung to her skin in the places he touched.

"What have you chosen?" he repeated, his face mere inches from hers.

"Death. I have chosen death." Niren's, first. Tuer's, soon. She jerked up and paced away from him, hugging her arms around herself in the freezing wind. He didn't follow.

Lightning crackled on the distant horizon, and for a moment the wind smelled like rot and worms. Fear cut through her.

But the next moment the sky was dark again, and the scents faded to nothing more than smoke from the fire and the icy mountain air.

Tainir appeared with two squirrels, stepping past Eda with

a brief glance at her chin and a raised eyebrow. Eda flushed hot, rubbing her hand against the place Morin had touched her over and over until she felt sure the paint was gone.

Then there was dinner to make and eat, and the moon was halfway up by the time they'd finished. Just like last night, no one seemed in any hurry to crawl into their bedrolls, so Morin made more tea, and they all sat around the fire.

Tainir began to sing, a quiet thread of melody that was almost more like a sigh than a song. Glints of gold danced around her lips, and when she raised her hands more appeared, echoes of the fire glimmering on her fingers.

Morin noticed Eda's stare. "There has always been magic in the mountains. Tainir *feels* it, in a way I've only ever felt when I'm speaking with the ayrrah. Our mother was like that, too. She never came to harm, until now."

"You want to bring her back, don't you?" said Eda.

Grief touched his face. "The dead are the dead. It isn't my place to bring her back. But I would like to see her one more time. My father, too. I'd like to know they've gone to their rest, that they're not suffering. That they're together."

"And you have faith that the gods will . . . let you see them again?"

He shrugged. "Perhaps."

She kicked at a clod of dirt. "Does Tuer often send you visions? Do you always do what he tells you to?"

"I never vowed myself to him, if that's what you mean, but the gods have always been part of my life. I go up to Tal-Arohnd on feast days. I bring offerings to the temple. I listen for Tuer's voice. He never spoke to me, before the other day, but I always knew he was there."

A knot pulled tight inside of her. "How?"

"I just do, Eda. I can sense him, watching over his mountains, watching over his people."

"You still think he's benevolent, even after everything I told you?"

Morin sprawled out on the stone ledge, propping his head up on one hand. "I think you only know one side of him."

"And you know another?"

"It seems I have heard different stories than you."

"Tell me one," Eda challenged.

Morin glanced up at the spangled sky as Tainir stopped singing, her glance passing between the two of them.

Morin shut his eyes. "When Tuer first saw Raiva, she was so beautiful he thought that she must have been born of the Stars themselves. In a way, he wasn't wrong. Raiva alone of all the gods and goddesses had touched the Stars and not been burned— save Caida, who was the Stars' keeper. Their light had sunk into Raiva. Become part of her. And so she was the embodiment of light and truth and beauty. Tuer didn't know it then, but love woke like a flame inside of him, and the more he knew her, the more it grew."

Eda kicked at the dirt clod again. Morin clearly wasn't telling a thinly disguised story meant to flatter her. She was no Raiva, and no one would ever think that about her. Ileem's face rose unbidden to her mind, and she bit back a curse. If anything, she was like Tuer. Selfish. Possessive. Guilty.

"She was gentle and wise," Morin continued, "and yet also fierce as a flame. She taught mankind music under the shadow of the Tree, and she mourned the falling of it, the division between them and the gods. She withdrew, for a time, to her great wood, where she watched mankind from afar and sang every night to the lesser stars the songs she had learned at the beginning of time.

"From deep inside his mountain, Tuer heard her sing, and he took to emerging every evening to better hear her. He could see her shining among the trees, and, little by little, he began to descend from the mountain and venture into the wood.

"One evening, he came very near to where she was, standing ankle deep in a pool of water, her face tilted up toward the sky. She turned and smiled at him, then bowed very low. 'Won't you join my song, my lord Tuer?'

"'My lady, I do not know it,' he replied.

"'Then I shall teach you.'

"And she did. When he had learned it, they sang together, and their voices were like starlight and earth, strong and bright.

"'Come again tomorrow, my lord,' said Raiva. 'The wood is beautiful, but I am lonely.'

"And so the next day he came, and the next day and the next. Always she looked for him, and they sang together. Sometimes they sat and took bread in the shadow of the trees. Sometimes they drank deep of the wine of wood and earth. Sometimes they simply were with one another, content each in the other's presence.

"Raiva's heart warmed to him, and she knew that she loved him, as she had seen the men and women of the earth love each other. But she saw in him a great and heavy sorrow, and it grieved her.

"'My lord,' she asked. 'What troubles you?'

"The god of the mountain bowed his head into his hands and wept. 'You were there,' he said. 'You saw my greatest sin. You were there the day I slew the man Tahn, who stole the seed from the Tree. It was I who began everything: death, time, sorrow. It was I who put to naught everything the One meant for Endahr to be.'"

Eda squirmed with discomfort. She had begun everything, too: Niren's death, the Empire's fall, Ileem's betrayal. She hated Tuer for reminding her of herself.

But Morin wasn't finished. "'Not everything,' Raiva argued. 'There is still life and light and music. There is still love.'

"Tuer couldn't bear to look her in the eye, because he was not brave enough or strong enough to ask her if she loved him as he loved her. 'I wronged gods and men alike that day, and I have made no recompense.'

"'Have you entreated the One?' Raiva asked. 'Have you asked him what you must do?'

"'I dare not show my face before him.'

"'If you do not ask, you will never know,' Raiva told him. 'I have known the One's mercy; I have seen his heart. You need not fear him.'

"But Tuer couldn't hear her. 'I must atone for the life I took. I must restore Tahn to Endahr. I will find his soul, Lady of the Wood. I will bring him back.'

"'Tahn's soul has been at peace these many centuries. It is folly to seek him. It is evil to drag him away from his rest.'

"'It is what I must do. It is the punishment I deserve.'

"Raiva sighed, because she knew she could not sway him, but she took his hand in hers and kissed his brow. 'Then do what you must do, my lord, but make haste. The light in the wood will be dimmer in your absence.'

"And then he turned and went up into his mountain. He never came back."

The snap of the fire sounded overloud as Morin stopped talking. Eda stared at him across the flames, her discomfort sharpening to anger. She *was* like Tuer. There was little difference between them. And now here she was, seeking that very mountain, seeking to drive a knife into his heart. Isn't that all Ileem had wished to do? To end her cruelty, her mistakes, as she intended to end Tuer's, Rudion whispering in both of their ears?

"What's wrong?" said Morin.

She jerked her eyes away. "You're right. I've never heard that story. But it doesn't make me think better of Tuer than I did before."

"You forgot the ending," Tainir admonished her brother. Golden sparks were dancing all around her face and her shoulders. She raised her hands to reveal more flecks of light cupped in her palms. She blew on them, gently, and they drifted up into the night like so many fireflies.

"What's the ending?" asked Eda. Pain pulsed through her.

"After a year of waiting in her wood, Raiva went into Tuer's Mountain. She went after him."

"But not even she could save him," Eda guessed. Her eyes found Morin's of their own accord, and this time, she didn't look away.

Tainir lowered her hands to her lap again, and the sparks around her faded. "So it would seem."

Chapter Thirty-Three

THE SPIRITS WERE HUNTING THEM.

Every day the stain on the horizon grew larger, and the wind from the east brought with it the stench of rotting things. Sometimes, from the corner of her eye, Eda thought she saw Rudion: his flaming crown, his jagged teeth, his dark-feathered wings. Yet every time she turned her head, there was nothing beside her but empty air.

The days fell into a rhythm: flying most of the morning, with a break midday for the ayrrah—and the humans—to hunt and eat. Then flying in the afternoon and making camp just before sunset. It was always Tainir who went hunting, always Morin and Eda who stayed behind. She felt perpetually awkward around him when they were alone—she didn't know what to make of him, and more importantly didn't know what *he* made of *her*. So she talked to him about little things. Unimportant things. Just to fill the silence until Tainir came back, her eyes straying always to that stain on the horizon, in constant dread of dark wings and bone swords filling the sky.

Every time they stopped, Morin marked their progress on one particular well-worn map, showing Eda where they were, how far they'd flown.

"When did your mother become a cartographer?" she asked him on the fourth day. The ayrrah had put them down for the night on the very tops of enormous pines, and they'd had a long climb down to the forest floor. There was sap in Eda's hair, and she'd scraped both arms on the rough bark. She felt a little safer, under the cover of the trees.

"My mother could draw before she could talk," he told her, brushing pine needles from his trousers as he knelt to make a fire. "My father said she was born with a pen in her hand."

Eda helped him arrange the wood, then struck a match and set it to the kindling. "What about you?"

"The year I turned seven I contracted a terrible fever and was confined indoors for months. I was restless, so my mother let me try her pencils and paints. I'd had no interest in them before, too busy climbing rocks and learning to speak to the ayrrah. She showed me how she sketched her maps, traced the outline with thick black ink, filled them in with watercolors. It fascinated me, and I discovered a talent for it. On my next birthday, my mother gave me a beautiful set of colored pencils she'd sent for all the way from Pehlain. I used them so sparingly I still have a few of the stubs somewhere back home."

"You miss her so much," said Eda across the crackling flames. "I'm sorry."

"I can't believe she's gone. I can't believe she just . . . fell."

"Is that how she died?"

He shuddered. "Her back was broken. Her neck, too. She must have fallen."

Eda read the truth in his face, and her heart wrenched. "You dug her grave. Alone."

"I didn't want Tainir to see." He bowed his head into his hands, his shaking shoulders the only evidence he was crying.

Something compelled her to go around to his side of the fire, to take one of his hands in her own. His skin was rough and warm, and for some reason that startled her. She let go.

He looked up at her, his face shiny with tears. "I'm afraid, Eda. I feel the world weighing on me—I feel it splintering apart at the seams. And I feel my mother's soul, wandering, lost. We can't get to Tuer's Mountain fast enough. I don't know if we can even get there at all."

Eda crouched on her heels beside him, the fire popping and sparking, the light dancing on Morin's hair. "I feel it too. The weight of the world."

"Every night when I dream, I see spirits slipping through cracks in the world. They devour all life, and Endahr dies, and its light is put out, and all is nothing more than wheeling dust in the void."

"We're going to find Tuer," she said, with more conviction than she felt. "We're going to put your mother's soul to rest. We're going to fix this."

"I thought all you cared about was making him pay for what he did to you."

"I've found I can care about more than one thing," she told him simply.

His eyes met hers in the flickering flames, and she felt a sudden, fierce kinship with him.

Somewhere out in the boundless night, something screamed. The scent of decay crowded her nostrils and she shuddered.

Morin grabbed her arm, squeezed tight. "I know they're out there. I know they're following us."

"What are we going to do when they catch up?"

"Keep going, as fast as we can. Trust that Tuer is stronger than they are."

"Do you think he is?"

"I think he wants us to reach the Mountain. I don't think he would have brought us this far just to let us fall."

Eda took his hand in hers, lost in Morin's eyes, in the strength of his faith in the god she hated.

And then Tainir came through the trees with a fat hare draped over her shoulders. Eda let go of Morin immediately, but his hand remained on her arm for half a dozen heartbeats before he drew away.

Two days later, the ayrrah circled the cliffs for a long while, looking for a place to deposit their riders as the sun slid too quick down the rim of the sky. The air smelled like dead things, and the eastern horizon was writhing with shadows. At last, Morin blew a series of notes on the horn that hung around his neck, and the birds approached a narrow rock ledge barely wide enough to stand on. The ayrrah hovered awkwardly while Morin dug climbing spikes from his pack and hammered a few into the cliff. Dread shot down Eda's spine, and it only deepened when Morin clambered off his ayrrah to perch precariously on the spikes, clinging to the rock with his fingers.

"Sit tight," he called to Eda and Tainir. "They'll take you round a few more times, and then I'll have the hammocks ready."

"The *what?*" said Eda, but Filah had already shot into the sky again. "He surely can't mean we're sleeping on the side of the cliff!" Eda called to Tainir.

But Tainir didn't seem to hear her.

The last rays of the sun were glinting off the mountain when the ayrrah returned to Morin's perch. He'd rigged three hammocks on spikes pounded into the rock, and had somehow managed to put his climbing harness on. He waved Tainir over, and helped his sister climb off her eagle and join him on the cliff. She put her harness on, too, and settled into one of the hammocks.

Filah flapped her wings uneasily, clearly ready to find her nest for the night. Eda would have preferred to take her chances sleeping with the giant eagles, but Morin held out his hand. "Come on. It's not quite as terrifying as it looks. We'll be safe here." He glanced at the darkness behind them. "As safe as we can be."

Eda gulped and took his hand, lunging off Filah's back and colliding with Morin on the impossibly narrow rock ledge. For an instant, her feet slipped and she thought she was going to fall, but Morin wrapped his arm around her chest and held her tight. She could feel his heartbeat, rabbit quick, pulsing in time with her own.

"All right?" he said into her ear.

She was too shaky for speech, but she nodded. He helped her put on her harness, which he secured with another climbing spike and a length of rope into the rock. She sank gingerly into the central hammock, expecting it to rip off its moorings and plummet to the ground below, but it held.

Morin climbed around her like a spider and took the hammock on her right, while Tainir got comfortable in the one on her left.

"We've done this before," said Morin, digging about in his pack. "There's always a chance the ayrrah can't find anywhere flat for us to camp, so we learned to make do."

"You'll find it's really quite comfortable," added Tainir.

There was no possibility of tea, but Morin had squirreled away some dried meat and an apple for just such an occasion, and divided the fare between the three of them.

Eda watched him cut the apple with his knife, the blade flashing in the light of the rising moon, and for some reason couldn't stop thinking of peeling an orange in Ileem's chambers in Eddenahr, back when she'd thought he could be a friend.

The night deepened and the moon brightened, illuminating half the sky while the other half lay plunged in darkness that looked thick enough to touch. Tainir began to sing, raising her hands to the cliff above them. Gold light swirled round her.

"She's singing to the cliff," said Morin, "asking it to guard us from the spirits as we sleep, strengthening the ropes with the old Words of Power."

"Where did she learn to do that?"

"She said the wind taught her, when she was small. I think perhaps she's spoken with the wind gods, Mahl and Ahdairon, although she's never told me as much."

Eda thought of the Itan priestesses and suppressed a shudder. She studied Morin in the moonlight, the planes of his face swathed in silver, and thought he looked like the chiseled image of a young god. Some impulse made her want to reach out for him, touch his face, pull him close.

But then she thought of Ileem, crushing the orange under one knee, promising his fealty as he plotted her downfall, and she hated herself. Instead she turned to Tainir, who continued to sing to the mountain, ancient magic flowing out of her.

When Tainir finished, all three of them settled down into

their hammocks. Eda pulled her hat down over her ears and tried not to feel the wind ripping past the cliff, making her hammock sway in an extremely horrifying manner. At the moment, she feared the fall more than the looming shadows.

"I'm never going to sleep up here," Eda muttered, without really meaning to. Her head was pointed toward Morin's hammock, but she couldn't see him—all she could see was the blur of darkness below her, concealing the plummeting drop.

"We just need another story," said Morin. "Tainir, tell us about Raiva going to find Tuer."

Eda shut her eyes, her body pressing up against the cliffside.

"Raiva went into the mountain," came Tainir's voice. "It was dark and stank of shadows. She called Tuer's name, but he didn't answer. She walked and walked and walked, ever deeper into the mountain, and she came to a door. It was locked, but it opened for her, because she was bathed in Starlight from the beginning, and there is almost no power greater than that.

"She went looking for Tuer beyond the door in the Circle of the Dead, where lost souls moaned and cried, for many of the race of mankind had died since Tuer slew Tahn, centuries ago. Raiva knelt by one of these souls, a young woman with shining hair, and she touched her forehead, imbuing her with Starlight.

"'Go,' Raiva told the young woman. 'Gather the others. Bring them on to the One, who will give them rest.'

"And the young woman kissed the hem of Raiva's gown and went and did as the goddess instructed her. She was the first Bearer of Souls."

Eda shifted uncomfortably. Though she'd realized she did in fact mean to try and fix the tears in the world when she found Tuer—she still didn't want to be the Bearer of Souls. She didn't want to be bound to the Circles and the gods in such an inescapable way—she couldn't think of a worse fate.

"Raiva did not forget her," Tainir went on. "When the first Bearer had gone about her task a hundred years, Raiva herself bore her beyond the Circles of the world and brought her to her own rest.

"On Raiva went and came to another door and another. She passed through both of them and found Tuer, chained and weeping in the Circle of Sorrow."

Eda's heart seized. "She found him?"

"Yes. But she couldn't free him, though she tried for a century. Because Tuer had trapped himself there. Tuer had forged his own chains and bound himself to Sorrow, to atone for his crimes. So he couldn't see Raiva. He didn't even know she was there. He thought he was alone.

"And there he is still. Raiva goes as often as she can to see him, but she despairs that he will ever be free. She despairs, because she has the power to do so many things, but not to save him. Never to save him."

Tainir lapsed into silence and Eda rebuked the tears that pressed suddenly behind her eyes. She tried to hold on to the fact that she hated Tuer. That he'd sent Rudion to take everything from her. That he deserved to die.

But she couldn't deny the stark understanding of everything he'd done, and everything she'd done, and how they were nearly the same. She thought of how she'd wanted to touch Morin's face, to pull him close. She couldn't do that to him. Couldn't entangle him in her web, so that he would lose himself like Raiva in the dark of Tuer's Mountain. Morin was good, and she was not. He couldn't help her. Not that way.

But she was still on the side of the cliff, held up by a few lengths of rope, trusting her life to him.

"How can you sleep," she said, "knowing you might fall in the night?"

"The stakes are deep and the rope is strong," Tainir returned. "And we fear death. *I* fear it, more than my ancestors ever did. Because the doors are shut. There is no Soul Bearer now to guide me to paradise."

Eda could almost feel the bands of the gods' fate closing around her. She swallowed. "That is not very comforting."

She heard the quiet thread of Morin's laughter in the dark. "What Tainir means is, we won't let you fall."

Somehow, Eda slept, and when she woke the next morning she was still secure against the cliff face. Darkness roiled behind them. She thought she could see the outline of shadowy figures, the flash of white swords.

Morin and Tainir packed up in a hurry, hanging in their harnesses from the rock. Eda clung to Morin as he helped her out of her hammock. It was freezing on the cliff, but his proximity made her flush with heat. "I dreamed that you were searching for me," she told him. "That you were calling my name in the dark."

He looked at her intently, opening his mouth to say something. But the ayrrah arrived in a rush of wings, and in another few moments Eda, Morin, and Tainir were all hurtling on into the silver sky, away from the grasping shadows.

The spirits loomed large behind them, close enough for Eda

to make out dark wings, the glint of talons, the bleached white of their swords. The stench of them choked Eda's breath away.

The ayrrah didn't stop for their midmorning rest. They flew on into the afternoon, as, bit by bit, the spirits gained on them.

All at once, a mountain peak in the near distance emerged through the clouds; it shimmered and danced in the watery sunlight.

The ayrrah flew closer, revealing the mountain's impossibly colorful rock layers, ranging from crimson to cerulean to a deep, rich green, its top a glistering yellow. As they drew nearer still, music curled strange through the air, a chorus of wind pipes and throaty percussion, a tinkling of bells and harsh splatters of lightning. And above it all, a wordless, mighty voice that seemed to shake the world.

Eda glanced over at Morin to see his expression; his face was wide with awe.

Tainir's words echoed in her mind: *Tuer made it for Raiva, in the days before the Stars were plucked down from heaven.* The Singing Mountain.

For a moment, the spirits were forgotten.

The music rose and fell in waves, sometimes deafening, sometimes whisper quiet, but always mesmerizing and impossibly, achingly beautiful. Eda got the feeling that perhaps all of Endahr had been like this, long ago when the One who was before the gods had first formed the earth.

Morin pulled pen and parchment from his pack and started madly sketching the scene in front of them. Tainir opened her mouth to join the mountain in its song, her lips sparking with gold. Eda just stared and stared. She couldn't get her fill.

The ayrrah flew even closer, until Eda could see the thick,

velvety moss that covered the mountain and gave it those impossible colors. Every part of her yearned to stand on that beautiful peak, to let its music seep into her and fill her up, to think of nothing else for the rest of her days.

It seemed the ayrrah were drawn to it, too. Filah shot toward the mountain with terrifying speed; the music swelled to a roar, overwhelming her senses.

And then the spirits broke on them with the strength of a crashing wave, and the music was suddenly cut off.

The world went dark. The smell of decay enveloped her.

Something collided against Filah with a horrific *thud*. And then the ayrrah was screaming and Eda was falling through empty air toward the valley far, far, far below.

Chapter Thirty-Four

E DA PLUMMETED DOWN, DOWN, WITH SICKENING SPEED. She didn't even have the breath to scream and so the terror swallowed her whole and she was helpless and falling and falling.

The last thing she saw would be the Singing Mountain, a blur of color, silenced by the shadows.

She had failed.

Tuer and Rudion had won.

The Circles were broken and there would be no rest for her.

No rest, no rest.

Then all at once a hand closed around her arm and Morin was there, still astride his ayrrah, but his bird was falling, too. One of the spirits was tangled up with him, its bone sword lost somewhere, its clawed hands ripping at the ayrrah's wings. Eda clung to Morin, her fingernails digging into his arm as he struggled to hang on to her. The spirit shrieked and snapped its broken teeth at Morin's head. He ducked in time to save himself, but the spirit's teeth sunk into his shoulder. Eda screamed. Blood ran down Morin's arm.

They fell and fell.

Rock and dirt rushed up to meet them. Eda and Morin, the ayrrah and the winged spirit, collided with the mountain, skidding to a stop in a tangle of earth and blood and feathers.

The spirit leapt back into the air, joining two others who shrieked and spat, their teeth dripping red. They wheeled above the mountain, preparing for another strike.

Morin scrambled to his feet, drawing his dagger, and Eda loosed the knife the Itan priestess had given her from her belt. It was too small to wound the spirits, a needle against dragons. She stood beside Morin, bracing for the attack, trying not to focus on his blood-soaked sleeve.

The spirits pinned their wings to their sides and dove. Eda thrust upward with her blade, but she missed. One of them collided with her, talons raking her shoulders, tearing a line of pain from her neck to her ear.

She scrabbled backward as the spirit bared its broken teeth. *"He told us we may not kill you,"* it hissed. *"But he did not say we may not harm you."*

"Go back to the *void*," she spat, lunging with her knife.

The spirit launched himself backwards into the air, easily avoiding her blow, laughing at her. *"Your companions are not needed. Our lord Rudion only wants you. Their deaths will be your fault, as so many others already are."*

Eda shrieked and leapt from the mountain, grabbing the spirit's taloned feet with one hand as she used the other to plunge her knife into its shadowy breast. The spirit roared in pain. She let go, tumbling back to the ground as it wheeled away from the others and disappeared into the clouds.

Gasping for breath, Eda scrambled back up to where Morin was fighting another of the spirits. There was a jagged scratch down one side of his face, and he was guarding his ayrrah as he fought, the bird too injured to protect himself.

The winged spirits laughed, a sound like steel scraping stone, and gathered themselves to dive again.

Eda stood shoulder to shoulder with Morin, her hand tight around her knife hilt, blood gushing down her hand. She glanced at Morin and he nodded, grim. They couldn't survive another attack.

The spirits rushed toward them, all shadow and malice and clacking bone swords; Eda and Morin raised their puny blades high.

And then something leapt past them and collided with the spirits head on, and the spirits were fighting that something instead of Eda and Morin. Eda stared, dumbfounded.

It took her a moment to make sense of what she saw in the whirl of shadow: the creature who'd come to their defense was a cat of some kind, a leopard perhaps, light colored and spotted, with massive paws and huge sharp teeth.

Morin sagged with relief beside her, and Eda realized that he wasn't surprised by the leopard's presence. He adjusted his grip on the dagger and ran forward to help.

The spirits drew back, screeching and seething and dripping shadow blood, and then they beat their black wings and flew away, leaving Morin and Eda alone with the spotted cat on the mountain. The leopard stared after the spirits, crouched and ready to spring again if they were to return.

"It's all right," said Morin, stepping up to the cat and laying his hand on its shoulders. "They're gone."

"He must have called them back," said Eda. "Rudion must have called them back."

And then the leopard let out a long strange sigh and glinted suddenly with sparks of gold light. Its body stretched and strained and *changed*, and a moment later Tainir laid there, trembling, claw marks raking all down her bare shoulders.

The wind was searing cold on the mountainside, and Morin took off his poncho and pulled it over his sister's head. She shook and shook, unable to get warm.

It was Eda who stumbled about in a daze, gathering wood for a fire, finding flint in her pack, laying the sparks and coaxing them to burn.

It grew swiftly dark, and Morin and Tainir and Eda huddled round the flames, Tainir still trembling uncontrollably. Morin's ayrrah perched with his huge head on Morin's knee, his wide dark wing broken, unusable. Eda's and Tainir's ayrrah were nowhere to be found, and Eda knew, without wanting to know, that they wouldn't be coming back again.

"Tainir's not usually like this when she changes," said Morin, his voice low and tight. "Fighting those spirits has weakened her, like their shadow stuff has poisoned her blood."

And Eda realized that Tainir must have shifted into her leopard form—a snow leopard, Morin told her—almost daily on their journey, every time she disappeared to go hunting. "Our father could change, too," said Morin, as he wrapped his arm around his sister and held her tight. "He did it only rarely, but I saw him once—he transformed himself into a mountain goat. But he didn't like it. He said it made his head feel odd, his thoughts go dim. He was afraid if he changed too often he wouldn't be able to become human again. I was always jealous of Tainir—her changes are usually so effortless."

"But you can talk to birds," said Eda, part of her thinking absently that it turned out Tainir *was* part mountain goat after all.

Morin laughed a little, though his face was creased with worry and pain. "Yes. Yes, I suppose I can."

Eda's eyes went to his torn and bloody shirtsleeve. "You'd better let me have a look at your shoulder."

He let her peel the sleeve away, pull the shirt up over his head. His bare skin pricked with gooseflesh in the frigid night. The cut was jagged, and deep enough Eda glimpsed Morin's bone. Nausea rose acrid in her throat.

Morin peered at his wound in the firelight, and Eda thought he turned a little green.

"Tell me how to fix it," she begged him.

He took a breath, and told her to dig the medical pouch from his pack. "Can you sew?"

A fair question. Empresses definitely did not, but her mother had taught her embroidery as a child. It was different, stitching Morin's flesh back together. Bloody and wet and awful, and she knew with each prick of her needle she was causing him more pain. But finally she pulled the wound closed, and tied off the thread. She bandaged it clumsily, and then helped him pull his shirt on again.

She felt more awkward around him than she had in days.

"Now let me look at you," he said.

She acquiesced, flushing furiously as she shrugged out of her poncho and let him examine the cuts on her own shoulders. She drew off one sleeve, hugging her poncho fiercely to her chest and turning her back to the firelight. She'd never felt more exposed in her life.

"The scratches aren't deep," he assured her after a moment. "The one on your neck is the worst." He smoothed salve on all her cuts with his quick fingers. The salve tingled. Her skin sparked where he touched her. She was relieved to draw her shirt on again, to tie her poncho tight around her throat.

His eyes caught hers across the fire. Something pulsed between them. Something she didn't want to name. She thought of a wicked smile in the ballroom. Hungry kisses on a rooftop. She closed herself off, turned her face away. She was Tuer, shut in the mountain. She wouldn't let Morin be Raiva, calling her name for an eternity in the dark.

"Even with Tainir's help, the spirits should have destroyed us," she said. "Why did Rudion call them off? What are we going to do when they come back again?"

"Maybe it wasn't Rudion," said Morin. "Maybe Tuer was protecting us."

"Tuer doesn't care if I live or die."

Morin raised an eyebrow. "We both know very well that's not true."

She didn't answer.

They passed a fitful night's sleep on the mountainside, Eda and Morin taking turns keeping the fire going while Tainir tossed and turned on the hard ground, tears leaking from her eyes. Eda slept for the few hours before dawn, and woke to find Tainir awake and kneeling beside Morin's ayrrah.

"You're still too weak," Morin protested, hovering over his sister like a mother hen.

But Tainir shook her head. "I have to try. It might already be too late, and he saved you, back there against the spirits. It's the least we can do."

Tainir shut her eyes and put her hands on the ayrrah's broken wing, a song spilling from her lips. Those golden sparks danced around her face as she sang, and the ayrrah's wing knit itself back together, the blood fading from the feathers, the bones growing straight again.

When Tainir finished singing, the ayrrah bowed his head to her, as if she were an Empress, and then he gathered his wings and leapt into the sky.

Tainir crouched back on her heels, looking after him. "He's gone to find the others."

"I hope he does," said Eda, though she knew in her heart he would be searching for them the rest of his life.

Morin gave a sharp nod, his eyes flicking to Eda and then away again. "What now?"

Eda knew the answer to that, too. She hardened herself to it. "I continue on foot, alone. You two go back."

Morin and Tainir exchanged glances.

Tainir shook her head. "We're with you until the end, Eda. We're not leaving you."

"You can't just abandon us on a mountain peak miles and miles from civilization," said Morin, trying for lightness.

It was hard for Eda to look at him. She couldn't stop thinking of his hands, gently spreading salve on her wounds in the flickering firelight. She forced herself to stop, to close herself off to him. "I can't ask that of either of you. I won't ask it."

Morin's jaw went hard. "You're not asking it, Your Majesty. We're offering."

It hurt to hear him call her that, a rigid wall of formality suddenly between them.

Tainir gripped Eda's arm. "We're not discussing this any further. The three of us are stronger together than we would be on our own. We're coming with you. Now. Morin. Do you know where we are?"

Morin glanced once at Eda, as if expecting her to protest further, but she didn't.

She was glad they were coming. She wouldn't have been able to bear it if they'd agreed to her going on alone.

Morin pulled the map out of his pack and unfolded it, tracing their journey along Tuer's Rise with one finger. "The spirits knocked us a little off course, but I think we're past the Singing Mountain here, which just leaves a day's climb that way"—he pointed westward— "until we reach the end of our mother's map."

Eda shivered. "And then?"

"Then we'd better hope we find Tuer's Mountain," he said grimly. "And not tumble off the edge of the world."

It was strange, hiking up the mountains after so many days of flying over them. Strange and awful and *slow*. None of them had breath to spare for talking, so they climbed in silence, winding their miserable way up and up, over a treacherous path of snow and rock. The sky stretched wide above them—it seemed close enough to touch—and the air grew thin. Eda felt like something heavy was pressing against her chest; she couldn't get a deep breath.

Clouds gathered dark and fast, and snow came down in thick, smothering flakes. It grew worse the higher they climbed, until Eda couldn't even see a foot in front of her. Morin had them all stop and put their climbing harnesses on, and then he tied the three of them together with a length of rope before they trudged on into the blinding snow: Morin in front, Eda in the middle, and Tainir behind. Eda was relieved to be tied to Morin with something as solid and tangible as the rope. She wished she could see him, walking just a pace in front of her, but it was enough to know he was there, that the storm wasn't going to rip him away from her.

"I should change into the snow leopard," came Tainir's voice, the wind whipping it strangely around them. "I could lead us."

"We can't afford to have you weakened again," Morin called back. "We can't stop."

Eda knew that was true—they had to go on, had to hope they found shelter before they collapsed from exhaustion.

Not half an hour later they stumbled into a cave on the side of the mountain. It was out of the wind, out of the snow: a miracle. And there was another miracle: a bundle of wood stacked neatly just inside the entrance.

"The gods are watching out for us," breathed Morin.

Anger buzzed down Eda's spine, but she didn't say anything. Morin was right—there was no other explanation for the cave and wood to be there.

Tainir built a fire, and the three of them crouched together around it, their clothes steaming. They drank melted snow and tea. There was no more food in Morin's pack, and neither he nor Eda would even hear of Tainir going hunting.

BEYOND THE SHADOWED EARTH

"I could go," Morin offered.

"Snow leopards are built for the cold," Tainir argued. "You'd just get lost and tumble off the mountain."

"I'd rather go hungry than lose either one of you," Eda interrupted.

Morin jerked his gaze to hers and she was startled to find how much she meant it.

"No hunting, then," he said, and made more tea.

Tainir changed the bandage on Morin's shoulder while Eda poked at the fire and told herself it made more sense for Tainir to tend him, that it shouldn't upset her.

"Neat stitches," said Tainir appreciatively.

Morin caught Eda watching and held her gaze. "Not many people can boast of being stitched up by the Empress of Enduena herself."

"Former Empress," Eda corrected.

"Still." He smiled at her, and it warmed her from the inside.

Night fell somewhere beyond the snowstorm. Tainir sat in the cave's entrance, her back to the fire. She whispered words out into the snow, the thread of her voice tangling with the wind. Gold sparks leapt from her fingers, and Eda thought the gods must be listening. The snow lessened. The wind grew less fierce.

"The spirits are still out there," said Eda as Morin settled beside her. "Still watching us. They'll attack again, when Rudion tells them to."

"They won't touch us." Morin's voice held an easy confidence. "At least, not until we reach the Mountain."

"You really think we'll find it?"

There was a sudden warmth on her knee, and Eda glanced down to find Morin's hand there, his heat reaching even through the thick weave of her trousers.

"The gods are leading us there like a hound on a leash. They brought us to this cave, didn't they? It's not an accident."

"I know."

"Are you scared, Eda?"

At last she turned to face him. There were freckles around his eyes, and she wondered that she'd never noticed them before. "I'm terrified."

"Of failing?"

"Of succeeding."

"Why?"

She stared at his hand, lying so gently on her knee. "Because I don't know if I have the strength for what comes after."

"I'll help you."

She thought of Raiva, wandering in the dark. Of her Barons and Ileem and everything she would have to do to reclaim her throne. She thought of the solitude that would come with her return to power. The loneliness. "Oh Morin. You can't help me."

And she moved away from him, forcing him to drop his hand, putting measured distance between them.

He didn't approach her again that night, didn't attempt to pick up the threads of their conversation.

Her heart cracked. She'd wanted him to.

By the morning, the snow had stopped. The three of them trudged on up the mountain in an eerie hush, and Eda couldn't shake the feeling that something was watching them. Morin hadn't spoken a word to her since they woke up. She tried to tell herself that's what she wanted, but that was a lie. What she wanted was for him to take her arm, to walk beside her, a solid, steady presence. Peace. Strength. But she knew that was not what the gods had for her. That was not what she had for herself.

Tainir kept up a constant stream of ancient Words as they walked, gold glints pouring from her lips. Morin's fingers went constantly to the horn on the cord at his throat. Eda knew he must feel vulnerable, without his ayrrah to call on anymore. She kept her own hand wrapped around the hilt of the Itan priestess's dagger.

As they climbed higher, lights began to flash in the distance, glimmering on and off in shades of blue and violet and green, like lamps lit and then instantly blown out. A jarring music rose on the wind, eerie and high and tangled with screams.

Morin's jaw tightened, and Tainir's face blanched with fear; they saw the lights, heard the awful music, too.

They went on, shoving through rock and snow, struggling ever upward. The wind tore at Eda's hood, slipped under her collar and shot icy, grasping fingers down her neck.

And then she looked up and Niren was peering at her from around a curve in the trail, the hem of her white gown whispering over bare toes.

Eda screamed and stopped short.

Instantly Morin's hands were on her shoulders, his eyes frantically searching hers. "Are you hurt?"

She pointed ahead of them, but Niren's ghost had vanished. The lights winked on and off, the music and screaming jangled in her ears.

"Who did you see?" Morin smoothed his thumbs over her cheeks, his touch tethering her to the mountain.

"I saw my sister." The words were ash in her throat.

Morin nodded. "I've seen my mother around every turn in the trail for the last hour."

"I've been seeing Father," said Tainir beside them, her voice cracking. "Their souls are waiting. They've nowhere to go."

Eda tried to breathe, tried to steel herself for what came next. "Then we must be close. We must be close to Tuer's Mountain and the door to the Circle of the Dead."

Morin nodded, his hands still touching her face. "Let's go find him. Let's go find Tuer."

Chapter Thirty-Five

A STRANGE MOOD SEEMED TO SEIZE ALL THREE of them. They climbed on, up and up, faster and faster. Eda understood now that every time Morin drew a sharp breath or Tainir's jaw hardened, that they were seeing their dead, just as she was seeing hers: Niren, around nearly every bend in the trail. Her parents, flushed with fever. Rescarin, his fingerless hands dripping blood onto the snow. The Emperor, peering at her with sightless eyes, as poison dribbled from the corner of his mouth.

The lights grew brighter on the mountain ahead, sparking to life and no longer winking out, like impossible, multicolored lanterns suspended in thin air. The music rose to a jangling cacophony, and Eda knew it for what it was: a thousand voices singing all at once, every one a different melody, every one adhering to a different time. It was beautiful, and it was horrible, and it seemed strange that it could be both at once.

Night fell behind the clouds, darkness hemming in. There

was no discussion of whether or not to make camp; Eda, Morin, and Tainir just kept desperately, frantically climbing.

And then, without warning, they reached the top of the peak, stepping up into what felt like the sky itself, the music and the lights suddenly vanishing. The clouds had broken apart enough to show a sliver of stars, and the three of them stopped and stared, panting and shivering in the frigid wind.

"There's nothing here." Tainir's voice sounded deafening in the silence. "There's . . . there's *nothing*."

She was right. Beyond the peak there was no stretch of snowy mountain winding downward again. There was only a dark kind of blankness. Like they really had climbed all the way to the edge of the world.

Eda shrugged out of her pack, letting it thud into the snow. She walked slowly toward the blankness, one hand outstretched. She'd only taken a dozen paces when she knocked against something cold and hard. She touched it with both hands, peering into the dark. Morin and Tainir crunched through the snow, coming up behind her.

"Ice," said Eda. "It's a gods-damned wall of *ice*."

She dropped to the ground in a fit of laughter, her whole body shaking. She laughed until she cried, while Morin and Tainir stood staring at the translucent wall in sober, stoic silence.

When Eda grew calm again, Morin flopped down beside her, hugging his knees to his chest.

"We should make camp," said Tainir. "Decide what to do in the morning."

They spread out their bedrolls and crouched on them miserably. There was no wood on the barren peak, and so no possibility of a fire. Tainir didn't offer to go hunting, but Eda didn't even really feel all that hungry. There was a hollowness inside of her, an ache. Nothing more.

Tainir got up and paced toward the ice wall; the thread of her song whispered back to them on the wind.

"The gods wouldn't have brought us all this way only to fail now," said Morin after a while.

"Yes they would," said Eda bitterly. "They've done worse."

Morin regarded her with a sudden intensity that made her uncomfortable. "Have you ever wondered if you've been looking at it all wrong? If it isn't the gods who have done all of this to you?"

"But the deal I made——"

"Maybe it was never about that. Maybe your deal meant something different than you thought it did. Maybe it's just been about you and the gods all along. *Just* you. No one and nothing else."

The thought shattered her, terrified her. She thought maybe he was right, and she didn't know how to answer him.

She watched Tainir walk back and forth in front of the ice wall, glittering gold pouring from her lips.

"I can't let go of my anger," Eda said at last. "I—I don't even want to."

He nodded. "I know."

"And you don't . . . think less of me for it?"

A smile touched Morin's lips. "You don't strike me as the kind of person who cares what other people think."

"But I do." She realized as she said it how *much* she cared. How much she had always cared. She'd never stopped being that nine-year-old child, screaming for a place in the world after her parents' deaths. Longing for affection and meaning and simply to be noticed. Making a deal with the gods and clawing her way onto the throne, just so she could feel wanted. Needed. Necessary to others' lives. And then it had become about control and she was always grasping to hold on to it, grasping and failing because it had never really been hers. All that she'd had was an illusion. An illusion she didn't know if she could ever get back, even if she succeeded in plunging a mythical knife into Tuer's heart.

Morin studied her, reading more in her face than she could ever express. He reached out for her hand and she let him take it, let him clasp it so tightly in hers she could feel the faint echo of his pulse. This time, she didn't pull away.

"I feel like we've come to the end," he said. "That whatever happens tomorrow will be the last thing that ever happens."

She looked back at Tainir, still singing to the ice wall. Suddenly she saw Niren's face, pressed up behind the ice, all awful gray shadow and haunted dead eyes.

Eda shuddered. "Morning can't come soon enough."

Morin rubbed his thumb over her fingers. "Yet as long as it's night, the end isn't here. And no." His eyes found hers. "I don't think less of you. How could I? The gods called you, same as they called me. We're both wrapped up in things beyond . . . well, beyond this Circle of the world."

Another tremor passed through her, and she laid her head on Morin's shoulder, almost without meaning to. She fell asleep that way, her head tucked under his chin, their hands clasped tight together.

In the morning, they tried to break through the ice.

Weak, watery sunlight illuminated the peak, the ice wall

shimmering and shining as it hadn't done in the dark. It stretched out of sight to the right and the left, following the slope of the mountain, and up into the sky, never ending. It was massively thick, and its surface had dips and ripples, as if once it had been a flowing curtain of water that had frozen in an instant. It smelled, strangely, of roses and smoke.

They battered at the wall with their climbing spikes and hammers, throwing all their strength into it.

But nothing happened, not a chip, not a dent.

They couldn't climb it without footholds; they couldn't go around it. For a while they tried digging under it, but no matter how deep they went, the ice was still there, as if it ran all the way through the mountain.

They went back to trying to break through it.

Sweat pricked Eda's shoulders and poured down her face. She cursed and threw her dagger; it hit the ice and bounced back, slicing her cheek. She touched the cut and her fingers came away sticky, red.

Tainir and Morin stopped their own assault on the wall, looking over at her.

Eda wiped the blood off and onto her trousers. "Is this it, then? How it ends? The gods mocking us so close to our goal?"

Morin paced up to her, brushing one hesitant finger along Eda's brow. Eda felt again that faint pulse of heat in her forehead.

"Maybe you should appeal to Tuer," Morin said. "You are gods-touched, after all. Maybe he'll let you in, if you ask."

Eda swallowed another curse and stepped up to the wall. She looked at Tainir. At Morin. She could still feel his heartbeat, pulsing near hers, still feel his breath in her hair, the warmth of his arms when she'd woken up beside him, a crick in her neck from sleeping on his shoulder all night.

"Say something," said Morin.

Tainir nodded. "A Word. A prayer."

Eda didn't know any of the ancient Words, and prayers made her too angry. But she splayed both palms flat against the ice and shut her eyes. "Tuer," she whispered. "Tuer, let me in."

Heat pulsed all at once from her forehead, blazing through her body, down her arms, into her hands. It seared into the ice wall and for one moment, two, nothing happened. And then the ice shattered with a horrific *crack*, the force of it knocking Eda backwards. She ducked her head under her arms to protect herself from the shards of ice flying out in all directions like deadly rain.

"Should have tried that earlier," Morin quipped.

Tainir gave her brother a dirty look.

Eda barely registered them. Because beyond the wall of ice stretched an expanse of snowy ground, and beyond that—

Beyond that stood a plain peak of dirt and rock, wreathed all in clouds, and she knew without a doubt that they'd found Tuer's Mountain.

Eda grabbed her pack and stepped across the shattered ice. She was tight with fear and hope and triumph, and overwhelmed with a desperate need for haste. She broke into a run, feet pounding across the snow, not even glancing back once to make sure Morin and Tainir were following.

The sun rode high in the sky as she ran. The snow turned to

slush and then mud and then bare dirt. Somehow, it was warmer now. She shrugged out of her pack and her poncho, dropping them heedlessly to the ground as she ran on and on.

The ground began to rise again. The clouds melted away. Morin and Tainir kept pace at her heels.

She ran and ran, the mountain growing larger against the sky until she could no longer see the top of it. She felt smothered by the clouds, by something strange on the wind she didn't have a name for.

A jagged crack split the air away to her left and the noxious scent of decay filled her nostrils. A host of spirits flew through on dark wings, jaws gaping, teeth flashing, bone swords raised high.

Eda tore the priestess's knife from its sheath as behind her came a sudden snarl—Tainir, changed into her snow leopard form.

Morin's hand wrapped around Eda's wrist. "We have to run."

They hurtled headlong up the mountain, hand in hand, Tainir bounding beside them on four paws. The spirits pursued them, shrieking and laughing, mere heartbeats behind.

Eda didn't dare look back. She held tight to Morin. They came to a worn stone path, moss growing bright between the cracks, and kept running. The very ground seemed to hum.

The path ended abruptly at a stone doorway that looked into yawning darkness. Eda, Morin, and Tainir skidded to a stop.

Behind them, the winged spirits circled, preparing to attack. But something kept Eda standing there, staring through the gaping entranceway, frozen, unsure.

An ancient altar stood just past the doorframe, a simple plinth of carved stone, with an empty spot at its base where a petitioner could kneel. There had been a cushion there once, perhaps, but it had long since rotted away.

On top of the altar rested a basket of grain, a bowl of wine, and a loaf of bread, all as fresh-looking as if they'd been set there a moment ago, though Eda knew very well that was impossible. Had the gods preserved them, somehow? She felt suddenly foolish, small. She had brought no offering to the god of the mountain. Why did she think he would hear her?

"Do you think you need an offering? You, the god's chosen one?"

She blinked and a shadow stood beside her, black feathers brushing against her arm. She looked up into Rudion's face and he smiled.

Beyond him there was no one else: not Morin, not Tainir, not the host of spirits. Just Eda, and Tuer's Shadow, the altar, and the door to the mountain.

Eda clenched her jaw, her hand wrapping around the priestess's knife. "Why are you hunting me? I'm here. Where you wanted. At the doorway to Tuer's Mountain."

"I'm not hunting you," said Rudion. "I'm driving you. And if my people devour your companions along the way, so be it. What is two less of the race of mankind on the earth? You should have come with me when I asked. Perhaps that would have saved them."

Fear for Morin and Tainir seized her, but she refused to rise to his bait. "Your *people?*"

"The gods cast my fellow spirits into exile. I am merely restoring them to their rightful place."

"With you as their king?"

His crown pulsed brighter. "As you say. But what are you waiting for, little Empress? I think you had better run."

Lightning split the sky and thunder roared, shaking Eda

from her vision. She jerked her head back to see another crack opening in the world, more and more spirits coming through.

"Eda!" Morin cried.

The spirits shrieked, pinning their wings to their sides.

They dove.

Eda grabbed Morin's hand and pulled him through the yawning doorway into Tuer's Mountain, Tainir at their heels.

Part Three

STARLIGHT AND SORROW

At last they reached the doorway to Tuer's Mountain, but a spirit with a burning sword barred their way.

Chapter Thirty-Six

E DA RAN BLINDLY INTO THE DARK, MORIN beside her, Tainir at their backs, her claws clicking on stone.

The spirits came after them, teeth snapping, wings scraping the sides of the passageway. Ahead, there was nothing but blackness.

"Light." Eda breathed it out like a prayer. "Just a little light."

Her forehead pulsed again with heat and started to glow, enough so she could dimly see a foot ahead of her, no more.

She ran faster, and Morin matched her pace, stride for stride.

She glanced back. A mistake.

The spirits were only a heartbeat behind, forced to come one at a time through the narrow passage. One of them leapt at Tainir, who met it head on with a roar, slashing at it with her huge paws.

Morin clung to Eda's hand. They hurtled on.

Whispers echoed far off. Laughter coiled near. Lights flickered into being and winked out again, in shades of violet and blue and green, like they had yesterday out in the snow. Eda thought she saw a blur of faces in the lights, dead eyes, moaning lips.

Terror coursed through her, and she tightened her grip on Morin's hand, nails digging into his skin. She wished they'd had time to put their climbing harnesses back on. She got the feeling the darkness had grown hands and wanted to separate them.

They ran on, their footsteps echoing overloud in the stone tunnel. Tainir loped at their heels, a blur of white.

And then Eda and Morin and Tainir ran through a carved wooden door that slammed firmly shut behind them, an iron bar locking into place across it. The spirits clattered shrieking against the door, scraping it with swords and teeth and talons.

A shadow person stood beside the door—the one who'd shut and locked it. A girl, no older than Tainir and so faded that Eda could see all the way through her. She bowed her shadowy head and pointed on down the tunnel.

They didn't need to be told twice—the door would not hold against the spirits forever. They ran on.

The passageway widened around them. Lanterns sprung up in the dark, illuminating a cavernous hall. Massive stone pillars stretched up from the floor and were lost somewhere far above. More shadowy people crouched behind the pillars, peering at Eda and Morin and Tainir as they raced by. Eda realized they were ghosts, souls lost and wandering with no one to guide them to their rest. Anger twisted sharp between her ribs. She hated that, despite her best efforts, her world had expanded to contain more than her thirst for vengeance. She wanted justice, now. Justice for all these wandering souls, and for the ones she'd killed as well: the Emperor. Rescarin. Niren.

She'd killed them because it suited her. She'd traded their

lives for an Empire. And yet Eda was brazen enough to seek out a god, to demand he answer for his crimes when she had yet to answer for hers.

She kept her gaze fixed ahead as she ran, but she was still aware of the ghosts, more and more of them, leaving their pillars, following silently in line behind her and Morin and Tainir, like the strange wistful tail of a kite.

"Look," said Morin softly, pulling her to a stop. Tainir pressed up warm against the backs of their legs.

They'd come to the end of the hall, where a rectangular wooden door stood shut beneath a carved stone frame. An . . . entity stood beside the door. It was something like a tall silvery figure, its form angular, thin, but at the same time it had no shape. It wavered like water or smoke, the only thing solid about it a pair of fierce bright eyes.

"You have come to the end of the Hall of Memory," said the figure, its voice brittle as ice and piercing as high bells. "You may not go farther."

"You are a spirit." Morin's voice was hushed with awe. "A servant from the beginning of time, one of the few who did not betray the gods."

"I guard the door, by command of the Lord of the Mountain."

Eda set her jaw. "We're here for Tuer. Take us to him."

"The Lord of the Mountain is out of your reach. The doors are sealed. Not even he can pass through."

The spirit brushed a translucent hand across Eda's forehead. She felt that familiar pulse of heat under her skin, and also the faint touch of the spirit's fingers, soft as rain. "You are gods-touched, bright one. There is Starlight in you."

"Starlight?"

"You burn with it. Can't you feel it?"

Eda shuddered where she stood. She thought of the shattered ice wall, the light that had guarded her through the dark. The spot in her forehead grew suddenly, unbearably hot, as if there were a live coal under her skin.

"What god was it who touched you?" asked the spirit. "I have not seen one such as you in millennia."

"I spoke with Tuer's Shadow when I was young."

"It was not Tuer's Shadow—Rudion has not that power. Perhaps one of the gods looked in on you when you were born. Perhaps that is why you do not remember."

Eda brushed its comments off, even though they made her roil with a sense of uncertainty and violation. "If Tuer is behind that door, that's where we're going. Now let us pass."

The spirit seemed to shake its head. "You may pass, bright one. The others may not. They have no Starlight in them. They could not bear to step through that door. It would rip them apart, and not even a Bearer of Souls in all her rightful power could save them."

Morin caught Eda's arm. "You can't go in there alone." There was panic in his face, a desperate helplessness.

She fractured inside, felt every break, every splinter. Her soul cried out for his, but she thought of Raiva, calling Tuer's name in the dark, and she closed herself off. She couldn't do that to him. She *wouldn't*. "I started this journey alone, Morin. It's only fitting I should end it that way, too."

Behind and around them, the throng of ghosts began to scream and wail, and Eda glanced back. Her heart nearly stopped. The dark spirits must have battered down the door in the passageway; they were flooding into the cavernous hall, shrieking with triumph, cutting through the ghosts with their bone swords as they careened toward the greater door. Rudion stood in the midst of them, fire licking his crown and raging all down his sword. His eyes met Eda's. He smiled.

And suddenly Eda couldn't step through. Couldn't leave Morin and Tainir here to face Rudion, and their death. "Morin—"

But his expression hardened. He touched her cheek, the barest pressure of warm fingers against her skin. "Go. Tainir and I will be fine."

"But—"

"I'll see you again." He pushed her, gently, toward the door. He smiled, and the smile broke her yet again. "Go," he said. "Go!"

The dark spirits shrieked and dove at Morin and Tainir, Rudion at their head.

Eda let out a fierce cry and leapt through the door.

Chapter Thirty-Seven

S HE WAS STANDING ON A DARK HILL beneath a sky strewn with stars. Beyond her sprawled a wide, endless land, all hills and valleys and broad-leafed trees that smelled of rich honey and the tang of fire.

It was . . .

It was *beautiful*, and its beauty pierced her through. The darkness was deep, but not all-consuming, and it made her feel strangely at peace. She stretched her free hand out in front of her, her fingertips buzzing at the icy touch of the air. She knew it must be frigid enough to shatter bone, and yet her body pulsed with the heat emanating from her forehead. The cold couldn't touch her.

Starlight, the spirit at the door had told her—there was Starlight inside of her. Her whole body hummed with it.

She descended the hill and strode through a wooded valley, the broad trunks of the honey-fire trees shimmering violet and silver in the faint light emanating from her forehead. She touched one of the trees as she passed, and yanked her hand back with a startled cry—it was sharp as teeth, and blood dripped red from her fingers.

After that, she was more wary.

She walked on and on. The Circle of the Dead grew no less beautiful, but its utter, desolate loneliness cut deeper and deeper until its beauty didn't matter anymore. She wanted to collapse under one of the honey-fire trees and never get up again. But the Starlight compelled her to keep going.

She broke through the forest all at once, and came into a valley that was somehow darker than the wood had been, like the light from the stars far above couldn't reach it. The ground was writhing with shadows. They slithered over her feet like eels, and they stank of moldering stone, of dead, rotten things.

Eda trudged through them as fast as she could, shuddering.

Is this what it would mean to be the Bearer of Souls? To command this domain, know every hill and valley, every shadow, every tree? How good it must feel, to have the power of a goddess at her fingertips. To have a place, a purpose. But how cruel of the gods, to offer her all that in exchange for a lifetime of all-consuming loneliness.

She ran, shadows screaming and flopping to get out of her way. She tread dozens of them under her feet, desperately trying to ignore the pop and squish of them, the thick darkness that splashed all the way up to her knees.

And then she was running out onto a wide desert plain. White sand glittered and flashed, a field of stars stretching endlessly before her.

One of the shadows clung to her boot. She tried to shake it off and fell to her hands and knees. Pain seared through her, and she leapt to her feet again—the sand, like the trees, was sharp. Blood ran down her legs and arms. The light from her forehead wavered.

"Bring me to the door," Eda whispered, nearly sobbing. "Bring me to the door. Please."

She ran on.

A silver ship sailed through the sand in front of her, and it was filled with a host of the dead. They wept and wept, scores upon scores of them. Somehow, Eda knew the ship had been sailing in circles, searching for the door. And she also knew that the dead would never be free, that way.

She ran farther, and saw a mass of silver ghosts walking together across the brutal desert. The awful slithering shadows from the valley were hanging from the ghosts' shoulders, sinking sharp teeth into gray flesh, devouring them unawares.

And Eda knew, as she had known about the ship, that the dead did not feel. That they didn't know the shadows were there. That they would be eaten for all eternity, unless someone showed them the way to the door.

Eda ran past them, agonized. But she couldn't help them, not yet. Not until she found Tuer.

She ran on, through a tunnel of writhing trees and into a great empty darkness. Screams and weeping echoed around her. Chains rattled, unseen creatures hissed and roared. There were more shadows here, and they were larger, tall as men, every inch of their bodies covered with jagged silver teeth.

Groups of dead souls were huddled together, weeping and weeping, because they couldn't find the door, couldn't go to their rest.

In the center of the darkness stood nine shining figures: tall, fierce women, with hair in different shades of cerulean and coral and sea-foam. They circled round a mass of the dead, flaming swords in their hands, fighting back the shadows that sought to devour their charges.

All the dead of the sea, Eda knew, protected by the Billow Maidens of legend. But even they could not hold back the shadows forever. Even they would eventually fall.

And then suddenly Eda was hurtling back out onto the dark hill under brittle stars. It was the same hill, or seemed the same, but she knew it could not be, for the sound of roaring water reached her ears.

And she was not alone.

A woman stood at the brow of the hill, looking down to where the water flowed. Dark hair blew loose past strong shoulders, and bare brown feet peeked out from beneath the hem of a silver gown.

"Niren," Eda breathed.

Her sister turned, and Eda saw her face—haggard, weighed down and aged with sorrow, with fear.

"The door is near." Niren's voice was hollow, expressionless. "I have been waiting for you. Come."

And she turned and descended the hill. As Eda followed her she saw it: a dark river *made* of those vicious shadows, a writhing mass of snapping teeth and hissing jaws.

Niren led Eda to the bank, and Eda balked. "Where are you taking me?"

"The door is in the midst of the river."

"But we'll be devoured."

"There is no other way."

"Then my journey ends here? Eaten in a river in the Circle of the Dead?"

Niren's face went hard. "Even now you think only of yourself.

This story isn't about you, Eda Mairin-Draive. It never was. You took things that didn't belong to you, things you were never meant to have." She brushed cold fingers across Eda's forehead, and the Starlight pulsed hot. "*I* would be devoured if I went into that river. But perhaps you will not. Perhaps the Starlight is enough to save you. Or perhaps you will be eaten. But if you're too much of a coward to even *try*, I'm pushing you in anyway."

Eda took a step backward, afraid of the darkness in Niren's eyes, afraid of *Niren*. For the first time since she had entered the Circle of the Dead, Eda felt the cold. She stared at her sister, and ached. "I'm sorry. For everything I did to you in life. For bargaining you away to the gods. For dragging you to the capital. For forcing you to be my friend. And you're right. If I don't go in there—" Eda glanced at the writhing river. "If I don't, all this will be for nothing."

Niren gave a sharp, final nod. "Then go. While there is still time."

Eda wanted to pull Niren into an embrace, to cling to her and weep with her and tell her they were really sisters. But Niren was like a stranger here, as cold and unreachable as a god.

Eda bowed to her, very low, and then stepped past her, pacing down the bank and into the river.

Instantly the shadows were on her, jagged teeth tearing into her legs, her arms, her sides. They tugged her down, down, pulling her under the shadowy current. She couldn't breathe, or see, or hear. Terror and pain burrowed deep. In another moment the shadows would swallow her whole. In another moment, she would be lost forever.

But her hand found the priestess's knife, and she thrashed it about, slicing through the shadows. She fought her way to the surface again.

Still the shadow creatures twisted and shrieked and tore at her flesh. Slimy clawed fingers closed around her throat. Poison crept into her veins.

And then something compelled her to touch her forehead. Her body blazed with heat, with light. It poured out of every part of her.

The shadows screamed in agony and fell away like so many husks.

Blood poured down her arms and back and legs. The heat of the Starlight could not quench her all-consuming pain.

But before her stood a doorway, carved in stone and pulsing with the same light that burned inside of her.

She shook the dead shadows from her feet, and stepped through the second door.

Chapter Thirty-Eight

"*E*DA? EDA, ARE YOU LISTENING? SOMETIMES I swear on Tuer himself I don't know *where* your mind goes."

Eda turned from the window, where she'd been looking down at the sea. She'd lost herself for some moments in the mesmerizing waves, watching them break with white foam on the rocks. She must have slipped into some kind of daydream, but not the pleasant kind. The kind filled with darkness and shadows and fear. She didn't want to think about it.

So she smiled at her father and hopped down from the windowsill, climbing onto his lap and cuddling with him in his favorite chair. It had been a lovely day and tomorrow would be just as lovely. It was spring, and her father wouldn't be leaving to give his report to the capital for some weeks yet. Her mother was happy in her garden, so Eda mostly had him all to herself.

"Such a sad story, Father," said Eda, tucking her head under his chin. She listened to his heartbeat.

"Erris should not have made a deal with Tuer that he didn't

understand," her father said gravely.

"Still," Eda murmured, "Tuer must have known what Erris meant. He didn't *have* to be so cruel."

"No. I suppose he did not. But that is the way of the gods, my love. Their ways are different than ours."

"Their ways are cruel."

They shoved her screaming into the carriage. She fought and kicked. She sank her teeth into her newly appointed regent's arm and bit him, hard. Rescarin swore and slapped her face, twisted her arm, told her he'd chop off every one of her fingers if she wouldn't be still, if she wouldn't let Baron Lohnin take her back to Eddenahr.

She was still.

The carriage rattled away and she didn't cry. Her dead parents were to be buried tomorrow, and no one had thought that she should attend their funeral. No one remembered she was a child whose parents had died. She was simply an inconvenience. A nuisance.

Lohnin dozed in the carriage on the seat across from hers. His spittle caught in his beard. She hated him almost as much as she hated Rescarin. She thought about what it might be like to kill Rescarin. To take a knife and drive it straight into his heart. His eyes would grow dim, like her parents' had. He wouldn't bother her anymore. She could go home.

But she didn't think she could kill him. There would be a lot of blood, and she didn't like blood. And besides, killing was an offense against the gods, and the gods were the only ones who could help her now.

She was careful of the words she spoke to Tuer when he came to her in her family's temple, her knuckles aching and bloody where she'd pounded them against the stone altar. "My life in service," she promised him, "to make me Empress in my lifetime." She was proud of that last phrase. Erris hadn't thought to make any such addendum, and look where that had gotten him.

But she hadn't thought Tuer would ask for anything more.

She hadn't thought he would ask for Niren, whom she loved best in all the world.

In one heartbeat, she decided.

In the next, she bargained away the life of her friend.

She celebrated her sixteenth birthday in the evening alone in her small palace room. No one knew, or no one cared, and her passage to womanhood went wholly unnoticed. She slipped from her balcony and climbed up onto the roof. She lay back onto the tiles, feeling the latent heat of them burn her shoulders through her thin silk top. She stared up at the sky.

She had waited for the gods. Waited and waited for them to uphold their end of the bargain. But her years in the palace had slid unremarkably by. She was no closer to being Empress than she was when she first made her vow.

She had decided to stop waiting. The crown prince had died that morning in a hunting accident, and with the Empress almost a decade gone herself and the Emperor unlikely at this point to remarry, there would be no more heirs. It was rumored that Eda herself was the Emperor's illegitimate daughter, and though she had found no proof of that, she could use it to her advantage.

Perhaps the gods had been waiting on her all this time. They'd given her the pieces she needed. She just had to act.

She drew a small vial from the pocket concealed against her breast, and studied it in the moonlight. It was odd, to hold a man's death in her hands.

The room was hot. Stifling. The Emperor lay dead beside her, his body already stiffening. She looked at him without regret and stood from her chair, calling for her attendants to make her resplendent. A sense of rightness burned in her; this is what was owed to her, this is what the gods had promised. She went to take what was hers.

She was climbing a cliff, driving spikes into the rock. Sweat dripped down her back even though the air was frigid. There was music on the air, brimming bright with gold. There were wings beneath her, wide and warm.

She was wandering through the dark and the shadows had teeth. They sank into her, gnawing her ankles down to bone. But a light in her burned and burned. It drew her onward.

She stood on a high mountain, the sun blazing hot above her, the wind slicing through her thin frame. She was hollowed out by age and time. Her body was frail, brittle. She could feel the life in her ebbing away, bit by bit. But she had wanted to see this view one last time: the sun from the mountains. Tears streamed down her face but she didn't mind them. They dampened her cheeks and made her think of her life, everything she had done and undone. Every wrong she had righted.

"The gods can take me, now," she whispered. "I am ready to travel the Circles once more. I am ready to go home."

And she shut her eyes and let herself fall from the cliff, fall and fall, as Uerc had done long ago.

The air rushed past her. It was time, and she welcomed it.

She fell and fell. Her heart rushed into her ears. Darkness folded over her, and she was screaming.

She lay in the dark.

The shadows had teeth.

They were eating her.

She couldn't get free.

Chapter Thirty-Nine

"EDA, ARE YOU LISTENING? SOMETIMES I SWEAR on Tuer himself I don't know *where* your mind goes."

Eda turned from the window, where she'd been looking down at the sea. She'd lost herself for some moments in the mesmerizing waves, watching them break with white foam on the rocks. She must have slipped into some kind of daydream, but not the pleasant kind. The kind filled with darkness and shadows and fear. She didn't want to think about it.

And yet—and yet she *must* think about it.

She hopped down from the windowsill and passed her father's chair, wandering out into the rest of the house, that sense of darkness pressing down and down.

She stepped through the door into a world of swirling shadow. There was no sun, no wind. The sky was dark and writhing. The grass was brittle underneath her feet.

She turned back to the house but it crumbled away at her touch, falling to dust.

She stood alone in a whirling void, the darkness clawing at her hair, her clothes. She bowed her head and fought her way forward. She knew she could not stand still—she would be ripped apart.

She walked for an eternity, and another after that, and she thought she saw ahead of her a glimmer of shadow, but not the kind she feared. It was luminous somehow, and she knew she was meant to follow it.

She did, quickening her pace, desperate not to lose the shadow into the nothingness of the void. It turned back, once. She saw sad eyes in a kind face, and she remembered stepping through the door into the Circle of Time, jumping from memory to memory. She remembered her journey. She remembered herself.

"Wait!" she cried, as the shadow turned away from her again and winked out like a candle flame. "Please wait!"

But the shadow had brought her where she was meant to be: a wide green valley, mountains stretching above her to graze the brilliant sky.

Before her was a patch of grassy earth mounded with stones, a throne in the midst of them, a man sitting on it.

It was then that she remembered everything.

The man's hair and beard were white as wool, pooling about his shoulders and all down his lap onto the grass. His clothes were the barest bits of rags, but there was a crown on his head. His startlingly blue eyes stared into nothing.

Her gaze dropped to his knees. A knife rested there in a tooled leather scabbard, the edges seeming to glow with a faint light. The handle was made of a twisted white wood, roughly hewn.

Lumen's knife. The godkiller.

Eda knelt beside the throne, hesitant fingers curling around the scabbard. The man on the throne didn't stir. He hardly breathed. He didn't seem to know or care that Eda was there, claiming the knife forged to kill a god. Perhaps he'd never known Lumen had laid it there in the first place.

Her pity twisted sharp. "Oh Erris. You poor fool. I'm going to stop Tuer, and heal the world and free us both from the deals we never should have made. Thank you, for keeping this safe for me all these years." And then she bowed very low, as to the king he'd wanted so badly to be, and stepped back.

She was once more alone in a whirling void.

Shadows spun about her feet, leapt at her, sank their teeth into her arms.

She shook them off and broke into a run, drawing Erris's knife from its scabbard, holding it out in front of her. It buzzed and grew warm, bright, the godkiller's light piercing through the void, illuminating her way.

Hands reached out for her in the darkness, snatching at her sleeves and her heels. She shook them off again and again, but one hand grabbed her jaw, forcibly turned her head.

And Eda found herself staring into her own eyes.

She screamed and scrabbled backward, but the other her followed, grabbing her arm. "You have not seen it all," the other her hissed. "You have not seen all the seconds of your life, every drop of memory, every breath, every tear, each creating one of us. And now you are here with us forever, and we will lead you through your memories for all of Time. Come, come!"

From the shadows of the void stepped thousands of figures that were all Eda, every one wearing a white gown trimmed with silver, every one reaching out for her.

"Get away!" Eda cried, raising the godkiller.

But her other selves didn't fear the knife. They surrounded

her, swept her up like a shell in the tide, and hurtled her forward.

"Come see, come see!" they shrieked all together, laughing as they ran.

Eda struggled and screamed, but she couldn't get free.

Her other selves brought her through the void to a dark field thick with shimmering pools, and as they came close, Eda saw that the pools brimmed not with water, but memory. *Her* memory.

Gleefully, her thousand selves plunged her into one.

She was being born, her mother screaming, the goddess Raiva watching the birth. The goddess brushed her fingers across Eda's forehead as the midwife laid her into her mother's arms. And Eda cried and cried, because heat seared through her, her whole body burning.

She was thrust up and out of the pool, gasping for breath, and her thousand selves plunged her into another.

Her father was telling her stories as the wind blew up from the sea. "Eda, are you listening?"

A desperate gulp of air, another pool.

She poisoned the Emperor.

Another.

She sent Talia away.

Another.

She ordered the guards to cut off Rescarin's fingers.

Another.

She was falling and falling from a high cliff, a witness to her own death.

Her thousand selves never stopped, never slowed, hurtling her out of one pool and into the next until she couldn't comprehend what she saw or what she felt or even who she was. Pain seared her. She was being pulled apart, bit by bit, unraveling one thread at a time. Soon, there would be nothing left.

But her thousand selves kept going, an unstoppable tide. Time crushed her. She couldn't break free.

Another pool closed over her head. She couldn't bear another memory. She shut her eyes. *No more, no more*, she thought. She gave herself over to oblivion.

A light shone suddenly before her, piercing and bright, and a hand that was not her own closed around her wrist.

She was pulled suddenly, violently upward, and flung upon a grassy bank, where she lay sobbing for breath. She shook and shook, and then she lay still. The gods had mercy after all. They had let her die.

"You are not dead, daughter of dust."

Eda lifted her head to see the goddess Raiva standing between two of the awful memory pools, wind stirring through her hair and gown. "I am sorry," said the goddess. "I did not mean to let you wander here for so long." And she reached out and pulled Eda to her feet.

Eda stared at Raiva, still trembling, and wiped the tears from her face. Somehow, she still held tight to the godkiller. She hadn't lost it in the wretched pools. "You saved me." Eda's voice was as shaky as the rest of her.

"Yes, child." The goddess smiled, wan and sad. "Come. It is a foolish thing to say in this Circle, perhaps, but time grows short. And there is yet more that you must see."

Raiva turned and paced between the memory pools and Eda followed, careful to step just where the goddess stepped and nowhere else. She could still feel the grasping fingers of her other selves and was not even tempted to look into any of the pools.

The goddess led her to a shadowy tree that stood in the center of the field, and Eda gasped, overwhelmed by its beauty and its sorrow.

"You know it," said Raiva.

"The Immortal Tree. Planted by the One at the beginning."

"It is a memory only, as all things are, in time. But it is all that is left of the Tree now, in any Circle of the world, and so I think it beautiful. Come. Touch the Tree. See what it will show you."

Eda looked from the goddess to the Tree and back again. She raised her hand, laid it gently on the trunk.

A vision enveloped her with the strength of the memory pools, pulling her under, drowning her.

There was a great darkness, the three Stars flaring to life, Endahr formed in the midst of them. Then the world came into being, the Tree, young and strong and shining. Tuer stood on his mountain, joy and pride searing through him. She felt his strength, felt his awe at the life he was given, the world he was made to command.

The other gods and goddesses came forth. They lived and thrived beneath the Tree. Tuer's heart was fixed on Raiva; he longed to dwell with her among her trees and be a part of her song forever.

The spirits sprang to life, thousands upon thousands of them, each formed with a drop of Starlight, no two quite the same. There were some with wings and some with scales and some with both. There were dark spirits and bright spirits and shadow spirits. Every one was beautiful. One bowed at Tuer's feet and pledged himself into the god's eternal service.

And then mankind awoke beneath the shadow of the Tree. They grew and flourished. But they became discontent, longing to see more of the world. A boy called Tahn stole a seed from the Tree, meaning to carry it west and build a life apart from the gods.

Tuer seared with rage at the boy's rebellion. He struck Tahn down, grinding him back into the dust, his blood seeping into the earth.

Men and gods warred against one another. Death crept into the world.

And Tuer mourned. His sorrow was piercing and dark. It ate at him.

Ages of the world spun away. The god went into his mountain, creating the Circles as he went. She felt his pain and his agony. Felt the silence in the Circle of Sorrow, felt his overwhelming despair as he sent his Shadow away from him, out into the world to do his bidding.

The vision ripped away from her like a knife from a wound and Eda wrenched back from the memory of the Tree, gasping. Her face was damp with tears she didn't remember shedding.

Raiva met her eyes, face drawn with sorrow. The goddess brushed her fingers over the trunk of the shadowy Tree, and a doorway appeared, illuminated in silver. "This is the way to the one you seek, the last door. Do what I cannot. Free him. Heal the breach. Unlock the Circles. And if you cannot do that either—" The goddess's eyes snagged on the godkiller. "Then do what you must."

Eda stared at the door, the knife trembling in her hand. "Why would you show me all that? How can I face Sorrow, when it's even bigger than Time?"

"That you might understand him a little better," said Raiva gently. "And because it needn't be. Now go. Time grows very short."

For a moment, Eda didn't move, helplessness and panic tangled up inside of her. Tuer was only a door away.

She bowed to the goddess, tightened her grip on the godkiller, and stepped into the Tree.

Chapter Forty

E DA STOOD BEFORE AN IRON GATE IN a high stone wall, illuminated only by the knife in her hand. Behind and on either side of her was a horrid nothingness that she knew somehow would swallow her whole if she stepped into it, no matter how much Starlight flowed through her veins.

There was only one way to go.

Eda pushed on the gate. It creaked open, and she went into the earthen passageway beyond, the godkiller casting eerie shadows on the floor and walls. There seemed to be no ceiling, but neither was there any sky—just that same hungry nothingness, kept uneasily at bay by the gate and the passage.

In the darkness ahead of her, someone was weeping, the anguished cries of the utterly hopeless. Eda set her jaw against the noise—she was not about to let Sorrow consume her, not now when she was so close to her goal.

She hurried down the passageway, her footsteps echoing on the hard-packed earth. Eyes watched her from the wall above;

she thought she heard the whir of feathers, the clack of claws. Another voice joined in the weeping, somewhere ahead—a man's voice, brittle and broken.

She went faster, running past the openings to several new passages that branched off the main one.

And then she saw Niren just ahead, the hem of her silver gown whispering over the stone.

Eda cried out and ran to catch her.

"Niren!" Eda stumbled into an alcove that she recognized with confusion as Niren's sitting room, back in the palace. Rain poured outside the window, and Niren sat at a carved ebony table, sipping tea. The air was rich with moisture and the scent of cardamom.

Contentment settled over Eda—Niren was here, alive, well. Tuer's Mountain was nothing more than a bad dream.

And yet there was anger in Niren's eyes. She rose from the table, her hands shaking. She was holding a silver chain that dragged along behind her on the ground—a chain made of sorrow. Without a word, she paced toward Eda and hung the chain around her neck.

Then both Niren and the room wavered, disappeared, and Eda was standing alone in the dark of Tuer's Mountain, something scrabbling in the blackness behind her.

The chain was heavy and bitterly cold, and no matter how hard she tried, Eda couldn't seem to shrug it off. She started running again, as fast as she could with the chain weighing her down.

Behind her, wings scraped stone. Beaks clacked. Something gave an awful shriek. Talons grasped her shoulders, digging down to bone. She yelped and slashed blindly above her with the godkiller, and whatever creature had grabbed her let go again.

She glanced back as she ran to see a mass of dark carrion birds filling the passage. They had long necks and blood red, featherless heads. Their black wings oozed shadow that pooled hissing on the floor and they watched her with cruel, sneering eyes.

And then she slammed hard into a packed earthen wall—the abrupt dead end to the passageway. She fell backward, all the wind knocked out of her.

The carrion birds crept toward her, claws clacking on the ground. *"A labyrinth,"* they hissed all together. *"She did not know. She did not count the turnings. She's caught like a rat in Tuer's maze. Her sorrow will taste so sweet. So sweet."*

Eda scrabbled to her feet again, and raised the knife high as she barreled back the way she came.

The carrion birds screamed, flapping their awful wings and flinging themselves away from the godkiller's light.

She ran, trying not to feel the icy sorrow of the chain that seemed to be sinking into her soul. She turned right at the first passage she came to, then left into the next one. The birds had spoken truly: she had not counted the turnings. She didn't know which passages might lead her back out, and which ones led to the center of the labyrinth, where she was sure Tuer was waiting.

All she could do was keep running.

Suddenly, her surroundings shifted a second time, and she found herself in the palace dungeon. Rescarin lay on the floor of his cell, cradling his fingerless hands against his chest as his forehead poured with sweat, with fever. Eda hated the guards for not doing a better job tending his wounds. She hated herself for her careless order to mutilate him. But even more than that she hated that she cared that he was dead. That his death was *her fault.*

Rescarin forced his trembling body upright, a silver chain in his bloodied palms. He draped it around her shoulders and was gone, the dungeon fading with him.

The darkness was deeper than before, the chains too heavy to allow her to run. So she walked, as quickly as she could, down another passage and then another. She felt the weight of Tuer's Mountain, the weight of Tuer's sorrow. Behind her came the scrape and clack of the carrion birds.

She wasn't surprised when her surroundings shifted a third time and she stepped out onto a terrace that overlooked the palace rose garden. She was glad to get out of the dark, away from the carrion birds, if only for a few moments. It was a fierce, hot day, the sun high in the sky, and the Emperor was lounging in a woven reed chair, a pair of attendants holding an awning over his head. He was younger than she'd ever seen him, not yet twenty, and she was surprised to find him almost strikingly handsome. His dark hair curled slightly over his ears, and his beard was neatly trimmed. A shrewdness shone from his eyes, and a lazy smile curled on his lips.

He beckoned her over. Eda went, and sat at his feet on a thick orange cushion.

"Your aspirations do you credit, my dear. I always admired you, you know. I wished you were mine. I would have instructed you. Groomed you. Taught you how to rule the Empire and not lose it." He gave her an admonishing glance.

"It's not like *you* held onto it," Eda grumbled.

"Only because you poisoned me, my dear. An interesting choice. I thought the sores in my mouth were making my food taste odd, not the other way around." He shrugged, and took a long drink from his wine goblet. "Live and learn, I suppose. Or rather, die." He laughed more than his strange joke merited, and it took him a moment to sober up again. "The point is, you took something that did not belong to you. And now you must pay the price."

"The gods promised me the Empire. I made a deal with them."

"Ah, yes. But it is a tricky thing, is it not, dealing with the gods?"

Eda fidgeted on her cushion. "I held up my end of the bargain. They didn't hold up theirs. And in any case—" She jerked upright and paced over to the balcony, wrapping her free hand around the sun-warmed stone railing. "In any case, what did the gods even do for me? *I* bargained with and bribed my supporters. *I* forged documents and mixed the poison into your food. *I* got rid of Talia and built the temple and rescued Niren—"

"You mean 'killed Niren,' I suppose."

Eda wheeled on him. "I *saved* her. And then the gods took her anyway."

"Hmm," said the Emperor. "That's one way of looking at it."

"And what's another?" Eda spat.

The Emperor's face creased with pity. "That you are a scared, lost child, who threw a fit when she didn't get what she wanted. The gods don't exist to *do* things for us. They exist to guide us, to shape the world, to keep it, as the One instructed them at the beginning. They do not bow to our whims. They don't care if we build temples or carve statues or sing hymns. They care for the things of their own domain, and they expect us to care for ours."

"My domain was taken from me."

The Emperor shrugged. "And so was mine, but you don't see me whining about it." He took another draught of wine. "Just take care, my dear, that the thing you think you're seeking is not the thing you actually find."

He rose from his chair, another chain lying silver in his palms. He seemed almost apologetic as he hung it around her neck. "I wish you hadn't poisoned me. We could have had so many things to talk about."

And then the Emperor and the terrace were gone.

The chains were so heavy now she could barely walk. She shuffled forward, angry at the dark of the labyrinth, terrified of the carrion birds whose wings came quick behind.

She went on, her chains scraping against the stone, and then she was stepping into her childhood bedroom, a window looking out to sea, the waves crashing white on the shore. Her books were there, stacked on shelves, and lined up in neat rows in front of the books were her wooden toy soldiers that her father had carved for her and her mother had painted. Eda had given them needles for swords and sewn tiny blue sashes for them, so they looked like the Emperor's Imperial Guard.

Her parents stepped in, death clinging to their wasted bodies. They held shimmering chains in their hands, and their faces were drawn and angry.

Pain stabbed under Eda's ribs. "What wrong have I done you?"

"You lived," said her father.

"And we died," said her mother. "We are trapped forever because of you, and so you shall be also."

They hung their chains on her, wrapping them round her arms and legs.

She sank to her knees.

Her parents vanished, but the room did not.

Another figure appeared before her, his back bent with

long sorrow—Niren's father, nearly a decade gone, now. Chains weighed heavy in his hands. For an instant, Eda didn't understand why he was there. And then she looked into his eyes and saw her own eyes staring back at her, and remembered. Because he was her father, too.

He wrapped his chains around her head, over her eyes and ears and nose. The room at last faded and she lay gasping on the ground in utter darkness. The chains bit into her skin, crushed her bones.

But that wasn't why she writhed in agony, weeping until there were no more tears and then heaving dry, wracking sobs.

She felt, for the first time in her life, the full weight of the sorrow she had inflicted on those around her. It ate at her, ate and ate, until she wanted to die but she *couldn't* die because the chains were binding her to life, binding her to the sorrow so that she could never escape, so that she must feel every grief, every pang until the end of time itself, and beyond.

Because sorrow is greater than everything, even time.

Dimly, she was aware of the sound of wings, of an awful, hissing laughter.

"Her sorrow is so sweet. So sweet. Let us taste it. Let us gorge ourselves."

The carrion birds leapt at her, talons locking around her arms and legs, hooked beaks tearing into her flesh as if her chains were not even there.

Pain burst hot in every part of her, a deep, soul-rending *agony*.

Her vision blurred. The carrion birds crushed her as they devoured her, grinding her body into the stone.

She was drowning in chains and feathers, and she couldn't

even scream, because when she opened her mouth she tasted dark wings.

Pain and sorrow, sorrow and pain. There was nothing else, and there could be nothing else, because she had left Death far behind her. There was no way back.

And then a hand, closing round her wrist, pulling her up through the gnashing birds as Raiva had pulled her from the memory pool.

But it was not Raiva who stood there.

It was the man from her dream, long ago in the holding cell in Evalla. Gnarled, ropey scars ran all down his face and arms. His eyes were piercing, dark, his grip steady.

The carrion birds shrank before him. "Be gone," he commanded them. "You do not belong to this Circle of the world, nor any other. Go into the void, and there be undone."

The birds hissed and screamed but did as they were bidden, gathering their wings and hurtling into the nothingness above the passageway.

"Come," said a deep voice. "I will lead you through the labyrinth."

She could not stand on her own; the chains were too heavy. She crumpled back to the ground, peering up at the scarred man between the links of sorrow. "I cannot move," she said, utterly wretched.

The man smiled at Eda, though his expression was sorrowful. "Do not fear, daughter of the dust. I know you cannot—I will carry you."

And he scooped her up into his arms, chains and all, as if she weighed no more than a handful of jasmine flowers. He carried her on through the labyrinth.

"They are not heavy, you know," said the scarred man.

"What are not?"

"The chains. They are your sorrows, and so the only one they weigh upon is you."

Eda shut her eyes, tried to shut out the pain, but she couldn't do it.

The scarred man seemed to walk for an eternity. At last he stooped beneath a wooden doorway, and bore her into a vast dark hall.

He vanished like smoke and she tumbled to the ground, landing painfully on hard stone. Her chains, like the scarred man, were suddenly gone.

She could see nothing either ahead or behind her, but the sound of someone weeping drew her deeper into the chamber.

And she knew, without even having to see him, that it was Tuer, chained somewhere ahead in the dark.

She gripped the hilt of the godkiller, and went to find him.

Chapter Forty-One

A SHADOWY LIGHT FLICKERED SOMEWHERE IN THE DARK hall, enough to illuminate the host of mirrors in the center of it, and the god who knelt weeping before them, hung with chains.

Eda sheathed the knife, not wanting Tuer to see she had it, and paced up next to him.

There were hundreds of mirrors, perhaps thousands—she couldn't see properly in the shifting light—and they looked into peoples' lives like the pools in the Circle of Time had looked into Eda's memories. In one, a woman clung to a boy's bloodied body, sobbing. In another, a girl in a drawing room clutched a letter that clearly contained ill news. In yet another, an old man held the hand of an old woman who lay shuddering on a thin mattress piled high with blankets; silent tears ran down the old man's face.

Eda couldn't bear to look very long into any of the mirrors, but she found she couldn't wholly look away. She saw a young boy crying over his dog who'd been slain by a bear. A girl standing stoic as she watched the man she loved wed someone else. Two Itan girls kneeling in a mountain temple, pleading for the gods to bring their father safely home.

But there were smaller sorrows, too: broken limbs and lost toys, grownup children striking out on their own and leaving their parents in empty, echoing houses. A flower, dying in the heat of the sun. Loneliness.

"All the sorrows of the world," came Tuer's voice, low and heavy at her ear.

Eda jumped and turned.

The god of the mountain, on his knees, was taller than Eda. His hair was white as snowy peaks, his skin speckled gray like stone. His eyes were a startling, vibrant green.

"All the sorrows of the world are my fault," said the god. "And so I sit here, and watch them, so I will understand the gravity of what I have done. So I will feel every wound and every tear. The One did not see fit to punish me. And so I punish myself."

Eda stared at him, the old anger rushing back. "You did this to *yourself*? Locked the Circles? Trapped the Dead? The world is tearing itself apart because of you!"

"I bound myself to the world's sorrow—those are the chains that keep me here. I cannot be free of them, even if I wished to be. Locking the Circles happened by accident. I never meant to trap the Dead, never meant to poison the world."

"The world is *dying*! Spirits are breaking through the cracks, escaping from the void where they were banished. Your Shadow—Rudion—is leading them. They're murdering people. Devouring life."

"Soon they will swallow the sun."

Eda followed Tuer's gaze to one of the mirrors, which showed a score of the winged spirits attacking a village by the sea. Bodies were strewn like rag dolls on the beach; the spirits' bone swords dripped crimson. She had to shut her ears against the screaming. "THIS IS ALL YOUR FAULT!"

"Yes, it is." Tuer crouched back on his heels, watching her sadly. Knowingly.

Eda paced around him, itching to draw the knife and be done with it, but she didn't have her answers yet, and she forced her hand to be still. "Why did you make Rudion call me here? Why did you take Niren and the Empire from me? *Why*, when I did everything you asked? I built you a temple. I began the priesthood again. I would have reinstated religion across the Empire if you'd given me a chance. Instead—instead, you ripped everything away. My husband, my home, my country, my—my *sister*—"

"You did not do everything I asked," said Tuer quietly.

Eda wheeled on him. "Yes. I did."

He shook his great head, a strange light of humor in his eyes. "It was never about the Empire. It was never really about Niren. It was always about you, Eda Mairin-Draive. All the sorrows of the world play endlessly before me, and sometimes, they allow me to see the future. And so I knew you would make a bargain with me. I knew that, in your mind, I would fail you. And I knew that it would make you so angry you would be compelled to journey all this way. To find me. To have your revenge."

"So you could make me the next Bearer of Souls," Eda snapped. "I know."

"The Bearer of Souls?" Tuer frowned. "You are not the Bearer of Souls."

Something wrenched inside of her, and Eda grew suddenly

still. "Then who is?"

"Niren, of course. The gods chose her as the Bearer long ago. I thought you had figured that out by now. I allowed you to think you were sacrificing Niren, when you promised her to me as earnest, but the gods would have taken her without regard to any deal you did or did not make. Niren's life was never yours. It was never hers. It always belonged to the gods."

Eda's world shifted sideways. "She deserved a choice."

"And she was given one, but that does not concern you, little one."

"Don't call me that. I'm not a child anymore."

"Dearest, you are all children to me."

She scowled at him, her nails digging hard into the hilt of the godkiller.

"When I came here, centuries ago, I did not realize what my self-punishment would inflict on Endahr. I did not know that with every strand of sorrow I drew from the world and bound to myself I chipped away at the doors I had made, until they shut and locked and could not be opened again, not even by the Bearer of Souls. They've been sealed twenty years, now. But Raiva made a plan, as Raiva always does."

Pain creased the god's forehead, but Eda's anger only grew.

"Did you know she's tried to free you countless times? Did you know she's come here, sat with you, knelt with you, wept with you? That she couldn't find a way to free you?"

"I know," said Tuer heavily. "Of course I know. I can see her light, always. It gives me strength. But there is only one way to free me, and I would never ask it of her, so I pretend I cannot see her. I pretend I do not know she is there, because if she knew— if she knew, she would sacrifice herself for me in an instant.

There are many sorrows I can endure, many pains I could bear, but I could not bear that."

Eda hated the pity that twisted through her, almost as much as she hated him. "Why is *your* sorrow, *your* suffering, more important than anyone else's? Why would you not allow her to free you, when it could unlock the doors and heal the cracks in the world and stop the spirits from leaking out? How can you be so SELFISH?"

"What will you do, little one, when you have killed me?"

Eda realized she'd drawn the godkiller by accident. It wavered before her, its light flashing white-hot. She gritted her teeth. "When you are dead, I will journey back the way I came. I will return to Enduena, and raise an army, and take back my Empire. I will pull your temple down stone by stone and burn whatever is left to ashes. Because the people do not need the gods. They only need themselves and their Empress. I will lead them into a golden age. I will conquer all the world, and it will bow to me."

"And that will make you happy?"

The god's quiet voice echoed oddly in the vast chamber. Eda stared at him, biting her lip so hard she tasted blood. "Why did you call me? WHY DID YOU CALL ME?"

With infuriating calm, Tuer picked up the threads of his story. "Raiva made a plan. The gods chose the next Bearer of Souls as she grew in her mother's womb. In centuries past, the Bearer was given a pendant imbued with Starlight, which she has always used to unlock the doors. But when the doors were sealed, the pendant no longer worked. Raiva planned to draw some of the Starlight from her own soul and put it into the Bearer—into Niren—on the day of her birth."

The truth was beginning to dawn on Eda with an awful,

twisting horror. She thought of the memory she'd seen in the Circle of Time, of Raiva, touching her forehead the instant Eda entered the world. "Raiva didn't put the Starlight inside of Niren. She put it in me instead."

"I could see the future, and I knew it must be you who came to me. I sent my Shadow to distract Raiva, to keep her here in the mountain until the day of Niren's birth had already passed. She went to Evalla on the day of *your* birth, and she thought—"

"She thought I was Niren." Eda brushed her fingers across her forehead, and heat pulsed through her. "It was a mistake. All of this was a mistake. I'm not important and I never was. I'm here on the whim of a mad god, who spends centuries weeping over the sorrows of the world instead of getting up and *fixing them himself.*"

"Child, I told you. I cannot get free. And it wasn't a mistake. Not really."

"If Raiva had put the Starlight in Niren, the Circles would be unlocked. The Dead would be free. There would be no tear in the world, no spirits devouring all life. I would be Empress and I would be—"

"Happy?" said Tuer. "But you would not be. Because Niren would not have been free. Unlocking the doors and healing the tear in the world requires something more than merely passing through the Circles, or my Shadow or Raiva would have done it long ago."

Dread ate away at her. She didn't want to ask, but she did anyway. "What does it require?"

"Freeing me," he said heavily.

"And how would one free you?"

The god took a long, long breath. "By taking my place."

Chapter Forty-Two

"YOU CREATED ME ONLY TO DESTROY ME," said Eda.

"Little one—"

"You are the spider at the heart of the web, and you lured me here because—and only because—I am so insignificant that my life means nothing to you. It never did. Raiva was too precious. So was Niren. But I don't matter. I don't matter at *all*. I am just a tool. A key. To be used and abandoned and forgotten."

"Eda."

Her name in the god's heavy voice broke her. The knife was hungry in her hand.

"I did not call you here to torment you, but to give you a choice. And so that you may truly choose, I now release you from our deal."

"Our *deal*," said Eda viciously. "What deal is it, exactly, that I made?"

Tuer blinked at her. "Your life in service in exchange for being made Empress."

"I made *myself* Empress. You did *nothing.*"

"Perhaps, if you choose to see it that way."

She looked at the mirrors, and understanding dawned. "My life in service. My *life.* This is what you meant."

"I have little use for temples."

She thought of Erris, moldering even now on his throne. She hadn't specified that she wanted to be Empress for the rest of her life. She thought she'd been so careful. She thought she'd been so wise. "But it wasn't even you I made a deal with, was it? It was Rudion. It was always Rudion. In the temple, in the ballroom, on the ship, on the mountain. It was never even *you.*"

The god shut his eyes, pain creasing his forehead. "It was me. Always. Because I didn't have to listen to my Shadow. I didn't have to let him stroke my ego, make me feel more than mankind, above my duty to them. Everything he has done I am guilty of, from the beginning until now."

Tuer brushed his fingers along the surface of the mirror before him. "Little one, I would tell you a story. Listen, and understand.

"When the world was young, a god and his Shadow watched as a man stole a seed from the Tree.

"'How dare he,' the god's Shadow whispered in his ear. 'How dare he stand against the gods, against *you?* He does not deserve to live. He does not deserve to dwell any longer under the Tree.'

"And the god listened to his Shadow, and struck the man down.

"'Make me a king,' pleaded a boy called Erris. 'Make me as high as my brother. Make me mean something to him.'

"'What will you give?' asked the god's Shadow.

"'My life. My time. My heart.'

"'Then you shall be king,' said the Shadow.

"The god did not like what his Shadow had done, but the

Shadow slinked round him, easing his sorrow. 'How dare a man resent the will of the gods? It is why his brother was made king, and he was not.'

"And the god understood the truth in his Shadow's words, but still sometimes he looked into the mirror that showed Erris on his throne, king of nothing, ruler of no one, all the years of his life robbed away, and more. The god mourned. But he could not undo the things that his Shadow had done in his name.

"As the centuries spun away, the god forgot it was his Shadow who had done it at all. He imagined himself on the mountaintop, making a cruel bargain with Erris that Erris did not understand.

"And so he came to blame himself wholly, and the Shadow stayed.

"More and more, the god's Shadow left him alone in the Circle of Sorrow to go out and do his bidding in the world. More and more the god sent him, more and more the god wished him back.

"And when one day the god's Shadow whispered in his ear that the world was dying, that the Circles were closing and the earth fracturing apart, the Shadow offered him a solution, a chance at freedom, at absolution for everything he'd done. He only needed to find someone, to find *no one* to take his place. Because the god was the only one who could heal the world.

"Rudion knew that. He slipped into the Circle of Time and looked into the future. He saw Niren, the chosen Bearer of Souls. He saw Eda, who was unimportant but strong, and he knew he'd found the one to take the god's place. The god agreed. For even though he had meant, in his heart of hearts, to pay an eternity for his crime of bringing death into the world, he longed for freedom. He longed to be rid of his chains, to walk in the winds of Endahr and be joined at last, at last, to Raiva, who held his heart in her hands.

"And so he told Rudion to bring the girl to him. After all, she was nobody. She didn't matter.

"And yet.

"The god watched her grow up. Saw her joys and her sorrows. So many sorrows. And he pitied her, but he could not turn back from his path. Because without her, all the world would die.

"It was just that one should suffer so that the world could live.

"The god would make that choice, if he could. He longed to make that choice.

"But instead he watched as her parents died. As she made a deal with his Shadow. As she grew up and seized the Empire his shadow self had promised her.

"And he watched as his Shadow stole her friend into death, the one she had bargained away without meaning to.

"He watched as the man she loved betrayed her for his Shadow.

"He watched and he watched and he watched.

"And at last.

"At last, you came."

Eda blinked, coming wholly back to herself in the Circle of Sorrow, the spell woven by Tuer's story suddenly broken. "Why did you tell me all that?"

"So you would know everything."

"So I would pity you," she spat.

Tuer shook his head. "I mourn the pain you suffered on my account. I mourn the things my Shadow did to you. But he succeeded in doing what I asked of him. He brought you here. And now that you are here, now that you know the whole of the truth, you must choose. What will you do? Time grows short.

Soon my Shadow and his fellow spirits will devour the world, and there will be no choice left for you to make. Choose."

Eda flicked her eyes to the mirrors, to the god who crouched before her. Her fury sharpened. She did pity Tuer, pitied him as much as she reviled him. Like she pitied and reviled herself.

"Choose, little one. Before time is gone."

"I will not be bound by your chains," said Eda. "I choose to live. But I will not leave the world to perish because of your mistakes."

Tuer shook his head. "You cannot make that choice."

The third way is to kill the god.

Eda grimaced. "Watch me."

And she leapt at Tuer, driving the godkiller upward, toward his heart.

Pain burst inside of her, and she gasped and fell to her knees.

Somehow, the godkiller had missed its mark.

Somehow, it had pierced her own heart instead of Tuer's.

Dimly, she was aware of blood pouring from her chest onto the ground. She couldn't stop staring at the knife hilt, protruding from her own body.

How strange to see her life spill out of her, so red and hot.

And yet how cold she was.

Darkness crept in at the edges of her vision. She couldn't feel anything now, not even pain.

I've given my life to Tuer after all, she thought.

And then the world shifted sideways, and shadows swallowed her whole.

She was standing in a low room in the hull of a ship. The vessel rocked gently beneath her feet, but the motion didn't bother her. The scarred man sat at a little table writing in his book, his pen scratching rhythmically across the page. He looked up at her, and smiled sadly.

"Oh, little one. I am sorry that you have come here. This is not the story I wanted for you."

She was clothed in a gown of white and gray, and when she lifted her hands before her eyes, she could see through them. "Am I dead?"

"In a manner of speaking." He wrote a few more words in his book, then closed it and stood, pacing to a porthole in the side of the ship.

Eda went to stand beside him. She peered through the porthole, up into a circle of starry sky. She remembered the feel of a knife in her hand, then pain, her life dripping red on the ground. "The godkiller. It didn't work."

"It could not pierce the chains of sorrow that bound the god of the mountain, but it thirsted for life, and so it took yours."

"Then it has all been for nothing. My life. My death. It's fitting, that I end this way—I made myself. And I've unmade myself, too."

His eyebrows lifted. "Do you truly think you shaped your own life?"

"Tuer, then," she said bitterly. "Tuer and his Shadow have been toying with me since the moment I was born. Perhaps it's better this way, that my death has deprived him of the thing he's been striving for so long."

"You blame Tuer, then, for everything that's happened to you?"

She looked at him, truly *looked*, and something stirred deep inside of her. "Who are you?"

"Do you truly not know me, little Empress? I was there from the beginning, watching over you. Who do you think stayed the hand of the plague that took the lives of your parents? Who do you think protected you at the palace, allowed you to ascend to the throne and rule an Empire? Who do you think turned the gaze of the Denlahn soldiers, allowing you to escape the revenge of their prince? Who do you think unlocked the door to your holding cell, and watched over you on your voyage and your long journey? Who do you think called the spirits away on the mountain and brought you to Erris on his throne?"

"Not Tuer," she said.

He smiled. "Not Tuer."

"You dwell outside the Circles," said Eda. "You must, or you could not reach me here. You are not one of the dead, and you are not a Bearer of Souls."

He studied her, waiting for her to parcel it out.

Her shadowy body began to shake. "You are the One above the gods. You have come to destroy me."

"No, dear one. I have come to offer you peace, rest. To bring you to my dwelling place beyond the Circles of Endahr, if that is what you wish."

The old anger flared. "Why did you not come to Tuer? Break him free of his chains? Heal the world and stop all of this from happening?"

"I did come to Tuer, many times. He would not hear me. He would not accept my forgiveness. He wanted to suffer, and so he did, making his own plan of escape only when he saw he was poisoning the world."

"Me. I was his plan of escape."

"Yes."

"But now I am dead and there is no one to free him." She looked up into her companion's face, tracing the lines of his scars with her eyes, seeing the depth of his wisdom and his age and his power.

"You do not have to worry about Tuer and his Shadow and their schemes any longer. Come with me, little Empress. Be at peace."

"What will happen to the world if I come with you? What will happen to the dead and the living? To Morin and Tainir? To Enduena?"

There was an immeasurable grief in his eyes, the weight of it dragging on him. "The world will end, dear one. Endahr will be no more, and time itself will be unwritten."

"And you think I am selfish enough to trade my own comfort for the end of the world?" she demanded.

He smiled. "Are you?"

"I murdered the man I always hoped might be my father just so I could take his Empire. I destroyed the rightful Empress's life because I hated her. And I bargained Niren away when I was still a *child*. Of course I'm selfish enough."

"Are you?" he repeated.

The ship was beginning to waver around her, the pull of death very strong. "What will happen if I do not go with you?" she whispered.

"Then I will send you back to the mountain. Back to Tuer, and another impossible choice. It may be that you can free him, and heal the breach between the Circles, saving the dead and the living, too. And it may be that you cannot, and Endahr will come to ruin anyway."

"And even if I do all that, it will still mean——"

"It will still mean that you will be bound in Tuer's place, bound to all the world's sorrows."

"Forever."

"That is your choice, little one. What will you choose?"

She looked at his book, which lay shut on the table. "What have you written for me?"

"Would it alter your choice, if you knew what it would be?"

Outside the ship the world seemed to shake. Stars fell from the sky and into the sea.

"Send me back," said Eda, tremulous, small. She bowed her head. "Send me back."

He brushed one finger across her brow, and the Starlight inside her pulsed warm at his touch. "Do not fear the sorrow, little Empress. It may yet save you. Farewell, until we meet again. Farewell."

Darkness closed round her, and something was ripped red-hot from her chest. She screamed in agony.

But then metal clattered noisily on stone, and the pain was suddenly gone.

She opened her eyes to see Tuer staring down at her, the godkiller lying on the ground between them, its blade rent in two.

Chapter Forty-Three

BUT THEY WERE NOT ALONE.

A silent figure paced toward them from the outskirts of the hall. It was Raiva, her gown dirty and torn, her face streaked with tears. Eda wondered how long she had been watching them.

"It should not fall to a mortal to mend a god's mistakes," said the goddess, and Eda recognized something inside of Raiva she hadn't seen before—anger.

Tuer bowed his head, and did not look Raiva in the eye.

"All this time, my Lord of the Mountain, I could have saved you. All this time the doors could have been unlocked and Endahr allowed to flourish. All this time, you could have spoken with me, and yet for centuries you let me think you could not hear or see me, consumed with your own wretched sorrow. Look at me now, my lord Tuer. Meet my gaze and speak my name. Tell me why you left me so long to languish in misery."

Tuer lifted his eyes, and Eda saw his shame. "I could not lose you," he told the goddess. "You are all I hold dear upon Endahr, and I could not bear it if you were gone."

"But you did this to *yourself*!" Raiva flung her arms at the mirrors. "*You* broke the world, then concocted a mad scheme with your Shadow to mend it because you were too proud and too stubborn and too selfish to admit that you were wrong!"

Eda took a step backward, a bystander in a story that wasn't hers.

Raiva shook with rage, and Tuer seemed to shrink before her.

"What is my life?" said the goddess. "What is it next to saving the one I love? Next to saving the world that I love? I would have given it to you a thousand times over."

"That is why I could never tell you," said Tuer.

"And why were you the one to make that choice? A choice that affects more than you—a choice that should have been mine? You cannot control everything and everyone you wish to. You are not the One who was before us. You are not all-seeing, all-knowing, all-powerful."

Tears dripped from Tuer's face. "I was the first thing the One formed on Endahr. The strongest. The wisest. And I failed him."

"And so you punish yourself," Raiva scoffed, "and all the world with you? That is not wisdom, my lord. That is foolishness."

A horrific *boom* shuddered through the hall, a crack opening jagged in the empty air above Tuer's mirrors. Wind came rushing through it, bringing with it the stench of death. There came the sound of leathery wings, the clatter of bone swords, the mingled clacking of thousands upon thousands of broken teeth.

Raiva looked at the crack with resignation. "Endahr tears itself apart. The spirits from the void will come even here, my lord, into your prison of Sorrow. Your Shadow will make sure of that. But I am no longer content to stand by, and do nothing."

She swept past Tuer, even as the god leapt to his feet. "My lady, no. Raiva—"

But Raiva reached up into the air, grabbing both ends of the rip in the world. Words poured out of her, a great song that filled Eda with despair, and Starlight came rushing from her fingertips, weaving around the crack, pulling it together again.

But the Starlight did not hold. No sooner had Raiva finished pulling one part of the crack together then it unraveled again, light hanging frayed around the edges. The stench of death grew stronger, the crack wider.

"Raiva," said Tuer, his face heavy with grief.

She stopped her singing, turned to him. "My power wanes. I cannot heal the world this way. So I will take your place. Hang your chains on me, my lord Tuer. Do not deny me."

But the god shook his head. "Sorrow is powerful. It can extinguish love and life, death and time. It would put out your light. Destroy you."

"My lord, there *is* no time. Give me your chains."

"You do not understand. You have poured too much of your Starlight into the crack. There is not enough left. If I hung all the sorrow of the world on you now, it would turn you to dust in an instant. The doors would stay locked. The spirits would break free. The world would still die."

"And so it is down to me," said Eda bitterly. "As it always has been."

The god and goddess both turned to her with surprise, as if they'd forgotten she was there.

Eda felt herself collapsing inward, crushed by her insignificance, which somehow had made her so, so important. "My life, for the world's. It's not a choice. You haven't given me one. You never have."

"And yet you are still here," said Tuer.

Raiva clasped the god's hand in her own. She looked frail now, smaller than she had been.

Eda paced in front of the mirrors, the crack in the world shuddering and groaning above her head. Images flickered through the glass: Niren, wandering the Circle of the Dead. Her parents, drowning in a river of shadows, clawing and fighting to reach the shore. The nine Billow Maidens with their flaming swords, guarding the dead of the sea. Morin and Tainir, clinging to each other as the earth cracked beneath their feet, as the sun fell from the sky and winged spirits devoured all the world. Rudion, tearing more cracks in the world with his bone sword, letting his brothers and sisters flood through.

"I wanted more than this." Eda gestured at the mirrors, at Tuer's chains. "I deserved more than this."

Tuer watched her, his piercing eyes ancient and powerful and deep.

She turned to the god, heavy with her own sorrow. For all her anger, there was only one choice she could make, the same choice she had already made when the One had sent her back. She had to try, to save Morin and Tainir, to save her parents and Niren and the world. "Give me your chains, Lord of the Mountain. I accept them for my own."

"Is there no other way?" said Raiva.

Tuer's face was stricken. "There is no other way."

He knelt before Eda, putting his huge hands on her shoulders. "I am sorry, little one. When I caused Raiva to put her light in you, when I sent my Shadow to draw you here, I did not know I would come to care for you, as I watched you grow, as I endured all the sorrows you endured. If there was any other way, I would choose to sit here for all eternity in your place. But there is not, not anymore. I am sorry. When it is done—when you are bound and the world is free, perhaps we can find a way to save you. And perhaps we cannot, but know that we will honor you, always."

Eda ground her jaw. "Bind me, then. Before I change my mind."

"Take my hand, daughter of dust. Close your eyes."

She did as she was told, folding her slender hand into his much larger one. She felt his pulse underneath his wrist and thought it odd that a god should have a pulse. She shut her eyes.

"I am sorry," Tuer repeated.

That was all the warning she had before a dark, raging pain seared through her, from her fingers down to her toes, and all the way up her spine to the roots of her hair. She screamed, thrashing, trying to break free, but Tuer didn't let her go.

The pain continued to fill her up. Heat and cold, knives and stone, a thousand stinging scorpions—her body writhed on the ground, unable to contain the full weight of her agony. Because Tuer was giving her his chains, his sorrow. She felt his grief, his rage, his helplessness, every last ounce of every dark emotion he had experienced for the centuries he'd been here, bound in the dark.

She couldn't bear it. She screamed at him to stop but still he held on, still his sorrow poured through her.

She was broken. She was remade. She was broken again. She would splinter apart, and there would be nothing left.

And then suddenly, the pain stopped. She opened her eyes. Tuer and Raiva stood towering above her in the full weight of their immortal power, and they were both so bright she could barely look at them.

"I am sorry," said Tuer yet again.

Raiva brushed cool fingers across Eda's forehead. For an instant Eda stared at her, shocked to see wrinkles pressed into the goddess's face, age weighing on her as it would on any mortal.

And then Tuer and Raiva turned and were gone, leaving her alone in the darkness.

The mirrors flashed and whispered before her. The jagged crack in the world writhed and groaned above her head.

It was only then, as she unconsciously tried to stand, that she felt the chains, heavy, cold, unbreakable. The chains that bound her forever to the Circle of Sorrow.

Chapter Forty-Four

THE CRACK IN THE WORLD GROANED AND shook above her. In every one of Tuer's mirrors a similar crack split the sky, and winged spirits poured through. The screams of a million souls filled her own, broke her and broke her again. But the chains bound her where she knelt, and the only thing she could do was lift her head.

Above her, a single shadow flew through the crack: Rudion, crowned with fire. Flames licked along his brow, but did not consume him. His eyes hungered for her. "Little Empress," he hissed. "How do you think to save the world, when you cannot even save yourself? The god has tricked you yet again. He is free, and you are not, and you will perish, here, in the depths of sorrow."

"It was *you* who tricked me." Her throat was raw from screaming; every word was pain. "It was always you. You tricked me, just as you tricked Ileem, just as you tricked Tuer. How did you do it? How did you make him think you served him, when really you plotted to keep him in chains as you worked to free your own kind?"

Rudion laughed and paced near her, his wings folded against his shoulders. In the dim light from the mirrors, he seemed almost to shine. "The proud are always the easiest to fool, because they think themselves so very wise. Especially a god."

Dimly, Eda was aware of one half of the godkiller lying just past her knee. "And yet for all your scheming, you have lost," she said. "Tuer is free, and he goes even now to unlock the doors. When he has done so, the cracks in the world will heal, and you and your kind will be sealed forever into the void."

Rudion put his bone sword to her throat. Cold burned her. Cut her. Blood trickled down her neck, sliming her chains with red.

He dragged one clawed finger down her cheek. "Little Empress, little fool. Queen of Sorrow and ruler of shadows. How small you are. How very, very small. I wanted you here. I meant for you to take his place. You are the last piece holding the world together. When I kill you, the Circles will fracture apart, and not even the god can repair them. Soon, all my people will be free: an army as vast as the stars. Mankind will fall, and the gods themselves will bow at my feet. How much agony will you feel, I wonder, as your body is torn apart? Perhaps not more than you feel right now. Perhaps your death will be a mercy." Rudion laughed again and raised the sword, swinging it toward her.

Eda shrieked as her hand closed around the half of the godkiller, and she thrust it hard into Rudion's chest.

The bone sword clattered to the ground. Rudion screamed and jerked back. Darkness poured from his wound like smoke, more and more until it consumed him, and his fiery crown clattered to the floor. For an instant he stared at her, shock written into every line of his frame. His wings lay dark against the stone, some wind she did not feel stirring through black feathers.

"I told you," she hissed through her agony. "I told you I would kill you."

And then his body fell all to ash, and the wind blew him away.

Eda shuddered, the chains weighing on her, pain splintering every inch of her. She wiped the blood from her neck and looked again into Tuer's mirrors.

She saw Tuer and Raiva pacing together through the dark of the mountain. As they walked, Raiva aged with every step, until at last she turned to dust, a shimmer of Starlight in the darkness. Grief weighed heavy on the oldest god, but he did not stop to mourn. He could not—his task was unfinished. He reached the door to the Circle of Time, and with the touch of his hand and a Word of ancient power, he unlocked it.

On he went through Time and unlocked the door to the Circle of the Dead. Then, at last, the door to the Circle of the Living. There the other gods were waiting for him: Mahl, Ahdairon, and Hahld. Together, they stepped from Tuer's Mountain.

Tuer's power weighed on him like a heavy mantle. He burned with it. And as he stood on his Mountain, the other gods with him, he called the spirits.

They came in a rush of dark wings, pulled by the strength of his power. There were thousands of them. They all knelt before him, trembling. Tuer spoke a Word, and a crack split the sky above him. Darkness wheeled beyond.

The spirits screamed. Begged.

But Tuer lifted his hand and they were silent, cowering before him. "We bound you once, for the crimes you committed against Endahr," said the oldest god. "Now we bind you once more, and this time, there will be no escape." Tuer looked at the other gods and nodded.

Together, the four of them began to sing, an ancient song they had learned at the beginning of the world, woven together with Words of power. They sang and sang, and the mountain shook and the spirits shrieked as they were flung against their will into the void. The song went on and on, until every last spirit was swallowed up. In their wake they left a field of bones, the only remnants of those they'd slaughtered in their brief moment of freedom.

Wind rushed over the peak, and Ahdairon, Mahl, and Hahld turned to their lord Tuer, and bowed to him. "How will we seal them?" asked Ahdairon. "How will we make certain this will never happen again?"

"With the blood of a god," said Tuer. For a moment, he seemed to look through the surface of the mirror, straight into Eda's eyes. "I am sorry, little one. Forgive me."

And he drew from his breast the other half of the godkiller, and plunged it into his heart.

"NO!" Eda screamed.

But the god fell from the mountain.

The crack in the sky vanished.

"Tuer!" Eda cried at the mirror. "TUER!"

But he didn't answer, and she didn't expect him to.

Tuer was dead.

She sagged back on her heels. Darkness clamored at the edges of her vision. There was nothing left. No Tuer, no Raiva. No one to save her.

There was only sorrow, and that's all there ever would be.

Eda looked into the mirrors, looked and looked, for she found she had no will to turn away. Mothers wept and fathers died. Women cursed, men raged. A serving girl curled in a corner of a grand house, aching with loneliness. A child sobbed, a bruise in the shape of a handprint on his face. A daughter found her father ripped apart by beasts in a forest.

All was *ache* and *torment*. All was sorrow, sorrow, sorrow.

The grief continued in an endless parade before her eyes. She wept until she was emptied of tears, and then she wept even more.

She fought against the chains, raged against them. But they only pulled tighter, only bound her closer to the mirrors.

Time lost all meaning. She had been bound in the Circle of Sorrow for an hour, or perhaps a millennium. She did not hunger, did not thirst, did not sleep. All she did was *feel*. And all she felt was *pain*.

She lost herself to it. She became sorrow, she *was* sorrow. That was all she ever would be.

Her life and her self slipped away. She forgot Niren and her parents and the Empire. She forgot Morin and Tainir and her long journey to find Tuer's Mountain. She forgot anything had ever existed besides pain. She felt every tear shed in all of Endahr. Every hurt. Every grief.

There was nothing else.

Sometimes, the ground seemed to shake beneath her feet. Once, she thought she saw a host of shadows pass through the hall beyond the mirrors, led by a woman who shone like a Star.

She couldn't properly hear or see them. They didn't even make sense to her, because within them pulsed something other than sorrow, and that was impossible.

It was sorrow that bound the world together.

Another time, she thought she saw a man on a throne of mounded stones lift his head. He blinked and sighed and looked around him, confusion creasing his brow. He stood from his throne, and strode away from it, turning, as he did so, to dust.

There came a time when perhaps her mind wandered away from her body and she dreamt, if dream it was, of a wide green land. Of shadows shining bright under a brilliant sky. Of rest, release, joy.

But she didn't know what joy was. She had never felt it. It didn't exist.

She thought she saw an old wrinkled man, his lips bloated from poison, step onto the shores of the green land and grow whole and young again. He ran through the grass like a newborn lamb, wobbly and rejoicing.

She saw a man and woman who had perhaps once been precious to her. They sat together on the shore, the woman laying her head on the man's shoulder.

Nine shining figures and a host of shadows came to the green shore. All of them radiated something that she didn't understand. Something that was the opposite of sorrow.

And then she was drawn back into her body and she knew herself, knew that she sat chained in the god Tuer's place, and that he was dead, and she would never be free.

She wept, for her sorrow, and for the world's. She would never stop weeping.

All the grief of all the world poured through her, eating her, but never consuming her.

Darkness. Pain. Weeping. Sorrow.

My life in service, in exchange for being made Empress.

My life in service.

My life.

My life.

A voice, strong as a storm: "It is too much for her. The sorrow has swallowed the Starlight." A sudden vision of the wind god Mahl, his white hair crowned with lightning.

Another voice, gentle as the rain through the trees, the wind goddess, Ahdairon, all rippling feathers and yellow hair: "Not all of it. There is a little left. It is enough, I think, to save her."

Save her.

Save her.

She was falling from a cliff, feathers in her hair. The world was a blur of gray and green, stone and trees.

A ship rocked beneath her. Nausea climbed up her throat. Rock, rock, rock.

A scarred man, writing in a book, ink flowing thick and dark from his pen.

Do not fear the sorrow, little Empress. It may yet save you.

A girl, sitting all night between her parents' bodies, so stiff on their tables of stone, so cold and blank and empty.

A man, pulling her away from her home, stuffing her into a room in the palace, a room far too big for her and far too empty.

Loneliness, eating away at her.

Slipping into the stable, saddling a horse, riding and riding and riding until her house appeared, stark against the horizon.

A temple in a hill, beating her fist against the stone, blood dripping down her knuckles.

The god.

Her deal.

My life in service.

My life.

My life.

Waiting and waiting. The loneliness threatening, always, to swallow her whole.

But she didn't let it. Planning, waiting. Bribes and promises. Searing jealousy.

Lonely, lonely.

A vial of poison, cold against her breast.

Dark drops poured between papery lips.

His last rattling breath.

A crown, heavy on her brow.

The people kneeling before her.

Still so lonely.

Niren—there and yet not there. A shadow. A fear.

Dark eyes and dark skin shining in the moonlight. Lips pressed warm against hers. Fingers tangled in her hair.

Happiness.

The bite of a knife under her jaw.

He never wanted her.

It is too much for her. The sorrow has swallowed the Starlight.

There is a little left. Enough, I think, to save her.

Do not fear the sorrow.

It may yet save you.

It may yet save you.

In the dark before the mirrors, Eda lifted her head. Starlight pulsed still inside of her, a faint, tremulous spark. She reached for it, reached and reached, and when she had caught it, she held it tight, an ember burning. Hope.

Sorrow is powerful, Tuer had said. *It can extinguish love and life, death and time.*

And perhaps, perhaps—

It could free her.

She stretched her hands out toward the mirrors, holding on to the Starlight inside of her. She reached for the sorrow, calling it into her, into the Starlight.

The sorrow came and came. The Starlight ate it, swelling until it blazed out of her with the fury of the summer sun.

Still it ate, and still the sorrow came. The chains fell off, link by link. The mirrors shattered outward, shards of glass piercing her heart.

And then the Starlight could eat no more, but the sorrow wasn't finished.

On it came, swelling inside of her, more and more and more, fusing together with the Starlight in her soul. She burned with pain and grief, with a strength her body could not contain.

Her bones stretched and cracked. Thorns pierced her knuckles.

All was a twisting, awful agony, and a rush of dark wings.

She burst upward, away from the mirrors and the chains, through the rock and earth of the mountain, up and up and up, hurtling through the dark, through a door in a tree.

The Circle of Time seethed before her, all color and glitter and show. The pools of memory wheeled by her, but she didn't even turn her head. They couldn't stop her. Couldn't even slow her down.

She flew up and up, and burst through a door into a whistling dark emptiness that pulsed with hunger, with wanting. She could see definition in the darkness, feel the ache, ache, ache. But she had no pity to spare for Death. It had had its time, and it had had its fill, and it was just a stop along the journey, now.

She hurtled onward, the strength of sorrow searing every part of her.

On and on, through one last door into the darkness of the mountain, then up and up, her body boring through the very stones of the world.

She screamed with a voice that was not her own.

And then—

She broke through rock and earth.

Beyond was sky.

Stars.

Air.

But still the sorrow clung to her.

She was free of chains and mirrors. She was free of the Mountain. She was free of Death and Time.

But she was not free of Sorrow.

It twisted through every ounce of her, engraved on her very being.

She screamed at the sky.

It listened, and shrank from her.

Chapter Forty-Five

S HE HAD NEVER FELT SO STRONG, THOUGH the strength twisted
through her with the bite of knives. She was pain and fury
and rage.

She could brush the stars with the edges of her wings, and
swallow the world with her power.

Her *wings*.

What was she?

She flew through a dark sky, the blur of trees beneath her.

She wanted, she *ached*.

Her body had stretched and grown and changed.

The sorrow had made her something else, something more.

Dark feathers.

A heart filled with fire.

She wanted to hurt everyone who had hurt her. She wanted
to make the world bow at her feet. She wanted to pour her sorrow
and rage into the stones of the earth.

Because she couldn't hold it in. It was tearing her apart.

Wind rushed past her wings, and on the mountain below were two figures: a boy with a creature beside him, pressed up against his knee.

The sight of him sent fresh pain searing through her, though she didn't understand why.

He must have wronged her. He must have sent her into the mountain to die.

She let out a shriek that rattled the sky and dove toward the boy.

She crashed into him, knocking him backward into the side of the mountain. She ripped at his shoulders with her talons, tearing into his flesh, watching his red blood pool on brown earth.

She felt his sorrow, a rush of intense horrific power that nearly overwhelmed her. She closed herself off; she could not contain his sorrow along with everything that already raged in her soul. She sent it back at him.

He screamed and fell to the ground, clawing at his skin like he was burning from the inside.

She'd forgotten his creature: a spotted cat. It lunged at her, snarling, and raked claws across her chest. Pain ripped hot into her body.

She screamed and scrabbled backward, almost falling from the cliff.

And then somehow the boy was there, though he still shuddered with pain, pulling her back onto level ground. He stroked her wings with gentle hands, and his voice, soft and certain, coiled around her like honey. "Eda. Eda. Be still, be still. You're here, and you're safe. Be still."

His blood yet dripped into the dirt, his face twisted with the agony that convulsed through his body.

And yet he was so gentle.

The spotted cat crouched and snarled, but the boy held it at bay. "Tainir, hush."

She shuddered and shook. Pain, in every part of her, tangled with the power of her sorrow.

But she didn't want to feel it, not anymore.

Her body cracked. Burst apart.

Heat and pain and light.

Feathers falling round her like dark snow.

Huddling against the stone of the mountain, shuddering with terrible, terrible cold; her wings were gone and there was nothing to warm her.

Gradually, Eda became aware of herself and her surroundings.

She was naked, curled up in a ball, icy stone pressing against her shoulders, frigid air biting at her exposed skin. She was human again, or at least had resumed her human form, the huge dark feathers of whatever winged creature she had been scattered around her like ashes.

But the sorrow hadn't left her; it raged still inside her soul, and power crackled through her like harnessed lightning, barely contained.

The snow leopard who was Tainir came toward her over the freezing ground. The leopard's body straightened and changed, paws stretching out into legs and arms, feline head and ears shifting into dark hair and red-brown skin and sparkling eyes.

Tainir was naked, too, but only for a moment; Words poured

glinting gold from her lips and she was clothed again, in a plain linen shirt and trousers that would do little to shelter her from the bitter cold.

Eda couldn't clothe herself; she didn't know what Words to say. She just shuddered against the mountain, the sorrow eating and eating and never getting its fill.

And then Morin was there, hesitant. Careful. He shrugged out of his own poncho and offered it to her, turning around so she could pull it on without him watching. When he turned back, his face was gray with pain.

A tremor went through her. Tears dripped down her cheeks. "What was I? What did I do to you?"

"You were a great black bird. Bigger than the ayrrah. Bursting with power." His words were soft and slow, but they held no fear.

She bowed her head; she couldn't look at him. "How did you know it was me? I could have been one of the winged spirits. I could have destroyed you—I nearly did."

"I just knew."

"The spirits are gone," said Tainir softly, kneeling on Eda's other side. From somewhere she produced a blanket, and Eda wrapped it gratefully around her frigid toes. "And I know it's because of you. We saw our parents. We bid them farewell, and then a woman with a star on her forehead came and took their hands. They faded away. I know they've gone to their rest."

Eda couldn't stop trembling. She stared at Morin's hands, which were balled into fists, knuckles straining under tight skin. "You're still in pain," she whispered.

"I can bear it."

"No." She shook her head. "It will destroy you. When I

touched you, I felt your sorrow. Every grief you'd ever endured in all your life, and it was *strong*, Morin. I didn't mean to but I sent it back at you. I think—I think I almost killed you. And it's still there, under your skin. It will eat at you and eat at you, until there's nothing left." She should know. Something had happened to her when she'd drawn all the sorrow inside, something that allowed her body to endure when she should be lying dead before the mirrors. But Morin had no such protection.

Tainir looked from her brother to Eda and back again. "Morin."

"I'm fine. Really."

But Tainir went to him, touched his shoulders, and tilted her forehead against his. She began to sing, glints of gold pouring from her lips and sinking into his skin. As she sang, Morin relaxed, his whole body sagging with relief, with release.

Eda wanted to claw her way into the mountain, let the rocks crush her, never come back out. She had never hated herself more.

At last Tainir finished singing, and sat back on her heels.

Morin gave Eda a wobbly smile. "Good as new, you see?"

But he made no move to come close to her again.

Tainir built a fire, and the three of them sat around it, sparks flying up into the new-fallen night.

Eda told them what had happened to her inside the mountain, piece by piece, as best as she could. But there were some things she didn't know how to put into words: her vision of the One, drawing the sorrow into her heart. The power that even now surged through her.

Both Morin and Tainir listened intently, a crease in Morin's forehead, faint gold sparks buzzing around Tainir's fingers.

By the time Eda was finished talking, the night had deepened, the fire burned low. Neither Morin nor Tainir said anything, and anxiety formed a tight knot in Eda's chest. She broke the silence, because her companions would not. "How long has it been since I left you outside the door?"

"A month," said Tainir.

That was all? Eda couldn't imagine the torment Tuer had endured, chained before those mirrors for untold centuries. The wind whipped through her hair, tangling it around her shoulders, biting icily down her spine. "What happened when I left you?"

"The spirits attacked," said Morin. "We fought them before the door."

Something haunted came into Tainir's face. "The ghosts were screaming. The spirits were—"

"Eating them?" Eda shuddered.

"Yes."

"And then?"

Morin fiddled with his knife, the blade glinting white in the embers of the dying fire. "The spirit who guarded the door leapt at the winged spirits, allowed itself to be eaten instead of the ghosts. We ran."

"Out of the mountain," Tainir continued, "back past the ice wall."

Morin stared off into the distance. "There was a massive tear in the sky, splitting the world in two. The spirits came and came, until there were so many of them we couldn't see the sun anymore. Tainir shifted into her leopard form and we huddled against the cliff. I'll never forget the noise they made. But then the ground shook and we heard a sound like a great brass bell, and the crack sealed itself, the shadows dragged back into the void, screaming. The wind tasted sweet and there was a sense of—of—"

"Of release," Tainir finished for him.

Morin nodded. "You did it, Eda." His eyes met hers, and fixed there. "You saved us all."

She shuddered and shuddered. "It wasn't me. It was Tuer."

"No." Morin still didn't look away. "I know it was you."

The three of them bedded down for what was left of the night, Eda curled up against the cliff wall. There had been no discussion, but Morin and Tainir slept away from her, on the other side of the fire. She didn't allow herself to feel that hurt, because the sorrow of all the world still pulsed inside of her. What had she become? What had Tuer and the One and the Starlight made her? Why was she sent back into the world if she was . . . broken? Perhaps this was her punishment for the lives she had taken. Her penance. To live once more among those she cared about, but to carry still their sorrow with her as if she yet knelt chained before Tuer's mirrors.

Could she . . . could she never touch anyone again without causing them pain?

She listened to Morin and Tainir breathing. She watched the fire, the flames shrinking as the wood burned low.

She got up and paced along the edge of the cliff, letting the wind and the snow and the stars wrap around her like a cloak. She was so different. And the world was the same.

What was she supposed to do now? Where would she go? What was she even fit for?

She shut her eyes and saw Eddenahr, its gleaming spires and blue-tiled roofs; she felt the sun burning her skin, caught the scent of jasmine and honeysuckle, tasted fresh orange slices, tangy and sweet. She saw a pair of dark eyes that once were dear to her, a lanky form sprawled over the roof tiles. She felt soft lips pressed against hers under the inky sky. Why did she miss him, even now? Why did she miss something that had never been hers, had never been real?

Sorrow pulsed inside of her, and it was not the grief of the world but her own grief, sharp and bitter and piercing as a spearpoint.

She knelt on the side of the cliff, her shoulders shaking as she wept for the country and the family and the friend and the husband she had lost. She wanted to go home. She wanted to go home so badly it *hurt*.

But how could she?

She crouched there all the long night, watching as the dark turned to dawn, the stars fading in the greater light of the rising sun.

As light poured golden onto the cliff, the power stirred inside of her. She could feel the monstrous bird, just under her skin, ready to fly free at her bidding.

She didn't turn when Morin came up beside her, but she was glad of his presence.

"Do you think I'm a monster?" she asked.

"No." His answer was quick and fierce.

"But you're afraid of me."

"No."

"Liar."

"Eda."

Her name on his lips made her gaze find his. There were tear stains on his face, as if he'd been crying unaware in his sleep.

"Come back to the village with us. Stay with Tainir and me. We discussed it at length—we want you to stay and make a home with us. To—to make a home with *me*, if you wish."

A knot pulled tight in her throat. She knew what he was saying, without him actually saying it. "Morin, you hardly know me. And I—I almost killed you yesterday."

"You can't journey with someone for weeks without coming to know every piece of them. I *do* know you, Eda. I know you've been alone nearly your whole life. You don't have to be, not anymore."

Beneath her skin, the power surged and stretched, whispering her name. "I don't think I can even touch you." She hadn't meant to say that, but the words had tumbled out anyway.

Something hard came into his face, and he held out his hand to her, palm up. His jaw was set, determined, but his fingers trembled.

She reached her own hand out, laid it on his.

His sorrow pulsed through her, staggering, strong, and she gasped and let go before she accidentally sent it back at him.

But even that brief touch was enough to make him crumple to his knees, his forehead creased in pain.

She bit back a sob.

"I'm all right." He gulped air like a drowning man, and forced himself to his feet again. "Eda, I'm all right."

The sorrow inside of her screamed to get out, and she stood shuddering on the cliffside. "I can't come with you. I'm a danger to you. To Tainir."

"Maybe you can learn to control it. Maybe—"

"I can't, Morin. I'm sorry." Her voice cracked. "I'm going home. The gods have cursed me anew, but at least they gave me what I always wanted."

He looked at her unhappily. "And what's that?"

"The power of a goddess." The words tasted bitter on her tongue.

Morin drew a deep breath. "There will always be a home for you, here in Halda. If you change your mind."

She forced a smile for him. "Goodbye, Morin. Thank you for everything."

"Eda—"

But she turned and launched herself from the cliff before he could see the tears pouring down her face, and gave herself over to the creature inside.

She welcomed the pain, and when the agony of her shift was over, she spread her wings wide, and flew east into the rising sun.

Chapter Forty-Six

S HE FLEW EAST AND SOUTH, THE SUN warm on her wings. She didn't look back; she couldn't bear it.

All day she flew, not stopping once to rest or eat. She didn't feel hungry or tired. There was only the sorrow inside of her, compelling her on.

Night came and she flew on, stars sparking to life all around. Tuer's Rise lay dark and distant below. She tried not to think of Morin standing on the cliff, looking after her. She tried not to think that he must be glad she had gone, he *must* be. She tried to tell herself that she was glad, too.

The days and nights slid into each other; her wings never faltered. After a time, she left the mountains behind her and came to the sea. Ships waited in the harbor, tall vessels with sails and riggings, stout iron steamers pouring choking smoke into the sky. She tried not to think back to that day, so long ago it seemed now, when she'd attempted to convince her council that steamers were the future—the way for them to conquer Denlahn.

But she did think about it, and everything that came after. Sorrow tugged at her. Her own, most of all, but the other sorrow too, that impossible, unshakable mass burning forever in her soul.

She was lonely. She longed for home. For a place that belonged to her.

She told herself, staring down at the ships, that what she most wanted in the world was to reclaim her throne, to drive every last Denlahn from her shore and all her worthless Barons too, while she was at it. She could do it so easily—send the full weight of sorrow into anyone she touched. It would break them. She didn't need an army, only herself.

But that was not what she wanted. The thought of truly using her newfound power in that way sickened her.

She went on, across the sea. Sometimes, she flew low enough that the ocean spray brushed her wings. She liked the sensation— it made her feel alive. It allowed her to pretend she was full when she knew she was profoundly, utterly empty.

Days became weeks, and still she flew, never tiring, never hungering. The sorrow ate her, and yet it sustained her, too.

And through the long nights and the longer days, all she could think of was Morin, standing on the cliff, the rising sun gilding his face with scarlet.

One day, the shore of Enduena glimmered into being on the horizon. She'd thought she'd feel triumph at the sight of her homeland, or at least a strong sense of relief.

But inside there was only a pit of ever-widening despair.

She flew past the seaport to her childhood estate in Evalla, landing in a rush of dark wings in the inner courtyard near the stable. She allowed her human form to envelop her, then pulled a shirt and a still wet pair of trousers down from the obliging clothesline and shrugged into them. She felt frail, small. The stones underneath her bare feet were hard and strange after so many weeks of endless, empty sky.

A banner flapped from the highest tower of the house, and Eda craned her neck up to peer at it: the symbol of a single Star shining from a red field. It was an old Enduenan flag, not the Imperial crest.

She considered it, uneasy.

A young female attendant stepped out into the courtyard, yelping with surprise when she saw Eda. She gave a hesitant, uncertain bow. "Your . . . Your Majesty?"

"What's happened?" The words were cracked and dry from a throat that hadn't spoken since the cliffside. Since Morin. "Why do you fly the Enduenan flag?"

The girl clutched the doorframe, clearly too frightened to come any closer. "There is no Empire anymore."

Sorrow and rage burned behind her skin, ready to lash out at the girl, ready to consume her—she had a right to be frightened. But Eda forced herself to be still, to speak softly. "What do you mean?"

But the girl shook her head. "I don't know. The steward took down the Imperial flag a month ago. He ordered it burned."

"Burned?"

"That's all I know, Your Majesty. He didn't say anything else."

Eda gave her a bewildered nod. "I'll go to Eddenahr. Find out for myself." For an instant, she almost let the dark bird burst through her skin, but then she held it back. She had had enough of the sky.

She took a horse from the stable, and the serving girl brought her sandals, a change of clothes, and a pack of provisions for the journey. Eda found herself suddenly ravenous, and wolfed down half the contents of the pack. She swung up onto the horse, a young dappled gray gelding, and thanked the serving girl.

The girl watched her with wide eyes. "What will you do when you get to the capital?"

Power raged inside of her, sorrow curling black around her heart. "I don't know." She put her heels to the gray's flanks and he sprang away, down the road to Eddenahr.

The horse was young and swift, but he had to stop to rest and eat, which forced Eda to stop as well. She hated it, regretting her decision to keep the bird caged inside. In her human form, she tired and hungered as well, but not as much or as often as before the sorrow had grafted itself onto her soul.

She arrived in Eddenahr early in the morning, four days after leaving Evalla.

The city was quiet, the sun pouring onto the cobbled streets and refracting off the whitewashed buildings. Eda followed the winding road up to the palace, ducking her head in an attempt to keep her face hidden.

Unease washed over her like a brittle wind. The banners that snapped from the palace roof and from the shops that crowded the street all bore the Enduenan crest. There wasn't a single Imperial flag anywhere in sight.

What had happened here, while she was lost in the world of gods and stories?

She passed through the gates into the lower palace courtyard, handing off her mount to a stable boy with hardly a thought or even a glance. Her heart roared within her.

What had happened?

She paced up to the grand palace entrance, where over a year ago she had made the envoy from Denlahn wait in the pouring rain.

A single guard stood there, a spear in his hand, but he didn't move to block her way, just gave her a bored glance. "You're a little early for petitioning, Miss, but you can wait inside. An attendant will show you."

"Petitioning?" Eda echoed.

"Petitioning the council. That is why you're here, isn't it? Every third week the delegates hear petitions."

"Oh, of course. Certainly that's why I'm here." Eda plastered on her falsest smile. How could he not recognize her?

The guard waved her inside.

A young Enduenan boy wearing a red sash sprang up from around a corner. His lips were wet, crumbs clinging to them, as if he'd been having a quick snack on the job. He smelled faintly of cinnamon and honey. "This way." He trotted off down the corridor Eda knew so well.

She felt like a ghost, wandering the palace, unknown and unseen. There were more people occupying each room than she was used to: a handful in the music room, playing on various instruments, another handful in the parlors and receiving rooms. All seemed to be dressed plainly, no distinguishing marks of jewels or rings.

The boy led her into the ballroom, which had been vastly redecorated since that night Ileem's soldiers burst in: ancient Enduenan tapestries covered the walls, and the dais at the back of the room had been carpeted over in velvet and arranged with two couches and an ornately carved ivory bookcase. Eda blinked at the figure on one of the couches, a young Denlahn woman, her dark head bent over a book, a tiger lounging at her feet, half asleep.

"It'll be a while yet, Miss," said the boy, "but there will be tea soon." And then he vanished back into the corridor.

The Denlahn woman on the dais lifted her head, and Eda knew her even though the breadth of the room stretched between them: Liahstorion.

It seemed Liahstorion knew her, too. She laid down her book. "Hello, Eda."

Eda crossed the ballroom, lingering at the base of the dais, where she had so often sat with a crown on her head, looking out into a crowd of dancers. Liahstorion was dressed in the Enduenan style, wearing a loose pair of violet silk trousers, a cropped beaded top, and an airy gold sash. But it was the resemblance Liahstorion bore to her brother that made Eda's throat close: those same fierce eyes, those same stark brows.

Power surged through Eda, straining against her skin, but she kept it in check. "What happened?"

The question hung echoing between them. Liahstorion rose from her seat, and took the two steps down from the dais to stand on even footing with Eda. The tiger rose as well, pressing against Liahstorion's knee. They paced together out onto the open balcony.

Eda followed.

"My brother held Eddenahr for ten days, until the Barons' combined regiments arrived. They took the city back in six hours."

Eda hated herself for asking, but she did anyway. "What about Ileem?"

"He called for his god in the midst of the battle, but Rudion did not come. They cut his throat. Left him to choke on his own blood in the dust." Anger hardened Liahstorion's frame.

Eda felt sick. No matter what he'd done to her—he didn't deserve to die that way, abandoned by the Shadow he'd served as a god. "What then?"

"Then the Barons realized they could not agree on who ought to be Emperor. More fighting broke out. A resistance of commoners was raised. The Barons were united in fighting *them*, only they couldn't extinguish the spark of rebellion against the idea of royalty at all. Agreements were struck. I was let out of my cell." Liahstorion shot Eda a baleful glance, absently stroking the tiger's head with one hand. "The Empire has been dissolved. We're trying our hand at democracy."

"'We'?"

"The peace treaty between Enduena and Denlahn stands. I am here to ensure no vengeance is sought because of the things my brother did."

Clearly there was more. Eda waited.

"I'm to marry Domin."

Eda was surprised.

"He's been elected Governor of Enduena, and I am to stand beside him."

"Why call him Governor and not King?"

"The people don't want a king, Eda. Or an Emperor. They want to be free." Liahstorion leaned out on the railing, shutting her eyes into the warm embrace of the sun. The tiger rubbed against her leg.

"What do you want?" Eda asked her.

"What I've always wanted. Peace. Now I have it."

Eda considered her, her strong shoulders and lithe frame, muscular arms used to holding a sword, and wielding it. And yet it would be so easy to overpower her. So easy to drive her down onto the floor and make her scream, make her suffer for all the things her brother did.

But Eda didn't move to touch her. She just stood there, the sorrow eating her up from the inside. She had power now, power she had always wanted. But she was still that lost little girl, wanting to find a place to belong. She knew in her heart of hearts that Enduena was better off without her, that perhaps it always had been. And she realized that place she longed for, the belonging she had always craved, was no longer here.

"I am sorry about the temple," Liahstorion said.

Sorrow burned. "What happened to the temple?"

The former Denlahn princess turned to look Eda in the eye. "They tore it down. Burned it to ashes. It was the one thing everyone agreed on."

Chapter Forty-Seven

S WEAT PRICKLED EDA'S NECK AND SHOULDERS, DRIPPED down into her eyes. The temple steps remained, but the rest of the building had indeed been torn to pieces. A scorching wind swept through the empty shell of it, smelling incongruously of incense and honey.

Eda paced to the center of the temple's floor, sitting cross-legged on the once-polished marble. It was strange, to be back where it all started, in the temple she'd built to appease the gods, to assuage her guilt for bargaining away the life of her sister. It would end here, too, and that seemed only right.

She shut her eyes and waited, as the sun beat down on her and the wind spat dust into her face.

She waited, as the day spun into evening and the scorching sun sank beyond the western rim of the world.

She waited, as the stars came out and the moon rose beyond the northern mountains.

And then at last she heard a step, and knew she was no longer alone.

She opened her eyes.

Niren stood there, silver skirts whispering about her knees, Starlight in her forehead blazing bright. She didn't look like a shadow anymore. She brimmed with life.

And yet Eda knew her sister had not rejoined the land of the living.

"I've been waiting for you," Eda said.

Niren smiled, and sank to the temple floor across from her. "I know. I came as fast as I could. The miles pass slowly when I am trying to reach my friend."

"Then we are friends?"

Niren brushed her fingers against Eda's shoulder. "Always."

Eda smiled back. She hugged her knees to her chest and stared out beyond the ruined temple to the starry desert plain. "What happened to you?"

"Tuer and Raiva found me, wandering in the Mountain. Raiva poured the rest of her Starlight into me. Made me Bearer of Souls, as she meant to from the beginning. I have been busy, gathering the dead, leading them through the Circles to paradise beyond."

"Are you happy?" Eda whispered. She shuddered at the memory of Death and Time and Sorrow. She still thought it cruel of the gods to bind anyone to such a fate.

"I have found my purpose," said Niren. "I am content, Eda. I always knew I was meant for something more."

It felt wrong to say it, selfish, childish, but Eda did anyway. "I don't know who I am anymore. I don't know what I want or what my purpose is."

"Eda."

She looked over at Niren's gentle face.

"It's over. You saved Endahr. You saved me. That's who you are."

"But where do I go? What am I to do?"

"You no longer wish to reclaim your crown?"

Eda thought about the city, glittering on the horizon. How fragile the Enduenans were. How easy it would be to destroy them. "I don't want to sacrifice anyone else like I did you. I know that isn't the point, that it was never the point, because the gods had other plans for you, but—but if I do, I will sacrifice others over and over again, until my soul is truly gone and I'm nothing but a cruel empty shell wielding the powers of a goddess. I don't know what I want. But I don't want that."

Starlight pulsed from Niren's brow. She nodded gravely.

"Can you forgive me? For what I did to you?"

"My dearest Eda. You didn't do anything to me."

"But I intended to. I traded your life away without a thought. It doesn't matter that the gods meant for it to happen. I still did that. To you."

Niren closed the distance between them, and folded Eda into a tight embrace. For an instant, Eda's whole body tensed, anticipating the rush of pain that accompanied the feeling of someone else's sorrow. But all she felt was Niren, solid and warm, her heart beating steadily.

"You can't hurt me," Niren explained, when she'd drawn back. "Just as I can't hurt you. I'm not exactly living, you know, and you're not exactly . . . you're not exactly mortal anymore."

Somehow, this didn't come as a surprise. Eda had felt it, when the Starlight and the sorrow had woven themselves into her soul.

"But that isn't all bad," Niren went on, her tone over-bright. "It means that no matter where you go, I can find you. Speak with you. We can be friends, as we haven't quite been since childhood."

Eda didn't miss the quirk of Niren's lips. "Did you always know I was your sister?"

"I suspected for many years, and I knew for certain when I met our father in the Circle of the Dead. You frown the same way he used to frown, you know. You laugh like him, too. Although it has been a very long time since I heard you laugh."

Eda wanted to laugh, but she didn't know how. She found herself yearning to know the father she had known, and yet not known. "Tell me about him. Tell me everything."

Niren did, as the moon rose and sank again, as the stars faded and the sun climbed bright into the sky. And for the first time in a long, long time, in the ruins of the temple she had tried so hard to build to save her friend's life and quell her guilt—for the first time, Eda didn't feel alone.

Epilogue

SHE ALWAYS FELT MORE ALIVE UP ON the cliff.
There was a certain ledge unreachable except by half
an hour's treacherous climb that she visited nearly every
morning, tucking herself between the rocks, watching the ayrrah
soar in the air currents as the sun poured over the mountain peaks
and warmed her face like nothing else could.

This morning, clouds were gathering fast, and the sharp
wind carried with it the promise of snow. She would have to
climb back down before the weather hit in earnest, but she had
a few minutes more of peace. Perhaps today was the day she
would finally take the path to the village in the valley below the
monastery, finally go and see Morin again, make her peace with
him. She couldn't deny he was part of the reason she'd chosen to
settle here, a permanent pilgrim in Tal-Arohnd, weeding in the
garden or gathering eggs, not speaking a word for weeks together
if she didn't wish to.

Life in the monastery suited her, and it was easier being close to Tuer's Mountain, in case she was ever called upon to return. She was safe here, too. Secluded from most of the world, where she need not touch or be touched, where there was no danger of the sorrow inside of her killing anyone.

Two winters had spun away since she'd come back here, begging sanctuary from Torane. Two springs, two summers, too. Tainir had climbed up to see her several times since her return.

But not Morin. Never Morin.

She wanted to go down to him, wanted to accept the offer he'd made her so long ago. But there was so much grief burning up her soul, she didn't know if there was room for anything else.

The wind bit colder, and the first few flakes of snow fell wet against her cheek. She turned her back to the staggering drop and began to inch her way down the cliff. She climbed slowly, the wind tugging at her body, the snow coming thick.

By the time she'd made it to level ground again, a thin layer of white already blanketed everything.

A path lay at her feet: to her left was the way back to the monastery, to her right, the road down to the village. She stood a moment, considering. She thought of the mug of tea she would brew as soon as she reached her tiny stone room, which she'd attempted to make more homey by plastering Morin's map on the wall and stringing beads on bright yarn from one corner of the room to the other. She thought of Morin and Tainir's little house, with the goats bleating in the pen just outside, and Tainir hanging a kettle over the fire.

Eda had healed, slowly, these last long months, but she was still uncertain of her steps. And though Niren came to talk with her often, even her sister could not ease her loneliness completely.

She looked up the path, and down the path: one way, a

comfortable solitude. And the other?

She drew a slow breath, hugging her poncho around her in the thickly falling snow. She didn't know, but she was ready to find out. She was ready to see if there was anything for her in Endahr beyond the sorrow that ate at her and was never full.

She took the downward path.

The snow fell, and the wind bit, but there was a fire burning in Morin and Tainir's hearth. When Eda stepped in through the door, tea was ready and waiting. Morin looked up at her with a swift, fierce smile. She went to join him by the fire.

Acknowledgments

THIS BOOK WOULD NOT EXIST WITHOUT MY amazing editor, Lauren Knowles, who, when I pitched the idea of a completely different companion novel for *Beneath the Haunting Sea*, was all: "Okay, but what if the companion novel was about Eda instead?" Initially, I didn't think Eda had much of a story to tell. And then I sat down to brainstorm possibilities and realized that she *did*, and things spiraled out of control from there. Lauren, thanks for the brainstorming phone calls, for always answering my emails, and for your boundless enthusiasm for this book!

Thanks to Ashley Tenn for creating such a gorgeous cover! Tolkien himself would be proud, and I can't stop looking at it.

Thanks to the entire team at Page Street for transforming my words into beautiful, book-shaped things, and for making my oldest dream come true three years in a row.

Thank you to my wizardly agent, Sarah Davies, for always championing me and my work.

Thank you to Hanna Howard and Steph Messa for reading *Earth* in its messiest, rough-draft form. Your enthusiasm and encouragement dragged me up from the depths of despair and enabled me to keep working on this book. Hugs and hugs and hugs.

Thanks to my intrepid critique partner, Jen Fulmer, for your invaluable notes on the second draft of *Earth*—don't worry, I changed that part about the floor tiles!

Thanks to Laura Weymouth, who, when asked for ideas of alternate travel methods, suggested "giant eagles like in Tolkien" and then proceeded to tell me everything she'd learned about eagles from nature documentary shows.

Thanks to Jenny Downer for the first line, for thinking this book sounds cool, for keeping me company while I was writing it, and for still being my BFF even after all these years. Here's to drinking many, many more cups of tea together.

Thanks to Anna Bright and Hannah Whitten who, along with Jen and Laura and Steph, make up The Pod, and are always there to cheer me on or commiserate or both, depending on the situation. All writers need a Pod, and I'm beyond grateful for mine.

Thanks to Amy Trueblood and every one of the incredible authors who make up the AZ YA/MG Writers' Group—you all inspire me beyond words.

Thanks to the band The Oh Hellos for your gorgeous, inspiring music. I listened to the albums *Eurus* and *Notos* on repeat ad infinitum whilst writing and revising *Earth*.

I would be remiss in not mentioning J. R. R. Tolkien and Megan Whalen Turner, whose words and worlds will never cease to inspire me. I like to think *Earth* could be the strange lovechild of *The Lord of the Rings* and *The Queen of Attolia*.

As always, thanks to my friends and family for their continued love, encouragement, and support. I love and appreciate you all more than words can say.

Thank you to my husband, Aaron, who is long suffering during the book-making process, and who has ridden this particular roller coaster enough times now to not take me too seriously when I bemoan to him that "This is the worst thing I've ever written." Thanks for encouraging me. Thanks for being proud of me. I love you.

And to Arthur, who is growing up so fast: thanks for taking such good naps while I wrote and revised this book! I really don't know what I'm going to do when you stop napping, but we'll figure it out together, okay? Love you always.

And last but by no means least, thank you thank you thank you to every single one of my readers. It means the world to me to share my words with you.

About the Author

J OANNA RUTH MEYER IS THE AUTHOR OF *Beneath the Haunting Sea*, which *Kirkus* described as "epic, musical, and tender," and *Echo North*, which received starred reviews from both *Kirkus* and *Publishers Weekly*.

Joanna hails from Mesa, Arizona, where she lives with her dear husband and son, a rascally feline, and an enormous grand piano named Prince Imrahil. She currently splits her time between toddler wrangling, teaching piano lessons, and writing, and her greatest obsessions are loose-leaf tea and rainstorms. One day, she aspires to own an old Victorian house with creaky wooden floors and a tower (for writing in, of course!).